MICHAEL HARTLAND

THE YEAR OF THE SCORPION

CORONET BOOKS
Hodder and Stoughton

First published in Great Britain
in 1991 by Hodder and
Stoughton Limited

Coronet edition 1992

All characters, government
agencies and events in this book
are fictitious and bear no relation
to any real person, government
agency or event.

Printed and bound in Great Britain
for Hodder and Stoughton
Paperbacks, a division of Hodder
and Stoughton Limited, Mill
Road, Dunton Green, Sevenoaks,
Kent TN13 2YA (Editorial Office:
47 Bedford Square, London
WC1 3DP) by Clays Ltd, St Ives plc.
Photoset by E.P.L. BookSet,
Norwood, London.

British Library C.I.P.

Hartland, Michael
  The year of the scorpion.
  I. Title
  823 [F]

ISBN 0-340-56458-X

What the Critics Said

DOWN AMONG THE DEAD MEN

'Cleverly plotted and impressive.' *Guardian*

'Credible characters, a plot that really hums along – all the signs of a future winner.'
Ted Allbeury

SEVEN STEPS TO TREASON

'A stunning display of diplomatic and under-cover know-how, SAS dare-devilry and global double-cross.' *Sunday Times*

'A taut tale of treachery.' *Punch*

THE THIRD BETRAYAL

'Very impressive . . . for devious depth this one beats the band.' *Observer*

'Criss-crossed with treachery – a winner.'
Sunday Times

FRONTIER OF FEAR

'The unmistakable stamp of authenticity.'
Western Morning News

'Fast-moving thriller of sexual blackmail.'
Today

Before taking up writing, Michael Hartland
spent twenty years in government service,
travelling widely in Europe and the Far East as
a diplomat, then working in counter-terrorism
and for the United Nations. He draws on this
experience to describe the secret world of
espionage with insight and great authenticity.

His four previous novels have established him
as one of Britain's leading thriller writers.
Translated into twelve European languages
and Japanese, they are also being adapted for
film and television.

Michael Hartland is married with two daugh-
ters and lives in Devon.

For Olivia

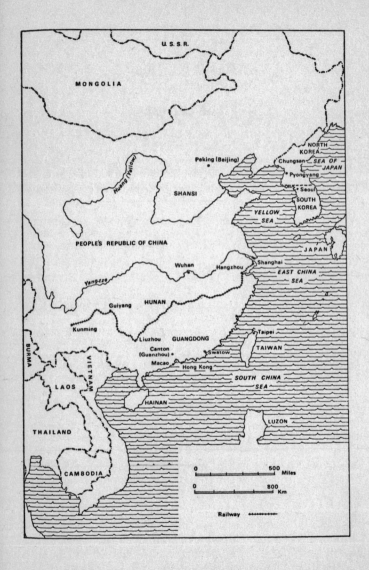

PROLOGUE

CHINA – 1950

The missionary struggled as two soldiers forced him to his knees, crying out in pain as they twisted his arms behind him until his shoulders were contorted like a cripple's. For a moment he was still, only a few seconds but long enough: the sword sliced through the air and his head bounced away like a football. The kneeling body slumped on the ground making no sound except a sharp hiss of air, a tyre deflating, and blood spurted from the neck, scarlet turning brown as it soaked into the dust.

The soldiers picked up the dead man and tossed him into the drain at the side of the road, where the body of his wife already lay. The others laughed and continued to ransack his covered wagon. One belched and an empty bottle shattered as it was thrown into the boulders on the slope. They were stragglers from the defeated Nationalist army, trying to escape into the hills south of Wuhan. Conscripted by Chiang Kai-shek, they had fought the bitter civil war against the communists and were now abandoned by the leader who had fled to Taiwan. Their homes were at least a thousand miles away, in communist hands, and they would never see them again.

The group had encountered the Europeans on the mountain road, a man dressed all in black and a well-made woman with flaxen hair, riding in a wagon with a canvas top, pulled by a mule. Already drunk, they had seized on the woman but she had struggled too much and her husband had fought them, so had killed them both instead. There was nothing much in the wagon: just bedrolls, some rice and water, a box of Chinese bibles and Lutheran hymn books. They took the mule, the rice and the water, then set fire to the wagon and reeled off into the hills. When they were out of sight, a small boy emerged cautiously from the boulders where his father had hidden him just before the attack. His eyes were wide with terror but he had obeyed: 'Whatever happens – even if they hurt *Mutti* and me – stay there until these evil men have gone. Be a good boy and stay quiet as a mouse.'

It was nearly twenty-four hours later that the other soldiers arrived, men in baggy green uniforms with red stars on their caps, singing *The East is Red* without enthusiasm as they marched. They found the child asleep, clinging to the cold body of his mother. He was dressed like a little Chinese, but European and about two years old.

PART ONE

HONG KONG AND MACAO

1

Forty years later, Ah Ming lay in the muddy water slopping over a paddy field. Swirling monsoon clouds hid the moon. She was alone in the darkness, freezing, transfixed by the line of white arc lights shining on the fence ahead. Although the air above her was warm and moist, electric with the imminent typhoon, her thin body shivered with cold and fear.

Ah Ming was only fourteen but she had made her way south alone, hiding by day, walking fearfully through the night. She had grown up suddenly when her father had become frightened after the massacre on Tian'an Men. Then he had taken Ah Ming and her brother from school and sent the whole family to live with relatives in a disgusting peasant village. He had pretended it was some kind of holiday but she sensed danger all around and had not been surprised when her mother was arrested. She and her brother had been confined in a youth compound that was little more than a labour camp, but Kwai-lan was barely ten and had refused to come when she escaped. She was surprised quite how much she missed him; every night she cried when she thought about him, and about her parents. She knew that this was the only way to survive, but in her heart she also knew that she would never see any of them again.

Now there were only a hundred yards to go, just a three-metre wire fence separating her from Hong Kong. She had wriggled past the last People's Liberation Army post ten minutes ago. She had hoped to see skyscrapers shining with lights, but she knew that those were still miles away. This was no man's land, dark and safe, but when she stood up she would be in danger again – more danger than at any time since she had jumped from the truck carrying her back to the compound from stacking jagged concrete blocks on the building site. Her hands had healed now, but then they had been permanently grazed and bleeding.

Ah Ming watched a jeep drive past on the track that ran along the other side of the wire, then crawled forward, trying not to splash. She flinched as she brushed against a duck, sleeping with its head tucked into its feathers, and cringed into the water as it flapped away quacking indignantly. But then it was silent again and she was resting on the edge of dry land, the fence gleaming in the light only thirty feet away with no sign of any guards. As she gripped the wire-cutters she had stolen in Canton she was suddenly tempted to go back, to try to swim across the harbour, but it was impossible for she had never learnt to swim. She crawled forward towards the blaze of light, keeping as near to the ground as she could.

She was close to the fence when she felt a slight breeze and sensed the clouds moving faster across the black sky. A crack in them opened to reveal the moon and pale grey light caught on her white singlet. In a surge of panic she started to run. There was a shout behind her and suddenly the whole world burst into white flame. A searchlight beam swept down with savage accuracy, blinding her as she rushed towards the fence, weaving in a futile effort to escape the glare. The first shot missed, but the second pierced her shoulder and she threw up her arms with a scream, twisting away from the searing pain and the pulse of warm blood soaking into her clothes. She managed to stumble the last few feet, gasping with the effort, and was clawing at the wire when the third bullet punched her into unconsciousness.

The Chinese private returned to the hut where his companion was still watching a cartoon on the portable television. He made an entry in the log. Sometimes his orders were to let them cross, sometimes to show that Peking had teeth. He shrugged – it was all politics and above his head. The Gurkhas from the other side could pick up the body at dawn.

Next morning the hydrofoil took an hour and a quarter to cover the forty miles across the Pearl River estuary to Macao. At first it was a bumpy crossing with a stiff breeze whipping the muddy waters up into waves the colour of milky coffee; but gradually the weather cleared and they landed in brilliant sunshine. Macao was not frenetic and jumpy like Hong Kong – a calm, old world Portuguese town washed up on the coast of the South China Sea. The tall American found it relaxing as he loped into town with a long stride. It was warm, but he was cooled by a pleasant salty breeze off the bay as he passed the seedy casinos and shanty towns of rusty corrugated iron huts with lines of bright washing hung across alleys full of rotting garbage. When Macao was a Portuguese colony they had been the home of thousands of refugees from Red China; and the refugees were still there even though this was now 'Chinese territory under Portuguese administration'.

The tin huts gave way to the *Praia Grande*, its avenue of shuttered buildings curving gracefully by the shore and shaded by gnarled banyan trees. The girl was waiting for him, long fair hair blowing in the breeze, long legs swinging above the breakers as she perched on the balustrade staring out to sea. He gave her an admiring glance, but there was nothing soft about this woman. A few years ago she would have been frail and beautiful; now she was striking, with an aura of physical strength that he found attractive but almost unfeminine, powerful muscle in her bare forearms and the tanned calves emerging below her white jeans. She gave him a broad smile, but there was something distant about her.

'Miss Cable?' he asked. 'Good to meet you, ma'am.'

13

'You must be Robert Gatti?' She replied with a crisp efficiency that took all the gloss off the carnal thoughts he had been about to have. When she stood up she was nearly as tall as Gatti. She in turn studied him: over six feet but shoulders slightly hunched even though she knew he was the right side of forty, faded jeans making him look more like a beachcomber than a commander in the US Navy. She smiled again, a hint of warmth and encouragement behind the cool exterior. Then she was brisk and businesslike again. 'Go down the second alley on the right and you will find a coffin-maker's shop – just walk straight in and they will be expecting you.'

'Is Foo there?'

'No, he is at home. But he owns the shop – he owns half of Macao these days. They will take you in their closed cart to deliver a couple of coffins and will drop you in the garage of Foo's villa. He's most concerned that no one should see either of us entering or leaving.'

'How about you?'

'I'll sit here for a little longer, looking like a tourist, then approach the coffin-maker's yard from the alley at the back. I am travelling with you – in the other box. They're quite comfortable, particularly if there's some padding.' She gave a throaty chuckle and for the first time seemed human as her eyes crinkled with laughter, but then turned abruptly back to the sea. He was dismissed.

In fact the journey was far from comfortable in the back of the cart as it jolted over cobbles pulled by a donkey. They lay in the two short Chinese coffins with their legs dangling awkwardly over the sides, staring up at the canvas awning that hid them from view. Sunlight filtering through turned their faces a sickly green. Outside were the smells of fish and the shouts of trawlermen as the cart plodded along the fishing wharf, then it grew quieter as they entered the wealthy residential area. When they emerged from the stifling space into a closed garage, Sarah Cable noted a large white Mercedes and a red Ferrari before they climbed up a flight of stone steps. She wondered where on earth they found to drive the Ferrari in a place only about one mile by five.

When they reached the terrace there were a few brightly coloured sun loungers and white metal chairs, shaded by umbrellas where the palms did not cast shadow – and a magnificent view over the South China Sea. A woman in her mid-thirties turned to greet them, a smile of genuine welcome lighting up a face more round than oval. She wore a cream silk dress that showed off her generous curves discreetly. Like the simple cut of her dark hair it had undoubtedly been expensive but she had an air of earthy cheerfulness that suggested the obvious signs of wealth were not important to her. 'I am Ruth Foo.' She smiled again: she had beautiful amber eyes. Gatti was puzzled – what the hell was this powerful Chinese doing married to an Englishwoman, and not a bad looking one at that? 'Welcome to *Lin Chiao* – my husband is on the telephone and will join us in a minute.' She hesitated, uncertain which of them was the senior, then turned to Gatti. 'Would you like a drink? Tea? Or perhaps a beer?'

Before Gatti could reply, Sarah said, 'Tea would be fine for both of us, thank you.' Ruth Foo nodded approvingly and turned to give an order to an unseen houseboy some-where inside. They sat in a corner of the terrace sipping green tea from small porcelain bowls. Mrs Foo gestured at a line of junks gliding bat-winged across the sparkling water.

'It's incredibly beautiful, isn't it?' she said brightly. 'You wouldn't think all those poor souls are still living in the shanty towns just a couple of miles away. There are some real problems here, you know, it isn't all tourist restaurants and casinos.'

At that moment Foo emerged from the house. He was very tall for a Chinese, with broad, lined features and grey hair swept back from a high forehead. The aura of dignity and power befitted his station in life, but it was belied by eyes that were always on the verge of smiling. He shook hands and sat down while his wife poured a fourth bowl of tea. From the way the couple looked at each other, Sarah sensed the powerful bond between them, but Foo's gravity was unbroken as his wife crossed her legs to reveal an expanse of brown thigh, which she hastily covered.

There was no more small talk. 'Thank you for coming to see me,' said Foo deliberately. 'I'm sorry if the last part of the journey was a little tiresome.' That engaging smile again, a piercing glance from eyes that could see right through you. 'As you may be aware, I once had a close connection with the intelligence service of your country, Miss Cable – which inevitably meant that I had something to do with your Central Intelligence Agency, Commander Gatti. That all came to an end more than ten years ago, when I left Hong Kong to develop my business interests here. It came to an end in very unhappy circumstances so I am somewhat surprised to see you here, but I knew Nairn well in those days and a request from an old comrade cannot be ignored. So how may I help you?' There was an awkward silence, broken when a roar of diesel engines followed a white speedboat pulling a water-skier across the bay.

Gatti put down his bowl of tea, for the first time noticing the delicate blue and white porcelain. 'I – I guess Mrs Foo is familiar with these matters, sir?' The meaning was obvious and there was another awkward silence. Sarah's lips tightened: why didn't the dickhead leave her to do the talking?

'She is.' A sudden coldness in the reply.

Gatti started again. 'When you were active, sir, I believe you ran an agent in China, one Tang Tsin?' Foo nodded, almost imperceptibly. 'The fact is, Mr Foo, he has been inactive for years, just the occasional snippet of information passed to his contact – now at the American Embassy – pretty low-grade stuff. Then six months ago he started to produce intelligence that was high-level, straight from the top of the Party and the government.'

'He is a high-ranking official.'

Foo's tone was so cold that Gatti's throat was suddenly

dry, his voice hoarse. He knew he was handling it badly. 'Recently he's also started to make demands – first money, then a safe haven for him and his family to leave China, support for the rest of his life, the usual kind of thing.'

After another silence it was Sarah who spoke and the atmosphere seemed less frosty, perhaps because the *tai-pan* was attracted to her. 'The problem, sir, is that his allegations seem very serious – but are they just fiction? Is he any more than a refugee with a vivid imagination who wants to settle in America or Australia with a bag of our money, not in poverty in a shanty town here or Hong Kong?'

Foo studied a rusty freighter heading into the estuary towards Canton, a red flag with five gold stars flapping at its stern, his face unreadable. 'What kind of allegations?'

'They are of a military nature, a threat to the interests of both our countries – from the only major totalitarian communist power still intact since the collapse in Eastern Europe.'

'That tells me nothing.'

Sarah sipped the green tea, now cold and horrible, eyeing Foo sharply across the rim of her bowl. She knew that he was nearly sixty but that athletic frame could have been fifteen years younger. 'I'll get clearance to tell you more if you can help us, but I've no authority to be more specific now. I'm sorry.'

'I'm sorry too, Miss Cable. It was Sir David Nairn who hounded me out of your service. If he suddenly needs my help, he should be here himself, not sending two – forgive me – relatively junior officers with only half the story.'

Sarah inclined her head respectfully. 'I will convey that message, Mr Foo.'

'Thank you. As to whether Tang is genuine or a plant – I recall him as a valuable agent, reliable and trustworthy. But of course he could have changed – or he might have been turned, acting under duress?'

'Exactly.'

17

'You may tell Nairn two other things. We are not totally cut off here in Macao and since Gorbachev came to power I see the governments of the West sinking into ever greater confusion. Peace seems to be breaking out all over Europe, communist parties collapsing from the Baltic to the Black Sea and giving way to some kind of democracy – though after the backlash not, it seems, in Russia itself.' Sarah and Gatti said nothing. 'And in China too things are different.' He gestured northwards towards Canton. 'We are on the edge of the biggest country in the world – with the biggest army and the biggest problems. In Peking the hardliners are still in power. There is tremendous opposition, as we saw at Tian'an Men, but make no mistake – those hard men aim to keep control. They are isolated and frightened; they have force on their side but they face strong forces too. It is a most dangerous situation, far more dangerous than the Gulf War or anything that's happened in the Baltic States, and your masters ignore it at their peril.'

Sarah nodded, suppressing her irritation at being given all this generalised bullshit when she had come looking for some hard facts. 'And the second thing, Mr Foo?'

'Tell Nairn that if he comes himself, here to my house, I shall try to help him.'

Foo insisted that they return to Hong Kong in his cruiser *A-ma*, the Goddess of the Sea, a large white vessel moored just below the villa. The quay was reached by a private tunnel under the road and shielded by a high wall. Sarah wondered what illicit cargoes might require such privacy. The crew of four ushered her and Gatti down into the saloon where they could not be seen and cast off in that slovenly but confident way typical of Chinese seamen. With a roar of powerful diesels, Gatti felt the sea rolling under the deck and watched Macao vanish in the spray at the stern. He turned to Sarah. 'That guy confuses me.'

'He confuses us all.'

'Where'd he spring from?'

'His father was a merchant in Shanghai who fell foul of the communists in the thirties. The whole family died in the civil war and the Japanese invasion – except young Benjamin who escaped to Hong Kong in 1948. He was only nineteen – and penniless – when he arrived, but in ten years he made a fortune, became a British citizen and indispensable to the SIS station. He actually ran it for eight years. He was a legend in our service until Nairn fired him in 1979.'

'Why was he fired?'

'Suspicious contacts with Red China, but no real evidence that would stand up in court. If he'd been British-born and driving a desk in London they couldn't have touched him. He took Ruth with him by way of revenge – she was an SIS officer and Nairn's girlfriend. I guess that's why he wants Nairn to come himself – Foo lost a lot of face and now it's Nairn's turn.'

Gatti faced her across the cockpit. 'Why the hell *didn't* he come himself? Foo treated us like shit, but wasn't he right to be offended?'

'Nairn's old and has heart trouble. He ought to be retired. I guess it's a long journey.' Sarah shrugged. 'If Foo's still bent it was a mistake to come at all.'

'Damn right it was – if I'd known Foo's background I'd have been against it. I didn't ask questions because I assumed Nairn knew what he was doing.'

'Maybe he does, but he *is* getting old, Bob.'

'Jesus, what a fuck-up.' Gatti shook his head in puzzlement. 'Has Foo forgiven your people – or is he still out for revenge twelve years on?'

'God knows. He's become rich enough to be immensely powerful. Maybe he's forgiven Nairn and it's all genuine. Or maybe he still has friends in Peking and it's a nasty little scheme with them . . . '

'How the devil do we decide which?'

'I don't know, Bob. But I tell you one thing – if we get it

wrong they'll crucify both of us. Maybe even if we get it right.'

Back in Hong Kong Sarah spent a couple of hours in the office but at five o'clock the typhoon warning was broadcast and she hurried home to Cheung Chau. Since being posted to Hong Kong a year ago she had lived in a rented apartment on the small offshore island. The ferry journey took an hour, but it was worth it to escape from the overcrowding and bustle of Central. Cheung Chau was shaped like a dumb-bell: two wooded hills rising from the sea, joined by a flat strip of land that formed the waterfront. The harbour was always packed solid with boats, mostly junks, square sterns of varnished wood rising high out of the water draped with washing and fishing nets with orange floats. Today everything was being thrust into lockers and the smaller sampans were scuttling for shelter, engines popping, sides hung with old tyres dripping with seaweed.

Sarah was swept down the gangway in a tide of Chinese. Usually the quay was crowded, the staccato bargaining in Cantonese deafening as women in black pyjamas and straw hats sold fish alive from pails, but today the typhoon was coming. The atmosphere was subdued as Chinese in vests and blue shorts put up shutters. She turned down the alley by the fire station and ten minutes later was in the second-floor flat near Nam Tam Wan, the Morning Beach. It was luxurious by Chinese standards – a living room with a balcony, separate bedroom, bathroom and tiny kitchen – and expensive, but the Queen thoughtfully paid everyone's rent on an overseas posting.

He was already there, shuttering their windows on the balcony, taller than Sarah, disgracefully handsome. She threw her arms round his neck. 'Nick! How wonderful – I thought you were still in Peking?'

'Got back this morning.' He kissed her in that tender, thoughtful way she loved so much. For a hard-nosed naval intelligence officer he was surprisingly gentle and had such kind eyes. 'Will the café on the corner stay open with the typhoon coming?'

'Ah Wong? Oh yes, he'll stay open till the last minute.'

'Good. I was going to surprise you by doing supper, but there wasn't time to buy anything. Shall we go to Ah Wong's instead?'

She went on cuddling him, nuzzling her face on his shoulder. 'Please. I wonder how long the typhoon will last?'

'At least two or three days. Whatever will we find to do?' They both laughed as instinctively their eyes turned to the double bed in the next room; but then the open door from the balcony started to bang urgently in the wind. 'Christ – I'd better go batten down those shutters.' Outside, the sky was already black and the gale rising, the sea no longer blue but leaden grey, angry waves smashing on the beach. Soon the alleys would be awash with garbage and driving rain.

2

But the typhoon did not arrive that evening. After a deluge of rain the wind dropped, leaving the colony hot, steaming and irritable as Bob Gatti worked late in his office on the Peak. Normally he was number two to the head of the CIA station, a retired admiral of nearly seventy – a staunch Republican political appointee who knew little of intelligence work. But last week the admiral had been whisked back to Washington for an operation on his piles and Gatti was taking his place. A massive heap of intercepts and files was waiting and it took him six hours to plough through them.

It was gone eleven when Gatti left for home and nearly midnight when he drove down the hill into Stanley. Only five miles away in Wanchai neon lights blazed, the humid streets were still thronged and girlie bars throbbed to Michael Jackson's latest. But here, the other side of the Peak, it was silent as a graveyard. Below Gatti the moon shone silver on a horseshoe of bay dotted with sampans and modern speedboats. The car windows were open, for the air was close and electric, and he could hear sea breaking on sand as the wind started to rise again. At the end of the town the road rose until he turned off into an avenue of white villas, looking down at the harbour through the ghostly shapes of swaying banyan trees. Gatti's house was at the end, two storeys with a big glassed-in verandah, hidden by a high wall. He parked by the wrought-iron gate at the side. For security reasons he drove an anonymous British Rover with ordinary Hong

Kong number plates, nothing to mark him out as a serviceman. Up here the wind was stronger, coming in fierce gusts, and he unlocked the gate with difficulty, pulling tired limbs up the steps to his front door.

The house was in darkness. Odd, because Sue usually left the hall light on for him when she and the boys went to bed. It also smelt very stuffy and there was an irritating buzzing of flies. Sweat started to pour down his body in the humidity and he realised that the air conditioning was off. When he switched on the lights nothing happened and Gatti felt his way to the kitchen where the fuse box was in a cupboard. By the sink he stumbled across something soft, peered at the floor in the moonlight and recoiled. Dropping to his knees he threw his arms around her but she was already cold. 'No – Oh Christ no!' He choked as his fingers felt blood caked around the wound under her torn blouse. In the grey moonlight slanting through the window the expression on her face was ugly, not mischievous and laughing as he remembered her that morning but twisted in terror. He stayed there kneeling for a long time, still cradling her head and shoulders, staring in disbelief, until he could force himself to turn away.

Clinging to his sanity, he stood up slowly, found the fuse box and reset the trip switch. Lights went on all over the house. Gatti knelt by his wife again and felt her wrist: perhaps there was still some spark of life? But the skin was icy and there was no pulse. The hiss of air conditioning had started but apart from that the house was in complete silence. The boys! In a burst of panic he leapt up the stairs, tripping at the top, his hand shaking as he gripped the banister to steady himself.

The two children were in their separate bedrooms. They were both dead with wounds in the chest. Little Chris had not woken up, but Edward had eyes glazed and mouth open, staring in pain and fear; the blood on his sheets was still sticky. Gatti staggered out to the landing, stumbling on a wooden train set, overwhelmed by waves of impotence and nausea. He felt empty, numb, forcing himself to the phone to summon help. The anguish of total loss, the grief and hopelessness he had seen in others would come later, much later. Now disbelief was giving way to a helpless, bitter anger; and a realisation that this was not a robbery that had gone wrong. Like any day of tragedy, this one had started routinely enough but he had blundered close to something that hard men were determined to keep secret – men who had reacted in hours by destroying his family to warn him off. Destroyed the only people that really mattered in his life. When he was in the office they had still been alive, eating frozen burgers and watching television. Now they were dead. The message was unmistakable. It was impossible, his mind could not grasp it. But the blood on his fingers and the stillness all around mocked him with the truth. He wanted to curse and scream, to blot out the agony that pierced his brain as if its fibres had suddenly become red-hot wires, but nothing could do that. Working on automatic pilot, he picked up the phone despite the tears blinding his eyes.

The police moved into Gatti's house within half an hour and stayed until four in the morning, taking measurements and photographs, trampling the shrubs in the garden, generally obliterating any clues there might have been to the killer. A Chinese inspector arrived and rebuked the uniformed sergeant, who had been first on the scene, for smoking and dropping dog ends on the carpet in the drawing room. Inspector Feng was young, intelligent, very understanding. But Gatti could see him starting to lose interest the moment he realised he was dealing with one of the funnies from the Peak.

Feng sat with Gatti in a corner of the big room, the curtains drawn back to reveal the twisted shapes of trees rocking in the garden, for now the wind was howling and rain lashing down. Efficient-looking Chinese police in khaki shorts bustled in and out on mysterious errands, ignoring him. Feng was thorough, writing down Gatti's answers to his questions meticulously in an old-fashioned notebook, but it was plainly a matter of routine. It wasn't a burglary that had gone wrong but a premeditated murder: not Triads but something political. The police would never solve it – probably higher authority would tell him to close the file in a week or two.

For the next few days Gatti was frequently to find people doing things around him, just out of sight, in an effort to be kind that was deeply wounding: treating him as if he wasn't there. The first time was while Inspector Feng was interviewing him. Without a word they took the three bodies away, his wife, his children, without his permission, without even telling him, without a moment to touch and kiss them for a last time.

'Not much night left,' said Feng at last with his staccato Cantonese intonation. 'Maybe you got someone stay with? Maybe few day?'

Gatti shook his head. 'I'll be okay here, thanks.' But ten minutes later, alone in the silent house, the sense of emptiness was unbearable. He walked restlessly from room to room, the wind screaming outside, pausing a long time in the boys' bedrooms where bedding and other items had been taken away, presumably for forensic examination. It rammed home the fact that he could never again pick up Edward or Chris and cuddle them; and he saw their faces so clearly, alive and smiling with Sue behind them, that he broke down again and wept. Even then the truth, the real truth, was impossible to accept. He lay down in the spare room expecting not to sleep but, despite the roaring typhoon, dropped off quite quickly from sheer exhaustion.

Sarah woke in Nick Roper's arms. He was turned towards her, half-smiling, still asleep despite the wind howling outside. His face looked very young, as if it did not quite belong to the muscular shoulders uncovered where the duvet had slipped. She moved his arm gently and slipped out of bed to peer through the slatted blind: she saw sea breaking fifty feet high and roof tiles flying down the alleys. Shivering, she pulled a dressing gown over her nakedness and ran into the kitchen to make coffee.

Nick was undoubtedly the best thing that had ever happened to her. They had met when she arrived in Hong Kong nearly a year ago. Sarah had been twenty-seven and a mess. Her relationship with the service veered between love and hate; and she had too much experience of being drawn to hopeless men, sex and the champagne life followed by periods of bitter loneliness. Then one day he had walked into the office bringing a package of documents for her from China: Lieutenant-Commander Roper, Assistant Naval Attaché at the American Embassy in Peking, about thirty, an inch or so taller than Sarah, devilishly good-looking.

Even so, at first he hadn't seemed quite her type. Nick plainly had a rather classy New England background – he came from Boston, Massachusetts, though he pronounced it 'Bor-ston' – and was a well-respected pro in intelligence circles. 'That Nick Roper,' they whispered in the spook bars. 'Going places, end up as Director of CIA.' To be viewed like that he had to be ambitious, but it didn't show. When he took her out she found that the all-American veneer hid a man as deeply cynical as Sarah about the profession in which they were both misfits and therefore naturals. He had an anarchic sense of humour, he was fun – and immensely kind. A year ago Sarah would have laughed at the idea that she would fall for a classy American with a body like a Greek god, but when they made love for the first time she felt so overwhelmingly desired that she wanted to cry. Then Nick had been ordered to spend half his time working for Gatti in Hong Kong and they had started to live together. Oddly enough, and despite the scepticism they shared, the more relaxed and comfortable – even dependent – Sarah became with Nick, the more she had become her own

26

woman in the service. At last she had started to pursue something like a determined career, although she had difficulty admitting it, even to herself. Carrying two steaming mugs she went back into the bedroom and half-opened the blind. Nick was awake and kissed her as she slipped back in beside him. 'You're too good to me, Cable.'

'How right you are.' She rolled on her stomach, burying her face in her arms so that 'Now it's your turn,' was half stifled. She spread her legs apart in invitation and gave a heavy sigh when she felt his fingers caressing the inside of her thighs. 'Mm, that's nice.' Sometimes she liked to dominate but today she wanted to be taken fiercely, from behind; as nerve ends throughout her body began to tingle she turned her toes in, wriggling and raising her bottom so that he could probe more deeply, sighing again – long and dreamily – as the storm raged outside.

At the border with China two Gurkhas struggled through torrential rain to pick up the tiny body spreadeagled out-side the wire. Splashing through the water, the oozing yellow mud was so slippery they could barely stand up-right; it clung to their combat boots like molten plastic however high they lifted them in an effort to shake it off. They rolled the girl roughly on the stretcher, securing her with webbing straps, and started to slither back to the gate in the fence, cursing quietly in Nepali.

3

The typhoon took three days to blow out, leaving Sarah
and Nick marooned on Cheung Chau. As the wind started
to die the islanders peered from their doors cautiously,
blinking like badgers emerging from hibernation, and Ah
Wong's restaurant reopened. For Sarah and Nick three
days together was a rare luxury; they talked a lot, made
love, opened several bottles of claret. The only drawback
was Sarah's chafing to get back and sort out Tang and Foo
– she always felt frustrated and irritable until she could see
some kind of shape to a case – so she was half-relieved
when she woke to a clear sky on Friday. Two hours later,
at eight thirty, she was walking through Central from the
ferry to her tiny office in HMS *Tamar*. The naval base's
undistinguished brick buildings clustered on the waterfront, full of cheerful sailors with white-topped caps,
white shorts and hairy pink legs. God knows what they all
did now there was such a small navy.

Sarah's room was like a slit trench, just big enough for a
metal desk, filing cabinet and a couple of chairs; but it had
a magnificent view across the harbour to Kowloon. She
could sit with her feet on the window ledge doing nothing
for hours, watching the sampans chugging between
anchored freighters and warships – usually American frig-
ates. After the storm the sun was dazzling on the expanse
of blue water, dominated by a massive aircraft carrier
flying the Stars and Stripes. In the far distance, beyond
the New Territories, she could see the wrinkled brown
hills of China. Sarah unlocked her in-tray. Irritatingly

there was nothing from London in response to her ciphered telegram about the meeting with Foo; she should have stayed on Cheung Chau and made a lazy weekend of it. It was typical – panic one minute, ignore you the next. She shrugged and started to plough through the morning's intercepts. Nothing of much interest was happening in China – or, if there was, it was going by secure landline not vulnerable radio.

After an hour she ran out of work and went for a chat with the Wren in the next office. Lynne came from Bristol; fair-haired, small and pretty she got through boy-friends like sex was going out of fashion and ten minutes of her reminiscences usually had Sarah falling about. Although Wrens were now going to sea for the first time, it was impossible to imagine Lynne on a ship. She was a secretary in uniform, working for Mary Devereux at the end of the corridor.

Sarah had never had cause to give the Wrens much thought before she was posted to Hong Kong. It was still a mild surprise to find them no longer confined to desks and radio-rooms – their officers now held the same ranks and responsibilities as men in the navy. Mary Devereux was an electronics engineer, a Commander and, at least in theory, senior enough to captain a frigate or submarine. She was very popular with her team of thirty, men and women all working on communications – radio links with ships and submarines, interception of Chinese signals – but she was unquestionably the boss. Like Nick, she was going places in intelligence and Sarah's job was to be a human junction box between the SIS station and Mary's outfit. Sarah envied the presence with which she swept in, all crisp in white blouse and dark blue skirt, the three stripes on her shoulders proclaiming authority. To make it even more unfair, she was still in her mid-thirties and good-looking: about five foot six, dark curls, English rose complexion, slim with fabulous legs. She was single; the whisper among the girls was that she had her moments, but nobody knew where or with whom.

29

Lynne's account of her torrid evening with a yuppie from Jardine Matheson was giving way to horoscopes and knitting patterns, when Sarah heard the phone ringing next door. She ran back into her own office, cursing the locked door, and picked it up.

'Sarah? It's Mason here.' One of the top brass from the office on the Peak.

'I'm honoured.'

He laughed. 'The Tang Tsin thing is limping into life again. There's a meeting with God at two o'clock, conference room B up here. I take it you can come.' It was a polite way of issuing an order.

It was a nasty little town in Shansi, only three hundred miles south-west of the capital but with all the worst features of provincial China. The buildings on the main street had an air of neglect and the atmosphere was dry and dusty; the usual vertical red and blue signs climbed up their façades but not many of them – and the shops had little to sell. Tang Tsin felt uncomfortably conspicuous as he emerged from the government guest house carrying his black briefcase. As he passed a building site on which young men in vests and shorts balanced like ballet dancers on bamboo scaffolding, the hostility and suppressed violence following him were almost tangible. After Tian'an Men he had reverted to wearing a grey Mao suit, shapeless tunic buttoned to the neck, which proclaimed him as one of the oppressors.

Tang was of average height, a little over five feet, his hair still black but thinning, his face pale and lined with fatigue. He had flown in yesterday for a tedious meeting with the regional police commander; Tang could not imagine why the man chose to operate from a dump like this – in the old days of Kang Sheng at least the security services had a certain style. At the end of the street he joined a crowded bus for the next town and the airport. Every seat was taken by women in black pyjamas and old men constantly expectorating on the floor; the smell of sweat was disgusting.

Barely a mile down the road the bus was stopped by an army roadblock. So the situation at the mine had not improved. Through the dusty window he could see the closed gates and a line of men in yellow plastic helmets staring defiantly through the wire. Some carried shovels or pickaxes as weapons. The soldiers outside outnumbered them by at least three to one and were advancing slowly behind an armoured car, AK-47s slung across their shoulders but swinging long wooden staves. The stand-off had lasted three days and Tang knew that this was the end – for the ringleaders a very final end for they would be tried and shot by evening. The bus fell silent – even the incessant spitting stopped – as its passengers watched in fascinated silence. The armoured car suddenly speeded up and rammed the gates, crunching the flimsy wood and wire beneath its wheels. As the soldiers rushed in, sun glinting on their steel helmets, the striking miners stood their ground swinging pickaxes murderously.

But the vicious hand-to-hand conflict lasted only a few minutes. The officer standing in the armoured car bellowed orders through a loudhailer and his troops ran back a few yards, turned and opened fire; not into the air but straight into the bodies of the strikers, three long bursts of hot metal. Suddenly there were men writhing on the ground and blood everywhere – Tang could hear their screams and curses as if they were only feet away. The soldiers clipped on fresh magazines and fired again. The strikers who were still standing turned and ran, pursued by uniformed men flailing staves with all their strength, and the bus drove on.

He arrived at Shoudu airport four hours later after a delayed internal flight. This time there was an official car to take him to the office; he did not reach home until eight that evening. Like China, Tang's house had no windows

31

to the outside world. It was built of stone and set around a small courtyard with a dried-up fountain at its centre. He had been lucky to be allocated it ten years ago and had grown to love it, even in winter when the roof tiles were covered by snow and the glowing stove heated only the main room adequately. But now it was spring, warm – and his house had become his prison.

He pedalled down the narrow alley, just wide enough for a car but he had never possessed such a luxury, dismounted and pushed his bicycle through the wooden gate into the yard. He felt awful, weary from the twelve-hour day and drained by the constant worry. It was six months since he had sent his wife and two children to relatives in the country for safety. At first they had exchanged letters every week, but for five weeks now he had heard nothing. He was sure that he was being watched round the clock and was loath to take the risk of visiting them and giving away their whereabouts. There was no telephone in his cousin's house – there was only one in the whole village, in the police post. It was unlikely the *Gonganbu* had hard evidence against him, but suspicion would be enough for them to take him when they were ready. On the other hand, if he could resist the pain of the interrogation and keep his mouth shut it would take them a long time to find his family – surely long enough for the underground or the church to get them to safety?

His fears for himself led on to his fears for the country. Back in the fifties he had believed that Mao's socialism was the way forward, that China's endless problems could be solved. But then Mao had gone mad and now there was nothing left at the centre but a clique of murderous old men dedicated only to destroying each other. The one objective they all shared was the need to cling to power and crush the currents of opposition stirring all over China. Tian'an Men had solved nothing and the bitter scene Tang had witnessed that morning was repeated somewhere every day. God knows where it would all end – or whether he would be there to see it.

Despite his depressed mood, the little courtyard seemed to offer a glimpse of tranquillity. As he sat under the curving green tiles of the eaves with his evening rice and vegetables he felt less imprisoned. He could hear the traffic on the main road, but only distantly. Everything he could see was in harmony: the proportion of the wooden windows that looked out from the house, now mostly shuttered, the low doorway, the creeper on the walls and the golden marigolds that had appeared in the stone trough for another year despite his neglect. As dusk fell he lit the lantern and poured himself a glass of *mao-tai*, followed by another as he became morose again.

It was dark and his head was swimming when he heard the hammering from the alley. The interlude of tranquillity was over. When he staggered over to open the gate a wave of fear shot through him like an electric shock – the yellow light from the lantern revealed three armed soldiers outside.

The conference room had no windows, its walls insulated with layers of polystyrene that were supposed to make it bugproof, and the air conditioning was icy. Tom Rumbelow, the station chief, sat at the head of the table huddled into a tweed jacket. Apart from Sarah only Mary Devereux was there, opposite an empty chair where Gatti should have been. The two women were stunned when Rumbelow told them what had happened. 'His whole family?' Sarah had thought she was hardened to violent death but her voice shook. 'Two little boys? It's horrendous. Has he gone back to the States or what?'

'No, he's still here.' Rumbelow shook his head. 'Says he has to stay on duty while he's head of station. Bloody fool. God knows what will happen – the funeral's tomorrow at Cape Collinson crematorium, if anyone wants to go.'

'I will,' said Sarah. 'But *why* did it happen? Was it *meant* – some kind of link with Tang and Foo? A warning?'

Rumbelow yawned. It was common knowledge that he was fifty-four and bored stiff; next year he would retire and he couldn't wait to occupy the cottage he had bought in Suffolk, near Southwold. 'A little fanciful, Sarah – it's important to guard against overdramatising, if you don't mind my saying so.' He smiled at her patronisingly, then turned to the other woman. 'Tell us more about this fellow Tang, Mary.'

'Tang Tsin is a Party member, sir, and an official in the *Tewu*. He was recruited as an agent by Benjamin Foo when he was still working for your people – about fifteen years ago.'

'How?' growled Rumbelow. 'I mean is he doing it for money or what?'

'He was brought up as a Catholic and still is one, secretly. I guess he just hates the regime. An awful lot of Chinese do, you know.' Rumbelow nodded vaguely; he had never really understood agents motivated by ideology.

'Shall I go on?' Sarah realised that she was listening more to Mary's classy voice than to what she was saying – she always sounded like the head girl announcing netball results. Sarah smiled inwardly and jerked herself back to reality. 'Tang had more natural reasons for contact with the American Embassy than the British, so they ran him. The product was shared.'

'*I've* never seen anything.' Rumbelow sounded puzzled.

'I expect it went from Washington straight to London. In any case, he hasn't produced much these last five years. We regarded him as dormant.' She looked at Rumbelow questioningly and he grunted for her to go on. 'Then six months ago he suddenly sends this postcard to one of the safe houses here, activating a procedure for a panic meeting set up by Foo who's been out of the business for twelve years.'

'That's when Roper went to meet him?' Sarah felt herself colouring as Rumbelow mentioned Nick – it still seemed odd to have a lover whose name cropped up at work. 'Turned up at the spot agreed with Foo twelve years ago?'

'Yes, by the lake in Zizhuyuan Park – near the zoo. Foo had planned it quite cleverly – Roper was to be there at set times, but all different, on Mondays, Wednesdays and Fridays until he turned up. Roper only had to go twice. He met him last October, exchanged passwords and bingo.' Mary smiled, as if encouraging Rumbelow to wake up and do the job he was paid for.

But the head of station looked steadfastly unimpressed. 'So what the hell was the panic about?'

'He said he'd been moved to a new post dealing with six major penetration agents in the West. All concerned with defence in some way.'

'I thought all that was passé?' Rumbelow pulled his jacket round him in an effort to keep warm. 'Everyone loves us since Tsar Mikhail took over.'

'The Chinese don't. They're the last serious communist power and they don't know what's hit them. They're edgy, scared, building up their networks to keep a jump ahead of the enemy – and that means us, and the Americans.'

Rumbelow nodded. 'Go on.' Although he still looked bored, Sarah sensed that behind the mask he was suddenly concentrating.

'Roper arranged to meet him a week later, but Tang didn't show. The following week he did and gave Roper photocopies of some documents – they turned out to be the minutes of one of their top intelligence committees. They set up a couple of drops, one in the park, one near Xizhimen station, and for five months Tang left top-grade material in them.'

'Where'd he get it from?' demanded Rumbelow. 'I mean what's his *job*?'

'Analysing material from these half-dozen agents in the West, linking it up with intercepts – writing reports for the top levels in the government.'

'Uh-huh.' Rumbelow sounded sceptical. 'Then he asked for another meeting?'

'Yes, but this time in Beihai park, near the Five Dragon Pavilion.'

There was an expectant silence in the room. 'Go on,' said Rumbelow softly. 'This was just recently, wasn't it?'

'Yes, a fortnight ago. In the last two or three drops he'd left notes saying he wanted out – asylum in the West for himself and his family. Now he pressed this – he said he'd helped us on and off for fifteen years and that had always been the deal.'

'But there was something else, wasn't there?'

'He said that he had a new responsibility, he was concentrating on reports from a major agent codenamed Scorpion.'

'With a naval background? Someone highly placed and concerned with Trident – maybe an officer on one of the new submarines or on shore running communications?'

'Not necessarily . . . ' Mary tried to interrupt but Rumbelow was in full flow, leaning back, staring glassy-eyed at the ceiling. 'The jewel in our defence crown. Our underwater launching platforms for all those nasty missiles and the means of activating them. The one weapon we're both hanging on to like grim death and could use against any government – Marxist, Islamic, sane or loony – that got tiresome in all this political chaos. Terrific. Clever old Johnny Chinaman.' He looked down at his papers, fingering a felt-tip. 'Don't suppose he had a name or anything useful like that?'

'No, he was reading himself in, boning up on low-frequency radio and the technical details of Trident so far as they know them in Peking. He thought he would be evaluating reports without ever knowing the agent's name. But the naval connection may be just *coincidental*, sir. The main target may be much wider than Trident, which is no doubt basic to our defences but not particularly relevant to China just at the moment.'

Tom Rumbelow stood up, arching his back with his hands deep in his jacket pockets, and studied the map of China that covered one wall. 'Shit. And they'll go spare in

London – Trident's the one thing that hasn't been penetrated so far as we know. Maybe we'll never use it, but by God we can't have a traitor running it. Why the hell does it have to be on my patch?'

Sarah and Mary Devereux exchanged glances of desperation. 'The problem, Mr Rumbelow,' Sarah interrupted firmly, 'is not Trident – we have to find this *Scorpion*.'

Rumbelow rounded on her. 'I know that, dear child – that's why I sent you to see *Foo*.'

'Which may have been a mistake.' Sarah spoke very deliberately, trying to look him straight in the eye. 'We showed our hand and Bob Gatti was warned off in a matter of hours.'

Rumbelow's face darkened angrily. 'I said we mustn't overdramatise, Sarah – there may be no connection at all.' His expression changed to slightly sheepish. 'But I did follow up your report, Sarah – a good report by the way.' He smiled patronisingly again. 'Made it clear that we wouldn't have consulted Foo if it hadn't been for his past connection with Nairn, that he'd reacted badly and there was no more mileage unless Sir David would meet Foo himself.'

That's right, cover your arse, thought Sarah. Aloud she said: 'Foo was kicked out twelve years ago for suspicious contacts with Red China and personally I still don't trust him an inch.'

'You may be right, but let's not overcomplicate. As you say, Scorpion's the problem and we just have to dangle some bait and catch the bastard.' Rumbelow snapped his folder shut like a gin trap closing.

'And then we lift out Tang?' Mary's concern sounded genuine. She was a decent woman as well as clever.

'Of course, Mary.' Rumbelow sounded pained. 'We always keep our word. Well, nearly always.'

4

Seven hundred miles up the coast of the People's Republic the sun was warm on the mountains and lakes of Hangzhou. Walking to the water's edge they made a handsome couple – the man tall, around forty, wearing only maroon boxer shorts that showed off a muscular torso. His face was thoughtful: ice blue eyes and hair still fair but thinning. She was Vietnamese, small and birdlike, thick black sampan-girl hair halfway down her back as she moved gracefully beside him. She seemed to glide over the ground, while his sandals crunched heavily on the gravel path.

Behind them the red pavilion shimmered in hot sun, gold dragons snarling at each corner of its roof, but the garden was green, full of shrubs and trees to cast shadow and cooled by a fountain. White umbrellas shaded a paved terrace. The sampans far out on the lake were unmistakably Chinese but otherwise, with the hills in the distance, they could have been in Italy or Switzerland. Apart from the cawing of crows in the trees and the lapping of tiny waves, the couple were surrounded by stillness. He flopped down on a canvas sunbed and she pirouetted before him: a tiny, taut body golden in a white bikini. She reached down to take his hand and pointed towards the lake but he shook his head. With a half-smile her almond eyes narrowed and she took a step away from him, peeling off both parts of her swimsuit and walking naked to the water without a glance backwards. He watched her, as he had so often in the past – head and back erect, the curve of her spine flowing into slim hips and legs that were long for a girl of her height. Her buttocks bunched and quivered rhythmically as she walked, ending in a short skipping run as she dived in.

He followed her and they swam for about twenty minutes, splashing and laughing. Back on the terrace she poured green tea from a flask and knelt beside him as he sipped it, leaning on one elbow. 'I missed you.' She spoke in awkward, sibilant English, for she knew little Chinese and he even less of her language. They had spoken English when he first picked her up in the bar in Hue and they had done so ever since.

'And I missed *you*, Josie.' He always used her bar-girl name, not Tuyet as she had been before. Putting down the porcelain bowl, he leaned back with a sigh as her fingers ran sensuously over his body, caressing, electrifying. 'But it is all going well and that bastard of a minister is pleased.'

'I'm glad, Luther. For both of us.' She put a finger to her lips and climbed on top of him, her face an inch from his, their lips brushing tantalisingly as her back arched and her bottom wriggled as she enclosed him. 'You *strong*. You *very* strong.' She giggled as she echoed the patois of bar-girls all over South-East Asia and he smiled up at her. It was an old joke between them. She laughed again. 'I can never believe there's no bone in it.' But then she sighed and closed her eyes as she felt him thrusting deep inside, gripping him tightly with bent knees, black hair cascading over her shoulders, panting, tiny body arching and twisting, eyes suddenly open and radiant as she soared into a series of frenzied climaxes.

Later they lay side by side on a softly woven Chinese rug, shivering a little as the sun began to descend behind the hills. Josie covered herself with a towel, for like most Vietnamese girls she was innately modest when not actively displaying her body. 'How long have we been together, Luther? Is it five years now, or six?'

'Just over five.' He took her hand and smiled. 'Are

you glad?'

'Of course. You rescued me from being poor and hungry – and from hating men.' She rolled towards him and kissed his chest, biting gently when her teeth found a nipple.

He ran his fingers through the thick black hair. 'You like this house, don't you?'

'It is our home, Luther. I like it best when we are alone here and I can look after you.'

'Would you mind if we went to live somewhere else?' He said it casually, seeming to study a long-necked cormorant as it bobbed on the water then dived for a fish.

She look puzzled and shook her head. 'I will go wherever you want, Luther. You are my life.' The words sounded natural and honest from her, as they never could from a European.

'Even away from China? To Singapore perhaps – or maybe Europe?'

'But why should we leave this beautiful place? You have lived in China all your life. The army found you as an orphan and Kang Sheng had you brought up – they've given you everything. This house.' She gave a throaty chuckle. 'Me . . . '

He stroked her face gently. 'But we don't need their permission to love each other and things are changing.'

'Changing? How?'

'I believed they were right, Josie, now I believe they are mad and I am becoming afraid.'

'You – afraid?' She gave a ribald chuckle, rolling towards him again. 'Never.'

'No, not afraid for myself. Afraid that something dreadful is going to happen here. The old men in Peking believe nothing any more but cling to power and there are great currents running against them. There has been bloodshed and there will be more. I can do nothing to change that, so maybe it's time to go? We have some money abroad, almost enough to buy a house and feed ourselves. Who else has that in China?'

She smiled and nodded, her movements still delicate as a bird, but the carefree joy had gone: suddenly there was real fear in her eyes. 'Do *they* know, Luther?'

'No, they don't – and they must not. I've recruited many agents for them, but they believe the one they call Scorpion will be very important. Now he is in danger and I must save him. The minister has promised me a large payment in hard currency if I succeed. It will be available in the Bank of China – in Hong Kong. With that, we have enough.'

She stood up and clutched the towel round her, uneasy, frightened, changing the subject. 'It's getting cold – let's go indoors.'

'But you will come with me?'

She did not meet his eyes. 'Yes, yes, of course. I am your woman.'

'And you will keep this secret – a great secret between the two of us, Josie?'

She bowed her head. 'I have forgotten already – I'm far too scared to speak of it, Luther, and I'd never betray you. If they knew we might leave they'd kill us both, I know it.'

'Yes – the next month is dangerous. After that we shall be two new people, living a new life.' He lit a Gitane from a blue packet, shielding the flame of his lighter against the breeze with cupped hands. 'I will destroy anyone who threatens that.'

'Was the American spy a threat?'

'Oh yes.'

'Does it matter that we did not kill him – only his family?'

'I meant you to kill them all, to warn the others that tangling with Scorpion is dangerous, make them confused and frightened.' He shrugged. 'If it was not enough you can always go back.'

She knelt and threw her arms round his waist, the towel slipping to reveal the satiny, almost transparent skin stretched over her fragile collar bone and a breast that was

41

small, but round and firm with dark pigmentation around the nipple. He kissed her tenderly. It was impossible to imagine her in action as she had been trained by the *Tewu*, the lithe killing machine that could take life silently and in seconds, with her hands or that long needle-like stiletto. He had never been there, but she had taken out more than two dozen for him – that tiresome CIA man's family in Hong Kong only a week ago – and she always came back at a peak of sexual arousal. He had never sent her out to kill simply for the pleasure she would give him on her return, but he had often been tempted to do so.

'We have crayfish with the evening rice,' she said, taking his hand as they walked back to the pavilion.

Nairn arrived at Kai Tak airport looking, as ever, like a down-at-heel commercial traveller. He had travelled from London on the British Airways 747 unaccompanied, first class because that way you could sleep but otherwise just like any business traveller. His suit was shiny at the elbows and frayed at the cuffs, flapping round a long bony frame. The gaunt, hollow face cracked into a smile as he opened his shoulder bag for customs and had his passport stamped by immigration.

'Sir David Nairn?' asked the uniformed Chinese girl, puzzled by the occupation shown as *Government Service*. The only civil servant she had heard of with a K was the Governor himself. 'How long you stay Hong Kong?'

'Just a few days.'

She stamped a one-month visa and he passed on, anonymous in the crowd, to kiss Sarah Cable. 'How the devil are you, my girl?'

'Fine. How're you? Rumbelow will be furious when he knows you've arrived without telling him.'

'He'll live with it. Let's find a taxi – I'm staying at the Mandarin.' They walked out into the heat together, a man in his sixties and a girl more than thirty years younger, but obviously fond of each other. Nairn had recruited Sarah seven years ago, before his appointment as head of the service had astonished Whitehall. Then a widower, he had been closer to her than was wise; and she remained half in love with him despite his acquisition of a new wife and small daughter. In the taxi he put his arm round her shoulders. 'How's your dad these days?'

Sarah sighed. She hadn't seen Nairn for over a year but they always picked up again as if it had been yesterday. Was Nick becoming like that? 'I saw him and Naomi when I was on leave about six months ago. They're running a post office on the Isle of Wight and growing a lot of vegetables. I believe they're very happy.'

'I'm glad. Are you happy, Sarah?' Of course he knew how tempestuous her life had been, but even for Nairn the question was abrupt.

'I – I think so, David. I'm glad you sent me here – it's a super place, even with 1997 so close.'

'Good. Can I get over to Macao today? I'd better see Foo and get it over.'

Sarah turned away from him, peering round the driver's neck into the wing mirror. The dashboard of the taxi was cluttered with Taoist charms and a tiny television set. 'Macao? That's easy enough.' She looked puzzled. 'David?'

'Yes?'

'I don't think you're quite as incognito as you wanted. We're being followed.'

'Who by?'

'A maroon Nissan with two Chinese in it.'

'No doubt our friends from the New China News Agency. Damn.' The Scots accent became very marked when he was irritated. 'I had hoped for twenty-four hours' privacy. How the hell did they know?'

'They probably watch every arrival – they're not short of people.'

'Maybe we can lose them at the Mandarin. I must see Foo without an audience.'

'How do we do that?'

The gaunt face creased into an evil grin as the taxi plunged into the tunnel under the harbour. 'I've done it before, my girl – remember this used to be my patch.'

The Sikh doctor adjusted his gold half-glasses and smiled down at the tiny Chinese policewoman. The girl in the high bed lay silent, unconscious as she had been for ten days. 'She had bullet wounds in the shoulder and thigh, WPC Wu. They are both healing well and no vital organs were damaged, but she has not recovered from the shock – she has never regained consciousness.' From the corridor came the sound of hurried footsteps and the clattering wheels of a trolley; they were in the Prince of Wales Hospital at Yuen Chau Kok in the New Territories. 'Do you know any more about who she is?'

The Chinese girl shook her head. Her khaki uniform was so well pressed it almost creaked as she moved. 'She is a refugee trying to cross from Communist China, but she carried nothing to show her identity. How long will she be unconscious, doctor?'

He scratched his head below the white turban. 'I cannot tell – it could be days or months. She is in coma. She may never recover at all. I'm sorry I cannot be more helpful.'

The policewoman put her notebook back in a breast pocket. 'Thank you, doctor. I shall call every day until she comes round.'

Private telephone lines were rare in mainland China but the Vietnamese girl and the European known as Luther possessed one. It was a professional necessity and they often regretted it, as they did next morning when it rang at eight o'clock. No sooner had their idyll begun than it was over – at least for a few days. Josie left alone, taken in a military car to Shanghai where she would catch an ordinary commercial flight back to Hong Kong.

44

5

The three soldiers in their baggy green tunics were polite
but firm, giving Tang Tsin time to lock up his house before
ushering him to a car parked at the end of the alley. He
did not recognise its make but it was large and black, with
a small flagstaff on the offside wing. The interior was
more luxurious than any he had ever seen: soft, deep
leather seats with white antimacassars and curtains on the
windows. They drove fast through empty streets, for it
was past midnight, until the car stopped at a gateway
guarded by soldiers with AK-47s. After a brief word from
the driver, there was a low hum and the steel gate moved
sideways on rollers. As they drove forward it closed behind them. Tang blinked as powerful lights went on: they
were in a kind of airlock, a space with bare concrete walls
and a steel gate at either end. Guards in smart grey
uniforms gestured to Tang and his four companions to
leave the car, lined them all up face to the wall and
searched them. As two guards led Tang through a side
door, the inner gate opened and the car vanished into
darkness. No one had spoken to him since they had left his
house and the silence continued as he was led down endless corridors and up staircases. He had no idea where
they were. At first he had thought they were taking him to
prison, then that it was a ministry. Could it even be
Zhongnanhai, the compound occupied by the leaders?
But no – he had been to Zhongnanhai before – this was a
secret place that he had never known existed.

Eventually the three of them passed through another

guarded door, into a book-lined study looking out on a
garden lit by floodlights among the trees. There were silk
hangings on the walls and a circle of velvet armchairs,
dark red with the ubiquitous white antimacassars. A jade
green vase decorated with gold dragons stood on a side
table. A stocky man rose to greet them with a smile and
motioned Tang to sit down. The two guards vanished. The
stocky man did not offer a name; he had thick black hair
and square horn-rimmed spectacles, a fleshy round face,
sweat on his forehead – could it be the secretive Qiao Shi,
vice-premier and head of all the intelligence services and
security police? Or had he been downgraded in the endless changes since Tian'an Men? There had been so many
that Tang couldn't remember. Whoever it was he had an
air of immense authority and Tang's feeling of inner terror
increased. The long tense build-up, the sudden change to
a warm cocoon, the cosy chat – it was just the scenario for
his final denunciation.

But he clung to his calm exterior, the gravitas that had
seen him through for fifteen years, inclining his head with
a smile as the man – could he be a minister? – poured
green tea into delicate bowls on a small lacquer table.
'Comrade Tang, thank you for coming to see me.' There
had been little choice, thought Tang bitterly, outwardly
smiling again. 'How do you find your new duties?'

'They are most interesting, comrade.'

'It is a position of great trust.' A long pause – was this it,
the knife thrust? 'And the Party is confident that you well
deserve that trust.' The great man smiled again and
poured more tea. Not enough trust to reveal his identity,
thought Tang, but perhaps he was just supposed to *know*?

'I am honoured, comrade. How may I be of service to
you?'

'The People's Republic is surrounded by dangerous
enemies, Tang – and there are also many enemies within.
It will not be easy to preserve all that has been achieved
since Chairman Mao proclaimed our victory in 1949.'

Tang inclined his head again, thinking of the millions

dying from famine as agriculture collapsed, the absurd backyard blast furnaces, the terror of the Cultural Revolution. 'No indeed, comrade,' he said gravely.

'Our need for sound intelligence is great – you have been analysing Scorpion's reports for three months now. What do you make of them?'

'I assume that Scorpion is a middle-ranking naval officer?'

'A fair assumption.'

'Then I would see his – or her – reports as useful for our defence. As he is promoted to senior command, with more involvement in political and strategic decisions, he will become of ever greater value.'

The heavily built man leaned forward confidingly. 'He or she *is* to be promoted soon and I wish you to become more than an analyst – you are to be Scorpion's controller, the executive head of Operation Scorpion. You will be promoted to Grade 5.' He smiled secretively. 'Before you leave here tonight, you will read background papers that are highly confidential. In future Scorpion will be your only responsibility.'

'I – I am very honoured.' How on earth should he address the bastard? He settled on 'Minister'.

'I am sure you will not fail me.'

Tang squirmed inwardly – did the man always speak like one of those awful Maoist propaganda films? Perhaps they lost all sense of reality when they joined the leadership, exhausted by the effort of fighting their way in, too worn out to rule, believing their own myths. He sat modestly with downcast eyes, struggling to hide his fear and contempt. There was an awkward silence – the best thing was to ask a question. 'Why is this Scorpion of such importance, comrade Minister? It seems a great deal of effort to devote to even a very senior naval officer?'

'Ah, but when he is promoted he will move to intelligence duties directed against the People's Republic.'

'Still as a naval officer?'

'Not necessarily.'

'I see. Will his reports continue to be copies of documents?'

'Usually. Scorpion has no radio himself – that might compromise him – and radios will never be used to transmit his intelligence from our missions: it will always come by bag, safeguarded by a courier. You will never meet him yourself, but you will have the services of a senior agent to act as intermediary.'

For the first time Tang started to relax. Maybe his fears of the past months had been groundless after all. He sipped his tea, staring out at the garden; in a corner the silhouette of an armed soldier stood out against the yellow light. 'May I know who is this agent?'

'Of course, my dear Tang. He is a European who grew up in our country – sadly his parents died in the civil war. Unlike a Chinese he can pass unnoticed in the outside world – as American, say, or German or Swede. His codename is Luther and you will meet him soon.' Behind the panel of one-way glass a tall figure sat on a hard chair, watching the two Chinese in the comfortable room. He was white-skinned, dressed in casual Western clothes, and drew on a Gitane, adding to the haze of blue smoke above his head as he nodded approval. Frightened little Tang would serve his purpose well enough.

Twelve hundred miles to the south-west, Sarah Cable lay back in a deckchair with her feet on the balustrade of her balcony. Cheung Chau was dark and quiet. Nairn had taken her out to a frugal supper at the Peak Café – he had never been one for expensive meals and the view was free – and listened to her account of what had been happening. She had left him at the Mandarin Hotel and taken the ferry home. Nick was still spending half his time at the Embassy in Peking and had flown back that afternoon for a couple of days, so she was alone.

Sarah went to bed early and dozed fitfully, her brain refusing to switch off. She had spent all day brainstorming in search of the elusive Scorpion and was beginning to fear they would never find him or her among the three hundred or more names she had listed. It was infuriating, frustrating, yet did it matter? True Trident was the most secret military secret going, but was it about that anyway . . . the real problem was Scorpion just being there . . . What damage might he do if he stayed in place for ten, twenty years, when China was disintegrating, a threat? Yes, it mattered like hell . . . on top of that seeing Nairn always disturbed her – why, oh God, why after all this time . . . and Nick had gone away just when she needed him. She imagined him locked in her legs, a master, or in her arms a child – damn him, oh Christ, *why* couldn't she get to sleep?

After tossing and turning for three hours she tried to lie still for a while, feeling sweaty and uncomfortable. She could feel perspiration dripping down her nose and all over her body, particularly in the small of her back. The green luminous figures on the digital clock showed it to be two in the morning when she admitted defeat and swung her legs out of bed. She always slept naked but it took only minutes to pull on jeans and a shirt in the dark. She padded out to the balcony in her trainers, down the steep metal steps and along the back alley towards the sea. She had a torch in her pocket but there was enough moon to see where she was going and she was on the beach in ten minutes, sitting with her back against an upturned boat and staring at the ghostly white shapes of waves breaking on the sand. The cool night air made her feel less clammy and the low, soporific pounding of the sea calmed her. She sat hugging her knees, gently rocking back and forward, and after a while started walking slowly back. The moon went behind a cloud as she reached the alley in which her apartment stood. Suddenly it was coal black all around and she hesitated at the corner, unable to see, afraid that she might trip over the crab pots or slip on the garbage that she knew to be everywhere.

The explosion rocked her as the Molotov cocktails

shattered a window fifty yards away. For a few seconds she was deafened, her eardrums stinging with pain. But then she heard a tinkle of glass and the angry crackle giving way to a roar as yellow flames shot upwards and lit the street like daylight. Doors were opening and puzzled Chinese faces peered out as she ran forward. The second floor of the building was ablaze, the rush of flames punctuated by the splinter of wood and muffled explosions. Wooden beams glowed red in the tongues of orange consuming the walls and Sarah flinched as the roof fell in with a sickening crash, filling the alley with red-hot cinders. She could feel the heat scorching her face. 'Jesus Christ,' she said as she ran back coughing from the smoke as Ah Wong from the café took her arm to steady her.

'You okay, Missee Sarah? You need help?'

Her head was swimming and she realised that she was swaying as he helped her to squat on a stool that someone had brought from their house. She managed a wintry smile at the concerned Chinese faces all around. 'I'm all right, thanks.'

'But is yo' place, yes?'

She nodded. 'Yes, it's my apartment. Thank God I was out.'

6

No one knew who Luther's parents had been, not even Luther himself. Forty years on he had only the vaguest memory of their deaths. He knew he had felt terror so deep that it could still resurface in nightmares, both when his father had been killed and when the communist soldiers carried him away afterwards. But they had been kind enough and he had grown up the only European child in an orphanage near Peking.

When he was ten, Luther had been playing on the swings in the garden when the matron had approached with a thin-faced Chinese dressed in the usual drab tunic; he wore a narrow moustache and horn-rimmed spectacles. The small boy had been flattered by the man's attention as they chatted, sitting cross-legged in a shady corner. Only years later would he learn that his visitor had been Kang Sheng, head of the new country's intelligence services, lover of Mao's wife Jiang Qing, the great Chairman's bitter rival for power.

From that day Luther's life changed. He left the orphanage and went to a boarding school for the children of high Party cadres. He mastered English and Russian. In his mid-teens he was trained for intelligence work, along with young Chinese men and women and a few other foreigners, in a camp on a disused airfield near Shanghai. He learnt how to discover information and how to transmit it, how to build a powerful short-wave radio from components you could buy in any high street, how to use codes, how to kill when necessary. It felt exciting to be

51

involved in these great mysteries; and flattering when he met Kang Sheng again. This time he knew well who the old man was when Kang summoned him to his head-quarters at *Zhuynan*, the Bamboo Garden, in north-east Peking.

The place was a complex of five large wooden pavilions, with much red lacquer, linked by covered passageways and surrounded by gardens with rocks, fountains and rare flowers. There were also armed guards, radio aerials and, so it was said, a vast underground bunker. Kang Sheng was now old but his eyes sparkled with life as he sat by a window open to the garden, peering through thick spectacles to paint a delicate plant in watercolours. By now Luther knew something of Kang's reputation for double-dealing and cruelty, but he did not sense evil as they sipped tea together. Kang told Luther, now eighteen, that he would be sent abroad for a year, with a West German passport, to Princeton University in America. He could start a degree in any subject he chose, but the objective was to perfect his English and get to know the country. He would be provided with money and someone from the Chinese Embassy would keep in touch with him discreetly, otherwise he was free to live his own life. And then came the unexpected punchline.

'You have been trained to work for our *Tewu*, Luther, because we need agents of European origin who do not stand out like a Chinese. I hope you will decide to return in a year and follow the career I have in mind for you – you will be serving the Party well and you will be rewarded. But if you decide to stay in the West, you will have my blessing.'

Luther often recalled his feelings of gratitude and disbelief as he travelled around America. But it seemed natural enough to return to China; it was the only home he had. Although a nominal Party member, he was sceptical about Maoism and Marxism – but the life of an intelligence officer with plenty of spending money and excitement seemed more attractive than making it on his own in America. It never occurred to him to defect. It never occurred to him, until years later, that the freedom to stay had always been unreal. He knew too much about the *Tewu* and if he had not returned they would surely have taken him out?

As he drove back to his apartment after observing Tang, Luther also recalled his last meeting with Kang Sheng. It was 1975 and Kang was plainly dying of cancer, his face and body wasted away, his breath so putrid from the decay within that it made Luther want to vomit. He had been propped up on cushions by the same open windows in the Bamboo Garden. Luther had paid his respects for a few minutes and left. He was already starting to feel trapped and bitter. They *had* been good to him after the tragedy that left him alone in a strange country as a child; but they had also kept him here to use him. Had they chosen, he could have been sent back to be with his own people, wherever they were – but twenty-five years ago it might not have been so difficult to trace a relative somewhere in Germany. Now he was condemned to this rootless Flying Dutchman life for ever.

From then on Luther had become more and more a mercenary – a loyal mercenary but a mercenary all the same. He served them to the utmost of his ability; but one day he would get out. Parking his Skoda outside the small modern apartment block, he was relieved to glimpse Josie's black hair in the light of the upstairs window. He was relieved that she was back safely but his eyes hardened as he locked the car. He hoped she had been more successful in neutralising the Cable girl than she had with Gatti. Those two were good, too good – a threat. He had no intention of allowing them to blow an agent he had cultivated for ten years, particularly when that agent was the price of a new life and escape from a country he had come to fear and hate.

* * *

WPC Wu visited the Prince of Wales Hospital in the New Territories every day, early in the evening. The girl remained in a coma, propped up on crisp white pillows, kept alive by a glucose drip. Dr Singh became less optimistic every time she spoke to him, but WPC Wu was doggedly persistent. Nearly three weeks had passed when she arrived on foot at seven o'clock. The Sikh doctor was hurrying down a corridor when he saw her, trying to retain his dignity by not quite running. He stopped abruptly. 'Ah, Miss Wu!' His grave expression did not change, but there was a hint of satisfaction in the soft brown eyes. 'Come with me, please.'

The narrow side ward smelt of antiseptic and the girl was still propped up in the same bed, but her breathing had changed. It was faster, more varied. 'It is Dr Singh again.' He spoke to her slowly and clearly in Mandarin. 'What is your name please?'

The girl's eyes flickered. 'Ah Ming.' Her speech was distant, hollow and she sounded painfully tired, struggling – but for the first time her lips moved. 'My name is Tang Ah Ming.'

Nairn did not travel to Macao after Sarah dropped him at the Mandarin. After three terse phone calls from his room, high up over the bobbing lights of the harbour, he went to bed and slept through to seven next morning. By eight he was on the ferry to Peng Chau.

The rocky islet lay in the shadow of Lantau, the largest of Hong Kong's islands, its spine of wooded hills covered in morning mist. The ferry scattered a flurry of sampans, each with its canvas-covered living space at the stern, nosing through water littered with garbage and rainbow patches of oil until it bumped against the slimy piles of the jetty. Nearby a motor junk was unloading bags of cement for yet more new housing but Nairn wondered how long that would last; he had already sensed the changed atmosphere, the resignation to takeover by China, the winding down, the fear. Conspicuous by his height he hurried through the crowded alleys of the village, jostled on all sides, past the stalls of fresh fish and fruit, deafened by the staccato clacking of Cantonese, narrowly avoiding a basket of quacking ducks hanging from a pole balanced across an old man's shoulders. *A-ma* was waiting at the end of the other pier, gleaming white hull out of place among the dirty weatherbeaten junks and sampans. Her engines started the moment the gaunt Scotsman stepped on the deck.

Benjamin Foo was waiting in the saloon, luxurious with mahogany panelling and brass fittings. He gave a formal bow of greeting, his lined face little changed in – what was it – twelve years? The cabin floor tilted as the big cruiser turned out to sea and Nairn grabbed at the table. 'Thank you for coming, Ben, it's good to see you again.' Although Nairn had come a great deal further, Foo remained impassive, gesturing at the bench opposite him and Nairn sank into deep leather cushions. A white-coated steward placed a teapot and two bowls on the table, raising the fiddles at the edge to stop them sliding off as the boat rolled, and left silently. Still Foo had not spoken. It was Nairn who broke the silence. 'She's a beautiful yacht, Ben – I congratulate you. You've achieved great things since we last met,' he paused, searching the other man's face. 'And how is Ruth?'

'My wife is well and so are the children.' Foo met the other man's eyes sternly and there was another long silence. 'I lost a lot of face, Nairn.' He paused to let the rebuke sink in. 'A *lot* of face – my work for your people was the centre of my life and you robbed me of it.'

Nairn nodded awkwardly. 'I know. It may be hard to believe but I *do* understand. I still feel badly about it, but I had no choice at the time.'

Foo remained stern. 'I have never been so sure about that.' He gave a dismissive gesture. 'Why have you come? What do you want?'

Nairn began to feel that his journey halfway round the

world had been a mistake. 'I am looking for your help, Foo Li-shih.' He deliberately used Foo's Chinese name as a mark of respect.

Foo did not reciprocate and remained formal. 'And why should I help you, Sir David? You betrayed my friendship, destroyed my life, which I have rebuilt with much difficulty.'

'Because we both care about the future of China – and of Hong Kong and Macao.'

'Which is why your government is handing back Hong Kong and its people to China, I suppose? You care so much that you will see the place eaten up by barbarians?'

'We had treaty obligations that gave us no choice.'

Foo's eyes remained cold. 'I disagree, it is an act of cowardice, but I ask you again – what do you want?'

Nairn shook his head. 'I'm sorry – perhaps it was a mistake to come. I should have realised how you would feel.'

He was almost knocked back in his seat by the gale of laughter and looked up to see Foo's eyes crinkling into a broad grin. The man had been taking the piss out of him – as well he might. 'You know, David,' he was still laughing, 'I think I won, for Ruth has brought me great happiness – I too felt bad when I took her from you. I think I won today as well.' He roared with laughter. 'So maybe honour is satisfied.' Suddenly he was smiling. 'I hesitated before meeting you again, but it is the past, my friend.' Foo poured two bowls of tea and offered one symbolically to Nairn. 'It is history and best put behind us.'

Nairn's surge of relief was almost painful. He sipped the aromatic green tea, then placed the bowl carefully on the table and reached across to take Foo's hand. 'Thank you, Ben.'

A few minutes later Foo led him out on deck where they sat under an awning at the stern. Sun had broken through the cloud and it was going to be a hot day. The cruiser was passing the end of Lantau, green hills rising behind the white lighthouse on the pier at Tai O, heading out to sea. Foo had been wearing a sober tropical suit in the saloon, but now threw off his jacket, which was lined with vivid blue silk. 'I hope you will come back to Macao and have lunch with me and Ruth? You would not find that – embarrassing?'

'No, it would be a great pleasure, after so long.' Tea had been replaced by two San Miguel beers and they sipped them pensively, two middle-aged men remaking a friendship wrecked by Nairn twelve years before. Once again it was Nairn who broke the silence. 'This was your territory, Ben, still is. So what the hell's going on? Some piddling source called Tang Tsin sends some decent intelligence for a change, there seems to be some kind of agent codenamed Scorpion. Everybody gets their knickers in a twist. So what? The Chinese have hundreds of half-arsed agents, so no doubt do we. But somehow this matters and they put the frighteners on – an American officer's family has been murdered, wife and two boys, horrible business. As I was leaving this morning I had a call to say there's been an attack on our girl Cable.'

Foo looked startled. 'When? Was she hurt?'

'Just last night. They firebombed her flat. She's shocked but not injured. By sheer chance she was out at the time, or she might have been killed. So tell me, Ben, what's all this about?' Nairn smiled inwardly at his own question; they could have been talking as colleagues twelve years ago, without the long painful rift. Foo was more generous than most Chinese, who could never have forgiven Nairn. Now his eyes narrowed as he stared at the waves. They were crossing the forty mile width of the Pearl estuary, both Hong Kong and Macao out of sight. *A-ma* breasted a big roller and spray spattered on the canvas awning.

'You are the intelligence officer, David – I'm just a humble merchant these days.'

'Stuff that.' Nairn struggled to light his pipe, giving up as the breeze kept blowing out the flame from his gas lighter. 'I can't imagine you're not better in touch than my man here.'

'Rumbelow? He does you little credit. But the Cable girl is good. Attractive too, but looks as though she may have been hurt in the past . . . ?'

Nairn gave an awkward cough. 'Yes, that's true, but stop evading the issue, Ben. I've come halfway round the world to talk to you. I'm listening. Tell me.'

Foo reached into a refrigerator tucked into the bulkhead for two more beers. 'Scorpion must be important?'

'Of course.'

'Somebody in Peking knows that Tang is a traitor and is desperate to protect Scorpion?'

'That makes sense, too.'

'There is a naval connection?'

'It seems so.'

Foo shook his head. 'That would be useful to Peking – they want to know about your missile-launching submarines as much as anyone else – but it's not enough. China's enemies are within, not out here.'

'Are they? Just how strong is the opposition – it's very hard to tell from London, you know?'

'It is *massive*, David. The Party and government are totally discredited. The leaders hang on because they use force every time opposition shows itself – not just at Tian'an Men but all over the country. Most of China hates them and looks enviously at what has happened in Eastern Europe, but people in China are poor and weak, disorganised. It is not so easy.' He paused, as if considering whether to go on. 'But there are networks of opposition all over the country, you know, there are plans . . . '

'How much do you know of them?'

Foo shrugged. 'I have some distant involvement. I can help with money, communications. I travel into China quite often.'

'Isn't that rather, well, *dangerous*?'

'It could be – I've had no trouble so far.'

'How will it all end?'

Foo spread his arms wide. 'God alone knows. Unless

58

there is some great change at the centre – a Chinese Gorbachev, which is surely impossible now – there will continue to be unrest and violence until the party collapses, whether suddenly or slowly. There are opposition leaders who favour using force – the army itself is very divided in its loyalties.'

'And where might Scorpion fit in?'

'I'd guess your Trident is not the final target. Useful, very useful – for they must see it as a threat. There are no Chinese submarines carrying nuclear missiles off *your* shores.'

'But you don't see that as enough?'

'No way. This Scorpion is going on to something more senior, where he – or she – can be manoeuvred into position as one of your main contacts with the opposition in China. The people of China will free themselves, like those of Eastern Europe, without your help. But they will want your goodwill and there will be increasing links as things get worse – you and the Americans have many interests to protect in and around Hong Kong. Anyway, some kind of breakdown or civil war in China would be like an earthquake – who knows where the shock waves would end?'

Nairn pulled on his beer, gazing towards an oil tanker flying the Japanese flag. 'There were close links between Western intelligence and the opposition in Eastern Europe for years before the end came.'

'Just so. Scorpion will become a key figure, where he will know the leaders and their plans – and can betray them.'

'But Peking must know already?'

'Not at all. They know of the vocal dissidents, students and the like, but those who are ready to lead when the time comes keep a very low profile. They are well hidden, but Scorpion has already betrayed at least half a dozen.'

Nairn started. 'How do you know – and who were they?'

Foo smiled inscrutably, ignoring the first part of the

59

question. 'You wouldn't know of them unless you are in close touch with China's problems – and I expect you have been preoccupied with Eastern Europe lately. They were middle-ranking officials, army officers, university teachers, potential leaders who have been jailed or executed – or just vanished.'

The cruiser was turning in a long arc towards Macao, a haze of green trees and low white buildings at the end of its peninsula. Something made Nairn feel suddenly uneasy. 'How mixed up in all this are *you*, Ben?'

Foo smiled opaquely. 'Perhaps more than I should be at my age, with a young wife and children yet to grow up. But China is in a Godawful mess, the economy is bad, there could be violent changes. None of us wants to see that – or Hong Kong and Macao drawn in and ruined.' He was suddenly fierce. 'This is my *home.*'

But which side of the border? thought Nairn. He agreed with Foo's analysis, but was suddenly sensing all the suspicion he had felt twelve years ago. Rumbelow must have been mad to consult Foo – he was surely Peking's man. Aloud he said: 'So you're in danger too Ben?' Nairn spoke quietly, almost casually. He could see a woman waiting on the quay below a large villa and knew at once that it was Ruth Foo: Ruth who had once been his lover. The smile in the familiar kind face seemed to travel across the water; but was it for him or the charismatic Chinese who had won her?

Foo was beside him at the rail. 'Oh yes, David, I fear I am in danger too.'

7

The tip-off was anonymous. They usually are. It came in a muffled telephone call to a police station in the Yau Ma Tei area of Kowloon: heroin with a street value of two hundred thousand Hong Kong dollars, concealed in an apartment on the island, near the coast at Deep Water Bay. The voice was Chinese and the sergeant who took the call yawned. Address? Name of the owner? Your name? She rang off. He logged it but he had heard it all before. Sometimes they were genuine, sometimes just loonies trying to screw their neighbours.

The apartment was in an ageing three-storey block. It was ten o'clock at night when the dark blue Land-Rover parked outside; the dim light from the street lamps caught the white *Police* on its side. Three men clambered out, a British officer and two Chinese constables all armed with revolvers in leather holsters. They adjusted their black peaked caps before marching in, boots clattering on the tiled floor of the entrance hall. The Malaysian caretaker emerged from his bedsitter wringing his hands and looked scared; he was wearing a filthy apron and smelt of curry. The officer gestured at him imperiously. 'Police. Hand over the pass key.' He studied the row of steel mailboxes, each labelled with the number of an apartment and name of the occupant.

The staircase was carpeted so their boots were muffled as they climbed to the top floor. The flat was number six and the officer motioned his men to silence as he turned the key and pushed the door open. Inside was a tiny lobby, fresh flowers on a pretty walnut table, a Canaletto of the Thames on the wall. An open door showed a comfortable drawing room but it was empty. The officer nodded silently to the others who drew their revolvers.

The crash as he kicked in the bedroom door shattered the quiet like an explosion. As the three men fanned out in the room a European woman whipped round, white face staring at them in horror. The shaded glow from two lamps reflected off Wedgwood blue walls and the rumpled black sheets on the bed. She was naked: flawless, slightly plump body twined around the golden skin of the Chinese, a girl in her twenties, pretty, thick black hair, almond eyes blinking in terror.

The Chinese girl shrieked and her hands drew back from the other woman's breasts. The three men paused awkwardly, one constable lustful, the other ashamed as they gazed at the women's bodies. The European stood up deliberately, turning away from them – the vertebrae on her spine stood out as she bent to pick up a short bathrobe from the floor, her buttocks full and white, giving way to broad tanned thighs, the flesh visibly trembling. She turned back, knotting the sash defiantly. 'What the hell do you mean by this?'

'Fucking dykes,' muttered the officer. Aloud he said: 'Shut up and stand by the wall, both of you. We have a warrant to search this apartment.'

'Why?' The woman's voice was shaking.

'I have reason to believe that you have an illegal substance in your possession.' The Chinese girl suddenly ran for the door, but the constables seized her. She struggled with one, scratching his face until blood flowed, but he caught her a punch in the kidneys that left her gasping and writhing on the floor. He turned her over roughly, one knee in the small of her back, and handcuffed her wrists together.

'Whose flat is this?'

The European woman eyed him defiantly. 'Mine.'

He gestured at the Chinese girl. 'What's her name?'

'Chang Xhisin.'

'Live here, does she?' Her classy accent irritated him and he spoke with a sneer.

The woman nodded wretchedly. 'Some of the time.' There were crashes from the other room as drawers were emptied on the floor and she sank to the bed, her face suddenly puffy and puce as the tears came. 'You bastards. You utter bastards.' She buried her face in her hands, her whole body shaking as she sobbed. The bathrobe fell open to reveal the triangle of dark hair between her thighs and she did not bother to cover herself again.

The police officer looked away in disgust. 'For God's sake control yourself woman – we have a job to do.' Two Chinese policewomen who had waited in the Land-Rover appeared in the doorway; he nodded and they started to ransack the bedroom. The search continued for two hours, when all five police returned to the bedroom. The European woman was still sitting on the bed in her bathrobe, staring into the distance as if in a catatonic trance. Her voice was distant, hollow. 'Well – did you find anything?'

'Not yet, madam. Now the policewomen will conduct a body search of you and your *friend*.' He pronounced the word with distaste.

'Like hell you will.'

The two Chinese women removed their tunics and advanced on her. 'We can take you to the station and do it there if you prefer.'

She gave them a glance of pure hatred. 'You bitches – gives you a kick does it, looking up another girl's fanny? Oh get on with it, we don't have any bloody choice, do we?' She stood up, turned awkwardly with legs wide apart and bent forward. The Chinese girl followed meekly, all defiance gone, and the police left empty-handed.

The officer saluted at the door. 'Thank you for your help, madam. I'm sorry you were bothered.'

'So am I,' said Mary Devereux. As the door closed, she went to the window and watched until they drove away, then rounded on the Chinese girl, eyes blazing with fury. 'Well? *Did* you have drugs here?'

The girl shook her head vigorously. 'No, never.'

'Nothing? Are you sure? For Christ's sake, they took the place apart, they body-searched us – it may be your way of spending a quiet evening at home but it certainly isn't mine. Nothing? Never? Not even some cannabis?'

'Well, maybe, just once, when you were away . . .'

Mary seized her by the shoulders and shook her violently. 'You bloody, bloody little fool! If this gets out it could ruin me, don't you know that?'

The Chinese looked truculent. 'They don' find nothin'. Is not crime to be gay.'

'It bloody well is in the Royal Navy. I could be court-martialled and kicked out – d'you realise that? I couldn't be an officer in the Wrens if they knew, I couldn't be in the Wrens at all, let alone work in intelligence. Every time they've security vetted me I've *lied*, don't you understand? Jesus Christ I've taken so much trouble to hide it and I've got away with it for more than ten years. I wish I'd never met you.'

Chang Xhisin leant forward and kissed her. Mary did not respond. 'Why should anyone know?'

'They must have seen my uniforms in the wardrobe.'

'They lookin' for heroin, not uniform.'

'God, I hope you're right.' Mary sat down heavily. 'I just bloody hope you're right.'

Nick landed in Peking knowing nothing of the attack on Sarah. After the three-hour flight a Chevrolet with a marine driver met him at Shoudu and took him straight to the Embassy. The naval attaché, Arend Meerburg, was a full captain who had spent most of his life at sea and kept his distance from Nick's arcana. This was Meerburg's last posting, tinsel on a solid if dull career, and he didn't want any unpleasantness. He appeared in the doorway as soon as Nick reached his office – weatherbeaten skin and shaggy grey beard flecked with white made him look like Charlton Heston playing Moses, except for the well-pressed blue uniform with splashes of gold. 'Going to a lunch at the defence ministry,' he explained apologetically, gesturing vaguely at his medal ribbons. 'Visiting senator from Iowa.'

'You look like a fag, duckie,' but Nick's grin was affectionate. 'Anyway, what's the panic? I was just in the middle of things down there – interesting case, beautiful girl, decent food for a change. Then you bugger it all up.'

'I wasn't sure how to play it, Nick.' Meerburg had a low rumbling voice. 'One of your people was emptying some drops yesterday – as you'd instructed, I imagine?'

'Sure.'

'One apparently contained some microfilm and a note asking for a crash meeting tomorrow – Thursday – in the Valley of the Ming Tombs. I didn't know what to do – seemed urgent so I called you back. I hope that was right?'

'Of course, Arend. Thank you – which agent was it?'

'I don't know, Nick. I didn't ask and I wasn't told. I prefer it that way.' Meerburg handed him a sealed envelope. 'It's all in there. Now, if you'll forgive me, I must attend to what are laughingly referred to as my diplomatic duties. Senator Rice is waiting for me to drive him for a tourist trip to the Forbidden City. Jeez, to think I once drove a battle cruiser.'

Thirteen emperors lay buried in the valley at the foot of the Tianshan Hills, thirty miles north-west of the city. Nick drove himself in a relatively anonymous Datsun from the pool – only relatively because most cars were owned by foreigners or party cadres – and parked under some pine trees after passing the Dragon-Phoenix Gate and the Seven Arch Bridge. The place chosen by Tang was not in the long line of tombs, each surrounded by its grey stone wall, but on a rough track circling the nearby Shisanling reservoir. Nick walked uphill for fifteen minutes after leaving the car, unmistakably foreign from his height and slightly greying fair hair, but unobserved on the empty road as his feet kicked up little clouds of yellow dust.

Tang Tsin appeared at his elbow without warning, stepping from the ruins of a stone hut, and fell into step. 'Thank you for coming, Mark' – he knew Nick only as 'Mark' – 'I suggest we walk on round the reservoir to where my car is parked.'

'Your *car*?' Nick turned to him with a smile. 'Good lord – things really *are* looking up!'

Tang trotted along beside the taller man. His lined face remained grave – Nick had never seen him smile – and his eyes looked frightened. He was wearing the baggy trousers from his Mao suit, some sort of cheap canvas shoes and a white shirt – he had abandoned his cap and tunic. 'Yes, Mark,' he replied in his customary funereal tone. 'I have been promoted. I have my own office for the first time, a secretary – plump with red ribbons on her pigtails and halitosis – and a Skoda.'

'Congratulations. Does this mean a change of job?'

'I am in the same department and I still report to Wang but, yes, there is a change.'

They paused in the shadow of some pines and watched a flotilla of ducks bobbing on the water. 'Tell me about it, then.' Nick's easy manner was slowly calming Tang's nerves. Nick always made him feel more confident, less in danger.

'I am to control an agent working in the West, in defence.' Tang sounded like a man announcing his own execution.

'What nationality?'

'I don't know yet – British or American. There is a naval connection – I think he or she must be a serving officer. I have been analysing some of his product, and you have seen it, but now I shall be his controller.'

Nick whistled. 'Now that really *is* something. I don't

66

suppose you have a name yet?'

'No. The codename is Scorpion. It will be a little time before I know his – or her – real identity.'

Nick put his arm around the Chinese's shoulders. 'Scorpion, you say? Hey – that's one hell of a coincidence. There's a lot of interest in this Scorpion at the moment.'

'I knew it was important – it is to be my only responsibility so it must be something big.'

'Big it certainly is, Tang. I shall want to see everything you can get for me. Will you be able to go on photographing documents?'

'I think it may be more difficult, the classification is very high, but I shall do my best. On the other hand I am more senior now and it would be natural for me to be invited to more functions at Western embassies. If you can arrange that, we can talk from time to time without arousing suspicion.'

'I certainly can and will, but is it okay to go on using the drops too?'

'We have three now, if you include the hollow tree in Tiantan. I can usually pass by one of them every couple of weeks. I think it's safe enough.'

They had passed the monument at the top of the long stretch of water and were walking downhill on the other side. In the distance a crocodile of children in red Pioneer scarves was climbing into a single-decker bus. 'This is excellent news.' Nick smiled encouragingly at the little man again. 'We owe you a great deal, you know, Tang – what you are doing is invaluable to both our countries.'

'So valuable that my own people will execute me if they find out,' muttered the Chinese drily.

Nick stopped and put his arms out straight, resting his hands on the other man's shoulders and searching his face with serious eyes. 'We know the risks you are taking, Tang. You are a very brave man and we do not expect you to run them for ever.'

'Then how long do you want? When will you help me and my family to leave?'

'If you are to control Scorpion, we'd like you to stay in post as long as possible – until you feel in danger.'

'I've felt in danger for at least nine months. That's why I sent my family out into the country.'

'But your fears were groundless, old friend! You've been promoted and given a position of great trust.'

'I know. I can't understand it.'

'Everyone doing this kind of work gets paranoid, starts to imagine they're being followed, phone tapped, betrayed by their closest friends.'

'I don't have any friends, Mark.'

'You have *us*; and plainly you're not under suspicion, never have been – you're going to be our top agent here and when you finally leave we'll give you a hero's welcome.'

Tang rounded on him irritably. 'Forget the hero's welcome. I'll stay in post until I have Scorpion's name, but then I must leave. You will get me travel documents for the whole family – you have all the details – so that we can go south by train one weekend and cross into Hong Kong. That's the easiest way. Then you will take us to America. Is that agreed? Really *agreed*?'

'Of course it is,' Nick's reassuring smile was working overtime. 'I'll get the papers you need – and the money for the fares. I've always said that we'll settle you with a new identity, a house, a pension for life.'

'San Francisco,' said Tang brusquely. 'That's where I want to go – San Francisco, somewhere on the bay.'

'No problem. Is that your car?' Nick gestured towards a brown Skoda, half-hidden in a pine grove a hundred yards ahead, patches of rust showing on its wings.

'Yes, I must get back to the office. I'd like the travel documents next week – I won't use them until I have Scorpion for you.'

'That may be a little soon, but I'll see what can be done.'

In the pine grove two men stood a little back from the car, one adjusting the lens of his camera. As Tang and the

68

tall American came closer he got them sharply in focus before clicking the shutter, not once but several times. He already had an incriminating photograph of the car. By the time Tang was unlocking the Skoda, the two men had scattered: one was strolling down to the main road, snapping the birds on the reservoir, the other – thin, like a matchstick figure – pedalling away on his black upright bicycle.

8

Sometimes the leaders of China's Party and government travelled anonymously, in unmarked cars or aircraft; no publicity, only guards to give them away. Their job was, after all, to govern and that could often be done best out of public sight. Sometimes the public did not even know the names of the high officials who controlled their lives. But today in Canton was different. The Prime Minister himself, comrade Li Peng, was showing the human face of communism, surrounded by cameras for national and overseas television: the first of a series of photo-opportunities that were supposed to make everyone forget the massacre on Tian'an Men. In his convoy of sleek black cars he visited a tractor factory and the Huifu Xila No. 2 Primary School: a small bespectacled figure in a dark blue Mao suit, in his early sixties, young by Chinese standards.

His last visit of the day was to the memorial garden for the Martyrs of the Canton Uprising, lush and green in the city centre. It was an uncomfortably hot and humid afternoon: the crowd of party luminaries stood sweltering as they waited. The fortunate had found shade under banyan trees and palms, a lucky few near the cool waters of the lake, but the speech was to be made outside the tomb of the martyrs, on a plaza open to the blazing sun. Several thousand young cadres had been bussed in from all over the province and stood in proud lines on the gravel: keen young faces, white shirts, carrying a forest of bobbing scarlet banners. When the procession of black cars drove slowly through the gate with its twin pagodas, the applause was more a sign of relief than enthusiasm. It was drowned by a military band playing *The East is Red*, growing into a deafening roar as the young voices joined in.

The Prime Minister's car stopped outside the tomb and there was a flurry of hand-shaking and slight bows. He mounted the dais, shaded by a canopy, with half a dozen other men in grey tunics, Party officials. A young woman with a clipboard and stopwatch fussily arranged the red flag with its five gold stars behind them for the benefit of television cameras on another raised platform. When the picture was satisfactory two children in red Pioneer scarves presented bunches of flowers to the great man. His wife was not there; indeed the secrecy around the leadership was such that almost nothing was known about her, except that she existed and was said to have three children. There was a burst of orchestrated cheering and the scarlet banners waved slowly from side to side like waves at sea. Li Peng stood behind the battery of microphones and started to speak in guttural Cantonese.

'Comrades. Friends. The Canton uprising took place more than sixty years ago, on 11th December 1927, under the leadership of our great Communist Party. Workers and soldiers seized the greater part of this city and pro-claimed the victory of the people, but they were tragically betrayed by the Kuomintang reactionaries in collusion with foreign imperialists. The rising was suppressed with much violence and bloodshed; we stand here on the ex-ecution ground that saw so many brave revolutionaries walking to heroic death. After the victory of the people in 1949, they were commemorated by this tranquil gar-den . . . ' He droned on, warning of the renewed danger from counter-revolutionaries and imperialists. In the heat and humidity there was little applause as his audience wiped sweat from their faces and used Party leaflets as fans. Even the horseshoe of officials sitting behind him on the platform seemed to be dozing. No one noticed the figure creeping forward from the crowd, slight, young, dressed in white shirt and black cotton trousers.

The girl had reached the foot of the steps before one of the uniformed guards noticed her. Suddenly she leapt up on the platform and rushed at Li Peng levelling a small pistol. The Prime Minister stood transfixed, then threw himself to the ground as three shots rang out. Another man screamed, clutching his chest, and collapsed. A soldier rushed forward and fired a burst from his AK-47 – the girl spun like a top, her cries unheard in the clatter of the gun, white shirt turning crimson, her pistol flying off into the crowd, collapsing in a pool of blood.

Before the shocked silence ended, the Prime Minister had been hustled back into his limousine which left at high speed flanked by police motorcyclists with howling sirens. Officials surrounded the cameras and seized their films at gunpoint. Pandemonium broke out as the crowd realised what they had seen. The most powerful man in China, apart from the godlike Deng, had been almost shot down before their eyes. One of the two most closely guarded men in the country had come within inches of assassination and no one could have penetrated his security without help from those in positions of trust. As the Party faithful turned to each other under the trees, they looked stunned, faces suddenly anxious and full of fear.

Luther was summoned to the minister within the hour. The compound was guarded even more heavily than usual. Luther was searched twice on the way in, armoured cars were standing in the gardens and the anti-aircraft guns, usually shrouded in camouflage canvas, had been uncovered: they stood on concrete plinths at the corners of the site, invisible from outside. The minister's plump face was sweating more than usual, eyes popping with fury behind thick-lensed spectacles; he looked desperately overheated with his tunic still buttoned up to the neck. 'There has been an act of gross terrorism!' He shouted as if he held Luther personally responsible. 'An attack on the

Prime Minister master-minded by the vermin who wish to bring down our state.'

'Outrageous,' agreed Luther dutifully. Somebody had been kicking the minister; he in turn was about to put the frighteners on Luther, a pattern that was sickeningly familiar.

'So what of Scorpion?' The man was sweating even more profusely, his voice a threatening hiss. Luther wondered why he didn't take off his tunic and relax in this heat. 'I have given you complete freedom – it has been an expensive and slow project, but you have guaranteed that Scorpion would achieve a position of great seniority, become our secret weapon to identify and destroy the leaders of the dissidents. Why has this not happened?'

'Scorpion's career has gone according to plan so far.'

'But it is all too *slow*. I need this agent in place *now*.' He was almost screaming with rage.

'Scorpion is already providing invaluable intelligence.' Luther met the wild eyes firmly, showing no anxiety, speaking quietly. 'Six months ago we identified the traitor Tang Tsin, and we are now feeding him with false information – he does not know it but he is working under our control.'

'To hell with Tang! *Scorpion* is not yet in the high position we need – and the threat is now. Not next month or next week, *now*. Does *Tang* know details of the opposition?'

'I'm certain he does not.'

'So what use is he to me?' The scream of fury must have been heard by the soldiers in the garden but they remained impassive.

'I did not believe that crushing the internal unrest was your only objective.'

For a moment Luther expected the flabby hand to strike him; instead the man stiffened and shuffled some papers awkwardly. When he spoke Luther almost felt sorry for him. 'Neither did I, but it seems to be all that concerns my colleagues at the moment.' Qiao Shi turned and gestured at the garden beyond the large windows. With the heavily armed soldiers, armoured cars and guns raking the sky it looked like a military camp preparing for war. 'They are terrified – and I need action to reassure them. I must destroy the opposition quickly now, or I shall be disgraced myself.' Suddenly the fear in his eyes changed to menace behind the thick lenses. 'And you are nothing without me, Luther – do you understand? Nothing.'

After the firebomb, Sarah was hustled away by one of the Cheung Chau constables and sat in the police post for an hour, shivering with shock, wrapped in a rough grey blanket, while long phone calls were made in Cantonese. Then a naval launch arrived and took her back to Central where Rumbelow – who for once seemed genuinely concerned – took her to his house. Next morning she was given the key to a government flat as a temporary home, saw a brisk Wren doctor at *Tamar* and did a lot of shopping, for everything in the Cheung Chau apartment had been destroyed. She spent a restless night, but the following day she was back in the office by nine.

Mary Devereux appeared in the doorway almost at once. Her white blouse was crisp as ever, but her face looked strained and there were dark rings under her eyes. 'Sarah – I'm so sorry – were you hurt?'

Sarah shook her head. 'No. It was a bit of a shock, that's all. Have I missed anything?'

'Not really. We're no further ahead on Tang, Foo and all that. But things are stirring in China – someone tried to assassinate Li Peng yesterday. Someone *did* assassinate General Zhang Zhiyang.'

'Who the hell's Zhang Zhiyang?'

'Governor of Yannan province down in the south-west, around Kunming.' She handed Sarah a flimsy stamped SECRET, an agent's report from a faint dot matrix printer. Sarah was still feeling shaky and had difficulty concentrating but read it through. There were just the

74

bare facts. She had never been to Kunming but they called it the city of perpetual spring and she had never heard of any trouble there, not even from the forgotten minority, the Islamic Chinese. But somebody had still blown the governor's personal aircraft out of the air with a well-placed bomb, scattering fragments of metal and human limbs over an area of two square miles. Sarah wondered who could have done it – for it must have required some sophistication – and why?

Nick returned from Peking that afternoon and Sarah met him at six o'clock, near MacDonnell Road station on the Peak Tram. Their temporary apartment was in a high-rise block wholly occupied by the navy, intelligence and senior civil servants, a kind of post-Raj ghetto, with an entrance hall guarded discreetly by armed Ministry of Defence police. After the terror of the firebomb at least it felt relatively safe. 'Come up and have a look.' She linked her arm with his as they strolled down the quiet street, almost empty, with its distinctly non-Chinese atmosphere. 'It's terribly posh.' The lift raced them up to the sixteenth floor and she opened the door into a white split-level room with patio doors leading out to a balcony. The furniture was provided by the MOD and sparse – glass coffee table, a sofa and some shapeless easy chairs in uninspired beige.

Sarah took two *Tsingtao* beers from the fridge in the kitchen and led Nick out to the balcony, which faced east and was now in shadow. They stood looking sideways at the harbour as she poured. 'Fantastic view. Classy area – that's the Masonic Hall down there. Oh damn. *Damn!*' Her hands were shaking and beer splashed down the front of her dress.

Nick took the bottle and glass from her and put his arm reassuringly round her shoulders. 'Steady, Cable – it's okay.'

She stared back at him, slumping into a plastic chair. 'Is it – how the hell would you know? You weren't bloody there.' Her eyes were bright in a face that had gone chalky-white. 'Oh God, I shouldn't have said that. You're kind and good for me, Nick, but I just feel so horrible.'

He bent down and kissed her. 'Of course you do. So would I if someone had tried to kill me.'

'I wish I could just have a good cry, but somehow it won't come. I've been feeling dreadful ever since the fire – scared, really scared. No, it *isn't* like me, it's never happened before.' She turned away savagely. 'But I get these black waves of depression that make me feel I just can't face any more.'

He finished pouring the beers and put the two glasses on the PVC table. White tower blocks clung to the hillside below them, falling away to the waterfront. The roar of traffic and clang of the trams floated up. She huddled into her dress as if cold, although it was a warm evening. 'Why does bloody Scorpion matter so much? It's not like an ordinary case – someone out there *knows* who's working on it, knows what we're doing, knows every fucking step we take. They take out Bob Gatti's family so he's walking about like a zombie and ought to be on compassionate leave. After the firebomb, Rumbelow wants me to pack it in and go back to England, wait for a new posting.'

'There'd be some sense in that.'

'You mean let them *win*?' Her voice shook with scorn and anger. 'All they've got to do is attack us as individuals and we chicken out? Not bloody likely.'

'I don't want them to win any more than you, but we aren't at war with China, you know. Does Scorpion matter so much?'

Sarah's hands had stopped shaking. 'It matters to *me*, Nick. China treats her people like shit and is going to fall apart, that's why it matters. I'm going to nail this bastard and I'm not going to be frightened off. Are *you*? You must be on their hit list too.'

He smiled; he had such kind eyes she wanted to kiss them. That face full of character and confidence: he would be even better looking when he had a touch more grey at the temples in his forties. He shook his head. 'No, Cable. They won't scare me off either.'

They went out to eat in Wanchai. The *dai pai dongs* had an inviting smell of sizzling pork and prawn under their green canvas awnings stretched across the pavement. Chinese cooks rotated woks over hissing butane stoves, sweating in the heat, their customers clustered on low metal stools shovelling in meatballs and noodles – bowl in one hand, clicking chopsticks in the other – with hurried jerky movements as if a famine had just ended. But it felt safer to go to a Chinese restaurant off the street. Sarah had nothing else to drink – she knew it would only make her feel worse – and the Peking duck seemed tasteless.

Back at the apartment she curled up on the sofa and relaxed in Nick's arms. His strength and gentleness were reassuring and she started to feel better. She remembered the first evening they had held each other like that, nearly a year ago on Cheung Chau. Over salt-baked Hakka chicken and green tea at Ah Wong's she had learnt that Nick Roper was from Boston, a Yale graduate and single. She had also sensed that he was not badly off. She had confessed that she had a lower second in physics from Liverpool and was normally destitute when not living on generous overseas allowances. They had laughed a great deal, something Sarah had not done for some time, and she felt reassuringly comfortable with him when they strolled back to the apartment and opened a bottle of Burgundy. Nick had put his arms round her on the uncomfortable broken-down sofa. 'Did you say your father lives on the Isle of Wight?'

'Yes. He retired early from our diplomatic service. My parents divorced when I was only eight and I travelled round the world with him for ten years. While he was in Vienna – '

'Vienna? Of course, *Ambassador* Cable?'

'I'm afraid so.' Sarah sounded embarrassed. 'He was

only ambassador to the United Nations organisations there, of course, not the real ambassador to Austria.'

'Sounds pretty good to me.'

'I don't think Dad felt quite that way. He fell in love with a Jewish girl twenty years younger and now they run a sub post office in Ventnor! At first I was madly jealous, but now I'm very happy for them.' She did not mention that the luckless Bill Cable had also been a failed intelligence officer, hounded out of the service under suspicion of cracking under enemy interrogation while on loan to the Australian army during the Vietnam War. The Vienna posting had been the last of a series of non-jobs – he had been a tragic figure, guilty of nothing that would warrant dismissal, but a lame dog who could not be trusted with real responsibility. It had taken Sarah years to understand that he had gone on – always feeling awkward, sometimes humiliated, enduring the fact that everyone around him *knew* – so that she lacked for nothing, had a decent start in life. As a girl it had been difficult with only a father – sometimes she must have been dreadful – but now she loved him painfully for it.

Even that early – they had known each other less than a week – she had sensed that Nick was nothing like her stereotype of a US Navy officer. He was doing a hilarious imitation of the racist, commie-bashing, redneck who ran the CIA station when the question slipped out. 'Oh God, Nick,' she was laughing uncontrollably. 'I don't believe it! However did this anarchist who's trying to feel me up get into the navy in the first place?'

'No choice, Cable.' He still sounded frivolous but she had touched a nerve. 'No choice. In Bor-ston – ' he emphasised the upper class pronunciation ' – we Ropers are very respectable people and the US Navy is nothing if not respectable.'

Sarah was surprised at the sudden venom in his voice and wished she had never asked the question. He poured more wine; she realised that he'd drunk a lot in the course of the evening and it was going to his head. 'I'm not sure I understand.'

'It's an old, proud, snobbish family, Cable. Quite dreadful. Father's a domineering banker and Mother's a kind of downtrodden housekeeper and hostess. Sorry if that sounds bitter, but I suppose it is.'

'It *does* sound bitter – and not like you at all. You're so good at what you do now, I can't imagine you as some kind of teenage rebel.'

'Rebel?' He snorted, but suddenly sounded serious, almost embarrassed. 'I wasn't. I had an elder brother who got killed when he was thirteen – drowned on a canoeing trip, very character building – and deep down, almost unconsciously, I guess I felt I had to be the kind of son they wanted in his place. I wasn't really a Yale and Annapolis type, but I guess I did it for them.' His speech was getting slightly slurred. 'Must have been out of my skull.'

'What would you have preferred?'

'Never quite knew. We were privileged, well-off – I felt guilty, wanted to break away, do something about the blacks and the poor.' He shrugged. 'But I didn't and now I guess they need defending just as much as the rich.' He gave a derisive grin. 'Peace is my profession.'

She kissed him. 'I don't believe it's that simple. *How* would you have done something about the blacks and the poor? As a politician? Social worker? Lawyer?'

He shook his head. 'Maybe some kind of social work and politics later – it doesn't matter any more, ancient history.'

'How did you end up here?'

'I was serving on a frigate with Bob Gatti as skipper when he was posted to naval intelligence about eight years ago. He invited me to join him and we've been following each other round ever since.'

'You're not at all like him.'

'Aren't I? Certainly I've got great respect for him. He got there the hard way – no free ticket like me. Bob comes from a poor Italian family in Chicago, but he was good on a ship and he's bloody good at what he's doing now.'

The thought of Gatti brought Sarah back to the present. Nick was running his fingers through her hair. 'I thought you'd gone to sleep, darling.' He picked her up bodily in his arms and she clung to him as he carried her into the bedroom and rested her gently on the bed. She started to giggle foolishly and he kissed her. 'What's so funny, Cable?'

'I just remembered, all your shirts and pants and things got burnt – what on earth will you wear tomorrow?'

He smiled, but his eyes still looked worried. 'Look darling, you need a good, long sleep – have you got any pills, something to really knock you out for eight hours?'

'Yes, the doctor at *Tamar* gave me some.' She hesitated. 'Perhaps you're right.' She tried to sit up but her head swam and she felt too enervated to do anything. Nick undressed her and Sarah felt easier than she had for days as the capsule took effect and she fell asleep in his arms.

On the other side of the island Bob Gatti sat in his silent living room pouring another whisky. Wandering through Wanchai to get away from the empty house he had passed Nick and Sarah two hours ago, but they had not seen him as they came out of the restaurant. He was still walking round in a daze, numbed by what had happened, endlessly thinking about Sue and the boys, blaming himself; but he was also starting to face the fact that life had to go on. Seeing Nick and Sarah so natural with each other, so happy, he had been surprised to feel more than a twinge of jealousy.

9

Despite the murder of his family, Bob Gatti had stayed in
Hong Kong – living alone in the echoing house in Stanley,
turning up grim-faced at the office on the Peak, working a
twelve-hour day, seeming emotionally anaesthetised. At
first Nick Roper had kept out of his way. 'I don't know
what to do,' he'd confided in Sarah. 'I've enormous respect for Bob, but he ought to take six months off. He's
obsessed with Tang, Foo and Scorpion. Vengeful. He's
not thinking straight and he looks so thin and gaunt – he
really scares me.'

'Haven't Washington ordered him back?'

'I'm sure they suggested some leave, but he's acting
head of station and they wouldn't push it. Langley trusts
him. We've already lost the ghastly admiral and none of us
really has the experience to run the office if Bob goes as
well.'

They had been in Ah Wong's. Sarah took a sip of green
tea and attacked the beef and black beans again. 'Can't
you take some of the load for him?'

'I suppose so – when I'm not in Peking.' And so Sarah
found herself working with Nick by day as well as sleeping
with him at night. It felt strange at first, but soon it was
not too difficult to divide her life into compartments.

Even so it was Mary Devereux, not Nick, who appeared
next morning with the news that Her Majesty's ballistic
missile-carrying submarine *Relentless* would arrive in the
harbour in thirty minutes. 'Since Scorpion may still have
some Trident connection, I thought you ought to know.

81

What should we do?'

'*Relentless* is one of the four Polaris boats, isn't she?'

'Yes, but her crew is the nucleus of one of the first Trident crews – this cruise is partly a training exercise for that.'

'I'll speak to Rumbelow.'

Half an hour later she stood at her office window watching the submarine cruising slowly towards the quay. She had never seen anything like it before. The Polaris boat was larger than many surface ships; she knew the data off by heart – 425 feet long, 7,500 tons, draught twenty-eight feet six inches. The resemblance to a huge killer shark was heightened by the black rubber acoustic tiles covering the hull like living scales. Two tiny figures in caps and shirt-sleeves stood on the high conning tower with its side fins, white ensign flapping from a short flagstaff above them, and the foreplanes were visible as two enormous flipper-like protrusions on each side of the fore-deck. The long aft-deck was steaming as seawater evaporated in the sun, no sign of the sixteen vertical tubes holding nuclear miss-iles. This was it, she thought: there were 143 men in that slimy black hull and just possibly one of them was a traitor. God knows why – money, sexual compromise, politics? The reason didn't matter, but if he was there they had to isolate him. She checked her appearance in the mirror – no make-up, long hair gathered into a neat knot at the back of her head – and hurried down as agreed with Rumbelow.

Relentless was already tied alongside. A semicircle of marines stood guard from bow to stern on the quay, cutting her off from intruders, and two launches were drawing a boom carrying a protective net round her on the seaward side. Sarah showed her pass to one of the mar-ines, who allowed her up the gangplank. A petty officer in white shirt and shorts stopped her as she reached the deck. 'Can I help you, Miss?'

'I have some documents for the commanding officer.'

'I'll take them down for you, Miss.'

'Thank you, but my orders are to hand them over personally. They need an immediate answer.'

'Very well, Miss.' He turned to a younger rating. 'Andrews, take this lady to the commander, if you please.'

Sarah climbed a steep ladder up the side of the conning tower, where a sailor helped her into the cockpit, then down another vertical metal ladder into an area full of pipes, dials and video screens. Sailors in white shirts or blue overalls scurried about, some looking at her curiously, as befitted men who had not seen a woman – except pin-ups – for over eighty days. Her guide knocked on a narrow door and she found herself in a small cabin panelled in light wood. There were some silver trophies in a glass-fronted cabinet and the chairs were covered in chintz. A stocky man rose from a tiny desk. 'Messenger from shore base, sir,' said the rating quickly, before saluting and scuttling out.

'Commander Thomas?' asked Sarah, holding out her hand.

'Yes.' He ignored her outstretched hand. 'What do you have for me?' Sarah handed him a large brown envelope and watched as he opened it with an ivory paperknife, taking out the sealed inner envelope which he slit in the same way. He was short, heavily built, with florid cheeks and a permanently cross expression. Like his crew he wore white shirt and shorts, three gold stripes on the shoulder flaps his only badge of rank, and sandals. He read the letter twice, his expression getting even more irritable. 'I'd better meet your Mr Roper as soon as possible, clear this up. What does he suggest?'

'Would noon be satisfactory? In the office here? Lieutenant-Commander Roper would be pleased if you'd stay with us for lunch.'

Thomas gave the slightest hint of a smile. 'Thank you, that's very civil – but I fear I'm too busy.'

*   *   *

Nick had borrowed a supposedly bugproof room for the meeting, underground with the usual icy air conditioning. After five minutes Sarah decided that she found Commander Ivor Thomas unsympathetic, after ten that he was absolutely poisonous. Nick explained the possibility of a leak in guarded terms. 'We can't be sure, of course, but the suggestion has come from sources in China and it has to be investigated.'

Thomas nodded brusquely. 'Why should the Chinese be interested in Trident?'

'I guess they're interested in anything that might threaten them if they get on the wrong side of us. Anyway – Trident may not be the main target. They could have compromised someone who's provided them with intelligence over a long period and just happens to be working on Trident for the time being.'

'I see.'

'We're looking at every link in the chains of command and supply of course, but we do have to consider your complement. You are, after all, training the nucleus of one of the first Trident crews.'

'If they ever finish building the damn thing, yes.'

Sarah had sensed that Thomas was a male chauvinist of the highest order and assumed a passive, note-taking role as if she were Nick's secretary. She sat at the end of the rectangular table with downcast eyes, ignored by the men who faced each other across the highly polished mahogany veneer, littered with cut-glass ashtrays and water carafes. Ivor Thomas plainly regarded brusqueness as an essential quality for senior command; he must be hell to work with and he talked down to Nick even though they were almost equal in rank. What on earth was a man like that doing on a Polaris? Nick edged into the next question carefully.

'I have to ask you this, sir, as you'll understand, on an entirely without prejudice basis. You have a crew of over one hundred and forty – is there a man among them whose loyalty you have ever doubted? Alternatively is there anyone who might be subject to blackmail?'

Sarah had seen the same question asked – and put it herself – many times. Usually people responded with a defensive 'no', after a transparent show of thought to show how responsible they were. It was always an embarrassing moment. But Thomas was not embarrassed, did not pause for thought and came straight out with it. 'Yes.'

Nick met his eyes in surprise. 'There is?'

'That's what I said. I was going to make a report before you asked for this meeting.'

There was a chilly silence. 'Then who is it?' Nick was trying to sound businesslike and unemotional.

Thomas's jaw tightened. 'My report will go up my own command structure. If they want you to know no doubt they'll tell you.' Nick flushed at the rebuke. 'Sorry, but you're not even an officer in my own service – you're in the navy of a foreign power.'

'An ally – your closest and most important ally. And I *am* investigating a most serious breach of security.'

'My report will be typed today.'

'Who will it go to?'

'The vice-admiral responsible for our submarine fleet.'

'Sir John Rusbridger in London?'

'The same.'

Nick restrained his anger. 'Could you possibly ask for permission to give me a copy – there is some urgency, you know.'

'You go up your own hierarchy, Roper, I'll go up mine. If your superiors agree with you on the need and the urgency, no doubt they'll get in touch with Rusbridger.' He stood up. 'Now, if you'll excuse me I have a great deal to do before we put to sea again.'

Nick stood up as well. 'Thank you, sir.' The irony was barely concealed. 'Thank you for being so helpful.'

Nairn flew back to London that evening, but fitted in a late lunch with Benjamin and Ruth Foo at a Chinese restaurant owned by Foo in Causeway Bay. They ate in a private room with delicate black lacquered furniture and red silk hangings; it was only their second meeting, only the second time he had seen Ruth since the painful parting twelve years before. Everyone was very friendly, Foo was as hospitable as he always remembered him – but Nairn would have felt less disoriented if he could have spent just a few minutes alone with the warm and generous woman who had once been his lover. The circular table littered with dishes, the delicate porcelain, Foo's aura of wealth and power: they were all part of her new life but alien to Nairn.

When the time came to go a government car pulled up outside to take him to Kai Tak. They all stood up, smiling and shaking hands, but there was a moment of confusion as they reached the doorway. The restaurant manager said something to Foo, who paused with his usual courtesy to reply. Nairn found himself among the jostling crowd on the pavement but alone with Ruth. She seized his arm urgently, eyes suddenly full of fear as Nairn made to kiss her goodbye. He drew back. 'What on earth's the matter?'

'You heard about Zhang Zhiyang, the governor of Yannan, David?' She was speaking fast, almost shouting above the clanking of trams and roar of traffic.

'The fellow who was assassinated yesterday?'

'Yes, but he wasn't "assassinated" – it was the *Gonganbu* who planted the bomb, their secret police. No trial, nothing to confuse the public.'

'You mean he was one of the underground?' Suddenly there were a hundred questions Nairn wanted to ask but no time. The driver opened the car door for him. 'How the devil do you know?'

Ruth met his eyes firmly, as if she had taken a decision for herself, a decision of which her husband would not approve. 'He was one of Ben's associates in planning a free China. Do you understand? *Do* you? Ben's in it up to his neck, David, he's taking the most terrible risks. I've been here twelve years and it's my home too now – I'm right behind him in wanting to see the end of that rabble in

86

Peking. But I want him to see it alive – what's the point if he's dead? Please find this bloody Scorpion, David, for God's sake find him soon before it's too late.'

As Foo appeared in the doorway Nairn gave Ruth a chaste peck on the cheek, and stepped into the car, his mind racing. He still mistrusted Foo – was the man deceiving his own wife? Or was Ruth in it with him, trying to throw her old lover off the scent? As the long black Daimler accelerated from the kerb, Nairn stared back at the pair of them, crossing the road arm-in-arm, vanishing into the crowd on the other side.

10

Tang Tsin was woken by the chanting. It grew louder while he dressed and made a pot of tea. When he wheeled his bicycle out of the courtyard he saw that the noise came from the street at the end of his alley – it was a demonstration, a long procession of students passing with red and white banners, shouting anti-government slogans in unison. In amongst the marchers was a crippled girl pushing herself along in a bamboo wheelchair. He cycled to the end of the alley where his path was barred by two soldiers in steel helmets, full battle order. Along the edge of the street a few people watched silently, but most had scuttled away, fearful of the violence to come. The soldiers noted Tang's grey uniform and spoke respectfully. 'Go back the other way comrade. You cannot get through with this rabble on the street.'

Tang Tsin nodded, but stood leaning on his bike as tanks appeared in the distance and blocked the path of the demonstrators. There was a clatter of boots on the cobbles and a file of soldiers trotted past, steel helmets glinting in the sun, AK-47s at the trail, gas masks bouncing on their chests. They looked as young as the students. The order to disperse crackled from a loudhailer somewhere in the distance: repeated several times, jeered at, ignored. Then the soldiers were firing, young men and girls fell to the ground, splashes of blood staining the white of their shirts. The chanting changed to screams and suddenly everyone was running for cover. Further down the street tear gas grenades were exploding and Tang retreated, covering his mouth and nose with a handkerchief, wondering why they had started shooting *before* using tear gas: surely it was the wrong way round? And as he pedalled away, very late for work, he reflected that he still did not know exactly what the demonstration had been about.

At Kai Tak airport, Hong Kong, nobody took much notice of the tall European queuing at the departure gate for Peking. Luther had entered the colony on his light blue Swedish passport twenty-four hours earlier and had had a reassuring meeting with Scorpion late last night. There had also been time to check on the funds in his accounts at the Hong Kong and Shanghai Bank. As the flight was called he swung his travelling bag over his shoulder and shuffled forward with a slight smile. He was winning.

In *Tamar* Sarah and Nick were huddled at the desk in her small office. Outside the sky was growing black and large drops of rain started to land in the waters of the harbour like stones. 'Not another typhoon?' he said.

'No. Just a nasty storm, it's been so humid and thundery lately.'

They both studied the document again. It was classified SECRET, with the additional privacy marking PER-SONNEL – IN CONFIDENCE, and addressed to Vice-Admiral Sir John Rusbridger. Signed in a bold hand by Ivor Thomas, it requested the withdrawal of Lieutenant Stephen Wainwright from his crew, on the grounds that he was a security risk. 'Do you believe this?' Sarah gestured at the close-typed page.

'His main crime seems to be coming from a working-class background in Leeds and keeping up with a few old friends. Thomas is an arrogant little snob. Wainwright's just not his type.'

'But Thomas does say Wainwright has this girlfriend Jo, mixed up in hard left politics, drugs, the lot. That seems a

89

little unwise for the communications officer on a Polaris?'

'Sounds highly exaggerated. How would he ever get through your positive vetting if his private life is like that?'

'Thomas says it's only just come to light.' Outside the rain was hammering down now, rattling the window, and sampans seemed to bounce on the water as gusts of wind drove high waves across the harbour. The submarine was still rocking at the quayside.

'You'll have to interview Wainwright – or one of you will – but I don't think he's senior enough to be Scorpion.'

'Reflects more on Thomas, would you say?' Sarah raised her eyebrows.

'Thomas is a shit – but I don't see him as Scorpion either.' Nick stood up in the cramped space and stretched his arms. 'At least I hope not.' He rubbed his nose with his right forefinger meaningfully. 'I've just found out that he's leaving *Relentless* and being promoted to captain. And he's coming back here – taking charge of all naval and military intelligence, joining the top table with the admiral and the dreadful Rumbelow.'

Sarah winced. 'You're not serious?'

'I am, deadly serious. He's been in intelligence before, turns out to have quite a track record – supposed to be good.'

She snorted. 'Thanks, Nick, you've really made my day. You know what I think? Cunning old Foo is running a massive operation against us for Peking and he's got an agent in the government who's in some kind of danger. All these hints about Scorpion having a naval connection are just hogwash, to throw us off the scent. Maybe there's no Scorpion at all?'

'Could be.'

Sarah closed the file with a flourish. 'So case solved. Chuck Foo in the slammer. Let's go and have lunch.'

'Sure. Did I mention Bob Gatti's coming back to life? He wants to talk with Mary Devereux? Is that all right?'

'Suppose so. Not for me to say – Mary's vastly senior to me, you know. *Why* does he want to talk to her?'

'Didn't say.'

Next morning found Gatti inside HMS *Tamar* with a crisp new plastic-covered pass that gave him access to all parts of the base. Curious eyes followed the tall, slightly stooped figure, dressed in casual blue shirt and crumpled white trousers. The sailor outside the office block had a gun belt strapped round his waist, the butt of a .38 revolver visible in the buttoned-down holster. Gatti showed his pass and the man scrutinised it carefully before saluting and opening the door for him. Inside it was cool after the blazing heat and his eyes took a few minutes to adjust to the absence of glaring sunlight. He passed Sarah's empty office, wondering what she was doing this morning. Strange how he wanted to see her again, envied Nick. It wasn't that he had stopped grieving for Sue, or loving her; he spent a lot of time every day doing both, but somehow he had taken to that girl with the hard shell and soft centre.

But today Gatti's objective was further down the corridor. He knocked on a door at the end of the row and a female voice called 'Come in.' Mary Devereux was enthroned behind a modern desk in light oak and her office was quite large – big enough to house a conference table with eight chairs. She stood up formally and extended her hand. 'You must be Commander Gatti? Do take a pew.' Classy accent but no sense of superiority. Businesslike but friendly.

'Thank you for seeing me, ma'am.'

'Not at all. It's my job to help you if I can.' She came and sat in the other armchair in front of her desk, crossing her legs and smoothing down the blue skirt over black tights. 'Security, you said?'

'Just so.' He pulled out a notebook and balanced it on the arm of the chair. 'I'm really with American intelligence, but this is a combined operation and Miss Cable asked me to speak to you. I guess you've been cleared to do so?'

'I have.'

'Fine.' He smiled encouragingly, equal to equal, to make it clear she was a fellow officer sharing his problems, nothing to hint at the real reason for his visit. He hadn't known what to do when his police informer had passed on a photocopy of the report on the drugs raid, so he'd shelved it for a week. Most Europeans with official positions would have complained like hell after that kind of treatment, demanded compensation, but there hadn't been a peep from Commander Devereux. When he realised why, Gatti had started to speculate on what other sacrifices she might have been forced to make to keep her private life private . . . Maybe there was nothing in it, but he put the drugs tip-off down to revenge by someone she'd fallen out with in the arcane lesbian community. Mary was eminently blackmailable and, behind that classy front, not quite straight – for she had lied every time she was positively vetted. But he was troubled and on dangerous ground – he did not want to damage her if she was innocent – so in the end he decided this was something he had to probe himself. Gatti smiled again, offering a cigarette.

'I don't, thank you,' she said. 'But you go ahead, please.'

Gatti put the packet away and shook his head. 'Time I gave up too. Let's cut out the preliminaries, Miss Devereux, come straight to the point. It seems that technical data on Trident are reaching a potentially hostile power, the Chinese. Possibly data on the Cerberus communication system – low-frequency radio and all the rest.'

'That's one of my responsibilities in Hong Kong.' She smiled back at him, suddenly looking ten years younger. 'Of course there are other groups preparing for the operational phase – in Britain, Singapore, San Diego and so on. The security here is pretty tight.'

'Surely, but you're the closest to China – and if technical stuff is leaking, what about other things?'

'You mean our interception of Chinese military

signals?'

Gatti nodded. 'Military, diplomatic, security police, whatever.'

'That would be very serious. I hope you're wrong – we follow all the usual security procedures, you know.'

'I'm sure you do. Maybe the leak is somewhere else, but is there anyone on your staff whom you've the slightest reason to doubt? Even for no reason, just a hunch?'

Mary Devereux looked thoughtful, staring out of the window at a motor junk crossing the harbour, petrol engine coughing as if about to expire. She crossed her legs again. 'No, I don't believe there is.' Her jaw stiffened. 'No, there bloody well isn't.' The upper class accent made her sound personally offended. 'I'd vouch for every one of them.'

Bob met her eyes with a smile. 'Sorry, but I did have to ask.'

'Of course, you must ask whatever you want. Would it help you to see the communications room? You'll find they have very little opportunity to copy anything or remove the manuals – it's all computerised, no paper is handled, no photocopying – and the technology is so complex most of the operators don't really understand it.'

They spent the next hour in an underground room where a mixture of white-shirted ratings and Wrens were sending and receiving ciphered radio signals. It was airconditioned, cool – and the atmosphere dry. At the end it was natural that they should lunch together in the mess, which was what Bob had planned. Mary had a lager with her rice and king prawns and was sparkling company when she relaxed. It was quite natural for him to ask her out for dinner one evening. She looked at him quizzically as if puzzled by the invitation, for she knew that he was recently widowed, but accepted graciously.

Tang Tsin's office was in a modern building off Xisanhuan Beila, near the China Theatre. Since his promotion he had been given his own room for security reasons. It was small, furnished with only a metal desk and two upright chairs, but there was a large safe with a combination lock. The only personal possessions he kept there were a vacuum flask for a constant supply of green tea and a small transistor radio. He was listening to the latter, turned down and with the door closed, just before his lunch break, but there was no mention of the demonstration in the news bulletin, nor of the deaths when it was broken up.

About twelve thirty Tang decided to buy a bowl of noodles from the stall on the corner and went downstairs, edging politely into the crowd pouring along the street. Before he had reached the corner two men fell into step with him, one on each side. They wore grey Mao suits similar to his. 'We have come to take you to the minister, comrade,' said one. 'There is a car just along here.'

Tang blinked in puzzlement. 'You could have telephoned me at my office? I would have come by bus.'

'A matter of security, comrade.' The man smiled as he opened the door of the ancient Volga and slid in after Tang. His colleague sat beside the driver. They drove slowly through the flocks of bicycles, speeding up when possible on the tree-lined boulevards, and in about twenty minutes arrived in the courtyard of a building Tang had not visited before. The two men had not spoken during the journey, but ushered him courteously through a steel door.

The corridor was painted a dirty yellow and the floor tiled. Curious surroundings for a member of the government. Their steps echoed as another door was opened and the three men entered a room with no windows, lit by two harsh spotlights. Another man in shirtsleeves stood behind a desk, a uniformed girl with a notebook perched on a stool to his right. Suddenly Tang Tsin understood, his throat going dry as he saw the blown-up photograph on the desk, himself and the American he knew as Mark deep in conversation near the Valley of the Ming Tombs.

11

Gatti's dinner with Mary Devereux was a quiet affair. She asked to be taken to one of the garish floating restaurants in Aberdeen Harbour; when he looked surprised she went pink and explained, 'I know it's a bit touristy but I've never actually been.' She looked good in a striped cotton top and tightish white trousers – and she was sparkling company. Gatti had not been out for a meal with anyone since his wife's death, but Mary chatted away inconsequentially and laughed a lot, like a teenager on her first date. Early on she said very gently, 'About your wife and the boys – I was so sorry, I know everyone at *Tamar* was. I'm surprised you're still here, not on leave or something.'

'I'm supposed to be, but I've nothing to go back to in Chicago and sitting around doing nothing just made it worse. So I'm giving myself odd bits and pieces to do.' He smiled. 'Like you.'

She laughed, showing two rows of shiny white teeth, but doing it unselfconsciously. 'Am I an "odd piece"? Sounds quite nice, a change from bossing everyone about.' The weak joke *was* self-conscious, as if she felt awkward below the charming, relaxed front and Gatti smiled encouragingly as she suddenly looked serious. 'Let's get the ground rules clear, Bob. If you want to talk about your family, please do – you must love them a lot and I'd be touched to listen – but if not that's fine by me. Whatever is easiest for you.'

He was parking his car by the water. Aberdeen Harbour was packed with sampans jammed tight around the massive floating restaurants, the Jumbo, Sea Palace, Tai Pak: all ablaze with coloured lights and heaving with customers, breathing out the noise of oriental Muzak and the pungent aromas of Chinese cooking. 'That's kind, Mary – I appreciate it and one day I *will* want to talk about them, but not yet. Is that okay?'

She squeezed his hand as she swung her legs out of the car. 'Quite okay. Let's just have a good evening.'

That evening Luther and Josie crossed back into Hong Kong. They travelled separately, Josie driven by car from Canton to Macao, where she mingled with the Chinese crossing to Hong Kong on the night ferry. Luther flew in via Taiwan; the immigration officials at Kai Tak barely examined his passport. The tall Nordic figure of company director Ulf Ericsson, carrying a passport issued by the Kingdom of Sweden, had become familiar in recent weeks.

Luther took a taxi into Central, where he paid it off and changed to a tram that clanked its way slowly through bustling streets towards Shau Kei Wan at the eastern end of the harbour. For the first ten minutes he stood on the packed lower deck, clinging to a leather strap as the tram stopped and started jerkily, surrounded by sweating bodies packed so close that the air was fetid and it was almost impossible to move. Eventually he managed to perch on one of the slatted wooden seats, alongside a grizzled Chinese woman in black pyjamas, peering out through the open window. The tram was inching along a narrow street, high tenements on each side with oblong Chinese signs climbing up them in garish red, blue and gold. At ground level were brightly lit shop windows and dense crowds of Europeans and Chinese trying to hurry along the pavement, dodging across the street between the streams of bicycles and Japanese cars. The noise of the traffic, pop music on transistors and raucous Cantonese was deafening: it had a cheerful vibrancy that he never saw across the border.

At the tram terminus Luther found a familiar alley and hurried past the open doorways of dark Chinese apartments, each with its flickering television set and smell of cooking oil. In the shadows of one or two living rooms he glimpsed the snarling figures of Taoist shrines lit by red electric bulbs. He crossed Wang Wa Street and vanished down a steel ladder to a basement where he knocked on a door; it opened a crack for a bloodshot eye to peer out, then quickly he was let in. The six men playing Mahjong under clouds of blue tobacco smoke turned and looked at him. The Chinese faces were blank and unwelcoming, but their eyes said that they knew they were about to make a large sum of money.

Tang Tsin's head was swimming from the barrage of questions and the pain where they had applied electric shocks to his penis. He perched naked on the stool they had brought when he collapsed, conscious of his thin pale limbs, embarrassed by the presence of the girl even though her eyes seemed fixed on her notebook as she scribbled down his answers. He winced at a blow to the head and stared into the glaring lights.

'Who-is-your-contact?' The interrogator's voice was slow, deliberate, full of menace. The other two men stood silently behind Tang in the fetid little room, stinking of sweat and urine.

'I told you.' Tang was almost inaudible and his words slurred. 'He is American, I know him as Mark.'

'What is his real name?'

'I don't know.' Tang stifled a scream as he was struck again, bursts of white light piercing the raw red of his brain like slivers of glass. His head lolled to one side and he wished he could pass out.

'How do you contact him?'

Tang groaned. 'Through drops – I've already told you again and again – and now I have a phone number. I've already given it to you. I suppose it's a private line – at the American Embassy.'

The young man came from behind the lights and looked down at him with contempt. 'Do you recognise these people?' He held out a photograph.

Tang Tsin started and made to seize it, but only succeeded in sending waves of pain up his arms, for his wrists were handcuffed behind his back. For the first time he started to weep. 'They're my wife and children.' He slumped in defeat. 'What are you trying to tell me?'

The interrogator curled his lip. 'They have been in our hands for three months.'

'But they are at our village! Until a month ago they sent me letters every week?'

'And I dictated those letters, comrade. If they wanted to eat, they wrote. If your wife wanted her children to survive, she wrote.'

Tang's face crumpled in anguish. 'What have you done with them? You bastards. You utter *bastards*. How long have you known about me?'

'Nearly six months.'

'I don't understand. That meeting with the minister? My promotion?'

'To reassure the Americans and the British that you were safe.' The interrogator gave a slight nod. Tang was jerked to his feet and dragged back to the heavy wooden chair bolted to the concrete floor. The leather straps were again pulled tight around his chest, his waist and his ankles, pinioned to the chair legs. The young man approached, smiling, waving the metal device that looked like a cattle prod but with a thick black cable that ran to the wooden box in the corner like a menacing snake. Tang's eyes flickered in terror between the brass plate with figures on top of the box, the lever running in a slit, the metal rod. He was defeated, humiliated. He ought to feel contempt for them: the interrogator might be about thirty, but the others were barely more than teenagers. All four had unlined faces with that impassive, hard look, typical of young Chinese in authority: you saw it every day under army caps on the streets. They had learnt no wisdom, did not understand that the power to destroy another being's mind and body was not one to be used so lightly. They did not know what they were doing. He should boil with hate and contempt; but he felt only shame and fear. He was too scared to think straight, consumed by terror of the pain he could still feel from the last time.

The interrogator's face was close, his breath stinking of rotting teeth and stale cigarette smoke. He was grinning, a chilling psychopathic look in his eyes – he was enjoying every moment. Tang Tsin jerked at the electric shock as the prod stabbed his chest: the pain seemed to stop his heart for a second and he felt sick. 'What is Scorpion's name, traitor?'

Tang groaned. 'I don't know, I truly don't know.'

'But you study the files, the reports?'

'Of course.' He screamed as another shock shot through his genitals, leaving him sobbing and panting. 'But I don't,' his voice slurred, he could hardly get the words out, 'I don't know his *name*.'

'You expect me to believe that? That your controller Mark should look so happy when you haven't told him the one thing he wants to know?'

Tang's head slumped forward. 'He wanted the name, but I didn't know it.' He screamed as another long shock burnt into his groin, filling his whole torso with biting pain.

'Very well,' the interrogator too was breathing heavily – he was getting a sick sexual thrill from using his power to wound and humiliate in front of the pretty girl who was taking notes. 'Very well, comrade Tang Tsin. I am going to check your answers now. If you have lied to me, you will pay for it. Meanwhile you will have a taste of what we can inflict if you do not co-operate in everything else that I ask.'

Tang felt a new wave of terror. 'There is no need for

that.' His voice trembled.

'There is every need, comrade.' He laughed. 'See it as the start of your re-education.'

Tang was pushed through a door into a stone-flagged passage that smelt of damp. They kicked him to the ground, seized his legs and dragged him down to the cellar, his head cracking on every step. He was hurled into a cell with padded floor and walls and felt his ankles locked into another pair of handcuffs. Then they tied his wrists and ankles together behind him so that his body was taut as a bow. He felt a prick in a vein on his arm and watched in fascinated horror as a syringe was emptied into it. The door closed with a bang, a red light came on behind thick glass in the ceiling and he lay there, sweating with fear.

The pain came suddenly. It was indescribable. Every muscle in his body seemed to be contracting, a thousand red hot needles were piercing his skin, his eyes bulged in their sockets. As his body arched and jerked, he felt that his chest was about to burst and there was no respite; the agony increased, wave after wave. He fought to get away, smashing his head on the floor to lose consciousness, but it was padded and his nervous system seemed only to increase in sensitivity. Every fibre of his body carried an electric current of pain, he writhed uncontrollably, panting, struggling for breath, surrounded by terrible animal screams that he knew were his own. The agony filled his mind and mingled with terror as he seemed to be surrounded by snakes with bared fangs, twisting menacingly in the red glow, and hideous reptile shapes that came at him from all directions.

12

Benjamin Foo disliked Tom Rumbelow, but he was the
top man at the station so it was Rumbelow he had to see
now that Nairn had gone. He had thought of approaching
the Governor, but that would involve many more people
getting to know – secretaries, military and political advis-
ers. Rumbelow might be a buffoon, but the secret service
ought at least to be capable of keeping a secret. When he
phoned, Rumbelow surprised Foo by suggesting an immediate meeting – not in the office on the Peak but a safe
house on Lamma Island.

They both travelled there on separate ferries. Foo
landed at Sok Kwu Wan and walked round the harbour,
past little waterside eating places – a few metal tables and
stools outside huts with a chimney and a delicious smell of
squid or prawns – and sampans tied up to piles hanging
with green seaweed. It was a rocky cove with a fresh, salty
smell, surrounded by cliffs, grey rock broken up by
patches of green scrub, small sandy beaches separated by
rock faces plunging sheer into the water. There were a few
Chinese about but no one took much notice as Foo passed
through them, nodding and smiling, to set out up the cliff
path.

Rumbelow was waiting in a stone building on the cliff-
top, out of sight of the harbour and looking back towards
Hong Kong island. On the other side of the channel a
police launch was leaving Aberdeen and the black and
white ferry was already ploughing back towards Central.
Foo opened the door without knocking and walked

straight in. Rumbelow was sitting in the window seat, but stood up and extended a hand in welcome. His thinning grey hair was untidy and his eyes very tired in a face that had little colour. Perhaps he was not so much idle as worn out after thirty years – or even ill?

Foo shook hands gravely. 'Thank you for seeing me.'

'Not at all, an unexpected pleasure.'

The building consisted of just two rooms, one above the other – the upper one reached by a metal ladder through a trap door – and Foo took in the thick stone walls. 'I think it was built as a naval lookout.' Rumbelow answered the unput question. 'Sometime during the war. It has stood empty for years.'

Foo nodded. 'Yes – I have been here before.'

Rumbelow smiled apologetically. 'Of course, I should have remembered. You once did my job.'

Foo gave a slight bow and smiled. 'Forgive my asking, but is the place still wired for sound?'

'No, I promise you it isn't, but we can talk outside if you prefer.'

'Please – you never know what the fellows from the New China News Agency may have installed.' Everyone knew that the agency was the front for Chinese intelligence in the colony.

They walked a little way along the cliff path, Foo more surefooted than Rumbelow. 'How may I help you?' asked the Englishman.

'First by assuring me that nothing I tell you will be written down except with at least a SECRET classification, nor circulated except to those who absolutely *must* see it?'

'We always work on a strict need to know principle, you know that. Everything you tell me will be properly safe-guarded, I promise you.'

'Then I will trust you, I have no choice.' Foo paused thoughtfully, the lined face grave: his eyes smiling, then serious as they bored into Rumbelow's, a silent message that promised retribution if Foo was let down. The two men faced each other hesitantly, black clouds blocked out the sun and suddenly it started to rain. By the time they had run back to the lookout it was pouring heavily. Inside, the rattle of rain on the corrugated-iron roof was so loud that Foo was less concerned about electronic eavesdropping.

They sat at opposite ends of the window seat, water streaming down the glass outside, and Rumbelow looked at Foo expectantly. 'Let's try again.'

Foo hesitated. 'You know of the Tenth October movement?'

'I know there is a large network of opposition groups in China, yes. Not much more than that.'

'There have been pockets of opposition for years, loose, disorganised, never quite sure of the direction the government might be taking. It once looked as if Deng Xiaoping would reform the country himself – a market economy, democracy, freedom – but since Tian'an Men there is no hope of that. The army has clamped down hard; and the opposition has become tougher and better organised in response.'

'We had guessed something of the sort from intercepts and our agents, but it's hard to know what is going on in that vast landmass over there.'

Foo nodded sympathetically. He did not mention that it had never seemed so difficult when he was in Rumbelow's job. 'I have a link with the opposition movement. In fact I have come to you on behalf of its leaders.'

'I didn't know it was so organised as to have leaders – at least not leaders for the whole country. Who are they?'

'I can't tell you yet: their only security from arrest has to be that nobody apart from the key men and women knows who they are.'

There was an awkward silence and Rumbelow looked puzzled. 'Why are you here, Mr Foo? What are you asking me to do?'

'Our leaders wish to see the end of the communists in Peking – and to this end they would like to establish regular contact with your government, the European Community and the United States.'

'You speak of revolution in the largest country in the world very matter-of-factly, Mr Foo – I cannot believe it will be easy, or pleasant. But that is your affair. Contact, you say? That will not be difficult. If you need more direct support that will be for someone more exalted than me to decide; ministers would have to be involved and our relationship with China is quite difficult enough already, what with Hong Kong reverting to them in 1997.'

'Contact will be enough at this stage. I've no idea how the opposition may develop – demonstrations, strikes, even military action by units that reject the present government. I have been a regular visitor to China until recently, but I cannot go on much longer. Our days as amateurs are over.'

'What are you asking for, Mr Foo?'

'I am inviting you, as head of the SIS station here, to come with me on my next visit to China. To establish contact with the opposition leaders – after all, some of them might be in government by 1997.'

Rumbelow's expression changed abruptly. He tried to remain nonchalant, leaning back in the window seat, gesturing vaguely at the torrents of rain outside, forcing his lips into a facsimile of an urbane smile; but his eyes showed naked fear. 'You know that I cannot enter China.'

'Why not? *I* did when I had your job.'

'Times have changed, Foo. In my head I carry every aspect of our intelligence work against China – I cannot possibly risk being arrested and interrogated. And if my presence was discovered there would be a major diplomatic row. Why not use somebody from our Embassy in Peking?'

'Because their travel is restricted and the *Gonganbu* have them all under surveillance. What I have in mind is something that would be unnoticed – the meeting would be secret and far away from Peking.'

'What about the Americans?'

'No doubt you would tell them – an American could be involved too if you want.'

Rumbelow stood up, slightly stooped, hands thrust deep into his jacket pockets. He stared gloomily through the window: Hong Kong island was hidden by grey mist and sheets of rain. 'I suppose I might be able to send one of my staff to meet your leadership and set up the means of future communication – by radio, couriers and meetings preferably *outside* China. But you are asking me to put whoever I choose into grave danger, you know – and to risk serious problems for my government if anything goes wrong.'

'But will you do it?'

'I will consult London.'

'Tell them they have no choice.'

Rumbelow started. 'Why on earth not?'

'Because handing back Hong Kong to the present Chinese regime could be one of the worst disasters your country has ever faced.'

'How so?'

'Oh come, Rumbelow. Look at the flood of talent leaving already! In the last few years before ninety-seven everyone will realise that life under China will be grey, oppressive, thoroughly unpleasant and possibly much worse than that. Your country will be pressed to take more and more refugees. The economy here may collapse, law and order break down – even before the Chinese arrive. Your country will be humiliated.'

'But there are guarantees – the Basic Law?'

'Worthless. When it comes to it the Chinese can do what they like. You have a problem and your government knows it. You will send someone with me, Mr Rumbelow, because the best solution would be for you to be dealing with a new regime in China, democratic and non-communist.'

'If my government tries to run with the hare and hunt with the hounds, we could face fearful problems.'

'But you will do it. You have no choice.'

'I'll take soundings. No promises, but I should have an answer in a week or so.'

Tang Tsin ached in every joint when they took him from the padded room, still conscious but confused and terrified. The interrogator, who said his name was Wong, ran through the precise locations of his drops again, making Tang Tsin identify them on photographs that must have been taken while he was in the cell. 'Which would you use next?'

Tang groaned as he moved. 'The crack in the wall near Xizhimen station.'

'Good. In future you will be working under my control. Now, I have some papers – how would you package them?'

'In an ordinary envelope, any colour, the sort you can buy cheaply anywhere.'

Wong nodded. 'Come with me.' They mounted the stone steps, then another staircase until they were at a barred window overlooking the yard. 'You will co-operate with me in every particular, Tang, for if you do not this is what will happen to your wife and daughter. The boy is too young.'

Outside, the yard seemed full of soldiers: green peaked caps with yellow piping, open-necked khaki shirts flapping outside their trousers but held in at the waist by leather belts. Below their crumpled dark trousers they all seemed to be wearing cheap canvas sneakers. A senior officer in a grey uniform with red and gold shoulder-boards seemed to be in charge. No one seemed to be taking much notice of the two figures kneeling in the centre of the yard, hands bound tightly behind them. A young man and a girl, both about twenty and wearing torn blue fatigues – they might have been students or labourers. They stared rigidly at the stone wall.

For a heart-stopping moment Tang Tsin thought the girl was his daughter, that Wong was going to make him watch

Hong Kong and Macao

his own child die, but then he saw that the young couple were unknown to him. They still looked far too young to be killed like this and he felt a wave of pity. 'What are they waiting for?' he asked as the minutes ticked by.

'The doctor and the ambulance.'

'Does that matter? Those two must be going through agony, they're barely more than children.'

The interrogator smiled at the older man's innocence. 'They are hooligans, counter-revolutionaries, Tang. The doctor will remove their kidneys as soon as the execution is over – they will be used for transplants later today.'

Tang Tsin felt a spasm of disgust and stared at him. 'Is that *normal*?'

Wong shrugged with indifference. 'Quite common. Organs are needed for the sick – these criminals might as well do something for others when they die. At present the supply is so good that we can earn hard currency from rich overseas Chinese who come to Canton and Peking for their operations.'

The chatter in the yard stopped as an ambulance backed in through a gate; several white-coated figures stepped out of its rear doors. An order was shouted and two soldiers carrying AK-47s stepped up to the two condemned, who turned and tried to smile at each other. The soldiers pressed the barrels of their guns against the necks of the man and girl, who flinched at the cold metal but then seemed to press back against it as if they had been told it was quicker that way. Another soldier held up a red flag; as he let it drop the two shots rang out.

The two figures jerked and tipped forward, still kneeling, hips in the air, an undignified way to go. The girl rolled over, plainly dead. The man's executioner must have missed the mark because he writhed on the ground with blood gushing from his mouth. A soldier stepped forward and kicked him in the head to hasten the bleeding and death. Wong laughed. 'The People's Republic can afford only one bullet for criminals, Tang – and their relatives will have to pay for that if they want the bodies to

107

cremate.' After about five minutes both victims lay still and were turned on their backs. Strips of paper saying 'executed for sedition' were pinned to their blood-stained chests and an official photographer's camera clicked. Orderlies rushed forward with stretchers and the ambulance drove away.

Tang Tsin stood wretchedly with head bowed. 'I will do whatever you order, comrade Wong. Anything. But may I see my family?'

13

That afternoon Rumbelow told Sarah that he had chosen her to accompany Foo into the heartland of China – very casually, as if it was routine, no risk, no danger. He did not summon her to the Peak but dropped in at her office in *Tamar* unannounced, mopping his forehead with a red and green Paisley handkerchief. 'God, it's hot out there.' He sat on the metal desk, swinging his legs, avoiding her gaze. 'We'll have a briefing session with Mary and Gatti tomorrow morning. Then I want you to take the train to Canton and fly to Kunming. Use your own passport – we'll get you a tourist visa, as if you were going on holiday.'

'On *holiday*? To *Kunming*?'

Rumbelow looked shifty. 'It's supposed to be very attractive, I'm sure they have a few tourists down there.'

'You reckon? A European woman will stand out a mile. I'll do it, if that's what you want – I don't have any choice – but wouldn't it be more sensible to use an ethnic Chinese – you could borrow one from Special Branch?'

Rumbelow shook his head. 'I thought of that. But I'm not quite sure I trust Foo,' he gave that familiar twisted smile. 'I want someone utterly reliable to go with him, assess the situation. We know far too little of the opposition in China – who are these leaders who think they can topple Li Peng? Are they credible? Are they loonies? Would it be wiser to have nothing to do with them?'

'Perhaps you should go yourself?' suggested Sarah sweetly. She enjoyed the shadow of fear that crossed

Rumbelow's face, then immediately felt guilty. He had done his stuff often enough in the past, taking real risks behind the Iron Curtain and in Africa; now he was entitled to live long enough to enjoy the thatched cottage in Suffolk that had become the end of his rainbow. She just wished he would be more honest with her.

'You know I'm forbidden to enter China, Sarah, none of us should go there.'

'Including me?'

'This is exceptional.'

'We aren't at war with them.'

'No, no of course not. But it would be very awkward if one of us was caught dealing with people they'd consider traitors.'

'Very awkward.' Sarah gave a brittle laugh and ran her fingers through her hair nervously. 'If I'm arrested I'll have no diplomatic protection or anything.' She was speaking very quietly, not trying to conceal that she was scared. 'For all we know Foo is Peking's man – and if he is they're bound to pick me up. They can chuck me in jail or shoot me, Tom – maybe they will, maybe they won't, but I'd prefer not to find out. I'm not a complete fool.'

There was a slight flush of anger and his eyes hardened. 'That's why you're going as yourself, Sarah. You must be known to our pals at the New China News Agency, we all are. But a few days holiday is perfectly plausible – they wouldn't expect us to send a known intelligence officer in under her own name for nefarious purposes.'

'Wouldn't they?' Sarah sighed. Through the office window Hong Kong harbour suddenly looked very beautiful, a place she did not want to leave. Safe. 'I hope you're right, Tom. It's my neck, not yours, and I just bloody well hope you're right.'

WPC Wu continued to visit the Prince of Wales Hospital early every evening. Each time she sat for an hour in the narrow side ward, holding the girl's hand. To begin with they kept each other company in silence, for WPC Wu sensed that Ah Ming's physical and mental pain had left her full of fear and mistrust. It was too early to ask questions.

After five days Ah Ming started to sit up and look around. She was soon eating a little normal food. WPC Wu went on holding her hand and brought her small gifts – a bar of chocolate, a spray of deodorant with a spicy perfume, a tiny charm of a black cat. It was partly natural kindness that made WPC Wu do this, partly her curiosity to know why a teenage girl should have been fleeing from China alone. Above all, perhaps, it was because ten years before WPC Wu had fled from China – alone and fifteen years old – after her father had been executed for counter-revolutionary activities and the rest of the family vanished into camps.

After ten days it was clear that Ah Ming looked forward to the young policewoman's visits and they were talking to each other. It was also clear that Ah Ming remembered nothing of her life before she woke up in hospital with two bullet wounds. 'It is a fugue,' said Dr Singh wisely.

'You mean she has lost her memory?' WPC Wu bit her lip with frustration. 'But how long will it last?'

The Sikh shook his head. 'I do not know, Miss Wu. I am sorry.'

Gatti spent another half day in Mary Devereux's radio rooms under HMS *Tamar*. He talked to a number of the Wrens and ratings who worked there and checked the security procedures. It convinced him that there was no sign of any breach, no copies of messages or intercepts being copied and smuggled out. There was nothing wrong with this set-up – it was leading him nowhere and irrelevant to the main problem.

There would be no official reason to see Mary again, which was a pity because she was good company. So that evening he asked her out for the second time and she went

with him, neat in jeans and check shirt, on the ferry to
Lantau. Before eating at one of the outdoor Chinese
restaurants they walked along the beach at Silvermine Bay
until they were alone. The sand was still warm to their feet
and Mary did not resist when he took her hand. When
they undressed she peeled off her jeans unselfconsciously
to reveal a black bikini that showed off her light tan and
ran splashing into the sea. After they had swum out a way
she raced him to a buoy with a powerful crawl, beating
him easily.

Stretched out on the beach to dry, Gatti smiled at her.
'You swim brilliantly.'

'I wasn't too good at anything else when I was a girl, but
I could do that and worked on it. I still enjoy a good swim
– helps me forget being on parade as the boss all the time.'
She turned lazily on her front and he admired her body.
The dark curls and brown eyes were matched by a skin
that took the sun easily. Small, firm breasts; long attractive legs, the slight swell of powerful muscles in the backs
of her thighs. She was beautiful, though the lack of flaws
made her strangely uninviting, even when she was nearly
naked. He ran his fingers gently down her spine and
kissed the back of her neck. He felt her buttocks tense
slightly under his hand, but she smiled at him in a friendly
way, neither discouraging nor inviting.

'Is it difficult?'

Mary's head jerked up and she looked puzzled. 'Is *what*
difficult?'

'Being a Commander, ordering people about and all
that.'

'Not bad. I'm used to it now but it's nice being taken out
by someone who's even bossier.' She sighed. 'Mm, do that
again please. Sometimes I wish I'd married and had a
family instead.'

'But you've done awfully well – I bet you end up as an
admiral or something.'

'They don't have women admirals, not yet anyway. Yes
– I've made it in a man's world, but I still get confused

112

sometimes – doesn't everybody? – and miss having a husband and children. It's sort of basic, if you think about it.'

'But you chose not to.'

'Actually I couldn't.'

'I'm sorry.'

'Well, maybe I could've but – oh forget it. Let's just relax and forget everything.' He reached out and she rolled into his arms, looking up at him like a lost teenager with a half-wistful look in her eyes. He kissed her gently on the mouth and she responded awkwardly, eyes closed, but gripping him hard. 'You're nice, Bob. I don't get asked out too often, you know.'

'I don't believe that, Mary – you're incredibly beautiful.'

'Don't be silly.' Even her laugh had that upper class tone. 'I'm not twenty any more you know. If I eat too much I get an awful tummy and my bum's positively fat.' They stood up slowly and shyly she put her arms round his neck. With one hand he pulled her to him, the other caressing her face as he kissed her. She responded but somehow he sensed that it was an effort, as if she really was lonely and grateful for his attention, but didn't quite fancy him. Or felt guilty? Or confused? Or perhaps it was his imagination?

Later they sat by the harbour in the dark, at a table lit by Chinese lanterns, a grove of high bamboo creaking in the breeze behind them. Mary had a gin and tonic, then lager with the clams and smoked duck. Her smile in the lantern light was young and eager as they talked more intimately than ever before about hopes, fears and insecurities. Gatti forgot the reason for their being thrown together and Mary was the first person to share his pain at the death of Sue and the boys. She told him about a childhood of genteel poverty in a vicarage. 'Mum and Dad were desperately undemonstrative. No feeling of love, but of course they did care. If it hadn't been for poor Daddy I wouldn't be here – he was determined we'd both get a decent education because he hadn't anything

113

else to give us.'

A waiter in a white shirt brought more lager. 'You from Engrand or 'Merica?'

'England,' Mary smiled at him. 'He's from America though.'

'You marry?'

'No, we aren't married.'

The waiter winked and grinned. 'Have go' time then.'

They walked back to the ferry arm in arm in the darkness. She nuzzled her curls into his shoulder. 'Thank you for a lovely evening. Hold me tight, Bob.' But he sensed that below the warmth there was a hollowness, a yearning for intimacy that was not in reality there. Puzzled and troubled he stroked her face gently. 'Oh Bob,' she whispered. 'I realised why we are here when we were having dinner. I ought to hate you, you bastard – but I don't. You're checking me out, aren't you? You *know*.'

'Know what, Mary?'

'Don't play with me, or I *will* hate you. You're on duty, aren't you?'

'I was on duty this morning. Not now. We're here because I enjoy your company, that's all. I haven't done anything like this since . . . I just wanted us to have dinner again – if it was a mistake, I'm sorry.'

She squeezed his hand. 'It wasn't a mistake. If things were different – for both of us, I mean – I think I'd fancy you something rotten, Commander Gatti.'

He smiled in the dark. 'That's mutual, then.'

'But you still tricked me. You *do* know, don't you?'

'Does it matter?'

'It's a crime in my service. It matters a lot.'

'Sure, I guessed.' Gatti hesitated. 'I wasn't planning to tell anyone else, if that's what you're asking.'

'Are you certain about that?'

'You can trust me. Sure, the thought crossed my mind that you might've been compromised. *Have* you been compromised, Mary?'

'No, of course not. Being gay doesn't make me a

114

traitor. I've always known that if someone tried to black-mail me I'd have to come clean, take the rap.'

'I believe you. I got that far some days ago – tonight is private, just for us. Okay?'

'You're sure you believe me?'

'Absolutely.' You shouldn't be doing this, nagged an inner voice, you shouldn't be here at all. She's a suspect, not some kind of friend – how the hell can you know she isn't lying? But Gatti pushed the thought away. He *did* believe her.

'You won't let me down?'

'No. Promise.'

'Oh Bob,' she whispered, clinging to him as his fingers felt the dampness of her tears. 'Can I really trust you?'

14

Sarah's briefing was in the same icily air-conditioned conference room on the Peak. Foo was not invited – she was to meet him with Rumbelow late in the afternoon, but for the morning he was an outsider. The previous evening she had been allowed to read a thick file that told his life story from birth in Shanghai nearly sixty years ago. The first nineteen years were obscure, but she could imagine the privileged upbringing – his father had been a merchant with a large house and servants – cut short by the violence of the civil war and Japanese invasion. His home in Shanghai had been destroyed in a Nationalist air raid, two sisters buried in the ruins. There was a note from the Hong Kong police inspector who had first recruited Foo as an informer in 1953: on coarse yellowed utility paper, the blue royal arms still clear on each sheet, the handwriting round and bold in a scratchy pen. It described Foo's only sign of emotion appearing when he recalled digging his sister Mei-ling out of the ruins, her fragile body crushed by a block of blackened concrete, and his parents fleeing up the Yangtze to Hankow on a crowded junk that was machine-gunned and sunk by the communists at a point where the river rushed through a ravine, so that those who survived the bullets were sure to drown.

Suddenly alone in the world he had made his own Long March south to Hong Kong. His progress from penniless nineteen year-old with no home but the streets, to SIS station chief honoured with a CMG and now millionaire made fascinating reading. She handed back the file with a

116

renewed respect for the man she was accompanying to China – she could see why the attractive Ruth had fallen for him and been ready to cut herself off from the West to share his life. And Sarah had sensed how much in love the ill-assorted couple still were. She had no doubt that Ruth Foo was a straightforward, honest woman who believed that her husband was involved with Tenth October, despite the very real danger, because he wanted to see an end to the bastards in Peking. Nairn dismissed them as empty, a spent force, but from what she had seen their loss of conviction had simply made them more repressive and murderous than ever.

And was Ruth deceived? Was Foo Peking's man? If so he wouldn't be the first expatriate Chinese millionaire to throw in his lot with the communists as some kind of insurance policy. Not a bad insurance, either, if you wanted to be in on the pickings after they reoccupied Hong Kong . . . And if Foo was Peking's man Sarah was surely going to see the inside of a Chinese jail, or worse – unless she flatly refused to go, which would warrant dismissal from the service, or contrived to break an arm, which would be bloody painful.

Now she huddled over a map of China as Rumbelow pointed to Kunming, in the mountains of the south-west towards the frontiers with Vietnam and Burma. 'Never been there myself, but it's on this plateau – mountains on three sides, Lake Dianchi to the south. Nearly fifteen hundred miles from Peking, nicely out of the mainstream.'

'Is that why someone blew up the Governor?' asked Sarah drily.

Tom Rumbelow looked embarrassed. 'According to Nairn he may have been part of this opposition network, taken out by the *Gonganbu* for Peking.'

'Terrific, so every soldier and secret policeman down there will be looking out for suspicious characters?'

'It's a big place – nearly two million with a mixed population, twelve different Chinese nationalities, Han, Hui, Yi, Bai, so on. A few Europeans – and foreign

117

tourists and businessmen *do* go there, so I think you'll be okay. It's a sensible choice for what Foo has in mind.'

Sarah said nothing. She was wearing a neat white blouse and dark skirt that made her look like one of the Wrens on *Tamar*, particularly as her hair was tucked up into a knot. In China she would wear it like that, covered with a straw hat: her height would still be a nuisance but at least that give-away long fair hair would be hidden. In the end she said: 'Just what *does* he have in mind?'

'He claims to be calling together three of the leaders of this obscure movement – they will come from all over China, to show us that some semblance of a national opposition really does exist. They call themselves Tenth October, after the date of Sun Yat-sen's revolution against the last Emperor in 1911. It started on the tenth of October. The Chinese are fond of using dates for political movements.'

'How interesting.' Sarah gave an ironic little smile.

'Yes, well – Foo wants you to stay in one of the larger and more anonymous hotels for two nights, then he'll pick you up and take you to a meeting place in the mountains, where you'll stay several days.'

'And just what am I supposed to talk to these jokers about?'

'I'd have thought that was fairly obvious, but Mary has written a brief – you can study it this afternoon. Basically we need to know how serious they are. Do these leaders have the necessary strength? What kind of jobs do they do at present? Do they have real influence politically? Numerical support? Money? Arms?'

Mary Devereux had just joined them. 'Perhaps most important of all, Sarah, how do they stand in relation to the People's Liberation Army? Are there army units that might support them? Better than that, are there generals commanding whole divisions that might? Or is the whole thing a sick joke?'

'And then I just fly back, like a tourist?'

'Exactly. You'll have to make some notes, but Foo has

undertaken to provide you with a Minox camera so that you can photograph them and he says he has the gear to reduce them to microdots. You'll do that and stick them on postcards to some addresses we'll give you, then burn your notes and dump the camera, so you come out absolutely clean.'

'How's Foo travelling?'

'We'll find out the details this evening, but he'll be going after you by a different route.'

'What time are we meeting him?'

'Six. Here. We'll pick him up in a closed van near Aberdeen.'

Rumbelow stood up. The briefing was over. As they knocked and the security guard opened the door, Mary Devereux turned and smiled at her. 'Good luck.'

'Thanks,' Sarah shrugged and laughed, but without humour.

Shortly before midnight Luther stood on the quay by the typhoon shelter at Chai Wan. He breathed in the aroma of empty fish boxes and crab pots, keeping out of the pale yellow light from the window of a fisherman's hut as the motor junk chugged away across the harbour, crowded with sampans, out into the sea. Her navigation lights were steady and correct, the fishing nets convincing, she would pass any inspection and with luck no one would even notice her until she landed in Red China in twelve hours time. He turned and walked back through the tin huts of refugee housing; it would be a while before he could find a taxi but there was plenty of time before his flight at five in the morning.

Sarah and Nick were leaving the lift of the tower block in MacDonnell Road, both mellowed by the chilled Chablis that had accompanied a candle-lit French dinner at Gaston's. They had barely mentioned China all evening.

She fumbled until her key found the lock and they collapsed on the sofa. Outside, the lights of Central and the harbour twinkled through the glass doors until Nick got up and drew the curtains. 'Coffee, Cable?'

Sarah shook her head and pulled him down to her. 'Not yet, Nick. That was a super meal – thank you. To be honest it was just what I needed – I'm scared about tomorrow, bloody scared.'

Nick's eyes looked troubled. 'I know – Rumbelow's off his rocker. We ought to know a lot more before risking this kind of thing – I don't trust any of it.'

'I'll have to go, you know – there's no way out.'

'Can't you refuse – go over Rumbelow's head?'

'Not if I want to stay in the service. They'll just think I've no guts.'

'But that's absolute rubbish!'

'Is it?' She snuggled up to him. 'I'm beginning to wonder . . . I'll be okay, but you're good for me, darling. Behind that cool Bostonian front you're one of the kindest men I've ever met – did you know that?' She kissed him. 'I wish you were coming too.'

'So do I.' His arms were strong around her, the eyes that met hers very gentle, full of character. In the bedroom they lay naked for a time, the tall girl burying her face in the chest of the even taller man, long legs twining and untwining.

'Oh Nick, I feel so safe with you.' She gave a dreamy sigh, kissing his nipples hungrily. 'It's been nearly a year, you know – I *do* love you.'

His fingers caressed her face, eyes smiling down at her. 'I love you too, Sarah.'

'Nick, suppose something goes wrong? I'd never see you again.' Tears were pricking her eyes as she lifted her face to kiss him again, wanting the warm closeness to last for ever, letting her body take command. Suddenly she was pulling him down, arching her back, gripping his waist with her legs, caressing his face and shoulders, eyes closed, trembling and panting with exertion as she felt him

entering her, deeper and deeper, starting to thrust. 'Oh
Nick . . . Nick . . . my love . . . ' In the long stillness they
clung together, heads side by side on the pillows, smiling
at each other. 'Oh I wish we could stay like this for ever.'
They talked for a long time until Nick went to fetch two
glasses of wine from the fridge. She enjoyed watching his
body, golden in the lamplight except for the sweet little
white strip across his bum; when he returned holding the
glasses, eyes smiling down at her, wide shoulders, penis
half-erect, he looked like a Greek god. He did not lie
down again but sat on the edge of the bed, not touching
her: both of them happy with the silent presence of the
other but enjoying the knowledge that the tantalising six-
inch gap would not last.

That second time she wanted to be taken roughly – if
Nick could ever be rough – and he responded, throwing
the sheet aside, pulling her up by the shoulders, arms
crushing her, tongue flashing into her throat. Suddenly he
tipped her back on the bed, drew her towards him and
knelt between her legs – spread wide apart, toes drumming on the floor – his tongue probing again until she
cried out, her whole body pulsing with exquisite sen-
sations. He lifted her thighs – so slowly that it drove her
wild with anticipation – until they were pressed against his
chest, long legs dangling over his shoulders. His hands
electrified her breasts and the kind eyes crinkled above
her. But now his face was too far away so she twisted like
an eel and kissed his arms again and again as his hands
cupped her buttocks and lifted them from the bed, feeling
shamelessly naked and vulnerable yet overwhelmingly
safe and loved as she clutched his hips and began to move
powerfully with him.

15

Next morning Roper let himself out of the flat at six thirty. Sarah was still asleep – she looked very young, half-smiling, fair hair tumbled on the pillows. The engine of his rented Toyota echoed deafeningly around the basement garage until he gunned the car up the ramp and roared down the street, still quiet and empty. As he sped by Happy Valley racecourse he was humming *The Battle Hymn of the Republic*, for no particular reason except that he felt absurdly happy. Last night had been important to both of them, an expression of mutual respect and admiration as well as mutual need; with Sarah he felt complete, a man in control of his life. He laughed out loud and smiled benevolently at two elderly Chinese doing traditional exercises, oblivious to passers-by, at the side of the road; but then he remembered the imminent danger and the purpose of his dawn journey and stopped smiling.

On past the Hong Kong Cricket Club, Wong Nai Chung Gap, down into Repulse Bay and along the coast to Stanley. Bob Gatti was still living in the same white house, silent and empty. Roper had been one of the dozen friends who had accompanied Gatti to the short cremation service at Cape Collinson and he still felt tears in his eyes when he remembered the numbing sadness: the bleak impersonal chapel, Sue's plain oak coffin, the two little white ones for the boys, the flowers that seemed somehow irrelevant. Gatti had just stood there, his face harrowed and lost, as if he had died with them. So much had gone: Roper could no longer imagine him in command of a ship, telling his dry jokes in a deliberately exaggerated Chicago accent or preaching the virtues of Coors beer. He wondered if Gatti would ever laugh again.

His friend was waiting on the terrace in front of the house looking down on Stanley harbour, a pot of coffee steaming on the white PVC table. 'Hi, Nick. I've got some croissants for you in the oven.'

Roper yawned. 'Great. I'm sorry to get you up so early.'

'I wake about five anyway, Nick. Better to get up and do something, otherwise I brood and that gets me down. Bloody depressing.' He hesitated. 'How's Sarah?'

'That's why I'm here, Bob. She's supposed to be leaving for China this morning – I want you to speak to Rumbelow, stop it.'

'Why?'

'Because it's dangerous, bloody dangerous, and not worth the risks.'

Gatti looked troubled. 'Look Nick, I know you and Sarah are close and you don't want to see her put at risk, nor do I, but she's supposed to be an intelligence officer. Has she *asked* you to do this?'

'No, she hasn't.'

'And Rumbelow's the head of station.' The harsh Chicago accent faded away as he lapsed into thought. Eventually Gatti shook his head. 'I can't see what I can do?'

'You can speak to Rumbelow.'

'He'll just tell me to go to hell. Quite rightly.'

Suddenly Roper was angry, very angry. 'But you could at least *try*!' Gatti sat in silence, not meeting his eyes. 'For Christ's sake, Bob, you've lost your grip. You need some time off, away from all this, but you can't just let Rumbelow go blundering on to disaster.'

Gatti poured more coffee and Roper was appalled to see his hand shaking. 'I guess I could try to ring that guy Nairn they had out here?'

'Bob, that won't do – we've served together, we're

supposed to be *buddies*. Speaking to Nairn, even if you can find him at the end of a phone, will take too *long*.' Gatti looked at him miserably – Roper had never seen him quite so broken and indecisive. 'There isn't *time*, Bob. For Christ's sake do something *now*.' He stood up abruptly, suddenly shouting. 'Well? What about it?'

As soon as he arrived at Shoudu airport Luther was driven to an unmarked building in north-east Peking. Its walls were a dirty yellow, with the rendering peeling off and the few windows to the street high up and steel-shuttered; the place was obviously some kind of prison or interrogation centre. He was let in through a wicket in the high double gates and within minutes was in Wong's office, watching Tang Tsin at exercise, walking round and round the empty yard. Wong treated Luther with the mixture of deference and suspicion that Luther was used to: Chinese cadres accepted him and respected his rank, but remained puzzled that a European should be working alongside them. Luther gestured at the sad figure shuffling below them. 'Is he broken? Will he co-operate completely?'

'I believe so, comrade. He fears for his family, he fears the red room for himself.'

'He won't try to use secret procedures that show he is under control?'

'That is highly unlikely. For one thing he has no method of contact except his drops and an open telephone line at the American Embassy.'

'No fail-safe procedures – something he must do every month or week to show he is a free man?'

'He says not, comrade.'

'Amazing, quite amazing.'

'Do you want to talk to him?'

Luther gave a slight smile. 'No, not yet. Let him become dependent on *you* – you have broken him, now become his friend.'

Wong inclined his head respectfully. 'In the end I take it

he will be executed?'

Luther shrugged. 'That is not my decision but I imagine so.'

The phone rang and Wong picked it up. 'A call for you, comrade.'

Luther took the receiver, listened, then laughed quietly. He put down the phone and walked back to the window, ignoring Wong. Everything seemed to have worked exactly as he had planned and he felt a sudden sense of triumph. He was about to rout the enemy, the adrenalin was rising, he wanted Josie's lithe body but she was still in Hong Kong. A slight shadow crossed his face but Luther's step was light as he descended the concrete steps back to the gate. Josie would be back that night – and at last he was winning.

Sarah left on the train for Canton later that morning. Although she was travelling on a legitimate tourist visa, Rumbelow had two other agents on the same train to watch her back. They were both Chinese, a young man and a middle-aged woman; they saw no sign that Sarah was followed or under observation. The man travelled on the same crowded bus from Canton station to Baiyun airport, sitting three seats behind Sarah, and watched her board a flight to Kunming. He reported back to Rumbelow on Friday evening that there had been three other Europeans on the flight and that they looked like tourists; hopefully Sarah's cover would stick.

In Hong Kong it was Sunday morning when the roof started to fall in. The long Flash telegram from London, classified TOP SECRET, came out of the machine about six o'clock, a roll of thin paper nearly four feet long. The Diplomatic Wireless Service operator was tired and bored; the night shift at weekends was deadly quiet once you had ciphered and despatched the routine stuff, floating away from the masts on the Peak to be picked up at Hanslope Park near Milton Keynes, north of London. He wanted to get off back to the flat in Kowloon where his Chinese girlfriend was waiting, so he was delighted to see that the long telegram – hundreds of numbered groups – was personal from Nairn to Rumbelow and for Rumbelow alone to decode. The despatch rider took it straight round to the chief's house, a white bungalow set in a luxuriant garden by the sea in Repulse Bay. He left his motorcycle at the kerbside and walked up the garden path swinging his helmet, taking in the blue swimming pool, the clipped lawns, the red sun-loungers, the barbecue. Rumbelow might be an idle sod but he did himself all right – his rent allowance must be enormous.

After ringing the bell for ten minutes, the door was opened by a middle-aged woman in a housecoat, pretty in a faded sort of way. She looked irritated, as if the chief only gave it to her once a week and he'd caught them on the job. 'Good morning, Mrs Rumbelow. Sorry to disturb you – urgent telegram for the boss.'

'Please come in, Keith.' She had a nice smile, nice tits too, must be about fifty. Her accent was still Lancashire. She gave him coffee in the kitchen, while Rumbelow dressed and appeared looking ghastly: unshaven and bleary-eyed, must have a terrible hangover. He unlocked the leather pouch and took out the long roll of paper.

'Why the hell hasn't it been decrypted?' Then he saw the heading. 'Oh Christ, it'll take at least an hour – you'd better wait, might need a reply. Have a swim if you like – Jean will find you some trunks.' He kissed her on the cheek, abnormally human for once. 'Sorry love.'

When Rumbelow emerged from the study an hour and a half later his wife was lying by the pool, trim in a modest one-piece black costume, and the despatch rider was swimming up and down; he climbed out dripping and started to dry himself. It was still only eight on Sunday morning. Rumbelow's face was grey: he seemed to have aged ten years. 'No reply, Keith. Thank you for waiting.

Are you on duty all day?'

'Only up to noon, sir.'

'Good, give you time for the beach this afternoon.'

As soon as the man had gone, Rumbelow's wife put her arms round him. 'Tom, love, what on earth's gone wrong? You look terrible.'

'I've made the most God-awful cock-up. That fool Gatti has been in touch with London behind my back and Nairn has just vetoed Sarah Cable going into China to establish contact with a bunch of dissidents. Says he believes she's blown and they're waiting to pick her up. But he's too bloody late. She went last Thursday. She flew to Kunming, been there three days already and I damn well sent her.'

'Can't you get her out?'

Rumbelow ran his fingers through greying hair. 'Just at this moment I don't even know where she is – if she's still free she'll be in a hotel or guest house somewhere in Yannan, but God knows which one. She arranged a link-up with a Chinese called Foo and for security no one else knows about it.' He looked at his watch. 'Oh shit – it's risky on an open line, but I'll ring him now. That might be the answer. He may still be here, in Macao.'

Back in the study, Rumbelow closed the hanging blinds against the sun which was already getting hot and dialled one of the numbers Foo had given him – the private one, straight through to his bedroom or study, the number that wouldn't be answered by a protective secretary or house-boy. It seemed to ring for a long time, then a voice answered in Chinese.

'Foo, is that you?'

'No, Mr Foo not here.'

'I'm sorry, I need to speak to him very urgently, a matter of business. Will he be back soon?'

There was a clatter as the receiver was put down and the sound of urgent exchanges in Cantonese. Finally a different voice spoke, Chinese but fluent, educated. 'Who is calling please?'

'My name is Smith, a business associate of Mr Foo's.'

'This is the Macao police. Mr Foo has vanished.'

Rumbelow fell back in his chair, breathing heavily; there was a sharp pain in his chest and he wondered if he was about to have a heart attack. 'What do you mean "vanished"?'

'There are signs of a struggle and he has gone. A houseboy has been stabbed to death. Mrs Foo appears to have been drugged in some way. She is still unconscious – found by a cleaner when she arrived early this morning. But Mr Foo has gone – he has been abducted.'

Tom Rumbelow stared into space. 'Who by?'

'I do not know. I have been here only fifteen minutes. But Mr Foo has gone – and I am sure he is no longer in Macao.'

PART TWO

PEOPLE'S REPUBLIC OF CHINA

16

Kunming was beautiful. The alleys down in the city were as filthy as any in China, but there were lakes and pagodas, mountains wreathed in cloud in the distance. The air was clearer and crisper than on the sultry coast, the streets less crowded. There seemed to be flowers everywhere – and shrubs, especially camellias and magnolia. The misty expanse of Dianchi Lake stretched away to the south, dotted with white sailing boats.

Sarah booked into the ugly block of the main Kunming Hotel, along with the other European tourists and businessmen on her plane. She arrived full of apprehension, still angry with Rumbelow's amateur aproach: whoever heard of sending a known intelligence officer into a dangerous country on a tourist visa? But after twenty-four hours she began to relax. She investigated the city, walking and on buses. The Chinese studied all Europeans with amused curiosity and, in the crowded market, Sarah was conscious of beaming women examining her clothes as they offered goods from their stalls. The men were plainly undressing her, intrigued by the sheer size and fleshiness of all European women, so different from their own. It occurred to her that Foo, with his northern Tartar build, and the smaller Ruth were an unusual combination.

But she felt reasonably certain that she was not under police surveillance and the man with the rimless glasses and gold teeth at reception didn't seem particularly interested in her passport and visa. It seemed that she was accepted as just another European tourist, so maybe Rumbelow's approach had been right. She was there legitimately, after all; so far no crime had been committed.

On the second day she followed Foo's instructions and took the number 33 bus from the Nantaiqiao stop near the hotel. It was packed with Chinese, but she found a place on the slatted wooden seat at the back, next to a young man who tried to chat her up in a dialect she did not know, in between long, hawking spits that landed several feet away. She smiled to herself: as Nick often said all Chinese had bad sinuses or bad manners. The bus wound southwards by the rippling waters of Dianchi, past the Dragon Gate shrine hewn out of a sheer cliff. It took more than an hour to reach the workers' sanatorium at Baiyukou, dropping off a young couple here, an old woman in black pyjamas and a basket of chickens there. At Baiyukou Sarah strolled away from the lake, up a lane shaded by pine trees. A Chinese girl in jeans and plain white shirt was waiting in the shadows.

Sarah hesitated. The first moment of danger had come; she sighed – it had been relaxing being a tourist for twenty-four hours. The girl said nothing but held out a coin, jaggedly cut in half. Sarah pulled the other half from her pocket and pressed them together. They fitted. 'I'm Sarah.'

The girl smiled: she was small and pretty. 'I'm Cheng Huiqing. Please come with me.' Sarah followed her through the trees to a rusty lorry loaded with sacks of fertiliser in a clearing. She hesitated again. 'Where are we going?'

Cheng Huiqing spoke perfect English. 'You are now the guest of Tenth October – I promise we shall take care of you.'

'But my luggage is at the hotel – I'm still booked in there. If I suddenly vanish it'll give the whole game away.'

The Chinese girl opened the cab door and smiled again. 'No. The head receptionist is our man. You have already been checked out, your bill paid and the necessary police forms completed for your return to Hong Kong. Your luggage has been packed and will catch up with you. Officially you will be back in Hong Kong tonight. It is all taken care of.'

Sarah suddenly felt very vulnerable. The trouble with going underground was re-establishing your status when you wanted to become legitimate again. She did not get in the truck. 'So how do I get out of the country when this meeting is over?'

'We shall take you to the Shenzhen Special Economic Zone and give you papers for a day trip from Macao – you will cross back into Macao with them and so to Hong Kong.'

'But Shenzhen is more than seven hundred miles away!'

'Don't worry, Sarah. I promise – we are better organised than you think.'

Sarah climbed in and sat beside her as she started the noisy petrol engine. She didn't like it, but she had to trust them. The lorry bounced along a track of dried mud until they reached a paved road, brakes shrieking with metal on metal. 'Sorry.' Cheng Huiqing gave a wry grin. 'Great socialist economy has no brake shoes for sale.' As the truck picked up speed they were surrounded by rattles, as if it was about to fall to pieces.

The Chinese girl drove carefully at about thirty miles an hour. The truck was of Chinese make and Sarah's head touched the roof of the cab. 'You speak perfect English,' she said. 'Where did you learn?'

Huiqing laughed. 'At Oxford. I did my Ph.D at Lady Margaret Hall. I am Hong Kong born, but I have returned to China.'

They were passing broken-down farmsteads with thatched roofs, a peasant in a straw hat driving pigs along the road, another wobbling along on an upright bicycle. 'Where are we going?' asked Sarah.

'Into the mountains, to some caves. They have been fitted out for meetings and have places to sleep and eat.'

'And who am I going to meet?'

'Some of our leaders. You will know them all by their cover-names at this stage, but they are empowered to deal with you on behalf of the movement.' She glanced in the mirror to check that the road was empty, then turned off up a dirt track that climbed steeply, shaded by trees. As she changed to a lower gear the engine rose to a higher, tortured note and the back wheels slithered on loose shingle, but they climbed on. 'It is still a long way – tell me about yourself, Sarah?'

'I'm Sarah Cable and I work for our Foreign and Commonwealth Office, stationed in Hong Kong.'

'Is that all?'

'It's all you need to know for the moment. Sorry – I'm not allowed to say more.'

'I quite understand. Then tell me about England – I have never been back and I often feel nostalgic. Have you ever been to the Trout at Godstow, on the Thames? It is one of my favourite pubs.'

Luther felt jubilant as he walked by the lake in Hangzhou. Josie would be back soon and he had just been telephoned from Peking. Kidnapping Benjamin Foo had been another of the minister's crude ideas – like the arrest of Tang Tsin – but at least it had been done efficiently. The old man was still unconscious from the sedatives they had injected, awaiting interrogation in Shanghai. Luther had planned to leave Foo free so that he could guide them to the leaders of Tenth October and at first he had been furious at the order to abduct him, but now the idiots in Hong Kong had sent Cable anyway. She would serve his purpose – and Foo should have plenty to tell them under interrogation.

Hearing a car in the road and the sound of its door slamming he hurried back to the house. Josie threw her arms round his neck, tiny Vietnamese features beaming from ear to ear, and he hugged her tightly. 'I've missed you, little bird. Did you come straight from Shanghai?'

Reluctantly she stopped kissing him long enough to be able to speak. 'Yes, they brought me all the way by car – a great honour. Foo is safely locked up. It was very easy.'

'What happened?'

'I climbed up to their terrace when they were alone at nearly midnight – the Foos were talking and heard nothing – and knocked him out with a stocking full of sand. Wah Cheong did the same for his wife. Then we injected them both and carried Foo down to the boat you hired in Hong Kong – ten minutes later we were in China.' She wrinkled her nose. 'The men you hired with the boat were very stinky. Oh – and a houseboy woke up and tried to interfere, so I had to kill him.' Luther followed her into the kitchen where she started to make a pot of tea. 'We shall have a day or two together now, yes? Before you go to Shanghai?'

They took the tea and two bowls out to the sunken gravelled garden just behind the house, under the red walls and golden eaves, perching side by side on a low wall. 'Did you check the bank accounts?' he asked.

She stiffened. 'Yes. All the funds are there in the Hong Kong and Shanghai. We have a lot of money, Luther, but I shall miss China. Must we leave – they will be so angry in Peking?'

'If we don't we shall go down with the rest in the violence.' He spoke brusquely, as if he was tired of explaining the same thing again and again. 'They will destroy the oppressors and that includes us. If we could stay here peacefully in this beautiful place, I would do so.'

'So we creep away to Australia or America? Just vanish? *Can* we vanish?'

He nodded and pulled her to him. The tiny pointed breasts pressed hard against her blue shirt, the nipples outlined in the cotton. His hand was large enough to cover one of her denim-covered buttocks completely, as his fingers gave her a friendly squeeze. 'We shall finish the job they are paying for – but it *is* the last one. They are realists in Peking, perhaps they will not pursue us.'

135

Her eyes looked frightened. 'We know too many secrets – they will follow and kill us if they can, you know that. We are going into great danger.'

'And we shall be in danger if we stay.' He smiled and shrugged. 'I'll take care of you, I promise.'

'Just don't leave me behind, Luther. If you betray them and leave me to answer for you, they'll treat me bad.' She grimaced, looking young and vulnerable, like a pretty teenager even though she was nearly thirty. 'Put in lousy prison cell, give lousy food, shoot in lousy neck.'

He stood up, towering over her, and put his arms round her, smiling protectively; his eyes said let's go to bed as he led her indoors. 'Later I'll take you to the Black Jade Pavilion for dinner. Would you like that?'

The complex of caves honeycombed deep into a mountainside about fifty miles north of Kunming. It was late at night when they arrived and Sarah felt stiff after the bonecracking journey. Cheng Huiqing still seemed fresh and cheerful, but she plainly possessed abnormal physical and mental stamina. Chatting on the long journey Sarah had learnt that she was the daughter of a refugee to Hong Kong who had made good and become modestly well-off on textiles. She had done well at school and he had sent her to Hong Kong university, but she had gone on to get a doctorate in chemistry at Oxford. Back in Hong Kong she had lectured at the polytechnic and helped her father in his business, until three years ago when she had become involved with the opposition.

Cheng Huiqing parked the lorry in a gully between some boulders, dim lights went on and Chinese figures armed with old-fashioned rifles surrounded them; a few brandished machine pistols and yellow lamps shining on their faces showed that half of them were women. She followed Huiqing into a cave while camouflage nets were pulled over the truck, down a tunnel to a tiny rock-hewn chamber with two camp beds, mosquito nets and a chemical toilet behind an oil-paper screen in the corner. 'Sorry it's a bit primitive,' apologised Huiqing, pouring steaming green tea from a vacuum flask. 'But I think you will sleep well.'

Sarah woke at about eight to find Cheng Huiqing gone. She washed quickly from a jug of water that stood on a tea chest, opened the wooden door and stepped out into a stone tunnel lit by bare light bulbs strung along its roof. The Chinese girl appeared almost immediately and led Sarah to the open, stopping just inside the entrance. 'No further,' she smiled. 'We do not want to be spotted from the air.'

'What is this place?'

'A kind of air-raid shelter built by the Nationalist army during the war against Japan. It was forgotten for many years until Tenth October opened it up again six months ago.'

Standing under the canopy of overhanging rock that concealed the entrance, Sarah could not take her eyes from the panorama of sunlit mountains and lakes. 'You have an incredibly beautiful country.'

Huiqing inclined her head with a smile. 'Thank you. But at present also rather poor and turbulent. We must find some more tea and something to eat.'

'When will I meet your leaders?'

Cheng Huiqing stopped smiling and looked a little awkward. 'There has been a small hold-up and they have not yet arrived, but I'm sure you will not have to wait long.'

Sarah had a sudden feeling of unease. 'You mean I've come all this way at their request and they're not even *here?*'

The Chinese girl shook her head wretchedly. 'No, I'm very sorry, but it is difficult to travel secretly in a country this size and sometimes things go wrong. Please try to understand. They will be here today or tomorrow.'

137

Sarah nodded as the Chinese girl turned back into the tunnel, but the cheerfulness with which she had woken up was gone. Something was wrong, troublesome, and she began to feel in great danger.

Nairn had a long and detailed memory, but he was getting old and sometimes it failed him. Ever since Gatti's phone call something had been niggling him, a piece of information from an earlier case also codenamed Scorpion, by the British or Americans not the Chinese. It had been ten or fifteen years back and he had handled so much since then, as his chest pains and increasing gauntness testified. In the end he walked to the window and watched the rush hour traffic piling up in Westminster Bridge Road. The evening sun was glinting on the sandstone of the Houses of Parliament across the river. After ten minutes he hesitantly picked up his private phone, a direct line that bypassed the switchboard, and dialled a number in Moscow. Within a minute he was talking to a senior GRU officer: an action only possible in the last two years, one of the quaint side benefits of *glasnost*. After the initial surprise she was really quite friendly. Was there any chance of a meeting, he asked, or maybe a secure phone call?

The woman's low Russian tone broke into a laugh. 'How times have changed, Sir David! Do you know, I happen to be going to Libya the day after tomorrow, spending a night in Rome on the way. Name a time and place and I shall be interested to meet you. No promises, but if it is a matter of mutual interest – as you say – who knows? Maybe I can help you a little. I don't imagine we need to involve our Embassies?'

'*Spasiba* – I'd prefer not,' replied Nairn in Russian. 'There is a café on the right at the end of the Via della Conciliazione nearest St Peter's Square; I forget its name but would that do, say twelve noon?'

'Near the Vatican?' She laughed again. 'Ah well,

nothing is the same since Gorbachev. What a frightful mess – we intelligence officers must stick together. *Dasvidaniya.*'

17

Retired Rear-Admiral Erwin Smith spent a few days at home in Maryland after leaving Bethesda Naval Hospital. The operation on his haemorrhoids had been far more painful than he had expected, but sitting on his rubber ring he found the reports from Hong Kong so disturbing that he decided he had to return. He arrived without warning the morning after Nairn's phone call to Moscow and invited Tom Rumbelow for a drink early in the evening. At six they were standing on the balcony of his office on the Peak, the skyscrapers of the mid-levels plunging away below them. The admiral sipped his whisky and met Rumbelow's eyes with undisguised contempt. 'So you cannot trace Scorpion, you have lost Foo, now you suspect the only really useful asset we have in Peking? Jesus Christ.'

Rumbelow's lips tightened. He detested the little man with the foxy face and slow southern drawl; Erwin Smith came from South Carolina. He had risen to the quaintly named rank of Rear-Admiral (Lower Half) in supply and never seen a shot fired in anger, but talked as if he had won the Korean War single-handed. But this was British territory and Rumbelow was head of the SIS station. Smith was only his equivalent in rank these days and the Americans were guests here; the bastard had no right to speak to him like that. 'This is a joint operation, Erwin, we are equally responsible.'

'It's still the fact that your outfit's the weak link, Tom, and that kinda worries me.'

'I totally disagree, but there's no point in arguing about it. The immediate problem is Tang Tsin.'

'So what the hell is wrong with Tang Tsin?'

Rumbelow stared down at the harbour for a while before replying. They were so high up that little traffic noise reached them: the cars and trams moved silently through Central, the Star Ferry crossing to Kowloon looked like a toy. 'I know you've only been back a few hours,' he said slowly, 'but did you have time to look at any of his material today?'

'Yeah – I read it.'

'Well – don't *you* find it puzzling?'

'In what way?'

'Before it was good but bitty – now it flows too easily. There's too much, it's too close to what we need. I believe he's working under control – he's no longer a free man.'

The admiral grunted and turned back into the cool of his office, lighting a small cigar. He sat down gingerly at his desk, leaving Rumbelow to find one of the upright chairs across it: Hong Kong might be British but this building was American and in real life he was the senior partner. 'Sure, I noticed the change. So what's your theory?'

'Scorpion has fingered him and the Chinese have locked him up; he's given them every detail of his work for us under interrogation and now they're filling his drops with doctored material.'

'I guess that's possible.' The admiral blew a smoke ring that floated up until the draught from the ceiling fan destroyed it. 'Roper hasn't seen Tang since the guy got promoted, been spending so much time here. I want him to go back to Peking for a few days anyway, clear up a few points, so he could check on Tang at the same time?'

'That would be a great help, Erwin.' Rumbelow got up with relief to go. 'Perhaps you'd let me know the outcome.'

The admiral did not stand up but turned to his file as if dismissing a subordinate. 'Sure. Any news of Cable?

Or Foo?'

'No to both I'm afraid.'

'Terrific.' The little man stared straight through Rumbelow. 'You wanna get off your ass, Tom, before someone fills it full of buckshot.'

The cell was windowless, below ground, damp and cold. A yellow light burned behind thick glass in the stone wall, but so dimly that the place was half in darkness. Foo sat in a corner, for there was no furniture, shifting his chained ankles from time to time. His head ached from the drugs and he was very thirsty. When he had worked for the British he had prepared himself carefully for this moment but it had never come; on his recent missions into China he had felt reasonably safe, but now they had taken him he was ready. He would stay silent whatever they did and he had already accepted that he was unlikely to survive. He thought a great deal about Ruth, David and little Hannah, for they were the focus of his life and if it came to it he would die loving them: but he would empty his mind of all that when the time came, for he must concentrate his whole will on resistance.

There was a jangling of keys, the door swung open and a guard in a peaked cap entered with a bowl of rice and a tin mug of water. He put them on the floor and left without speaking. Foo's hands were manacled like his feet so he reached for the water with difficulty; it was a relief to slake his thirst, but there was no spoon to eat the rice and anyway he was not hungry. And it meant that they were getting him ready for interrogation.

Sarah spent the whole day hanging about in the caves, growing more and more frustrated. In the morning she went for a walk on the mountainside with Cheng Huiqing; the vistas of rock faces and blue lakes were stunning, but Sarah felt edgy. They were a long way from Kunming, the only means of transport seemed to be the rusty lorry and she had spoken to no one except Cheng Huiqing since the night they arrived. 'Who else is here?' she asked casually.

'Just the guards you saw last night. They are here all the time.'

'So I've come all this way and there's no one to talk to?'

'Not yet – I'm sorry.'

'And where's Mr Foo? He's supposed to be joining us, isn't he?'

'I believe so, but he too has yet to arrive.'

Sarah's suspicions were growing. 'I can't stay for ever, you know – it's too much of a risk. If no one's turned up by this time tomorrow I'd like you to take me back, arrange my transport to Hong Kong.'

Huiqing looked hunted. 'But it is so important, Sarah – won't you stay a little longer?'

'If it's so bloody important why aren't they here? Where the devil are they?'

The Chinese girl smiled apologetically. 'I know they will arrive soon, travelling is so difficult . . . ' The two women had followed a circular route and were approaching the entrance to the caves again. As they passed a ventilator grille set in the rocks Sarah could hear the faint thudding of a generator; she had wondered where the electricity came from.

'Twenty-four hours,' said Sarah firmly. 'Otherwise all bets are off. Sorry, but it's just not good enough. Have you any conception of the danger you're placing me in? If you can't bloody organise your revolution or whatever you call it better than this, my government doesn't want any part of it.'

Major-General Kirova arrived at the café in Rome in a large Zil limousine with a flagstaff but no flag, followed by another car containing four bodyguards which stopped at the kerbside about fifty yards away. Since the meeting was supposed to be incognito, the limousine drove away hurriedly and parked in St Peter's Square at the end of the street. Nairn stood up as the grey-haired woman walked towards him in the spring sunshine. She was wearing a well-cut blue tweed suit and he recognised her from the photographs on her file, although she was much more attractive than he had expected. Once she had been very beautiful – now she was handsome, with eyes that were intelligent, penetrating and held more than a hint of compassion.

They shook hands and she looked into his face curiously. 'Sir David,' she said in good English, 'I have wanted to meet you for such a very long time.'

'And I you, General. It was good of you to come. Would you like a drink?'

'A Campari with soda, thank you.'

Two of the GRU gorillas stayed in their car, the other two stood guard, one to each side of the café to ensure that no one approached too close. Two more appeared from the car outside St Peter's and hovered watchfully. The white-coated waiter retreated inside after bringing a Campari and a whisky for Nairn. A passer-by, unaware of the elaborate security, might have put them down as an elderly couple on holiday together. Nairn raised his glass. 'Nadia Alexandrovna Kirova,' he smiled. 'Strange to meet you like this after such a long time. Congratulations on your Order of Lenin.'

'Thank you.' She smiled back. 'They still usually call me just "Kirov" in my service, but I will be feminine today if you wish.' She glanced at the dome of St Peter's, looming up beyond the fountains and flocks of pigeons in the piazza, topped by a cross glinting gold in the sun, and seemed about to refer to the irony of their meeting place but instead sipped her Campari. *'Na zdrovie*. I was sorry to hear you had been unwell.'

Nairn started slightly. 'Now how did you hear that, General – though it's kind of you to mention it?'

'From a mutual friend, Sir David.' She gestured towards the Vatican. 'Have you been here before?'

'Many times – and you?'

'Never. I have not left the territory of the Soviet Union and its allies for fifteen years. If my country was not in such a mess I should be very happy at recent developments.' She hesitated. 'Well, Sir David? You and I are two professionals who know a great deal about each other – I have always followed your career with great interest. I hope we shall be able to have lunch together and compare notes a little, but you had a specific problem. How may I help you?'

'You and I crossed swords about twelve years ago, General – in Hong Kong, if I recall correctly. You remember Golovkin?' The dissident Nikolai Golovkin had been shot down on the border between Austria and Hungary and died clutching the barbed wire within a yard of freedom, but neither of them was going to mention it.

'Yes I do.'

'There was something I recall about his time in the Far East – Manchuria perhaps or Korea – that might relate to a problem I have now. Since it concerns China, I thought our interests might coincide?'

She studied him thoughtfully, as if she had been expecting the question. 'Let's go for a walk, Sir David.' She stood up, the gorillas suddenly closing in to protect her. 'My ambassador has given me a pass that will allow us into the Vatican gardens.'

18

Far away to the north-west Nick Roper arrived back in Peking. It was the following evening, a crimson sunset as a marine drove him from Shoudu airport in a black Chevrolet. Nick was thinking of Sarah, wishing he knew that she was safe, wishing she was in his arms. Was it her strength of character or the excitement of her body that mattered most to him? Probably the first, though it was the second that he needed just at the moment. Roper sighed, staring through the car window at the endless flocks of wobbling bicycles, the floodlit hoardings with gigantic red and gold Chinese characters and idealised pictures of fearless soldiers of the People's Liberation Army defending peasants as they happily shovelled shit on the commune: How different from the reality. Up to a few weeks ago he had enjoyed Peking, for it was still the most beautiful city in the world, but now he found it threatening and oppressive. He was sick of everything to do with China and wanted to be far away, on the other side of the world with Sarah.

The car did not take him to the Embassy but dropped him near Guang'anmen station, from where he took a taxi. The last half-mile he walked, turning off the wide boulevard into the alley where Tang Tsin lived. He had not been there before, but Tang had described it and told him how much he loved the old building as a refuge from the world. He knew exactly which gateway was Tang's: a wooden door in a high stone wall, seven feet high and studded with iron bolts. No bell so he banged on it.

Although it was dusk and the alley was empty, he did not want to make too much noise and draw attention to himself, but when there was no answer he banged harder. If Tang was still at liberty he should be home by now.

After two or three minutes he saw a man approaching in the dusk, pushing a bicycle; at first he thought it was Tang but when he could see the face in the shadows he saw that it was not. The man wore the grey uniform of a cadre. Roper stiffened but the newcomer did not challenge him: in fact he seemed about to hurry past with eyes averted until Roper spoke to him in Mandarin. 'Does the same family still live here, comrade?'

The eyes that turned to him were frightened, flickering in a face that did not want to get involved with trouble. 'No, it has been empty for weeks.'

'Do you know where they went?'

'What right have you to ask?

'Just a friend, comrade.'

The man shook his head. 'His *friend* are you?' The sneer was ill-concealed. 'Well he went a week or so back and the wife and children went months ago. If you're a friend why don't *you* know where they are. I don't know anything.' He hurried away to turn into a neighbouring gate, his demeanour saying that he knew Tang Tsin was in trouble with the authorities and Roper ought to be too. Nick hurried away in the other direction, conscious of eyes watching him – but when he turned at the corner to look back the alley appeared to be empty.

Next morning it was raining, that drenching, penetrating rain you seem to find only in the East. From the entrance to the caves Sarah watched it slashing down, sheets of water washing pebbles down the mountainside, muddy rivulets as loose soil was washed away. She did not venture outside and Cheng Huiqing vanished down the tunnel saying that she was going to use the short-wave radio. She left Sarah squatting at the entrance, reading a faded copy of Eric Ambler's *Journey into Fear* which she had found in one of the caves. It was yellow with age, dated 1944, and must have been left behind by a British or American soldier in the war.

Various other figures in fatigues flitted in and out, smiling vaguely at Sarah, but no one except Cheng Huiqing spoke to her. The whole set-up was getting on her nerves. After about an hour the Chinese girl reappeared looking jubilant. 'Three of our council will be here in just an hour or so! You will be able to complete the business and leave tonight.'

They came for Foo when he was dozing uncomfortably, propped up against the corner of his cell. His watch had been taken away and there was no window, but his body clock told him that it was about midday. Two uniformed men: the usual peaked caps, olive green tunics, crumpled trousers and sneakers, the usual blank faces. They jerked him to his feet and pushed him roughly into the corridor, where he almost fell against the wall. 'Follow me,' snapped one in Cantonese. Foo shuffled along, the steel chains cutting into his ankles, and they helped him up the steps at the end of the corridor.

The interrogation room was at ground level, bare with a barred window looking out on a courtyard. Foo took in every detail: they must be in some kind of prison, possibly in Canton or Shanghai for the window was open and there was the noise of heavy traffic beyond the wall. He needed to know everything he could if there was to be any chance of escape. He stood in front of the wooden table, facing a man of about thirty with a smooth, impassive face, eyes totally devoid of feeling or compassion. The chairs were all wooden and heavy, bolted to the floor.

It was past three in the afternoon when Sarah heard the helicopters. Puzzled she ran from the tunnel entrance and peered into the sky. Three shapes were buzzing towards them, high against the sun, still about half a mile away. Cheng was suddenly at her elbow. 'I didn't know they were coming by air,' said Sarah. 'Bit visible isn't it? I thought they'd come by road.'

The Chinese girl had a pair of binoculars and studied the three shapes with them. 'Blast,' she muttered. 'I can't see anything – the sun's right in my eyes.'

Four other Chinese appeared and joined them, staring at the sky. They were carrying their old Lee Enfield rifles and looked worried. Suddenly so did Cheng Huiqing. 'On no!' She stifled the cry. 'That's not our council – that's the army. They've found us and they'll be here in a couple of minutes!' She turned to the other Chinese and snapped a series of orders in a dialect Sarah did not know. They ran back into the tunnel. 'Come on.' She turned to Sarah. 'We're going up the mountain to a secret place I know. We might just make it before they land – run like hell.' She shot off down the slope and up the other side of the combe, bent double, scurrying through the boulders like a rabbit, pursued by the taller figure of Sarah. As they climbed the clattering of the helicopter rotors came nearer and nearer. Sarah ran faster and faster, slithering on loose shingle, panting as they reached a narrow goat track, so scared that she could feel her heart beating painfully in her chest.

For the last hundred yards they were looking down at the cave entrance from at least four hundred feet above, crossing an almost sheer rock face by a path just wide enough for a single human foot. She clutched at tufts of grass for balance, breaking a fingernail as she slipped and grabbing at a crevice in the stone. At the other side Cheng Huiqing swayed on a wider ledge and pointed to a horizontal cleft in the rock about a foot high and twenty feet long. She laid her body along its lip, swung up her legs and slithered inside. 'Now you,' she hissed. 'Quickly!'

Sarah did the same, sliding into the crack and finding herself in a space that sloped downwards and rose to about a yard in height. It felt claustrophobic but safe. 'They can see nothing from below.' Cheng was out of breath as she pulled two water bottles from her pockets. 'All we have to do is keep quiet.' She wriggled forward and Sarah followed until they could see down to the tunnel. The noise of the helicopters was deafening as they descended, landing one after another in the combe outside the caves, their rotors sending clouds of dust into the air.

'What will happen to your friends?'

'They will hide deep in the complex. With luck the soldiers won't find them – if they do they will fight. Whatever happens they won't give us away. They don't know where we've gone and will deny ever seeing you. They know how important it is to Tenth October that our first adviser from the West survives.'

Sarah watched in silence as armed men in steel helmets poured from the three gunships. Orders were shouted and whistles blown as half of them spread out on the hillside, the others rushing into the mouth of the tunnel. Those who vanished inside were wearing gas masks, she noticed. There were no sounds of resistance, but she heard long bursts of automatic fire, rattling and reverberating round the stone walls and roof that she could not see, followed by low explosions. 'That will be grenades or tear gas,' muttered Cheng Huiqing.

After about ten minutes the soldiers reappeared with two of the Tenth October guards, hands raised and blood streaking their clothes as they stumbled in the smoke. They were knocked to the ground and Sarah could hear faint screams as they were beaten with the metal stocks of the soldiers' AK-47s. An officer appeared to be shouting questions at them, but getting no replies. A line of twenty or so soldiers was moving slowly through the rocks on the slope, weapons across their chests, plainly searching. 'They are looking for us.' Cheng Huiqing sounded confident. 'But they will give up after a few hours.'

She was right. They lay in the cleft, occasionally sipping

water, for another two hours while the soldiers ranged back and forth across the mountainside, but never coming closer than two or three hundred yards. At dusk they blew up the truck with grenades and climbed back into the three helicopters, taking the two prisoners with them. The engines throbbed back into life and the first machine rose in another cloud of dust, the clatter of its rotors deafening as it reached the level of Sarah's face; the other two followed at one-minute intervals. As the sound died away, the two women stared out at darkness and silence. 'I suppose the others were all killed?' asked Sarah.

'I'm afraid so.'

'Then we're on our own?'

'Yes, Sarah. I am sorry.'

19

Ruth Foo arrived, unannounced, at two thirty in the afternoon. The building had no nameplate but everyone knew it was where the funnies worked; the glass doors opened into a scruffy foyer where a Chinese policeman sat behind the reception desk. 'I've come to see Mr Rumbelow,' she said briskly.

The MOD policeman looked puzzled. 'Not sure we have anyone call' Rumberow here.' He was stalling – his instructions were to admit only pass-carrying staff and visitors named on his daily list of appointments.

'For God's sake,' she exploded, 'don't give me that routine, I used to work here. Just tell the head of station that Mrs Foo is waiting and wants to see him urgently.'

'Plea' sit dow'.' The Chinese pointed to a row of scratched metal and canvas chairs and picked up the phone. Ten minutes later Ruth was fuming her way through the process of having a Polaroid photograph taken by another Chinese policeman. 'Is this really necessary?' she asked through gritted teeth.

'Security.' He raised his eyes to heaven as if he thought it was crazy too, fitting the tacky print into a plastic holder and clipping it to her dress; but then it was straight up-stairs and into a conference room where Rumbelow was waiting. Talk to visitors in an empty room so they can't see what's on your desk and walls; in the past she'd done it often enough herself so she wasn't offended. 'Good after-noon, Mrs Foo.' Rumbelow smiled and pulled out a chair for her. 'Would you like some tea?'

'No thank you. I'll come straight to the point – what has happened to my husband?' Rumbelow sat down across the table and she noticed how tired and tense he looked. His thornproof jacket was frayed at the cuffs and one of the leather elbow patches was hanging off; although she had come to be aggressive she felt almost sorry for him.

'That's a question for the Macao police, Mrs Foo. I deeply regret what has happened, but I'm in no position to help. I'm sorry.'

Ruth Foo glanced around the room: on the wall was a faded print of the Queen, the windows looked out on a terrace with some cheap plastic tables and chairs. 'I don't believe that's true,' she said quietly, forcing herself to appear reasonable. 'My husband has been involved with the Tenth October movement for at least two years with never a hint of danger. Then he asks for your help and within days he's been kidnapped by Red China.'

'There is no proof of that. He might've been abducted by one of the Triads – I know nothing of your husband's business interests, nor of his enemies.'

Ruth almost lost her temper. 'Don't be bloody insulting – Ben has no connection whatever with the Triads, he's as legitimate a businessman as the chairman of Swires and you damn well know it.'

Rumbelow smiled apologetically. 'Sorry, I wasn't trying to be offensive, but the fact is neither of us knows – knows for a *fact* – who took your husband.'

'Of course we know!' Ruth banged the table and a carafe of water leapt in the air. Her voice was rising. 'He's somewhere in Red China and they'll interrogate him to get dirt on the opposition leadership – and on *your* government, Mr Rumbelow, have you thought of that?'

'Yes, to be honest I had.'

'Well, what the hell are you doing about it? He's my husband, for Christ's sake; he's sixty. If they mistreat him he'll die!'

'I can't imagine the People's Republic would use extreme measures . . . '

She smashed her fist on the table again. 'Of course they will – and you damn well know that too.' She took a deep breath. 'Look, Mr Rumbelow – I used to be in your service, I know the scene. If you don't get Ben out within days by diplomatic action – or by snatching him – your government is going to have a lot of egg on its face. And my husband might as well be dead. They'll get everything out of him and stage a show trial. Macao millionaire who used to be a British intelligence officer, condemned for plotting terrorism and subversion. A bloody good excuse to go back on all the meaningless promises they've made about preserving this place come 1997.' She gestured through the window at the skyscrapers and the harbour. 'Well – do you deny it?'

'No, Mrs Foo, you may well be right. Let me reassure you that I *am* in close touch with London and we are trying to locate your husband. If there is something we can do, believe me it will be done – the trouble is, he has no specific British connection.'

'He has a British passport and a British wife – isn't that enough these days?'

'He was living in Macao – Chinese territory under Portuguese administration. It's more than twelve years since he worked for my government.'

'So what?'

'It does not help. But please, Mrs Foo.' He had such frightened eyes – how on earth had he ever become head of an SIS station? 'I will do my best.' He walked her down to the entrance and shook hands. 'You're being very brave about it all. I'll keep in touch, I promise.'

In England it was seven thirty in the morning and David Nairn was walking his dog by the river at Chiswick. He did it most mornings when he was in London, strolling with the yellow Labrador from his block of flats, past the pubs of Strand-on-the-Green as far as Kew Bridge. It was low tide and the Thames flowed sluggishly between mud-flats;

the slipway by the sailing club was covered in dinghies, all sloping neatly in the same direction, halyards clanging on their masts in the breeze. On the river a tug belched smoke as she struggled upstream pulling a string of coal barges.

The tall man in the shabby suit was alone on the path, waving cheerfully as a boy cycled past with a bulging bag of newspapers. 'Hey, Wellington,' he called to the dog. 'Fetch, boy.' Nairn threw a stick along the foreshore and the Labrador retrieved it, tearing back and rushing round his master panting and splashing up mud. Nairn took the stick and the dog barked for him to do it again, long pink tongue lolling over sharp white teeth.

As he made to throw the stick, Nairn noticed two red buses standing in line on Kew Bridge; the traffic must be at a standstill, as it often was at this time in the morning. The pain came as he raised his arm: a sudden fierce stabbing in the centre of his chest. Before he could recover from the first shock, it soared into agony as if a white-hot poker was driving into his heart. The last thing he saw before he collapsed was the dog leaping up at him.

Ruth Foo telephoned Nairn's London office from her lawyer's suite in Central. Once David had been her lover which was, oddly enough, why she had hesitated to get in touch with him before. But Rumbelow was patently useless and she was desperate. The solicitor left her alone and she dialled the number direct. After a few clicks she was connected with the other side of the world, the city she had not visited for five years. A woman's voice answered. 'Sir David Nairn's office.'

'May I speak to Sir David, please? My name is Ruth Foo, it's a personal call.'

'I'm sorry but Sir David is not in the office this morning.'

'Will he be in this afternoon?'

'I – I'm not sure. You see, he's not very well.'

'He's ill? Is it serious?'

'I'm sorry, I really don't know.'

'Look – I'm phoning from Hong Kong and it's urgent. Will he be at home if I ring there?'

'I'm sorry, but I can't give you Sir David's private number.'

'I already have it, thanks.' Ruth rang off, fumbled in her handbag with nervous fingers and dialled another London number. This time it rang for a long time before the receiver was picked up. Another woman's voice answered.

'Hello, Alison Nairn here.' She sounded warmer than the other one – and worried.

'My name is Ruth Foo and I'm calling from Hong Kong – may I speak to Sir David please?' Despite her inner tension Ruth smiled; it was such a formal way to speak to the woman who was now David's wife, the woman he made love to in her place. Ruth wondered what she was like; I wonder if she's got embarrassingly big thighs like me, she thought, and a kind nature. She sounded nice.

'No I'm afraid you can't,' she was saying. 'David had a heart attack this morning.'

'Oh, no!' Ruth caught her breath. 'Is it – *serious*?'

'He's alive, if that's what you mean. It happened when he was walking our dog before going to work. A paper boy heard the dog whining and found my husband lying unconscious by the river. He was rushed to hospital and that's where I'm going now.'

'I'm so sorry – I do hope he recovers quickly. Please give him my – my best wishes, will you?'

'Of course. What did you say your name was?'

'Ruth Foo. From Hong Kong.' No sign of recognition – how odd. Could David never have told her?

'Yes of course I will. Forgive me if I go now.'

The admiral was at shooting practice in the basement of the CIA building. It was not necessary for his job but he enjoyed it, perhaps partly because he had never been in any kind of real action. For a man of over sixty he had a good eye and steady hand; as he blasted six shots from the Magnum the hardboard cut-out of a Chinese soldier rocked wildly. Covering the twenty yards with a swift stride, he counted all six holes in the grinning black shape of the head. When Gatti and Roper came in, he was at the crouch again, earmuffs on, blue baseball cap shading his eyes, both arms extended to grip the revolver. They watched as another six rounds splintered the target, covering their ears as the explosions echoed deafeningly in the confined space. Erwin Smith grinned at them. 'You want me, boys?' He was putting six more cartridges into the gun, snapping the chamber shut, taking aim again. 'One more time and I'll be with you.'

As the shots echoed away and the smell of cordite was cleared by the air conditioning, he led them back upstairs to his office. It was early evening and he poured three glasses of Bourbon. 'I read your report, Bob,' he said to Gatti, settling into the leather armchair. With its wooden panelling and bookshelves lined with morocco bindings, the room looked like a corner of a gentleman's club, except for the gold-fringed Stars and Stripes standing in the corner. 'Got the message on Devereux. Anything to add?'

'No, sir. I just feel a heel.'

'No reason why you should – now then, Nick?'

Roper sipped his Bourbon. 'Tang Tsin has vanished, sir. Plainly he's been arrested so everything we're getting from him is crap, carefully chosen for us by the *Tewu*.'

'Are you certain?'

'He's not at his office or his home and everyone around looks scared or shifty – yes, I'm pretty certain.'

'Shit.' The admiral puffed his cigar in silence. 'And Scorpion – you weren't impressed by this guy Wainwright, communications officer on *Relentless*, the one Commander Thomas fingered?'

'I wasn't impressed by him as a man – objectionable

little runt – but there isn't the slightest reason to doubt his loyalty. Thomas doesn't like him, nor does he like Thomas, but the fact that they hate each other is irrelevant. Neither of them is Scorpion – even if the British might be wise to get them both off a vessel as sensitive as a Polaris.'

The admiral snorted and splashed more Bourbon from a cut-glass decanter. 'That's *their* problem, Nick. I got plenty of my own. Foo's in the slammer, just a matter of time before he incriminates us and the Brits in trying to slice the goolies off his government. Tang Tsin's locked up too, so forget any help from that direction, and Cable's vanished somewhere in China. Terrific. I reckon the slanteyes might be winning, fellers, don't you?'

'For the moment.' It was Roper who replied; Gatti was lost in his own thoughts, as if he wished he wasn't there. 'They're getting well placed to find at least some of the leaders of Tenth October – and a show trial of Foo and Tang Tsin would do us no good.'

'Do us even less good if Cable's in the dock with them, a professional intelligence officer from a supposedly friendly Western power.' They talked round the problem for half an hour without reaching any conclusion; no more Bourbon was offered and eventually the two younger men left. Ten minutes later the admiral's secretary appeared with a sealed envelope.

'Mr Rumbelow sent this round by courier, sir.'

Erwin Smith tore it open and opened the inner envelope, for the classification was SECRET, and read the contents. It was a copy of a decrypted telegram from Nairn and the admiral looked puzzled. 'Deborah,' he said thoughtfully. 'See if Commander Gatti is still in the building.'

20

After the soldiers had flown away, Sarah and Cheng Huiqing lay side by side in the slit in the rock, each surprised that the other looked so terrified. 'We must stay hidden till dark,' whispered the Chinese girl hoarsely, as if the men in the disappearing helicopters might still hear. 'It was you and me they were after and they know we cannot be far off. They'll come back.'

The rest of the day passed slowly. By night they were hungry and the water bottles almost empty; the two women crawled out and sat on the hillside stretching cramped limbs. 'What do we do now?' asked Sarah. 'I want to get as far from here as possible by morning.' A full moon was rising, casting dark blue shadows round them in the darkness; there was no other light to be seen except a few pinpoints marking a village far below. They were surrounded by emptiness and brittle silence.

'I'm sorry, Sarah,' said Cheng Huiqing for the hundredth time. 'I would never have brought you here if I'd known this might happen.'

'Well it has – so *what do we do now*?'

'We need maps, torches, some food. I am going back into the caves, to see what I can find. Then we start walking.' They slithered down the scree of loose shale and picked their way through boulders in the moonlight until their feet found the path that wound up to the caves. When the moon went behind a cloud it was too dark to see anything and Sarah heard the Chinese girl curse quietly as she stubbed her toe and slipped. But silver moonlight had returned by the time they were at the entrance and Cheng Huiqing examined the wrecked truck hopefully. 'Maybe everything wasn't destroyed?' Fishing around in the ruins of the cab, she pulled out several items and threw them at Sarah. 'Some maps, a bit scorched at the corners but have a look at them if you can find some light.' She scrabbled around some more. 'Here's an electric torch but it doesn't seem to work.'

Eventually she wriggled backwards out of the twisted metal, cursing again as she caught herself on sharp edges. 'You stay here, Sarah,' she said briskly. 'I know the layout inside — I'll see if there's any food or water left.' She vanished into the tunnel and Sarah settled down by a boulder, hearing the Chinese girl's footfalls vanishing slowly as she picked her way in the dark. Now that Sarah had her night vision she could see the jagged black outlines of peaks all around; and there were quite a few pinpoints of light down on the plain. Perhaps they were not quite so isolated as she had thought.

The sudden explosion deafened Sarah, hurling her to the ground and stinging her eardrums painfully. There was an angry roar as flame and flints spurted from the mouth of the tunnel, followed by the crash of rock splintering and falling inside; the mountainside vibrated beneath her body. Raising her bruised head she heard the crackle of burning and saw flames from the tunnel glowing on the rocks around her.

Sarah struggled to her feet and stumbled to the entrance. The flames were already subsiding but there was enough light to show that the tunnel roof had collapsed in a solid wall of rock. Cheng Huiqing had been thrown backwards by the explosion. Her open eyes stared up in shock, arms thrown wide; she was buried up to the chest in splintered stone. Sarah knelt by her body, cursing herself; she should have expected a booby-trap and the Chinese girl was plainly dead. The flames flickered out as she stepped back into the open air, suddenly feeling afraid and very alone.

* * *

The news of Nairn's heart attack flashed through Century House. Gerald Clayton was installed in the chief's office by mid-morning. As David Nairn's deputy that was natural, but the change was received with more than a little apprehension. Forty-five, silver-haired, tough and ruthless, Clayton had two reputations: he was effective and he was a bastard. In the afternoon he called a meeting of all division directors, issuing orders and demanding reports like a machine gun. Everyone was mightily relieved when that evening he left for Hong Kong, even though it was for only forty-eight hours. The impeccable Savile Row suit climbed into the back of Nairn's official Rover and left for the airport.

Benjamin Foo was exhausted, his head ached and his eyes peered out through puffy slits, stinging from the bright lights. He had been strapped in this chair for at least eight hours, challenged by questions and threats from a series of interrogators, three men and one woman; she had been the best. Now the first man had returned. 'Don't be foolish, Foo.' He spoke quietly, reasonably. 'You have a wife and two children in Macao – tell us the name of every contact you know in Tenth October and you will be free in a day or two. You can go home. Yes, these people will be picked up, but they will only be treated in accordance with the law, none will die unless they are guilty of terrorism.' He paused. 'Do you understand?'

Foo stared back at him, saying nothing. He had not spoken since he had entered the interrogation room. He was determined to say nothing. He knew that whatever he gave them he would still die sooner or later; and once he started to talk it would be difficult to stop. The silence irritated the other man. 'You are doing yourself no good, Foo! This is the nineteen-nineties and we are not amateurs – we have drugs that will make you tell the truth, we have others that will induce agony worse than all the fires of hell.' As Foo continued to stare impassively, he gestured threateningly. 'And you may be old but I can still put massive electric shocks through your prick and up your arse!' He struck Foo across the face with his open hand, first one side then the other. 'Being rich can't help you – don't be stupid, granddad.'

Behind the window of one-way glass Luther and a Chinese in grey uniform watched. The tall German stubbed out a Gitane and lit another; the Chinese wrinkled his nose in disgust at the clouds of blue smoke. 'We need results,' snapped Luther in Mandarin. 'Your imbeciles in Kunming failed to arrest Cable, despite the precise information I gave them – now this old fool refuses to talk. I obeyed the minister's orders despite having grave doubts – but if Foo stays silent, what was the point?'

'He is a grandfather, Luther.' Qiao Shi's man had a high sibilant voice – like one of the palace eunuchs before the revolution. 'If we give him drugs or torture him he may die. Then how can we put him on trial? The minister is planning a big event.'

'The techniques are your problem, Zhang. He's going to die anyway, isn't he? I'd take a few risks if I were you, or we could still be sitting here when your master is disgraced by the Central Committee – or the committee is fleeing the mob.'

'*Our* master.' Despite his effete manner Zhang studied Luther with hard eyes, like an executioner measuring his victim for the drop. 'I will of course report what you say.'

21

'Who's this feller Clayton?' growled the admiral.

'Clayton?' Roper looked puzzled.

'Yeah Crayton – flom Engrand.' The admiral's mock-Chinese accent could become irritating, as could his domineering manner.

'You mean *Gerald* Clayton – Nairn's number two in London?'

'That's the guy.'

'Been in their outfit about twenty years; I think he was a regular dip before that – certainly looks very smooth. Doesn't get his suits from the Salvation Army like Nairn.'

'But what's he *like*?'

'He's good. Cuts through problems, trusted by the politicians. Ambitious – he's still only about forty-five and nearly at the top. As an operator he can be a real shit – ruthless with staff and agents. Suitable for the SS if they were still in business.'

'Uh-huh.' The admiral swung his feet up on the rosewood desk; Roper noticed that he was wearing cavalry boots under his trousers. 'See here, Nick, Nairn's had a heart attack and this Clayton's acting up for him. He's coming out here for a day or two.'

'A heart attack? Is it serious – is he okay?'

'Sure, he's recovering.' The admiral's tone suggested that whether Nairn lived or died was of no particular consequence. 'Nairn's one hell of a nice guy, but maybe this Clayton is what we need just now? They say there are three contenders for Nairn's job if this heart thing makes him retire – Clayton's only one of them, but if he wants to shine in the eyes of his political masters . . . '

'He's reckoned to be decisive as well as a shit.'

'Yeah. Good. Whad'you make of this tip Nairn got from the Soviets?'

'Puzzling, very puzzling. Let's see what Gatti brings back from Lantau; he's going over this morning.'

Bob Gatti took the ferry to Peng Chau where he weaved through the crowds to find the sampan from Tai Shui Hang, Trappist Haven. It was moored by a flight of crumbling concrete steps, below an old woman in black pyjamas squatting by the fish she was selling alive from pails: crabs, clams, red mullet and spotted eels wriggling in clear water. She grinned at him as he approached, displaying toothless gums, but spat when he passed her without buying.

The sampan was rowed across to the other island in five minutes and he started the slow walk up to the monastery. The track was stony and shaded by gnarled banyan trees; gossamer wings of butterflies darted between the shrubs on either side, vivid blue and orange against leathery green, and there was the overpowering scent of mimosa. It was like a corner of paradise, except that Gatti was sweating in the sultry heat as he climbed.

At the top he came to the plain white buildings, closed and silent except for the church. He stepped inside and it was welcomingly cool, with modern wooden pews and bright stained glass over the altar. A Chinese monk was arranging some pamphlets on a card table just inside the door; his white habit was made of light cotton and stained with earth at the front where he had been working on his knees in the garden. He smiled vaguely and went on with his work. Brought up as a Catholic in the Italian community of Chicago, Gatti genuflected to the reserved sacrament under its flickering red lamp and turned to the monk. 'Can you help me, Father? My name is Gatti and I have come to see Brother Bernard.'

The monk looked surprised. 'Brother Bernard? He does not normally have visitors – is he expecting you?'

'No he isn't, but I have brought a letter for him.'

'A letter of introduction?'

'No, a letter from me. Would you give it to him and ask whether he would be kind enough to talk to me?'

The Chinese took the white envelope awkwardly. He had a kind, wrinkled face and Gatti could see that he did not want to hurt his feelings. 'Brother Bernard is praying or writing at this hour,' he said. 'I shall take this to him if you would care to wait here – or in the garden – until I come back?' The old man hesitated, as if this had happened before. 'Tell me, my son – are you a journalist?'

'No, I am an officer in the US Navy.'

'Ah – so was Brother Bernard before he took his vows with us.'

Gatti found a cool spot on a bench outside, shaded by trees and with a distant view of the harbour. The monk was gone about half an hour. He reappeared in the door of the church, looked around for Gatti and hurried over. 'Commander Gatti,' he smiled. 'Do I have that right?' Gatti nodded. 'Good, Brother Bernard has read your letter and wishes to reflect on it. If you would care to return at the same time tomorrow he may be willing to see you.' He smiled again. 'I am sorry, we are here to work and pray, you know; we keep silence much of the time. But you look deeply troubled, my son – if it would help you to talk to Bernard I hope he will do as you ask.'

Gerald Clayton arrived at Kai Tak that morning. Rumbelow met him; even after the fourteen-hour flight Clayton looked fresh and relaxed. His silver hair shone, his lightweight suit – dark blue with white chalk stripes – was impeccable. The two men sat in the back of the official Daimler, glass screen closed to separate them from the Chinese chauffeur, but saying little to each other.

They reached the office on the Peak in twenty minutes and Rumbelow led Clayton up to his spacious office on the first floor. 'Have you been here before, Gerry?'

'Yes, but not for a few years. Is your deputy in the office this morning?'

'Barnie Mason? Yes, he is.'

'Good, I shall want to see him in half an hour.'

Rumbelow's room was furnished with a modern desk and conference table in light oak, some soft leather armchairs in the corner. To Rumbelow's surprise Clayton walked straight in and sat down behind the desk – *his* desk. He was about to utter a mild protest, but Clayton forestalled him. 'Close the door, Tom, come and sit down.'

Puzzled, Rumbelow obeyed. Clayton studied him: the lined, tired, face, the ineffectual eyes, the scruffy tweed jacket and greasy golf club tie. There were no polite preliminaries. 'You're not up to being head of this station.' He did not raise his voice but articulated each word carefully, as if he did not intend to repeat them. 'You sent an officer of this service into China in impossible conditions and she may be in great danger – it was utterly irresponsible. And God knows what you were playing at with Foo – what are you trying to do, start a war? China is a friendly power and we have a binding treaty to return Hong Kong to their jurisdiction in 1997. We have nothing to gain by interfering in their internal affairs.'

Rumbelow recovered from the first shock and tried to interrupt. 'What the devil do you mean? I disagree entirely!'

'Shut up.'

'What?'

'I said shut up – your disagreement is noted. But nothing can alter the fact that you have embarrassed your government and endangered your staff.' Rumbelow spluttered a protest and Clayton stood up abruptly. 'You are suspended from duty and will leave the service in a

month's time. You'll get your pension. It's all in here.' He
pushed a blue envelope across the desk. 'Now get out.'

Rumbelow stared at him open-mouthed, all the colour
drained from his face. After thirty-five years it was impossible that his career could be destroyed like this, in just
a few seconds.

'Your personal possessions in this office will be packed
tonight and brought to your quarters. Passages home are
booked for you and your wife in five days time.'

Rumbelow was starting to recover. 'You can't do this.'
He choked on the words. 'I shall appeal to the head of the
service.'

'For the time being I *am* the head of the service.' For
the first time Clayton raised his voice. 'Get out, you
bloody fool,' he shouted. 'Do it my way or you'll be
dismissed with no pension, nothing! The mess you've
made here is damn near criminal. God knows whether I
can salvage anything.' Tom Rumbelow saw his cottage in
Suffolk perilously close to vanishing and knew that he was
beaten. He was being cast out from the world that had
been his whole life. He would never enter this building or
Century House again; all his friends were in the service,
now they would treat him like a leper. He turned and left
without a word.

The policeman on the door was the only person who
spoke to him on the way out. 'Good morning, sir,' said the
young Chinese, as he always did when the head of station
left. 'See you later.' Rumbelow hurried past without
replying; he did not even turn his head. The policeman
and two passing secretaries watched in puzzlement as the
glass door slammed behind him. Mr Rumbelow was
usually so polite.

22

After Cheng Huiqing's death Sarah crept back into the tunnel to check her pockets. She hated doing it but it was important to make sure they contained nothing incriminating, for the army would be back soon enough. By the light of matches she felt in Huiqing's shirt, but the two breast pockets were empty except for a small electric torch, which she took. She paused to kiss the girl's forehead – already cold and clammy – before turning away. There was no time to grieve.

Sarah knew that Kunming lay to the south and the valley of the upper Yangtze to her left – that was where she could sometimes see lights far below. When she studied the map in the beam of the torch she felt that north was the way to go, for it was easier to hide in the mountains, but north to *where*? She had no food, the water bottle could be filled at a stream but she had no waterproof clothing and was wearing only canvas shoes. The death of a thousand cuts was too good for that lazy bastard Rumbelow who had landed her in this. She set out northwards, using the Pole star as a guide and following a ridge of rock in the moonlight; there was no cloud now and it was not too difficult to find a track. At first the lights of villages twinkled sporadically in the river valley, but as it grew later she could see only blackness, comforting and empty, above and below.

After three hours she was stumbling with tiredness, eyes aching from peering into the dark. The moonlight seemed to be fading, but she would press on for another hour. With the dawn she would have to find somewhere to hide, for a European woman wandering the mountains so far from a city would attract dangerous attention if she met any Chinese. When the first rays of light started to creep above the horizon she turned off the track she was following, scrabbling her way up the slope, occasionally using the torch. She had filled the water bottle from a stream about a mile back. Sarah found what she wanted after half an hour – a heap of massive boulders that formed a small cave. She wriggled into the space and lay down, hoping for a few hours sleep.

Gatti returned to the monastery by a different route, catching an early morning ferry to Silvermine Bay. He stood on the stern by two Chinese schoolgirls giggling over a soft porn magazine until the ship tied up at the new ferry terminal. There was still a surprising amount of new building going on: square white villas with smoked-glass windows and orange blinds over their verandahs. A mountain of sand was being moved from the quay to a nearby site, a confusion of brick and block walls rising inside a lattice of bamboo scaffolding. The sand was carried in baskets on small trolleys; some of the workers were young men, but there were also pairs of girls in jeans, older women in headscarves to keep off the dust, even a mother and her tiny son doggedly pushing a truck together. The queue was moving slowly and Gatti saw that two policemen were checking all the passports. When he reached them a brusque hand was held out. 'You got passpor', ID car' plea'?'

Gatti fished in a pocket. 'Why?'

'Is law. Everybod' mus' carry ID car' in Ho'Kong because of illegal refugee.'

He swung out round the bay, past the older and more humble Chinese homes of tin sheets nailed to a wooden frame, open doors showing crowded living rooms with families gobbling noodles round television sets, Taoist

shrines lit by red electric light bulbs in the background.
The noise of Cantonese argument, TVs at full volume and
wailing transistors was drowned by screams of rage and
pain as a fat Chinese woman burst from her home, flailing
at her small daughter with a long wooden spoon. It took
Gatti an hour to reach the monastery on paths through
paddy fields and woods. Another visitor was outside, a
short man with powerful shoulders, dressed in a check
shirt and denim shorts, his face and knees burnt dark
brown by the sun. He was smoking a pipe and reading the
South China Morning Post. He looked up from the
wooden bench.

'Morning.'

Gatti nodded. 'Hi.'

'You Gatti?'

Bob looked puzzled. 'Why, yes – who are you?'

'Bernard.'

Gatti did a double take. 'But I thought . . . ?'

The man laughed. 'You thought I was a monk. I *am* a
monk. These post-Vatican Two days we don't go about in
drag all the time – I've been working on the dairy farm.'
He beckoned. 'Come with me, friend. Let's go find some
quiet place to talk.'

Gatti followed the stocky figure through a door at the
side of the church, which he locked behind them, out into
another garden with more shade. An older man in a white
habit was sitting in a corner, lips moving as he said an
office from his breviary. Bernard led the way without
looking back: he was almost bald, with a cluster of white
hair on either side and a hook nose. He reminded Gatti of
a newspaper photograph he had seen recently of some
Israeli general or other, elderly but terrifyingly fit and
warlike as he worked half-naked in his orange grove. They
stopped in a corner of the garden where a stone bench was
shaded by a cluster of olive trees. The farm buildings were
not far away; Gatti could smell the cow dung and see a
herd of black and white Friesians grazing in a field.

The unlikely monk studied Gatti's face for a time. His

eyes were deepset and dark – full of compassion and highly intelligent. When he spoke there was still the hint of a Jew from Brooklyn, but none of New York's harshness. He had a soft voice and spoke carefully, as if a little out of practice; perhaps being in a silent order meant just that. 'What's your first name, Commander?'

'Roberto, Bob.'

'You a Catholic, Bob?'

'I was brought up as a Catholic.'

'I know what you mean. You're too pale for a seafarer, but you're in the US Navy, you say? You a spook, Bob?'

'I'm an intelligence officer.'

'How did you find me, how did you know I was here?'

'The British SIS station told my boss – I've no idea where they got it from.'

'Probably the Russians; I had a Russian here, like you, a couple of years back.' His smile was gentle, but with an ironic twist at the corner of his mouth. 'So you ain't the first. So how can I help you, Bob?'

'I'd like to talk about your time in North Korea – when you were arrested there about twelve years ago.'

'And tell me, Bob – how is that going to help anybody? What good will it do? Twelve years ago I was like you, Bob, a loyal servant of Uncle Sam, naval intelligence. Now I'm in this order and I guess I'll be here to the end of my life; I've taken lifetime vows and I'm studying to become a priest. I can remember the past well enough, but I'm suspicious if anyone asks me to. I suspect that out there some poor soul is going to suffer if I do. Am I right, Bob – who are you trying to screw?'

Gatti sighed. 'You won't believe it, but I understand how you feel – I may not be in the navy or intelligence much longer myself. If I explain why, maybe you'll understand why I'm here?'

'You have an honest face, Bob.' The monk, who Gatti knew had been born Israel Zimmermann in Brooklyn, looked into his face again, absently fingering a rosary. 'Tell me the background, *why* I should help you. Then if it seems right, maybe I will.'

As Gatti talked to the monk, Clayton's reign of terror continued; he stayed in Rumbelow's office on the Peak all day and late into the night, burrowing into the files, summoning Rumbelow's deputy, Mason, and the rest one at a time, issuing a stream of orders. At nine he went into a huddle with a senior Wren and the captain in charge of *Tamar*. At ten another Wren officer arrived at Mary Devereux's apartment near Deep Water Bay with two naval ratings, the dim light from the street lamp glimmering on their white-topped caps, white shirts and blue trousers tucked into white gaiters. Mary was alone when they rang the doorbell. She stared at them in horror when she opened the door, knowing instantly why they had come.

'Well, Cathy?' She sounded tired, resigned, as if she had been expecting them for weeks. 'Do you want to come in?'

In the elegant little sitting room Mary's friend spoke the words of arrest. 'Commander Devereux, I am ordered to arrest you for commission of a sexual act forbidden by Queen's Regulations, contrary to good order and discipline.' She took a deep breath as Mary stood with downcast eyes. 'Other charges may follow. You do not have to make a statement, but if you do – '

'For Christ's sake, that's enough, I know it off by heart!' Mary's face was white, her eyes burning, all pride and confidence gone.

'If you do, it will be taken down in writing and may be used in evidence.' She hesitated before adding, 'I'm sorry, Mary.'

They left the block shortly afterwards, Mary Devereux in uniform, handcuffed to one of the sailors, head bowed as she climbed awkwardly into the back of the waiting Land-Rover.

23

It took three visits to the monastery on Lantau before Bernard was ready to talk. On the second he listened intently while Gatti filled in the background, occasionally asking a question: about Sarah, Foo, Mary Devereux or Scorpion. The questions were incisive, for Bernard still had the skills of an intelligence officer, but somehow Gatti also found himself drawn to talk about Sue and the boys. For the first time he shared his pain; he kept telling himself that he was a hard-nosed intelligence officer questioning a dodgy source, but that seemed more and more irrelevant. It was impossible to hold back. Something far inside compelled him to confess the deepest agony – and the greatest love – he had ever felt; and as he did so Gatti felt embraced in a warm compassion that no one else had been able to offer. There was something not just kind and generous but almost mystical about this man with such an unlikely past for a monk, a profound capacity to turn despair into hope. Gatti returned to the empty house in Stanley having learnt nothing for the admiral – but that afternoon started him on his own road back.

The phone call came late that evening. 'Okay.' The Brooklyn Jewish voice rumbled down the wire. 'I've thought about it, Bob, and prayed. I guess too many people can still be hurt for me to keep my trap shut – can you be over at ten tomorrow?'

It was raining on the ferry crossing to Peng Chau. By the

time Gatti reached the monastery it had stopped, but threatening black clouds hid the sun. Bernard was waiting in the church, this time wearing his white Trappist habit and a cross made of two nails welded together. He led Gatti through to the garden where they sat on the same bench under the olive trees. 'I'll tell you what happened,' said Bernard. 'I don't know how much it will help – and I guess it's the reason why I'm here, so it's something deeply personal, which may explain my reluctance – but I'll tell you anyway. I trust you.'

'Thank you.'

'You may not thank me when I'm finished, Bob.' Bernard waited for another monk to pass, pushing a clattering lawnmower, then turned to Gatti. 'It was 1978. I was still Israel Zimmermann, lieutenant-commander in the US Navy, but everybody called me Joe. I'd served on a carrier and in intelligence, but then I was posted to South Korea as an adviser to their spook set-up for two years. Strange little country – the mountains and lakes are very beautiful but Seoul's a mess, tatty high-rise buildings, streets jammed with cars, prostitutes touting all the hotels and nightspots. Strange little people – their flat Asiatic faces just ain't as attractive as the Chinese or Japanese. The war had been over for years, but there's no peace treaty and everyone was jumpy. They used to have an air raid alert every week – sirens screaming, sheltering in cellars, the whole bit, just in case the North Koreans attacked again.

'Although I was born a Jew I wasn't brought up religious; at the time I guess I was agnostic. Oddly enough it was in Seoul that I first really noticed the Catholic Church – many Koreans are Catholic and sometimes I used to go to mass at the cathedral on Sunday evenings. It was always packed out and afterwards I dropped by a bar with some friends I made – near a shop where they sold grand pianos, I remember. Now who on earth wanted a *grand piano* in Seoul – but I guess someone did, for the stock in that window was always changing.

'For six months I did routine intelligence, watching the North. Pretty repetitive and dull. Then there was a big problem. We had an agent in Pyongyang, one Kang-Hong Cho. He was a Party member and an officer in the army, a colonel, apparently trusted by Kim Il-sung. I don't know whether Kim is crackers, as some say, but I do know he has this truly absurd personality cult – the whole darn country is plastered with portraits of the "Respected and Beloved Leader", everyone wears a little round tin badge with the bastard's face on it – and boy he's a survivor. Been in power since 1945, trusts almost nobody, so Colonel Cho was a real asset. He was on the North Korean general staff – our one-man early warning system against any preparation for a new invasion – and we paid him well for it.

'But, to cut a long story short, he came under suspicion and we agreed to lift him out with his family. It was a routine operation. The land border is shut tight of course, but small boats go up and down the coast all the time and we landed agents in North Korea, as they did in the south. At first I wanted him to fly to Japan, but he feared they might stop him at the airport – he couldn't tell whether or not he was under continuous surveillance – and anyway he could hardly take his wife and children too without attracting suspicion.

'In the end I decided it would have to be by boat. We were communicating by sophisticated short-wave radio – messages transmitted on tape in high-speed bursts that're almost undetectable, certainly not by the North Koreans who have little modern technology. I ordered him to be at a point on the coast near Chungsan at two in the morning on the third of September. I deliberately didn't arrange a pick-up near the North-South frontier, because both sides still had heavy forces there – it might reduce the risk to us, but he'd almost certainly get stopped before he reached the coast. North Koreans do *not* drive about on private business at two in the morning; for starters almost none of them has a car. On the other hand Chungsan is just north

175

of the capital, far enough up the coast for them not to expect foreign intruders, and Cho could get there quite easily so long as he wasn't actually followed from his house.

'I chose third September because that night Cho was going to a banquet given by Kim Il-sung for a visiting delegation from Russia. As a high-ranking officer Cho *did* have his own car and his wife and kids were going to hide in it in a nearby street while he was toasting the visiting comrades, then he would leave and drive straight to the coast; by morning they would be in Seoul. Easy.'

The clouds were getting blacker and they could feel spots of rain. 'Let's go on a little way,' said the monk. 'There's a summerhouse where we can shelter; I often use it to read or write.' In the small wooden building they sat down again as the rain fell harder and started to drum on the roof. In the distance Gatti heard the rumble of thunder.

'Now, where was I, Bob?'

'Lifting a Korean called Cho from the coast near Chungsan.'

'Ah yes. Well, Bob, the Koreans weren't too keen on this kind of job because if they got captured their northern brethren treated them real rough. Manicure with steel pincers and no anaesthetic that left them with no fingernails, electricity, twenty years in a labour camp if they were lucky – you know the scene?' Gatti nodded. 'So I decided to do it myself with a young British officer who was serving under me. He was a Welsh boy, from the Valleys, but you could hardly tell it after Dartmouth. Like me he'd been at sea – he was a submariner – and was doing time in intelligence. They must've thought highly of him because he'd been seconded to the US Navy for two years and that meant he was expected to reach the top, when it would help to be on easy terms with the Yanks.'

'What was his name?' breathed Gatti.

'Thomas. Ivor Thomas. Good sailor but an arrogant little sod.'

'How do you mean?'

'He was intelligent, but very mixed up inside.' Bernard seemed to be hunting for a way to explain. 'See – I'm proud of my folks in Brooklyn. They were poor but more or less honest, I guess his in Wales were too, but he seemed *ashamed*. He couldn't reconcile his present with his past. Somehow it came out as arrogance. He could be brusque, offhand, either he felt dominated by other people – or he dominated, even humiliated, them. Couldn't have an equal relationship. Had a wife with him – she was completely crushed. But I digress, Bob, this is all with hindsight – then my main concern was that he could navigate me up the west coast of Korea; and he was a darn good navigator.'

'What was his rank then?'

'Lieutenant. So on the night of second September we set out from Inchon as soon as it got dark, just the two of us in a wooden fishing boat with souped-up twin diesels. I guess we cruised up the coast about twenty miles out; the wooden hull wasn't likely to blip on their radar and if it did we'd look like what we were – a fishing boat. There was no moon, but we had good navigation aids and knew exactly where we were, even though we couldn't see the shore, and what the seabed was like below us. The engines were muffled and the sea was calm. It was all very straightforward.

'South of Chungsan I homed in on the cove we'd chosen. I was steering with one eye on the echo sounder, Ivor Thomas was in the bow with a boathook, ready to fend off any floating wreckage. We hit the sand just before two in the morning. Ivor went over the side, paddled ashore with a mooring rope and his torch showed them waiting on the beach: a little Korean guy in uniform, like a toy soldier, a woman with a suitcase and two children. Then the thunderbolt fell.'

'What happened?' Gatti was studying Bernard's face as he remembered; the memory was plainly still painful.

'Suddenly seachlights flooded the beach and the boat

started to rock like crazy as a coastguard cutter appeared from round the headland, a big bastard bristling with machine guns, churning up the sea. The Koreans on the beach were surrounded by armed men and someone called on me to surrender. They shouted through a bull-horn in English, so they knew we weren't Koreans.'

'Did you surrender?'

'Sure, we both did – what else could we do?'

'And what happened then?'

'We were all loaded into a truck – Ivor, me and the four Koreans – and driven into Pyongyang.'

24

When the rain stopped, Gatti and the monk left the summerhouse, and walked in the garden among shrubs and roses that sparkled with the film of water left on their leaves. In the distance a small herd of cows was swaying back to grazing after sheltering under the trees. 'What happened in Pyongyang?' asked Gatti.

'We were all separated. I never saw any of the others again. Years later I learnt that Kang-Hong Cho had been tortured and interrogated for about six months, until they'd pumped him dry. Then they hanged him in front of about five thousand soldiers, *pour encourager les autres*. His wife and children were probably killed within days of the fiasco on the beach, they were of no interest to the authorities.'

'What about you?'

'I was in uniform. Not my own but a rating's with paybook to match, in a phoney name, Joe Burrows – chosen because I answered to Joe naturally. They questioned me for days and I played dumb, pretended I couldn't understand a word of Korean. When they turned to English I said I was just the erk who drove the boat, and stuck to that.'

'Were you tortured?'

'I wouldn't say so. They beat me up several times and kept me for days without food – long enough to make even boiled rice and filthy water seem like a feast. It's no fun being kicked in the balls by a beefy guy with steel toecaps – they were rough but there was nothing systematic and after a few weeks they seemed to accept me for what I claimed to be. Unimportant. I'd been living like an animal in a camp near Pyongyang – they kept me in a hole in the ground covered by an open bamboo grille, so when it rained you got wet, but you could also see the stars at night and thinking of all those millions of light years helped to keep things in perspective when there was a lot of pain or when I wanted to give in. Then one day I was hauled out and taken to an office in Pyongyang. Some high-ranking Korean was there and a couple of Europeans, who turned out to be Russians. I vaguely remembered one of them hovering in the background when I'd been questioned a week or two before. They knew my real name, my real rank and my real job.'

Bernard gave a little smile. 'It was a bad moment. I was still reeling when they took me down to a yard – I thought I was going to be shot – chained me to a Korean prisoner and put us on a truck. No explanation. No nothing. We drove north-east for a couple of days, into the mountains near the Chinese border. As we got higher it grew darn cold. There was snow on the peaks and I still only had my rating's singlet and cotton overalls, so I felt pretty miserable. They took us to a camp high on a bleak plateau: log cabins surrounded by two electrified fences. It was full of American and British prisoners who turned out to have been there since the Korean War – more than twenty-five years, can you imagine that? The whole place reeked with despair. Hundreds, maybe thousands of them had died over the years – from starvation, typhus and other diseases – but those poor bastards were still there. They knew that everyone in the States believed they were dead, that they'd never go home. Every day we were marched out to work in a mine. They gave us padded coats that had some warmth in them, but the food was terrible. Boiled rice and runny stew that dripped off the plates – they only had flat ones captured in the war, no bowls. At any one time half the camp had dysentery. Those guys were like zombies, walking corpses, the living dead, just waiting to be buried. The guards were reptiles. If you collapsed they kicked you until you struggled up. If you couldn't they shot you on the spot. If you tried to escape they shot you too; quite a few of the prisoners ran away knowing they would be zapped by the machine guns. It was a way out, easier than committing suicide in the huts, so long as the shooting was accurate and you died quickly. To be honest I was surprised that so many struggled on, had done for all those years, for there was nothing to look forward to, just sickness and death.'

'Didn't anybody ever escape? How did *you* get out?'

'Most of those guys were in their fifties or sixties – they'd spent half their lives as prisoners, given up. I was only thirty and determined to survive. Even so it took me nearly ten years.'

'Ten *years*?'

'Sure, Bob, ten years. I thought that the American authorities would get me out, expected release every day for the first month, then the first year; even in the second I went on hoping. In the end I realised that they must have been told I was dead, that I was one of the zombies too . . .

'But come 1988 there were only fifty of us left in the camp. 1988, Bob. In Europe Gorbachev had already been in power three years, the Berlin Wall was cracking, but no *glasnost* in North Korea. Just living hell. Two hard winters had taken a toll and the Koreans were getting less and less from the mine. One day, again with no explanation, they loaded us on two trucks and drove us away. There were two rumours – one that we were being taken to another half-empty camp, the other that we were going to a mass burial ground to be shot. I never found out which was true, for at the first stop we broke out. Two or three of us had concealed tools from the mine in our huts, worked on them to produce knives and saws. The truck was a closed wooden thing with a sliding door on the side. We cut away the wood round the bolts as we drove along and as soon as the driver stopped for a pee, five of us kicked our way out.

'For a few moments the Koreans were taken by surprise and we opened the other truck. There was no plan. Most of us just ran for it, but some of the guys exploded with a quarter century of frustration, turned on the Koreans with rocks and knives, overpowering them, seizing their weapons. When I looked back they had some of the guards spreadeagled on the road, driving the truck back and forward over them as they screamed; there was blood and bodies everywhere. The other Koreans pursued us, shooting down everyone they could see. I just ran and ran – I think I was the only one to make it, the others were too old.'

'Didn't they hunt you down?'

'Sure they did, but I got away, hid in a ditch that night and next morning ran into some Koreans working in the fields. I thought they'd turn me in and by that time I was so knackered I didn't much care. But they hated Kim Il-sung and sheltered me until they could pass me on to friends. In a week they helped me to reach the border zone, travelling hidden in farm trucks, and guided me over one night.'

'What happened to Ivor Thomas?'

'That's just it, Bob. Back in Seoul I was about as welcome as bubonic plague. No one wanted to know about the Korean War prisoners – the guys who debriefed me said they just didn't believe it. When I persisted they put me under psychiatric treatment. But the thing that really fazed me was Ivor Thomas. The operation had been betrayed, Cho and his family had all died, someone had blown me to the Koreans and I'd spent ten years in a labour camp. But Ivor had been released only three months after we were captured. It was Ivor who'd told the Americans I was dead, so no one tried to negotiate my release. The Brits had given him some kind of gong – a military OBE I think it was – and promoted him. Now what do you make of that, Bob?'

25

In Peking Luther had once again been summoned to the minister. He was increasingly annoyed at being dragged into the confusion the man was creating within China. Luther's original concept had been sophisticated and he had nurtured Scorpion as a long-term agent, designed to become the high-placed source the Chinese needed. The crudity of kidnapping Foo was not for Luther; you could not defeat deep-rooted opposition by brutalising a brave old man. As he faced the sweaty round face in an office in Zhongnanhai, he had to control his anger and disgust.

'It was not my idea to abduct Foo, Minister. I advised you to leave him free, to let him lead us to your enemies. This country is the size of the whole of Europe, including Russia west of the Urals. There must be a billion discontented people out there, we do not know exactly how many, we are not even quite certain how many *villages* there are.'

'I did not summon you here for a geography lesson, *gwailo*.'

'My point, Minister, is that China is very large and the opposition can hide relatively easily; to trace its leaders we must penetrate the movement – and I have tried to do so both here and in Hong Kong. Foo was part of that strategy. But what use is he to us now? Then Cable came to Kunming – but some idiot tried to arrest her before she had made contact with the people we really want.'

'Where is she now?'

'How the hell should *I* know? Perhaps she is in the

mountains north of Kunming – she has vanished.'

'You will work with Zhang and see that she is found! We will put her and Foo on trial with Tang Tsin, show the people how the Western capitalists are trying to destroy us.'

Inwardly Luther despaired. A show trial would achieve nothing, but if the murderous old men wanted it, he would see that Cable was delivered to join Foo and Tang Tsin. So three good people would be executed, the West would be shocked and the leaders of Tenth October would grow stronger. Thank God he had started his preparations to leave two years ago. The minister pressed a button on his desk and the eunuch-voiced Zhang glided through a black and gold doorway. Qiao Shi gestured him to sit down. 'You are to co-operate with Luther, comrade Zhang. Find the woman Cable and bring her here to Peking. Bring Foo as well and apply harsh measures; if he is questioned here it should be possible to use our excellent medical services to keep him alive – I need him for public trial, but I cannot believe that he will not name his contacts in the underground first. Take him to the limit if necessary.'

The minister stood up and waved Zhang away. 'You may leave us.' The Chinese did so, glancing murderously at Luther. When the door had closed a girl in baggy uniform brought tea and filled two delicate porcelain bowls; Qiao Shi offered one to Luther with an ingratiating smile. 'Of course I understand that this will not solve the problem, Luther, but I must be alive to the feelings of the leadership. I pander to them – but I know your penetration agents in China and the excellent Scorpion in Hong Kong are still the real key to destroying our enemies.'

Foo was moved less than two hours later. Still stiff and exhausted from the hours of questioning, he was dozing fitfully in a corner of his cell when a guard shook him awake. 'Open your eyes, granddad. You're going on a

184

journey.' Unusually the young face was friendly and his
dirty uniform suggested that he might be less than fanati-
cal in his duties. He gave Foo a bowl of lukewarm rice and
a cup of water, returning after ten minutes with another
man. Foo was determined not to show his fatigue, but
could not prevent his chained feet shuffling along the
corridor and tripped as he pulled himself up the stone
steps, grazing his face because he could not use his
pinioned hands to save himself.

The building rose five storeys on each side of a cobbled
yard, shutting out the sun. It was mid-morning, but Foo
felt cold as they walked to the green prison van. He
climbed through the door at the back; inside the truck
there was a narrow corridor with five separate compartments on either side. Foo was pushed into one of them
and a steel door bolted behind him. The tiny cell was
barely two feet square and he perched awkwardly on the
narrow metal seat, trying to arrange his chained ankles
and wrists to minimise the discomfort; it was plainly going
to be an unpleasant journey. He stared through the small
barred window as the van started up and drove out into a
busy street.

Gatti and Roper were horrified when they heard that
Mary Devereux had been arrested. At first neither of
them believed it, but a few phone calls confirmed that it
was true. *Tamar* was agog with the news – the most senior
Wren in the place, the alabaster beautiful Mary in the
brig? For being a *dyke*? It was impossible. The petty
officers' mess rang to sniggers and jokes of predictable
crudity; there were sniggers among the Wrens too, but
mostly they reacted with disbelief. 'It's not bloody true!'
Lynne, Mary's secretary, was in tears. 'How *could* they
treat her like that?'

The two Americans went straight to the admiral. 'Well,
boys?'

'Why has Commander Devereux been arrested, sir?'

'I didn't know she had, Bob.' It was plainly untrue, but how do you tell an admiral he is lying when you're only a commander?

'I made a report, sir.'

'Sure you did, Bob. I read it – you got a tip-off, checked her out and said you thought she was squeaky clean, her whole outfit was. You also said she was a lesbian.'

'I mentioned that only because I felt it might have been noticed in the past, after all she's been in their navy fifteen years – and because I concluded that, even if it was true, I did not believe it had exposed her to blackmail. I said she was clean.'

'That's what you said, Bob.'

'It was a report for your eyes only, sir.'

'You said that too, Bob.' The foxy face was stiffening as he puffed a smoke ring to the ceiling in apparent relaxation.

'So how the hell did the British get it?'

'I naturally passed a copy to Clayton. This is a combined US-UK operation, we have no secrets from each other – I guess his interpretation is different from yours.'

'Sir, I would never have passed the comment if I had *dreamt* you would do that. I was recommending no action at all – not this. It's barbaric!'

Hard eyes suddenly burned into Gatti's. 'Forget all this holier than thou crap, Bob. You're not in a goddam kindergarten – we're hunting for a major Chinese agent and you implied Devereux had *lied* in every positive vetting they'd ever given her – five times since she first signed on. It had *not* in fact been remarked on before. Clayton had no choice but to do something.'

'But he could have spoken to her privately, a discreet confrontation – there was no need to send naval police to arrest her in the middle of the night!'

'For Christ's sake, Bob, Clayton had a reason – think about it. If that woman is being blackmailed by the Chinese, the only evidence we're likely to get is her own confession. I guess Clayton calculated that a big shock –

and boy she's had one – might make her talk.'

'And has it?' Roper too was blazing with anger.

'No. She's admitted she's a lesbian and that she lied in her PVs, but absolutely denies any suggestion of disloyalty.'

'So she'll be released?'

'I think not, Nick, not yet. It's plain to me that she's innocent and this guy Thomas is suspect; he has some real explaining to do and the Brits are keeping him under twenty-four-hour watch.'

'So why shouldn't Devereux be released?'

'I guess all the fuss will give Thomas a false sense of security? If he thinks we believe Devereux is Scorpion, he may give himself away?'

Roper looked appalled. 'But that's dreadful, sir. The poor woman's career is finished after this, but that's no reason to keep her locked in a cell, humiliated, pretend we see her as a traitor.'

'We're playing for high stakes, Mr Roper. We can't afford to piss about.'

Sarah woke with the dawn and continued northwards, swinging along the ridge and keeping the Yangtze valley in sight on her left. She felt hungry, but she was able to fill the water bottle from a stream where sparkling water tumbled over pebbles and her spirits were high as the sun came out. The mountain air was clean and clear, the emptiness around her intensely beautiful. Tiny, perfectly formed flowers clung to patches of moss in the rock face – scarlet, deep violet, primrose yellow – and the peaks in the distance glinted with snow.

For six hours she followed the path, seeing no other human being and no sign of habitation. The only living things she encountered were mountain goats and wheeling birds – and a buzzard circling above the body of a dead animal, already an unrecognisable mess of white ribs and torn flesh where other predators had attacked it. Late in the afternoon she could see a large town in the valley. An old-fashioned steam engine was pulling a freight train along a railway line and there was traffic on the roads. Should she go down and try to travel by train – she had enough money but no permit to travel? Sarah sat down by a rock, partly to think about it, partly to ease her aching legs and the blisters forming on her feet. Lulled by the sun she dozed off, waking with a sense of apprehension when she heard boots crunching on loose stones.

Sarah staggered to her feet, still half-asleep, and turned abruptly towards the noise. She felt a surge of panic and her mouth went dry with fear. Four men were approaching. They were carrying AK-47s and wore the green uniform and black peaked caps of the police.

26

Benjamin Foo watched for clues to his whereabouts, his face pressed awkwardly against the barred window. At first the van was passing through crowded streets: he could see Chinese in black pyjamas and bell-shaped straw hats, a few Europeans, flocks of bicycles and rusting old cars. When they passed side streets he caught glimpses of high office buildings that suggested Shanghai. But soon they were out in the countryside and he could see endless brown hills, sheets of muddy water covering paddy fields and bright green rice shoots. He assumed that they were going to an airfield for a plane to Peking, but it seemed to be taking a long time. The road was uneven and he was constantly jolted on the hard seat, but the sun on the metal roof made the confined space stifling and eventually he dozed off.

Even Polaris submarines can develop mechanical trouble and a fault in the hydraulics working her foreplanes was diagnosed when *Relentless* made a short training dive. Engineers were brought out from Faslane and reported that repairs would take at least a week. The crew were due for leave anyway, so most of them were flown home; the second crew would come out when the boat was ready to leave Hong Kong. For Ivor Thomas the change of crew meant the end of his command; instead of returning to England he was given a naval flat ashore and an office in *Tamar* where he started to read into his new duties. He said that he would go home for a couple of weeks' leave in about a month, but that his wife and children would stay in Tavistock as they had when he was a Polaris commander. Everyone seemed impressed with his keenness to get on with the new job; and it was now much easier to watch his movements. He suspected nothing.

Gerald Clayton also flew back to London, promising to return in a week if necessary, leaving Barnie Mason to tie up the loose ends. A team of twelve was assembled to keep Thomas under surveillance twenty-four hours a day. Mason and Roper met to study the reports every afternoon. Thomas appeared to lead a blameless life, working all day on the base, eating in the *Tamar* officers' mess, spending the evenings alone in the apartment. Roper prepared three documents classified TOP SECRET, giving plausible but false details of planned British and American naval movements in the South China Sea, and saw that numbered copies were sent to Thomas for information. He was hoping photocopies would crop up in China in a week or two and provide conclusive proof.

Foo woke with a start when the prison van stopped. He was still only half-conscious when he heard angry shouts outside, followed by the crash of glass breaking and a thunderous explosion. The van rocked, throwing him to the floor with both ears singing; his hearing distorted, the rattle of a machine pistol seemed to echo painfully inside his head. The van started to move again, then tipped sideways amid a tremendous fusillade of shots and the whine of bullets ricocheting. Someone was beating at the outer door, cursing and trying to smash it open with hammer blows that made the whole vehicle shake. He heard a shout in Cantonese: 'Can you hear, Foo? Keep away from the door, get on the floor, we're going to shoot it open!' There was another volley of shots, running footsteps, bolts clanged and the door of his cell was wrenched open with a screech of buckled metal.

A Chinese figure beckoned urgently, surrounded by smoke, face distorted by the stocking pulled over its head. 'Are you all right?' It was a woman's voice, speaking urgently in Cantonese. Foo struggled to his feet, swaying with giddiness and feeling warm blood trickling from a cut on his head. He stumbled to the rear door, slipped as he tried to climb down and ended up slithering to a spine-jarring stop on the steel step. The woman pulled out a pistol. 'It's okay – I'm just going to shoot off your chains. Could you spread your feet apart, please?'

Foo obeyed, deafened again by the explosion as she fired and grimacing silently as the chain split and the metal bands scraped the skin off his ankles; the pain was excruciating. He held out his wrists and gritted his teeth as she shot through that chain as well.

Head still swimming, swaying, he followed the woman along the side of the van which was skewed into a ditch. Rubbing his wrists to restore the circulation Foo could see that they were on an empty road lined by trees. A jeep with its engine running stood across the highway. All the glass in the cab of the van was shattered and two figures lay sprawled back covered in blood and broken glass. The door was hanging by one hinge and another stocking-masked figure was leaning through it, checking that they were dead.

A third man in uniform was groaning in a pool of blood on the ground. The woman levelled her pistol and shot him through the head. 'We are from Tenth October,' she said, pulling off her mask. She took some gauze from a pocket in the jeep and thrust it at Foo. 'Your head is bleeding – hold this over it and I think it will stop.'

The other Chinese was a man. He pushed Foo into the back of the jeep, tossing the police AK-47s after him, jumped into the driver's seat and shouted over his shoulder. 'Please hold on! We've got about twenty minutes to get clear.' The wheels spun and they shot off down the road in a cloud of yellow dust.

*　　　*　　　*

Luther left Peking with relief. The atmosphere behind the closed doors of Party and government offices was tense and steamy. The official press was full of good news, but everyone knew that rebellion was seething under the surface. Today there had been food riots in Sian, students in Hainan had occupied a police headquarters – releasing prisoners awaiting trial – and would have to be evicted by force; no doubt they were seeking martyrdom and would all die in the assault. What would tomorrow bring? The opposition was showing more strength than he had ever expected.

A government car met him at the airport and drove him back to the lakeside house and Josie. She greeted him with a flurry of kisses and they made love in a well-hidden corner of the garden. Afterwards she was pouring him a beer when the telephone rang. Reluctantly she handed him the receiver. It was Zhang, triumph in his voice as he reported the bad news.

'You mean they stopped the truck?' Luther caught his breath in disbelief. 'Killed the guards and got away with him? It can't be possible!' Josie frowned as she watched him. 'No, I shall not return to Peking – I've only been home ten minutes – but keep me informed.' He smashed the receiver down.

The tiny Vietnamese took his hand and led him out into the sun, two glasses of beer waiting on a wooden table. Her eyes looked frightened. 'What is wrong, Luther?'

'The millionaire Foo has escaped – and they have failed to find the woman Cable. That bastard Zhang is doing his best to discredit me with the minister – I'm only just realising, after nearly twenty years, that they can never completely trust a foreigner.'

'Are we in danger, Luther?'

'Yes. In Peking they are all terrified of the opposition and out to blame somebody else. I'm a natural target.'

'I'd like to kill that Qiao Shi.' Her eyes became dark slits as she made a stabbing gesture. 'Why should he treat you so bad?'

Sarah stood up as the four policemen approached, mind racing to find a plausible story; but she knew that there simply wasn't one. The first man called to her in an odd dialect that she thought was Putonghua, the new 'common speech' based on Mandarin that was supposed to become a national spoken language. She recognised her own name but tried to look puzzled and replied in English. 'Who are you? What do you want?'

'Are you Miss Cable?' This time he said it more insistently and in English.

Sarah knew when she was beaten. What was the Chinese equivalent of 'it's a fair cop, guv'? She nodded. 'Yes, that is my name.'

The man smiled in relief. 'Thank God – I am Cheng, from Tenth October.'

Was it a trick? Sarah continued to pretend confusion. 'I'm sorry, I don't understand.'

'Please – you can trust us. It was my niece who met you at Kunming. I'm sorry everything went wrong – we heard that the army had found the caves and feared that you were captured. Then we heard that you had got away and it seemed likely that you would come in this direction. We have been looking for you for twenty-four hours.'

'But why are you in police uniform?'

'Because we have to move you a long way and police uniforms will solve most problems in this country.'

Sarah suddenly felt lightheaded. Did she believe him? What else could she do? 'Who did you say you were again?'

Cheng met her gaze steadily. He had an honest lined face and must have been quite old; the other three were young. 'Please – you can trust us. I promise that we *are* from Tenth October and we *will* take care of you from now on. You will leave our country safely.'

Sarah sat down again with a sigh of resignation. The whole thing was a nightmare, cock-up after cock-up, punctuated by beaming faces enticing her to further danger. She hoped Tom Rumbelow would roast in hell. 'Will I?' she asked wearily. 'How am I supposed to get back to the coast?'

Cheng gestured to the town in the valley. 'The first stage will be by train.'

Sarah raised her eyes to heaven. 'Now I've heard it all! Not likely – I'll be arrested at the first station.'

'No, there will be other Europeans on the train and you will have correct papers. It is the fastest and safest way, truly. The four of us will travel separately but on the same train.'

The prospect of ever returning to Hong Kong alive was receding by the minute – how had fate ever mixed her up with this bunch of comic opera revolutionaries? 'Okay,' Sarah said at last, 'I have to trust you. Now tell me what you have in mind – *exactly* what we are going to do.'

27

Sarah was feeling more confident when the long train steamed into the station at nine that evening. Cheng had kept her hidden all day in a room behind the shop of a sympathiser. Perhaps they were not such amateurs after all, for he had taken a Polaroid photograph of her and returned after an hour with it stuck inside what looked like an authentic Canadian passport: her new name was Jeanne Hart, a journalist from Toronto. The passport was covered in the stamps of worldwide travel and he gave her a clutch of documents giving her permission to travel. 'How did you manage all this?' she asked.

Cheng's wrinkled face grinned wickedly. 'We have friends everywhere.' The weatherbeaten skin made it impossible to tell whether he was fifty or seventy and Sarah wondered how he came to be risking his life like this. He had a scholarly manner and spoke good but jerky English – could he be a university professor, a factory manager, even some kind of official? But this wasn't the time to ask – she stuck to practicalities. 'Where are we going?'

'To Guiyang, then south to Liuzhou. A long overnight journey, so in your part of the train – you are travelling first class – everyone will be asleep.' The wrinkled face smiled again. 'You will be quite safe but are proving quite expensive, for we have to pay sixty per cent higher fare for *gwailo*.'

'I'm sorry.'

'No – is my attempt at English joke. *We* are sorry. Your journey to China has been wasted and dangerous.

195

That is not what we planned.'

The locomotive was black with five huge red driving wheels and brass pistons belching steam. It had a cow-catcher and searchlight on the front of the boiler, like an engine in an old cowboy film, and there were three men in oily overalls and caps on the footplate; the massive loco-motive was drawing fourteen cars, dark green with two yellow stripes on the side and ventilators on the roof. As it came to a standstill Chinese poured from it, leaping through the windows as well as the doors with their cot-ton-wrapped bundles, while others fought to get on board.

With five or six other foreigners Sarah elbowed her way to the first class carriage and found herself in an oasis of chilly air conditioning with soft bunks, white sheets and blankets. The beaming conductor barely glanced at her ticket, took her passport, and showed her to an upper bunk; when she drew the curtains she was completely hidden. Maybe Cheng had been right. As she heard a long blast from the ancient QJ locomotive's steam whistle and the train started to move, *The East is Red* suddenly blaring from the tannoy in every carriage, Sarah lay back and opened her Thermos flask of green tea; this whole country was crazy but she felt cosy and relatively safe.

Mary Devereux faced the silver-haired man in shirtsleeves across the same deal table where he had questioned her for five hours last night, her face hollow with exhaustion. They were in a room at the corner of the guard-house in *Tamar*, a room with windows unlike her cell which had only a grating to the air about eight feet above the con-crete floor. Everyone else in the SIS station and naval security had bridled at questioning her and Brimson, the captain commanding the base, had supported his staff. 'I've no option but to arrest her, if you insist, until I get different orders from London, but I'll be damned if I do more than that. I feel thoroughly unclean at what you've done in my name, Clayton.' Clayton could have ordered one of his own people to do it, but that was no way to get results; he ended up doing the job himself.

Despite all the protests Commander Devereux was still lodged in a whitewashed cell, except when brought out for questioning. Clayton's eyes bored into her, but his voice tried to be soothing. 'You're finished in the navy, Mary. You've committed two serious court-martial offences – lying in your positive vetting as well as your sexual behaviour. If you tell me everything about the blackmail by the Chinese I'll see there's no trial, I promise. You'll be allowed to resign quietly . . . '

Mary's face was pale and hollow, there were red rings under her eyes, her hair was a mess and she was wearing crumpled blue fatigues. 'I've told you before, there *was* no blackmail. Everything you've tried to pin on me is complete nonsense. I hope you're enjoying this, you bastard – haven't you tormented me enough?'

'Do you really expect me to believe you?'

'Of course I bloody well do.'

'You're not helping yourself, Mary.'

'I'm telling you the truth – what more can I do?'

Clayton sighed. 'Look, let's try again.'

'Just forget it. I've had enough.' Mary stood up defiantly and turned her back on him. 'For God's sake take me back, I'm sick of looking at you.'

Clayton nodded to a face at the glass panel in the door and two well-built Wrens came in. Mary marched away down the corridor between them. 'Is there anything you need, ma'am?' asked one as she unlocked the cell door.

'I *would* like some clean underclothes and tights.'

The petty officer Wren hesitated, well aware of the regulations, then hung back as her assistant walked away down the corridor. 'Okay,' she whispered. 'You know I shouldn't, but I'll see what I can do.'

Sarah woke several times during the night when the train stopped, peering out through the window blind by her bunk at floodlit stations teeming with Chinese even at three in the morning, loudspeakers blaring martial music and *The East is Red*. At about eight she got up and refilled her flask from the glowing coal stove at the end of the carriage. She breakfasted in the swaying dining car, sharing a table covered in crisp white cloth with another *gwailo*, a tourist from France; Cheng and the three other 'policemen' were at a table further down the car. At Liuzhou she left the train and found the baker's shop, next to a pharmacist with a skeleton hanging in the window – the meeting place arranged with Cheng. As she entered, a woman in an apron streaked with flour looked up, seemed to recognise Sarah at once and beckoned her into a back room where faggots were burning under a brick oven. She sat sipping a bowl of tea until Cheng arrived, now wearing peasant clothes and a shabby cap.

'So far we win.' He gave a wry little smile, beckoning Sarah into a yard behind the shop where he made her lie under a heap of sacks in the back of an old pick-up truck; they smelt as if they had contained manure of some kind. Cheng climbed into the cab and headed for the hills.

They reached the village late in the evening. For the last fifty miles Sarah sat next to Cheng and listened to his life story, although she noticed that he left out salient details – she would not be able to identify him if it all went wrong and she landed in government hands. Cheng was not his real name, any more than it had been Cheng Huiqing's, but he came from Shanghai and had once been a Party member. His wife and grown-up children were still in the Party and had survived by claiming that he was dead. He had not seen them for ten years. Sarah sensed his deep sadness when he told her this; she guessed that he was about sixty, and warmed to his wry smile and apologetic manner. 'Officially, you see, I do not exist.'

'What did you do before, Cheng?'

'Before? That is so long ago it is like previous

incarnation. I taught nuclear physics at university in Shanghai but my cousin, who will shelter us for a few days, is farmer. He has been released from commune and is now allowed to run own business.'

The village was a cluster of wooden buildings in a hollow surrounded by hills. Cheng's cousin was a fat, bucolic Chinese with a thick droopy moustache; the scar on his face, and the knife thrust into the sash at his waist, made him look like a bandit. His wife too was cheerfully plump; they both laughed a lot and greeted Cheng and Sarah warmly. It was dusk and Sarah calculated that no one else would have seen the European woman arrive; no doubt she would also leave in darkness. Cheng parked the farm truck in a walled yard, where there was already an old American army jeep. 'Come,' he said to Sarah, 'I have surprise for you.' He led the way into the house.

The big living room was lit by oil lamps – there was no electricity – and a table had been laid for a banquet. Bowls and pairs of chopsticks surrounded steaming plates of pork, fish and rice. A Chinese in a long black robe stood up and Sarah took a step back. 'Ben! How on earth did *you* get here?' She threw her arms round him.

'I was brought here by our friends, just like you.' He kissed her in a fatherly way. 'I'm sorry it has been such a mess. When we are safely back in Hong Kong we shall have to try again.'

Sarah smiled at him, saying nothing. The last thing she planned to do if she got out safely was 'try again'. 'This fellow Cheng seems to be able to pull strings everywhere – is he one of the leaders?'

'No, but he is close to them.' *Mao-tai* was being poured from stone bottles and Sarah took a glass from Cheng's rubicund cousin. They were drinking some kind of toast and she joined in, feeling the firewater burn her throat like paintstripper. All around her Chinese faces beamed in yellow lamplight, the atmosphere was smoky and full of laughter. The noise must have penetrated all round the village, indeed the whole village appeared to be in this

199

room. She took another *mao-tai* to mask her despair, for her doubts about this crew were becoming deep and permanent: they might hate Peking but were they credible leaders of a revolution?

Luther jumped into his beige Skoda when the phone call came and drove as fast as he could to the police post five miles away. The coded message from Zhang was waiting for him, and he sat in a stuffy room with a sheet of squared paper to decipher it, resting each sheet on glass so that no trace was left on a blotter. It was typical of Zhang – he could have made a secure phone call, but he took every opportunity to make life tiresome. At least he had not sat on the information and Luther could barely conceal his jubilation from the constable who brought him tea.

They had traced Cable again, travelling south by train. A police officer who routinely examined the passports of foreigners at a station had recognised her photograph when it was circulated – unfortunately an hour or two later – by the *Gonganbu*. He could remember that the passport had belonged to a Canadian called Hart, though not where she had been going – but it should be enough. There was only one railway line. Luther smiled to himself as he asked for a phone connection to the police commander in Liuzhou.

After that morning's session with Clayton, Mary Devereux sat in her cell reading for a time. She moved from a Ngaio Marsh whodunnit to *Pilgrim's Progress*, but her mind was not on the words. She felt drained of spirit, crushed by everything. Her life had been going so well – the job was a success, she was in line for promotion and in love with Chang Xhisin. Now it was all destroyed. They would kick her out of the Wrens after a court-martial; Chang Xhisin would not want to go to England with her – after this she would probably never want to see Mary again. Wherever she tried to hide, people would find her out and snigger behind her back. She didn't know the name of the silver-haired bastard who'd been questioning her, but she had sensed at once that he was behind it all and in a wave of fury fervently wished she could strangle him. Then the anger gave way to tears as she relived the series of blows last night; she tried to rationalise, but the humiliation was just too cruel to bear.

She never took a positive decision, but she knew what had to happen as soon as she drew the new pair of tights out of the transparent plastic. As if in a trance she put on her clean things, systematically brushed her hair and smeared on some lipstick, recovering a little self-respect, then tied one end of the black material to the bars of the grating high in the cell wall, reaching up with some difficulty, for it was well above her head. Still standing on the stool she knotted the other end firmly round her neck. It was remarkably easy when it came to it. For a moment she hesitated, remembering a High Anglican childhood and wondering whether she should say a prayer or cross herself or something; but she did neither, kicked the stool away violently and jerked with a thud and startled gasp as her body fell about eighteen inches. Despite the shock she was still conscious enough to know that her feet could not touch the floor and to feel the choking band tighten round her neck. Her body twisted and convulsed as instinctively her lungs fought for breath, the pain in her throat and chest soared into a peak of agony and her eyes felt about to pop out of their sockets, but then the pressure seemed to lessen and, with a small sigh, Mary Devereux slipped away into unconsciousness.

28

The messenger came to Ruth Foo in Macao early next morning. He was an elderly Chinese, dressed in the blue shorts and singlet of a seaman, bony legs dark as mahogany, but with educated speech. This made the amah so suspicious that she refused to let him in when he appeared at the kitchen door, but he held out a sealed envelope and insisted he would wait while it was given to Mrs Foo. Ruth was still in her bedroom, forcing herself to get up and live a normal day as she had every morning since Ben vanished. She recognised the seals at once – the *chop* impressed in the red wax had been engraved on the signet ring he had worn since the day she first met him – and her fingers seemed to slip as she opened the packet. Five minutes later she faced the old man outside on the terrace, out of earshot of the servants. 'Where did you get this?' Her voice trembled slightly as she pointed to the rough cream paper and broken wax.

The old man bowed. 'From your husband's own hand, lady. He and the English girl Cable,' he had difficulty with Sarah's surname, pronouncing it 'Kabul', 'are now held by Tenth October. They are safe, but over three hundred miles inland – and the coastal area is full of troops. We hope that your English and American friends might be able to arrange transport for them?'

'Transport?' Ruth's brow furrowed.

'An aircraft perhaps?'

'Oh, I see.'

The Chinese hastened to explain. 'I daresay we could

get your husband and Miss Kabul out without help, but it could take some weeks. It is not easy to conceal a tall European woman . . . and time may be short. I fear there are powerful forces hunting them and they are in much danger.'

Ruth Foo had lived as a Chinese long enough to conceal her jubilation at the news that at least Ben was alive. She continued to stand in her long red robe, looking gravely out at a motor junk passing under the long bridge that soared across the harbour. She would handle this in a Chinese way. 'Would you like some tea?'

The old man inclined his head respectfully and she went inside for a few minutes, calling in Cantonese to the houseboy. When she returned Ruth politely invited the Chinese to sit beside her on a wooden bench in the corner, shaded by cherry trees. 'What is your name, friend?'

'Please call me Ling Boda. That is how I am known in the movement.'

The porcelain teapot was placed on a table in front of them and Ruth filled two delicate blue and white bowls. 'Thank you for bringing me news of my husband, Ling, but what do you suggest I do now?'

'We believe there is a Chinese agent working inside the intelligence services in Hong Kong, so we do not wish to take risks. Can you guide me to someone very senior – someone so senior we can be confident he is not this agent – and ask for help to bring out your husband and Miss Kabul?'

Ruth considered, then smiled at him. 'Of course – that must be the right thing to do.' She walked into the house and picked up a portable telephone, pressing the keys for the office number Rumbelow had given her. She started in surprise when a strange voice answered, a man's voice, plainly not a secretary; within a minute she was speaking to someone else who said his name was Clayton.

Foo and Sarah had also been woken early that morning.

Cheng looked worried. 'Military vehicles are coming up valley – army or police. We must go into hills.' There were no goodbyes. They ran through the big room, still heavy with last night's alcohol fumes, straight into the old American jeep and shot out of the village in a cloud of dust, hairpinning up the dirt road into the mountains for three miles until Cheng turned off, weaving through boulders until he could climb no further.

He ran the jeep into a gully and the three fugitives climbed out. They were screened from below by a ridge of massive boulders; when they huddled together at a gap they could see the village, tiny huts clustered on the plain like models. Four camouflage-painted trucks had stopped at its edge and a circle of figures surrounded the buildings: black ants closing in slowly, sun glinting on steel helmets and weapons. 'What will they do when they find us gone?' Sarah could almost hear her heart beating, felt the tension in her body. Cheng did not reply; he stood transfixed, face rigid as his eyes flickered to follow the events unfolding below. The tiny figures made straight for the house where Sarah and Foo had stayed, there were faint shouts and a burst of automatic fire. Suddenly she could see men and women being lined up in the street and smoke rising from the white building. Had Cheng's cousin set light to his own home to create a diversion or was that the army taking revenge?

The answer came as other houses burst into flames. Soon the whole village was ablaze, the villagers standing by helplessly in their fields as soldiers tossed in a few grenades to help the destruction. The explosions produced showers of red sparks and a plume of thick black smoke rose slowly against the blue sky. Sarah looked on in horror: if they did this to innocent people who had sheltered them, what would they do to her and Foo? Six or seven small figures were being loaded at gunpoint into a truck: it was too far away to see who they were. Cheng was still watching stoically, occasionally using a pair of field glasses. 'They are taking away my cousin.' His voice was hollow, betraying no emotion.

'I am so very sorry.' Foo gestured down at the burning village. 'I did not realise the risk your cousin and everyone else was taking.'

Cheng turned away. 'They knew it – and it is my responsibility. But soon those bastards will be up here searching for *us*.'

Foo nodded, showing no fear. 'Can we risk the jeep? Won't they hear the engine?'

Cheng shook his head. 'No, we are too far away. Come quickly, we must move as fast as we can.'

Ruth Foo and the elderly Ling crossed in *A-ma* to Hong Kong, where a government car met them at the quayside and Roper and Clayton, who had arrived back from London late last night, received them in an office on the Peak. Ruth took to Nick at once, just as she mistrusted Clayton. 'You mean you want us to go in with a helicopter or light aircraft and lift them out?' Roper responded at once, despite disapproving glances from Clayton.

'Exactly. Mr Ling says he can arrange a rendezvous and Tenth October will see that Sarah and my husband are waiting there in twenty-four hours or whenever you suggest.'

Clayton cut in sternly. 'It's not that simple. Of course we'll help if we can, Mrs Foo, but we're supposed to be a friendly government – flying into China in cahoots with these dissidents could lead to serious diplomatic problems.'

Roper shrugged his shoulders. 'Only if we get caught, Gerry.'

'That is a possibility we cannot discount.' Clayton's disapproval was icy: you did not speak like that in front of outsiders.

God that man's pompous, thought Roper; he turned to Ruth Foo. 'You can see that we have to discuss all this among ourselves and do a little calculating, Mrs Foo. Is there some place you can stay on the island – somewhere we can reach you later?'

'My husband has a small apartment in Shek Tong Tsui, near the university. We'll go there and I'll leave you the telephone number.'

As the same black car took Ruth and Ling Boda back down the Peak, Ivor Thomas was playing hookey. He had been reading files for several days in his temporary office, a Portakabin on the quayside, and decided that he would not be missed for a few hours; so he returned to his apartment and changed into civilian clothes, a sports shirt and rather old-fashioned slacks. When he emerged and hailed a passing Datsun taxi, he seemed unconscious of the four pairs of eyes watching from different vantage points in the street. They followed him in a dusty white Toyota, anonymous in the dense traffic, until his taxi stopped near the Outlying Islands Pier. Ivor Thomas appeared to be in no hurry as he paid the driver; but then, unaccountably, the four experienced Special Branch watchers lost him.

He was not seen for the rest of the day. At about six in the evening the microphones in his flat and telephone started to pick up speech – and tapes in the flat above automatically started to record. The two Chinese police who had been dozing there all day rang their superintendent, who reported sheepishly to Clayton; he had been furious when they lost Thomas and shouted down the phone that there would be hell to pay if it happened again. But what had Thomas been up to in the missing seven hours?

Half an hour later Gatti and Roper joined Clayton in what had been Tom Rumbelow's office. The admiral had returned to Washington for a few days, leaving Gatti in charge. There were no preliminary courtesies. 'What do we do about Foo and Cable?' asked Clayton abruptly, putting his feet on the coffee table; for the time being this was now *his* territory and he liked to demonstrate that he could do what he liked in it.

'I have no faith in Tenth October,' Gatti said. 'If we send in a helicopter it'll probably find they aren't at the rendezvous and then get into a shooting match with the People's Liberation Army. We won't get Foo and Sarah out – and we'll have a God-awful row with the Chinese.'

Clayton grunted and turned expectantly to Roper. 'Well, Nick?'

'I disagree. We can't possibly not try to rescue them. They're both in danger somewhere in mid-China and there's a massive hunt on. If we act in the next twenty-four hours we might just get them out – after that, who knows? If they're arrested, sooner or later they'll both say more than they should and I'd guess the Chinese will arrange a show trial to give our governments a bloody nose – teach us not to interfere in Chinese domestic affairs.'

'One vote for, one against.' Clayton sat with his fingertips together looking judicial. 'Either way, can we *trust* this fellow Ling? Is he genuine?'

'He brought the letter in Foo's handwriting, with his personal seal.'

'Not entirely conclusive,' said Gatti.

'Oh, I don't know – I think that's enough for me.' Clayton leaned forward, studying the map of China that covered the table and overflowed on the floor. 'We mustn't let personal considerations cloud our judgement, of course.' He shot a nasty glance at Roper, whose face darkened: how the hell did Clayton know about Sarah? 'But for my money the worst case is their being taken alive. Interrogation. Trial. Very damaging.'

'So what do you conclude?' asked Gatti stiffly.

'Fix a rendezvous, and send in a helicopter at night with four hard-arsed types from the SBS unit. They should be able to lift the delectable Sarah and octogenarian Foo out safely. If there's trouble, at least they can make certain neither of them survives to be arrested.' Nick Roper looked up sharply, staring at him in horrified disbelief. 'God knows what we'd do about the chopper and its crew in that case, but I daresay the dips could find some pack of lies to spin to the Chinese.'

Gatti shook his head vigorously. 'It's too dangerous, far too dangerous.'

'You're overruled and outvoted, Bob. It's not exactly enticing, but the *most* dangerous course is to leave them to be picked up by the *Gonganbu*. We can't risk that.' Clayton stood up. 'Get a plan together, will you, Nick? Talk to the SBS team. I want to see something on paper by ten tomorrow.'

29

Luther's stream of intelligence from Hong Kong seemed to be drying up, but he was still confident that they would catch up with Sarah – and he assumed she was with Foo since both must be following an underground route organised by the loose-knit and leaky opposition. But he had grave doubts about the reliability of the security forces in Liuzhou; he had been let down too often recently by inefficiency or downright obstruction. So Luther travelled south-west from Hanzhou himself, picked up by hissing Zhang in the minister's private aircraft. It was a small jet, well-appointed with wood panelling, red plush seats and the ubiquitous white antimacassars. The drawbacks were that there was no alcohol on board and smoking was forbidden. 'Qiao Shi does not like the lingering smell of tobacco,' explained Zhang solemnly, barely hiding his delight that Luther would have to chafe until they landed for one of his disgusting Gitanes.

After the burning of the village, Cheng drove east along dirt roads through the hills. Sarah sat beside him in the front of the jeep while Foo stretched out luxuriously in the back. The silence was tense and eventually she had to break it. 'What will happen to your cousin and his wife?'

Cheng gripped the steering wheel and continued to stare straight ahead. 'They will be executed. Harbouring terrorist is very serious crime.' He sounded so matter-of-fact that he could have been talking about people who were complete strangers.

'I'm sorry. You are all taking great risks for me and Mr Foo.'

'You were both taking a great risk by coming to help us.'

'But it was pointless – I've done nothing useful at all. There was no value in coming.'

The wrinkled brown face half-turned to her, his thin hair catching in the wind as he drove. 'It was important to us that you were *willing* to come – we desperately need contact with your government and the United States. Next time our security will be better, I promise, next time we shall achieve something – every day we are learning from mistake.'

But at what cost, thought Sarah. Maybe there were so many people in China they valued life less? She pushed the question away and scanned the road ahead: it was empty as far as the horizon, an unmade strip of beaten earth and yellow chippings, with low hills rising on either side. Away to the south she could see the scarlet and gold of a pagoda. The jeep bounced past a group of grazing pigs, watched by a teenage boy listening to a transistor. 'Where are we going this time?' she asked.

'To another village. I hope there will be answer to our request. Will your people send plane?'

'I've no idea. They may be too afraid of a confrontation with China. How far are we from Hong Kong now?'

'Not too far – about three hundred miles.'

'Then perhaps they will.'

Tang Tsin knew that his family were dead. No one had told him, but deep down he just knew it. For seven days now he had not been troubled: no more interrogation, no more torture. He was not displeased with himself. He had told them a great deal about Mark, but nothing about Tenth October; he had kept faith. Once they left him alone in his cell, he was glad of the solitude, content with

210

the thin diet of rice and water. There was time to think, pray and prepare for death. His cell was below ground but had a slit window, high up, and sun slanted in for about an hour every morning, when it was not raining – Tang Tsin was surprised how much he could value something that, a month ago, he would have taken for granted.

In Hong Kong Gerald Clayton continued to move with lightning speed. Roper spent half the night poring over maps and charts with a young marine lieutenant called Carstens. They presented their conclusions to Clayton and Gatti at ten next morning. 'It's not,' said Nick flatly, 'anywhere near as easy as we thought.'

'What do you mean?' Clayton might have doubts about lifting out these two bloody people, but if he decided to do it he did not expect obstruction.

'Foo and Sarah have just left a village near here,' Nick pointed to the map. 'East of Liuzhou, about two hundred miles from the coast and well over three hundred from here.'

'That's no distance at all.'

'I'm afraid it *is*, Mr Clayton. The fact is there's no airfield or landing strip, so we can't use a light aircraft. So it would have to be a helicopter – but there are no service helicopters in Hong Kong except Westland Lynxes used by the Army Air Corps. There's a frigate in harbour and most of them have a helicopter these days, but she doesn't.'

'Oh do get on with it,' yawned Clayton. 'What's the problem?'

'The Lynx has a range of only about two hundred miles. We have to cover over six hundred, there and back.'

Before Clayton could explode the marine intervened. 'Carstens, sir, SBS. There *is* a possible solution, but it's dodgy.'

'Yes?' Clayton eyed the serviceman irritably.

'It would be possible to lash-up a landing pad on the

frigate that's in harbour, sir – by this evening. We could then cruise down the coast, about thirty miles out, with one of the army choppers to a point in a direct line from Liuzhou.'

'You want to use a *frigate* – for Christ's sake this is supposed to be a clandestine operation!'

'Naval vessels come and go all the time, sir; we are still entitled to use Hong Kong harbour until 1997. In its way, using a ship of that size would be quite good cover – it would appear to be a routine movement.'

Clayton's mouth set in a hard line; he looked half-convinced. 'And then what?'

'We fly in with extra fuel tanks to bring the range up to about four hundred miles, flying low to minimise the risk of detection. With a bit of luck we'd be in and out in four hours.'

'Could it be done at once, tonight?'

'If the army and naval commanders both agree and get any higher clearance they need, yes it could.'

'Ralph – Lieutenant Carstens – has already sounded them out, Mr Clayton,' added Roper. 'It's not as neat as I'd like and there's no margin for error. But I don't see anything better. The only alternative is to leave Foo and Sarah to walk or take a bullock cart.'

'No.' Clayton shook his head. 'That just isn't on. Cable shouldn't be in China at all; I don't know why she ever allowed herself to get in this situation.'

'Because Tom Rumbelow ordered her to go.' Barnie Mason, Rumbelow's deputy who had been sitting quietly in a corner, spoke for the first time. 'She thought it was crackers and so did I.'

Clayton snorted. 'You're neither of you children – I still don't see why you didn't make more fuss – but this isn't the time for an inquest.' He shot a hard glance at Mason and his hands made a curious gesture, as if breaking the neck of a chicken. 'That comes later. For now I must get her out – I can't risk an SIS officer being arrested and put on trial. We may as well lift Foo as well, since he's

212

with her.'

'Does that mean we go ahead?' Roper started to roll up the coastal charts. 'If so we've one hell of a lot to do – and Ling Boda will have to send a short-wave message to his friends.'

'In one-time code, I trust? Sure – go ahead.' As the group dispersed, Clayton touched the marine gently on the arm. 'Stay just for a moment, lieutenant, when the others have gone.'

Cheng did not take Sarah and Foo to another village. They stopped at an isolated farmstead late in the after-noon, when some more Tenth October sympathisers produced a rough meal of rice and pork. But this time Cheng was taking no chances: no more alcohol, no more celebrations. Sarah sensed that he was worried, that they were barely one jump ahead of the pursuit. As they ate he popped in and out to the farmyard like a grasshopper, looking up at the sky; at one point he went out to the jeep, hidden under an open barn with a straw roof, and used his short-wave radio, running the engine to provide enough current. 'Why is he doing it, Ben?' she asked. 'Why are they all?'

'It's like Eastern Europe – there's a massive ground-swell against the regime in Peking. One day Cheng and his friends will bring them down.'

'But it's so disorganised. All this effort now to get us back to Hong Kong, but the great meeting we came for never happened at all!'

'That's never happened to me before, Sarah – whatever went wrong it was somewhere else in China, there was panic in the organisation, even Cheng does not know what caused it.'

'Hmph.' Sarah put down her chopsticks and pushed aside the plate of fatty pork, unable to force it down despite her hunger. 'How do you rate our chances, Ben?'

'About fifty-fifty.' He smiled cheerfully. 'They'll shoot

me of course, if they capture us. And Cheng. You might get away with a spell in jail or a camp.'

'Terrific.' Sarah changed the subject, it was getting depressing. 'Do you miss Ruth?'

'Of course, and the children.'

'You never mention them.'

'I *think* about them constantly. To discuss one's family is not the Chinese way.'

'Not even with someone who might share your firing squad?'

Foo laughed, but Cheng came back before he could reply. It had started to rain outside and his bedraggled clothes added to the gloom of his appearance. 'It is tonight, near here.' He sounded as if he was trying to convince himself. 'Your navy send helicopter.'

Sarah sensed his anxiety. 'So what's the *bad* news?'

'The army and police are all around. My friends believe Peking is determined to find us – and they still have at least twelve hours to do it.'

The admiral returned to Hong Kong that afternoon. His first action was to telephone Clayton and half an hour later they met at a spot near the Upper Aberdeen Reservoir, both driving themselves. Clayton arrived first and parked by the rippling grey water. When the American drove up, Clayton joined him in the front seat of the Chevrolet. 'Good trip, Erwin?'

'So-so. Washington are keen to use the Tenth October outfit as an intelligence source; they ain't so keen on us giving them aid and comfort – at least not till they're on the verge of winning anyway.'

'My people are more flexible but there's a lot of nervousness about upsetting the Chinese.'

'Yeah.' Erwin Smith lit a cigar and gestured at the barren hillside and cold sky. 'Miserable spot, this.' He pulled a flimsy piece of computer roll from a thin leather pouch. It was headed TOP SECRET – UMBRA, followed by a battery of symbols and numbers, then it turned into words with a number of gaps. 'Copy of an intercept made twenty-four hours ago – coded telegram from the New China News Agency here to Peking.'

Clayton whistled quietly. 'It's the text of the stuff we put together with Nick Roper and leaked to Thomas.'

'Just so. You still got watchers on the bastard?'

'Of course, but he's quite good at losing them.'

'I guess it'll soon be time to pull him in?'

'I agree, Erwin – just as soon as we've lifted out Foo and Cable.'

'That's still tonight?'

Clayton nodded.

'And who's in command?'

'The pilot is one of our marines called Carstens.'

'And does he know Foo and Cable are not to be left in China alive? Every effort to get them out, but if there's trouble . . .?'

Clayton gave a hard little smile. 'He has clear instructions.'

The frigate sailed as soon as it was dark, the Lynx lashed down on her aft deck and covered by canvas. Ralph Carstens, a sergeant and two other marines sat on the benches round the bulkheads of a nearby cabin, dressed in jeans, black tee-shirts and black canvas shoes. All British insignia had been removed from the helicopter and they would be wearing none. Their orders were to get back to the coast on foot if anything went wrong: only as a last resort should they turn themselves in and admit to being British special forces. They all carried sheathed knives, but four Heckler and Koch machine pistols, numerous magazines of ammunition and a variety of stun, smoke and combat grenades were already in the helicopter.

An oval steel door opened in the bulkhead and Nick Roper stepped in, balancing a tray of steaming mugs; he handed the coffee round and sat next to Carstens. The two men studied the map spread out on the wooden deck. It looked easy enough. Outside all lights were covered, except her navigation lights, as the frigate passed Stonecutters Island and headed out to sea. The rumble of the engines carried across the water, but the jagged black castle of her hull was already merging into the coast of China.

30

The coded short-wave message was relayed from Hong Kong to a butcher's shop in Hainan, to a teacher's house in Liuzhou and then carried to Cheng by hand. The pick-up was scheduled for between two and three in the morning. An hour after midnight Cheng drove Foo and Sarah about ten miles from the primitive farmstead, yellow headlamps criss-crossing an uneven track as the jeep yawed over potholes until he turned off and aimed at the crest of a low hill: a darker patch of blackness against a black sky, for there was no moon. The engine shrieked in pain as he engaged bottom gear, wheels spinning on loose gravel, then gripping and climbing slowly. Cheng stopped on a small plateau, checking his position with map and compass by the light of a torch. The three of them climbed out stiffly, gazing at a sea of darkness in every direction. 'Is this the right place?' whispered Sarah. 'How can you tell?'

'We have used before and I am here once in daylight.' Cheng pointed to another patch of darker darkness, a triangle against the sky a few miles away. 'That is Seven Dragon Peak and we are due west of it.'

Foo appeared beside them, clutching an empty sack round his shoulders against the cold. 'Will they find us?'

Cheng chuckled. 'Who? *Gonganbu* or your people?'

'The helicopter from Hong Kong.'

'I hope. I have infra-red lamp to guide. Tenth October not such amateur as maybe you thought.' He fumbled in a locker at the back of the old American Army jeep and pulled out a canvas satchel. A wind was rising, whistling eerily between the rocks and adding to the cold; Sarah and Foo got back in the jeep, pulled up the tattered canvas hood and huddled together in the darkness, sipping luke-warm green tea from a flask. Cheng crouched on a mound about ten yards away, fiddling with his lamps, teeth white as he smiled in the blackness.

Clayton and the admiral arrived in a long black Lincoln just after midnight. After a phone call, the sailors at the gate of *Tamar* allowed the car in, and directed the driver to a well-lit doorway a hundred yards away. The two men were met by a petty officer Wren, who led them down concrete steps to a communications room. The Wren had been in Mary Devereux's team and she knew who Clayton was: despite a smart salute the woman's icy distaste was almost tangible.

In the large underground chamber the atmosphere was as cold as the air conditioning. The dozen Wrens and ratings, faces reflecting pale green light from their flicker-ing computer screens, all knew that Mary Devereux had been cremated at Cape Collinson that afternoon, in a packed chapel with the service read by her widowed fa-ther, a bent old man in his late seventies who had paid his own fare to fly out. He had behaved with a simple dignity which, combined with a short address by one of Mary's sister officers, had left many of the normally hard-nosed naval congregation in tears.

At the end of the concrete bunker three officers stood by a wall-display of China lit from behind. A man in shirtsleeves, with a commander's three gold bars on his shoulder flaps, shook hands with the admiral and Clayton. He pointed to a red line that was appearing on the illumi-nated map, drawn by a hidden computer, starting out in the South China Sea and moving slowly north into China. 'The helicopter took off an hour ago, Mr Clayton, and should reach the RV in about fifty-five minutes. She's flying low, with muffled engines, and maintaining complete radio silence.'

'What's the weather like?'

'Cloudy – which is good because it means there is no moon. A bit windy, but basically just right for the operation.'

'Will they be able to find the place?'

'Should be quite easy. Lieutenant-Commander Roper went with them on the ship so that he and Carstens could compare the directions given by the Chinese with the configuration of the land when he could actually see it. They did a short flight together as far as the coast before Carstens left on the real thing.'

'Will there be some sort of lights to guide them down?'

'The Chinese say they have some infra-red lamps – impossible to see from the ground round about, but our fellows will pick them up with infra-red glasses.'

'Sounds fine.' The admiral looked questioningly at Clayton and the two men went into a huddle a little way from the others. The red line continued to inch northwards. 'Did Thomas get wind of any of this?'

'Just that it was happening, to maintain his credibility over there – and from the amount of military radio traffic between Liuzhou and Peking they'd already guessed that anyway. But no details – I want this to succeed. We've plenty of other stuff to hook comrade Ivor.'

'Is he a comrade, Gerry? Did they convert him or is it just blackmail?'

Clayton frowned, nodding meaningfully at the heads bent over computer screens all around. 'Just blackmail, I think. He cracked under questioning in Korea and they've held it over him ever since, but we can't discuss it here.'

'Should we stay?'

'Just until they've picked them up, I think – don't you, Erwin? I'll arrange some coffee.'

On the hilltop east of Liuzhou, Cheng and the two

fugitives huddled against the side of the jeep that was out of the wind; they had found the canvas hood too torn to provide much shelter. Cheng had set the three infra-red lamps in a triangle about twenty yards across, marking a flat patch of ground: they were switched on but the flashes were invisible to the naked eye. Thick cloud hid the moon. Occasionally there was a break that let through a shaft of grey light, picking out rolling hills in silver; but mostly there was nothing but darkness and silence all around.

Sarah felt Foo's arm round her and snuggled closer. 'God it's freezing. D'you really think they'll find us?'

'Before we all die of exposure? I bloody well hope so. This silence and lack of lights all around is suspicious – surely there must be a village or two out there?'

Sarah felt her body stiffen. 'You mean the army's closer than it looks?'

'I hope not, Sarah.'

She stood up slowly and peered into the blackness, pointing to the south. 'I suppose the sea is that way? I can't see anything moving on the ground. I can't see the helicopter either. Oh, Ben, are they really going to come?'

Sarah's watch showed 2.47 a.m. when she heard the faint noise of an engine under the whine of the wind. At first the whistling and gusting all around her made the sound come and go, but then it became a steady, muffled beat. 'That must be them,' she almost shouted in relief. 'Can you hear, Ben?' The three of them were standing up now, still huddled close together because of the wind, all peering into the darkness.

'Are the lamps still working?' Foo sounded edgy. Cheng snapped something in Cantonese that plainly meant *of course*. For about five minutes the low beat grew louder, but they could see nothing in the velvety blackness. Then the clouds let through a shaft of moonlight and

Sarah gripped Foo's arm, pointing to a tiny black shape moving across the sky.

Ralph Carstens studied the ground with the infra-red binoculars, leaving his sergeant in the right-hand co-pilot's seat to control the bucking helicopter. The powerful gusts of wind had slowed them down and made it difficult to keep on course; and the clatter of rotors made it impossible for the crew to speak to one another except through their chin-mikes and headphones. The other two marines were down in the hold, strapped against the sides as the steel floor jerked up and down when the rotors lost lift, then found it again. 'Down there.' Carstens' voice crackled urgently in all their headphones. 'About ten degrees to port. They're flashing from the top of a hill.'

'Can't see a bloody thing.' The sergeant had a thick Glaswegian accent. Beads of sweat stood out on his forehead as he struggled with the controls. 'Christ, this wind's strong! Can we use the searchlight yet?'

'In a couple of minutes.' Carstens addressed the corporal below. 'Duncan?' He waited for the crackling acknowledgement. 'When I give the order, be ready to focus the searchlight on a flat hilltop about ten degrees to port. Our passengers should be waiting there – I need it lit up before I can land.'

Forty seconds later he gave the order and the white beam raked across a hillside strewn with boulders, slashed by the dark shadows of gullies. The oval pool of light settled on an empty plateau at the top of the hill, picking out a black shape that must be the waiting jeep. 'We're there, chaps.' Ralph Carstens took the controls and the machine hovered. He issued orders tersely over the intercom. 'Open the door. Draw weapons. We're going down.' The Lynx started to descend, still bucking in the howling gusts of wind – the searchlight was waving about so much that it was almost impossible for Carstens to focus on the flat patch of land he had selected. 'I want to be off again in

twenty seconds, so get our passengers aboard as soon as
we touch. Then it's all lights out and back to the coast like
a bat out of hell. Is that understood?' He listened for the
three grunted acknowledgements then adjusted the stick
and continued to descend.

Each of the four men felt so tense that the descent
seemed to happen in slow motion, until suddenly the
helicopter bumped on the hilltop and a flurry of white dust
and white light shot up outside the cockpit windows. The
hold door was already open and the two young marines
crouched by it, one lowering a short ladder while the other
peered out clutching his machine pistol. Carstens
scrambled down the steps from the flight deck and joined
them. 'Where are they?' He could see nothing through the
glare of the machine's own searchlight so he switched it
off, jumped to the ground and ran a few paces into the
darkness. 'Miss Cable? Mr Foo?' he called urgently. 'Are
you there?' The words were snatched away by howling
wind and he shouted again, louder. 'Cable? Foo? Can you
hear me?' One of the marines slid down after him, canvas
shoes silent on the rock.

'Where the fuck are they, sir? What's gone wrong?'

In a lull between the gusts of wind the two men heard
Carstens' digital watch ping the hour: it was three o'clock.
They sensed clouds moving fast across the black sky as a
crack in them opened to reveal the moon. Pale grey light
picked out boulders and some figures about a hundred
yards away. 'Is that you, Foo?' called Carstens again.
'What the hell's holding you up? Are you hurt? Do you
need help to move?' There was a low whistle and suddenly
he was blinded as the whole world seemed to burst into
white flame. His black figure stood rigid with surprise as
three searchlight beams swept down with savage accuracy.

Carstens was still transfixed, shielding his eyes, when
the first volley of shots cut him down. As he fell he heard
shouts, the clatter of automatic weapons and the hammering of a heavy machine gun. A long tongue of yellow
flame lit up the edge of the plateau as someone fired a

bazooka, revealing helmeted figures clustered between the rocks; its warhead whined past and exploded in the helicopter's main engine, smashing the rotors and killing the co-pilot outright. The Lynx crackled into flames which spread hesitantly until they reached the fuel tanks. There was the thud of two explosions and the whole machine vanished in a roaring globe of orange fire.

The marine corporal knew that he was the only survivor as he knelt by Ralph Carstens, shielding his blackened face against the fierce heat: the lieutenant's shirt was soaked in blood and there was a bullet-wound in his face. The corporal struggled to his feet, throwing down his machine pistol and raising his hands, but there was no break in the firing. He screamed at the burst of pain as a dozen bullets tore into his chest and abdomen, tossing him backwards towards the blaze like a tailor's dummy. His clothes started to smoke and smoulder as red-hot ash floated down, but by then he was already dead.

31

It was barely three minutes after the first shots when a whistle blew again and firing ceased, leaving an over-powering smell of cordite and wraiths of blue smoke floating through the searchlight beams. The blaze in the centre of the plateau was already subsiding, leaving the black frame of the helicopter outlined by crackling lines of flame. A tall European and a Chinese officer emerged from behind a row of boulders. Luther pushed his flash-goggles up onto his helmet and the other man did the same. They advanced warily towards the wreckage, but it was plain that there were no survivors. Luther kicked over the first body with his boot. 'No uniform but obviously British or American.'

'I hope the film will develop well.' The officer was as wary of Luther as he was of the hot ash floating in the air. He had been astonished to find a European in the *Tewu*; and even more surprised that he had to take orders from Peking through him.

'It will.' Luther surveyed the scene in triumph, jubilant at another success that brought his final escape nearer. But openly he played the loyal servant of the state. 'You have done well, comrade! I shall see that your divisional commander is informed of that.' He sounded as if he meant it.

It was six in the morning before Clayton accepted that the rescue had failed. The admiral had stomped off to bed as soon as the helicopter failed to report a successful lift-off, taking the Lincoln and leaving Clayton to find a taxi back to his hotel. But Gerald Clayton stayed on hopefully; even when hope died he could not really believe it. The plan had been so simple – how could it go wrong, the kind of operation that had worked hundreds of times before? Were the marines dead or in jail? What had happened to Foo and Sarah? Confused and angry, he stared at the red line still cutting into the map of China, conscious of hostility all around. The whole communications room knew that four marines had been lost on a mission dreamed up by incompetent funnies. *Tamar* was sufficiently small for men and women sitting at the consoles only six feet away to know the men who had been in the helicopter, even though the operation was supposed to be secret: they played tennis with their wives, sent their children to the same schools. The funnies on the Peak were reaching a new level of unpopularity and the silver-haired chief funny was the pits. Even thick-skinned Clayton felt uncomfortable.

He left, fuming, at six thirty after a brief shouting match with Brimson, the captain of *Tamar*. Back in the Mandarin he flicked on the television before lying down for an hour's sleep. The early news from China showed massive food riots in some provincial city he had never heard of in Wuhan. He had seen it all before: students and workers with expressions of implacable hatred, teenagers with young, innocent faces screaming abuse and hurling bottles at official buildings – for the officials themselves were nowhere in evidence – then troops in olive-green helmets running at them swinging batons, retreating and firing live ammunition, not over the rioters' heads but straight into their bodies. The terrifying violence on both sides gave way to a repressive silence and empty squares littered with lifeless bundles of white soaked in blood.

Clayton's row with Paul Brimson had its result a few hours

later when Ivor Thomas arrived at his temporary office for the day's work. He left the crowded bus with relief, showed his pass at the main gate and hurried through the base shortly after eight thirty. The Portakabin on the quayside seemed curious quarters for a prospective captain with intelligence responsibilities, but he had not complained. Its security depended mostly on a large brass padlock. Thomas was surprised to find the padlock gone and the door open, but the shock came when he stepped inside. The cabin was already occupied by Brimson, in full uniform, and an exhausted looking civilian with prematurely grey hair.

Before Thomas could say anything Brimson rose and gestured him to sit down on a hard chair next to the desk. 'Good morning, Ivor, this is Mr Clayton from London. He wants to talk to you.' For the first time Ivor Thomas noticed a third person in the corner: another civilian who from his clothes might be an American. The sudden stress showed in Thomas's face as he sat down: his eyes looked downright scared and a vein stood out, throbbing on his forehead.

'I don't understand, Paul?' The captain did not respond to the too obvious use of his first name, looking straight through Thomas. 'What on earth's all this about?'

Brimson stood up again and the silver-haired civilian took his place behind the desk. He stared straight into Thomas's face, until the Welshman looked away awkwardly. 'Ivor, boyo.' He said it with heavy irony and a contemptuous mock-Welsh intonation. 'We want to talk to you, see. We think you've been a bad lad, Ivor. We think you're a nasty little shit who's let us all down.'

'I don't understand,' said Sarah again. 'Why did they land at the wrong place?' The three of them were still huddled by the jeep in the darkness, watching the blaze subside on a hilltop about three miles away. Half an hour before, they had watched in horror as the black shape of the helicopter swept down on the wrong hill – far too distant for their shouts to be heard – surrounded immediately by the red flashes of gunfire. The crash of explosions had followed seconds later, then the orange glow as the machine caught fire.

Benjamin Foo had a comforting arm round her shoulders. 'I don't understand either. Why did they land there? Why were the militia waiting? Unless *we* are in the wrong place?' There was an angry growl from Cheng. 'No. No, I'm sure we *are* in the right spot – and if we'd been over there we'd all be dead by now.'

Sarah was shivering from a mixture of cold, fear and exhaustion. 'What the hell do we do now?' Cheng returned to packing up his landing lights, a bent, defeated figure, silent and confused. It was Foo who made the decision.

'We must find some more petrol and head for the coast. When we see signs of the army or police we abandon the jeep and walk.' He called to Cheng in Cantonese and there was a muffled reply. 'He says we have enough fuel in the jerrycans for another two hundred miles. I hope he's right. I don't want to depend on the British *or* Tenth October – for the next forty-eight hours we'll win or lose on our own.'

The three of them climbed back in the jeep. This time Foo took the wheel, released the handbrake and they started to roll forward. The cloud had cleared and there was enough moonlight to weave between the boulders without switching on the lights. Nor did Foo start the engine, coasting down the dark hillside in silence. The three fugitives stared ahead tensely, without speaking. They had seen the strength of their pursuers only three miles away: how close were they now?

Nick Roper arrived back in Hong Kong at ten the next morning. He spent half an hour alone with Clayton and the admiral, but he knew even less than they. Once the helicopter had headed inland, the frigate had stood about twenty miles off the Chinese coast, steaming in a slow circle until *Tamar* admitted defeat and ordered her home. The locational beacon in the helicopter's tail had continued to transmit until after three in the morning, then suddenly stopped; there had been no radio message from Carstens.

After a couple of hours' sleep he joined Gatti in the naval base. The two of them spent much of the afternoon in a small office watching the interrogation of Ivor Thomas on closed-circuit television. He was in a room just down the corridor with Barnie Mason and a naval officer neither of them recognised. The three men sat round a table in shirtsleeves and Thomas looked a man on the run; his eyes were hunted but a transcript would show only a series of flat denials that he had ever had any dealings with Red China.

'This could go on for ever,' yawned Gatti. 'I'm worried about Sarah. What d'you think has happened to them?'

'I'm worried too. Foo will have to be darn clever to find a way out now, with the police and army so close to his tail. But there's nothing we can do – we don't know where they are and we've no way of finding out unless they use their Chinese friends' radio.'

'Foo and Sarah are too sensible to risk that. For my money they'll give Fred Karno's revolution a wide berth from now on.'

'And him?' Roper pointed at the small black and white television screen.

Gatti shrugged. 'He'll break. Don't you think so?'

'Maybe. It's a bit bloody late for Sarah and Foo.'

32

They drove non-stop through the night. Cheng guided the jeep through the spider's web of paved and dirt roads that make up China's communications, heading east instead of due south for the sea; he hoped this would reduce the chance of detection, for the army would expect them to go south, take the shortest route. Apart from that elementary precaution they abandoned attempts at concealment. The spymasters in Peking knew roughly where they were – the only hope was to move as fast as possible and hit the coast just east of Hong Kong.

Cheng was driving when they struck a long stretch of tarmac road and, for the first time, were able to move quickly, though still at barely sixty miles an hour. A line of shadowy lime trees at the roadside began to flash past with increasing speed in the dark. The narrow road stretched ahead in a straight line, empty except for the dim red tail-lights of a heavy lorry. After a few minutes they passed the lumbering truck and its cloud of diesel fumes, the jeep's engine roaring with effort, and sped on through a sleepy village, tyres drumming on rough cobbles, yellow headlights raking the long low shapes of one-storey huts.

Mostly they drove in silence, for the howl of wind tearing at the canvas hood was deafening. The rush of air snatched away the warmth of their bodies and the jeep had no heater; Sarah was shivering with cold when they hit a rough stretch again and had to slow down. For a few miles the road ran parallel to a railway; a long freight train was rattling by, drawn by a steam locomotive, and she envied the crew standing in the red glare from the firebox on the footplate. After three hours fingers of mauve and grey light started to clutch at the horizon. Cheng slowed down, bumped off the road and stopped in a grove of trees. 'We have come nearly two hundred mile. Now we sleep till is dark again.'

'You mean it's too risky to travel by day?' Sarah's heart sank; she had hoped they would reach the sea that night. 'Just where are we, Cheng? How much further do we have to go?'

Cheng searched for words, looking bewildered, then turned to Foo with a torrent of Chinese, speaking so fast that Sarah could not understand.

'He says it's about another hundred miles, Sarah. He's taking us in an arc to cross the Pearl river north of Canton, then striking south for the coast. The opposition has a cell between Swatow and Hong Kong and he's going to ask them to provide a boat for the last stretch.'

'Another *hundred miles*?' Foo could not see Sarah's face in the darkness but he knew she was aghast. 'How long will it take, Ben?'

There was another exchange and Sarah realised that she could understand even less because they had switched to Shanghai dialect. 'He says we can do it in one day.'

'Another day for them to find us.'

'It's a big country – that's a problem, but also an advantage. It makes it hard for them to guess where we are.'

'It still scares me, Ben. And where will we find petrol – and food – without giving ourselves away? We aren't in the mountains any more.'

'Cheng says there are sympathisers who can be relied on and will give us all we need. I think we must trust him.'

Sarah suddenly remembered Cheng Huiqing lying dead in the tunnel, this Cheng's lost family, the aura of sadness and courage that had struck her so forcibly when she first met him. They were both brave people, even if the sheer size and complexity of China often defeated them. 'Of course I'll trust him,' she said quietly.

*   *   *

In Hong Kong the next day was a nightmare of suspicion and fear. Roper and Gatti spent a lot of time together, frustrated at there being nothing useful for them to do. The shoot-up of the helicopter near Liuzhou had not been reported in the Chinese press, but intercepts of People's Liberation Army radio traffic confirmed that the crew had all been killed. They also suggested that Foo and Sarah had escaped, though it was not clear how.

Clayton had gone back to London leaving Rumbelow's deputy – grey Barnie Mason, the man nobody knew – as acting head of station. Mason was thirty-five and only six months in Hong Kong, so he had difficulty preventing the admiral treating him as an office-boy. Perhaps for that reason, in between joining the sessions questioning Ivor Thomas he vanished into his grand new office and dealt with other problems where the CIA was less involved. He finally called a meeting of the Scorpion team late in the afternoon. Nick Roper picked up Gatti in his rented Toyota. The suburban street in Stanley bustled with amahs bringing children home from school and returning from shopping, oblivious to the dragon waking on the mainland, the hapless Westerners being dragged inexorably into chaos they could not control. As they drove across the centre of the island Roper thrust a newspaper at Gatti; it was that day's *Standard*, open at page seven.

Gatti glanced at the short piece announcing the execution of two terrorist saboteurs in Peking. A smudgy photograph showed two figures, man and woman, contorted by arms bound behind them and pulled tight at the elbow, standing in a lorry with half a dozen armed police. They had been shot in public, said the report, on a rubbish tip near the edge of the city. 'I'm certain the one on the left is Tang Tsin,' said Roper.

'I'm sorry.'

'I guess he had a rough time – he probably wasn't sorry to go. He looks very calm in that photograph, unafraid. But I wish I'd recognised the danger; I *could* have got

231

him out before he was arrested.'

'Don't blame yourself, Nick. He knew the risk he was taking – he wanted to do it.' Gatti glanced down at the white skyscrapers of the mid-levels and the harbour glowing with evening sun. 'Poor bastard – I wonder what he told them before he died.'

'So do I.'

Sarah and Foo spent a long day hidden in a barn somewhere north of Canton: they had given up worrying about exactly where they were. The jeep was concealed under a heap of branches and straw. There was no farm or village in sight, but Cheng went off for several hours and returned with a can of petrol and a bag of boiled rice. At dark they set out again along busier roads, passing wobbling bicycles and trucks of farm produce.

They had driven about fifty miles when they breasted a hill and saw a cluster of lights ahead. Cheng reacted at once, signalled left and turned down a rough track shielded by bamboo. He stopped when they were out of sight and crept back to the road with Foo. Peering through the bamboo they could see a line of waiting vehicles, their headlights shining on a red and white barrier, uniformed figures and two cars with flashing blue lamps. 'Is that always there, or are they looking for us?' Foo spoke very softly for the checkpoint was only a hundred yards away.

'It is for us. We must leave jeep and walk.' Cheng spoke in Shanghaianese, relieved from his painful efforts to speak English to Sarah, whose Cantonese he found equally painful. 'Come.' They returned to the track and he drove the vehicle a mile or so further from the highway, then turned into a boggy area of mud, reeds and bamboo. It sank up to its axles and they piled on vegetation to conceal it.

The three of them stood back and looked at each other: 'Maybe they won't find it for a few days?' Foo sounded doubtful.

'What about *us*?' It had started to rain and Sarah's shirt was already soaking through.

'Cheng will guide us on paths away from the main roads and find us a boat – we must go on trusting him.'

'Sure.' Sarah sneezed violently. 'It's not trusting him that's the problem, Ben, it's feeling that I may die of exposure any minute; I don't know how you manage to stay so cheerful. At least being in jail might be warm and dry.' She felt the old man's arm around her and his coat being placed over her shoulders. 'No, you mustn't do that.'

He chuckled in the dark. 'We will share it.' Cheng was already a black shape six feet ahead, leading them down another farm track, then swaying along the dyke between empty paddy fields.

Ivor Thomas was equally tired, hunched at the bare table in a soiled white shirt that stank of sweat. He was seeing double in the glaring white light, exhausted from the hours of questioning by different faces half hidden in shadow. It was dark outside and he desperately wanted to lie down and sleep; his depression turned to despair when he saw that the team was changing again. The man he knew as Mason had come back. The others left the room.

'You must be tired.' His tormentor offered him a cigarette. Thomas shook his head but then took it and inhaled as Mason lit it with his lighter; he rarely smoked but it was something to do with his shaking hands. 'Look, Ivor, I have a problem – somehow Red China has got an agent in here and I believe it's you.' He held up a hand. 'No, don't say anything yet. Whatever happened in Korea all those years ago I'm sure you didn't seek it. I think they found a way of putting pressure on you, that's all, and I guarantee you won't be subject to any criminal charge if you come clean. It could happen to any of us, but I must *know*, Ivor . . . '

Thomas slumped back in his chair, eyes opaque in a

grey face. 'I've told all of you the truth . . . I broke when they interrogated me – there was no torture or anything but they threatened it, and told me I'd be shot. I was scared stiff and told them everything about the attempt to rescue Kang-Hong Cho.' His eyes pleaded for reassurance. 'Hell, they knew everything already, so what harm did it do?'

'Then why did they release you and lock up Joe Zimmermann for ten years?' There was a cutting edge to Mason's question, though his tone was still gentle.

'I don't know.'

'Did *you* blow Zimmermann?'

'I agreed he was an officer in naval intelligence, not a rating just sailing the boat, but I felt they knew it already.'

'When you were released, why did you say Zimmermann was dead?'

'They *told* me he was dead.'

'How? He was alive when you were captured.'

'They said he tried to escape from the camp and was shot by the guards.'

'Did you believe them?'

'Yes.'

'It never occurred to you that he was still alive? That you'd dropped him right in it?'

'No, it didn't. Really it didn't.' For the first time Thomas started to weep. 'Okay, I'm a coward – I was totally ashamed afterwards, couldn't face it, hated myself. I'm sorry – I just don't know why it happened.'

'I don't believe you.' Mason gestured to the corridor outside. 'An innocent woman hanged herself down there, Thomas, because we mistook her for you.' His expression became threatening, full of contempt as he leant back in his chair, lighting another cigarette; this time he did not offer one. 'You're not helping yourself, you know. I can wait all night if I have to, we've got all the time in the world, but I want the truth.' Suddenly he was shouting. 'The truth, Ivor, the *truth*.'

Thomas slumped forward on the table, his head lolling

on his arms, shoulders heaving, snuffling noisily. 'It *is* the bloody truth.' His voice was hollow, muffled by his arms, almost inaudible. 'Can't you see that *I'm* bloody innocent too?'

PART THREE

HONG KONG

33

Sarah and Foo covered the last fifty miles on foot. That first night they walked about half of it, leaning on each other in exhaustion behind the shadowy figure of Cheng. At dawn they lay down in a grove of creaking bamboo, on the edge of a chessboard of paddy fields – some covered in water, some dry – and remained hidden there all day. During the morning a few women in loose black smocks and trousers came to plant rice shoots, packed bright green in a handcart, but no one came near the bamboo. The three fugitives had nothing to eat, but there was still water in Cheng's bottle. Most of the day Sarah dozed restlessly. At one point she woke to see Cheng still kneeling upright, eyes flickering as he kept watch, first in one direction then the other. 'Where are we?' she asked drowsily.

'Somewhere east of Canton. Sleep, Sarah. I will wake you if there is danger.'

With the darkness they set off again. Fortunately there was no moon – the enveloping darkness gave a sense of security as Cheng guided them for mile after mile through narrow lanes and along the dykes between paddies, water lapping under their feet. After the first hour it started to rain, which made running into frontier patrols less likely, and all three of them were soaked. They finished the journey squelching through mud, wet clothes clinging to their bodies, stumbling with weariness as Cheng switched on the yellow beam of his torch to find the track down to an empty beach.

'Where are we?' asked Sarah again.

'On coast west of Swatow.'

'And what time is it?' whispered Foo. His teeth were chattering and he sounded ready to drop; for the first time he was showing his age.

Cheng looked at his watch in the torchlight, then switched it off. 'About five in morning.'

'Are you sure this is the right spot – where your friends will pick us up?' Somewhere north of Canton Cheng had made a call from a public phone at the roadside. He said that a boat would pick them up and take them to Hong Kong, but Foo was sceptical; everything Cheng touched seemed to crumble to dust. The doubt in his voice was impossible to conceal. 'Will they be able to *find* us?'

'It is right place,' snapped Cheng angrily. 'But there is bitter wind and we must find shelter or we shall all die of exposure.' The three of them padded across the sand until they came to a fall of rocks and huddled against them out of the wind and rain. It was painfully cold and they could see nothing in the dark except the occasional flicker of a white breaker crashing on the shore. The torch was not used again and they did not speak. They had been incredibly lucky in not encountering a single human being since midnight and Cheng was determined not to blow it. Pressed up against him for a little warmth, Sarah could feel the tension in his frame as he stared out to sea. Whatever he might have arranged, if a fisherman or coastal patrol chanced on them now they would be finished.

Luther knew that he *was* finished. Even if Scorpion survived, even if Sarah and Foo were recaptured, he had lost the minister's confidence. After the ambush of the helicopter he had expected Foo and Cable to be picked up within hours. When he realised they had escaped, Luther knew that the vile little man would never trust him again; it was one failure too many. Nerving himself for survival he had left Josie in the lakeside house at Hangzhou and returned directly to Peking.

Pacing up and down the suburban apartment, he hated the mean little room with its plain wooden furniture; but his options did not look too bad. He had funds in Hong Kong and six different passports to travel on. All he had to do was get out – and vanish. The Chinese would be apoplectic and determined to stop him talking to Western intelligence agencies; they would not hesitate to send a killer after him. But for years now he had rented a back street apartment in Causeway Bay as his personal safe house: a night or two in hiding and then – where? He favoured Western Australia. He would fly to Perth, get a one-month visa on arrival and then ask for settlement – he had nearly two hundred thousand US dollars and would claim to be starting his own business. In fact he *would* be starting one, industrial espionage perhaps or security *against* industrial espionage – that was almost respectable. The only outstanding problem was Josie; would the Australians let her in? He was deciding that they would bloody well have to when the telephone rang.

It was the minister – no secretary to put him through, but the man himself, angry and spluttering. Luther imagined the piggy eyes popping with fury behind thick lenses, sweat pouring down his face. There were no preliminaries, none of the usual courtesies, just a curt order. 'I must talk to you at once, come, now.' The line went dead and Luther felt a sickening tremor of fear. It was a moment of truth, a quarter century of trust suddenly shattered, and instinctively he saw the choice between survival and going under. If he went to Qiao Shi's headquarters he would not return. They would arrest him and investigate his failures, probably accuse him of treachery rather than incompetence. If he did not go they would send a squad of soldiers to arrest him within hours. He could not telephone Josie because it would be tapped;

anyway the lines were dreadful and it could take an hour to get a call connected. He had to walk out of that apartment and out of the country now, at once, without being recognised. There was no other choice.

Luther kept a West German passport in the name of Hans Richter hidden under a loose floorboard in the bedroom, together with a bottle of dye that could turn his hair black and make him look like a different man. He burnt his Swedish passport in the living room stove, breaking up the ashes with a poker to leave no trace – his other travel documents were all hidden in Hong Kong – and smeared on the hair dye in the shower room. When he left the apartment he descended the stairs to the door into the backyard that housed the garbage containers, sensing that he was unobserved. Any watcher would be at the front – where the lights in his apartment were still blazing and his Skoda was parked – and with luck they would not expect him to move so fast. The money he needed was distributed in bundles of notes around his pockets and he carried no luggage as he started the long walk to the central bus station. Twenty-four hours ago he had been driven from Shoudu in a government car with a chauffeur; now he was a fugitive on the streets.

On the beach near Swatow it had stopped raining but the icy wind cut through wet cotton and Sarah could not stop shivering. Foo and Cheng crouched on each side of her, gazing out to sea in the dark. No one had come near them; the only sign of life had been the navigation lights of junks trembling silently across the water, bat-wing sails the faintest of black shadows against the inky purple of the night sky. At the first light of dawn the wind dropped and thick mist descended, blocking the sea from view, bands of grey fog swirling around them like phantoms. 'Will the boat still find us in this?' Sarah was too cold and miserable to conceal her anxiety. Cheng did not reply and they relapsed into silence. Sarah felt more afraid than she ever had on the run – if the boat didn't show, they would be sitting ducks in the harsh light of morning, a Westerner and two strangers on an exposed beach and all high on the police wanted list.

Luther took the boldest way out, an empty night bus from the city centre straight to Shoudu where he bought a one-way ticket for Hong Kong. The concourse was quiet, a few passengers huddled on benches waiting for the first flights of the morning. His hands were sweating and his mouth dry when he approached emigration control, pushing his passport and ticket under the glass as naturally as possible. Were there more guards about than usual? Only a few yards away two young soldiers yawned as they pointed their Kalashnikovs at the floor, eyes tired under green caps, feet shuffling in the cheap canvas sneakers that made all army and militia other ranks scruffy these days.

The bored young man in the control booth flicked the pages of Hans Richter's passport sightlessly and stamped a page at random. Luther went on to the next hurdle, the security check. Would his lack of luggage attract suspicion?

As it grew lighter on the beach Cheng started to become agitated. He was at the water's edge, peering out to sea; on the beach above him Sarah and Foo huddled together like spare parts, unable to do anything useful, still freezing in their wet clothes. Sarah found Foo's oriental calm reassuring, his arm round her shoulders comforting; but the strain of the last few days had taken a toll. His face was grey with fatigue. Sometimes Cheng was hidden by the fog, sometimes visible in swirling chasms jumping about like a grasshopper. Sarah could see that he too was getting scared, fearful that the plan had failed. After trekking halfway across China, constantly tense and living on her nerves, she felt like weeping.

When the soft scraping sound came, followed by splashes and the crunch of boots on sand, her eyes were half-closed and at first she did not notice. It was Foo that brought her back to the present. 'They are here, Sarah!' He leapt up, pulling her with him, suddenly alive again. 'Move. For God's sake move! This fog may give us just enough time to be out of sight before daylight, but it will be touch and go.'

Suddenly she saw that there were three figures on the beach with Cheng. She had been expecting a sampan or fishing boat, but they were hauling a large rubber inflatable out of the sea. As the mist drifted round it she could see two outboard engines, swung up so the propellers would not foul – they were a curious square shape, must be muffled in kapok-lined boxes. One of the figures approached, all in black like a devil in a mystery play: wet suit, balaclava, even the tiny patches of skin round his eyes and mouth had been blackened. Only his eyes and teeth shone white. The eerie effect was lessened by the soft Yorkshire accent. 'You Foo and Cable?' Sarah stared at him in amazement. 'What the hell's the matter? I said *are you Foo and Cable*?'

Sarah pulled herself together. 'Yes. Yes, we are – but I was expecting someone Chinese?'

'Sorry if you're disappointed.'

'I don't understand.' Foo was already dragging her towards the boat, glancing anxiously at the sky.

'Your Chinese friend got a message through to Hong Kong. He arranged this – didn't he tell you? Just get in the inflatable and do exactly as I say. We're bloody pushed for time.'

Cheng was running beside them, grinning broadly. 'You see – we *can* do it! We learn from mistake. Tell them in Hong Kong we learn to destroy communist too. Tell them, Sarah!'

Sarah nodded in confusion, clinging to Foo. Standing in the breaking waves Cheng shook hands with them both and bowed politely as they clambered into the boat.

'Good luck!' he shouted through the wind. 'Tell them we are serious, tell them to help!' Sarah and Foo crouched on the planks in the bottom of the inflatable, feeling icy water swill around them and a wave sweep in under the rubber skin: the boat reared up and the three marines pushed it out to sea, rolling over the side in a practised manoeuvre. They started to paddle vigorously and one of them started the engines, which made a low popping sound – the muffling worked.

'I'm Cartwright, sergeant SBS,' shouted the man who had spoken to them on the beach. He tossed two thick anoraks at them. 'Put these on, it's fucking cold out there.' Sarah felt a warm fleecy lining as she pulled the thing over her head. Looking back she saw Cheng still standing at the water's edge, one arm raised in farewell as he watched them vanish into the mist. Would he manage to stay free?

She gave him only a fifty/fifty chance and felt a surge of tearful emotion. In his quiet, determined way he had saved her life – and Foo's. They had left in such a hurry that there had not even been time to say thank you.

34

Luther sat in the departure lounge undisturbed for nearly three hours, at first suffering agonies of fear every time an armed patrol passed, gradually realising that either the search had not reached the airport or his disguise was intact. His flight finally took off from Shoudu at seven in the morning. Looking down through the oval window of the old Ilyushin he saw the golden roofs of the Forbidden City glinting in morning sun, the vivid blue of the Temple of Heaven, the green park and lake around the Summer Palace at Wanshou Shan. It was incredibly beautiful and had been part of his life for thirty years. He would never see it again. At least he hoped not.

Fifteen minutes from land the South China Sea was distinctly choppy. The inflatable yawed sickeningly as it slid into the trough between waves and Sarah began to feel queasy. She was huddled against Foo in the icy water that slopped about in the bottom of the boat, while the three servicemen crouched around them; the Yorkshireman called Cartwright was steering. It was so uncomfortable that she felt quite relieved when the low popping of the engines died and the switchback motion gradually ceased. She sat up and turned to Cartwright. 'Why have you stopped?'

'Get down,' he hissed.

'But what – ?' As she felt his hand on her head, pushing it down sharply, she also saw the high side of the fishing junk about a hundred yards away. They had almost run into her in the mist but a puff of wind had suddenly cleared a passage between them. The junk was moving slowly, a long trawl net dragging behind her, and two figures stood on the high stern. They were speaking in a Hakka dialect she did not understand but she could hear them clearly. 'Oh God,' she breathed. 'If they turn round they'll see us.'

Cartwright dropped beside her. 'For Christ's sake keep *quiet*!' The inflatable rolled behind a wave and the junk vanished. 'If we all keep down they may miss us.' But the fishing boat reappeared giddily as spray dashed in their faces and Sarah saw that Cartwright was silently taking off the safety catch on his machine pistol; so were the others.

By midday Luther had landed at Kai Tak and reached Causeway Bay by a series of criss-crossing taxi, underground railway and minibus journeys. When he closed the door of the small apartment behind him, he was confident that he had not been followed. The flat was on the sixth floor of an old block near the Tin Hau Temple, occupied by a constantly changing spectrum of Europeans. He had rented it five years ago as a bolthole for this moment and no one knew of its existence, apart from Josie.

There was one living room furnished with just two armchairs and a television set, bedroom with a single bed, bathroom and kitchen with a cupboard full of tinned food. He left the fridge switched off when he wasn't there, but now plugged it in and the apartment filled with a quiet hum. When he lit a Gitane and stood at the window, shielded by dusty net curtains, looking down at the teeming crowds and traffic, he felt anonymous, safe. Breathing out a ring of pungent blue smoke he turned on the television, flicking the press-button switches until he found an English-speaking station.

Luther lay back in one of the armchairs and made a mental list of things to do. He would telephone his banks and get most of the funds transferred to Australia, but ask for ten thousand dollars in cash, to be drawn from a Hong Kong and Shanghai branch two blocks away. Getting a flight to Perth would be no problem. The problem was Josie. He wanted her with him, but she was in Hangzhou; for the first time it occurred to him that she might have been arrested but he brushed the thought aside. She would be safe enough – she was a citizen in her own right, had her own track record as an agent – but how could he contact her safely? How could he get her out?

The sound on the television was turned down low; it was a news bulletin and the presenter, a stunning Eurasian woman, mouthed at him silently like a goldfish in a bowl. Luther studied the screen vaguely, his thoughts on Josie. The announcer sitting at a studio desk was replaced by jerky film of a riot in China, the picture tipping giddily from side to side as if the cameraman had been hit by a missile. The newscaster was on screen again, then abruptly replaced by a black and white mugshot that looked familiar. Luther's musing was interrupted by an acute sense of shock. He was looking at his own face. He fell on his knees in front of the set and turned up the volume. ' . . . *German-born Manfred Luther,*' the presenter had adopted a grave tone, '*probably travelling on a forged Swedish passport in the name of Ulf Ericsson, escaped from custody in Peking while awaiting trial on charges of trading in heroin to the value of three million Hong Kong dollars. He is known to the Chinese authorities as a long-term drug trafficker and is now believed to be in Hong Kong. Anyone sighting him should contact the Royal Hong Kong Police at . . . *' The voice gave a phone number and the Eurasian newscaster was back on screen.

Luther sank back in his chair breathing heavily, stunned, angry but above all scared. He felt even greater fear than he had in Peking. The bastards! How had they discovered the details of his false passport? How on earth did they know where he was? Then he gave a twisted smile at the irony of them trying to use the Hong Kong authorities to turn him in.

For Sarah and Foo the voyage back to Hong Kong passed quietly once they had drifted past the fishing junk and the outboards were started again. At twenty miles offshore they were wet and freezing, but a naval patrol boat was at the rendezvous and picked them up. They settled down in two bunks below deck and went to sleep. A young sailor woke them with hot coffee just as they entered Hong Kong harbour in mid-morning, sun blazing on the water, ferries darting between Central and Kowloon, the Peak glittering with white tower blocks but with a halo of mist at the top. Sarah swung her legs off the bunk with a feeling of immense relief and was ushered up to the quay with Foo.

She kissed him – 'We made it, Ben; thanks' – and found herself in the back of a car driven by a naval rating that sped towards her flat in MacDonnell Road. For some reason Foo was taken off in another direction, but she still felt too exhausted to question why. It took only a few minutes to reach the block, where the driver – not a rating after all but a petty officer by his uniform, with an intelligent lined face – took her up to the apartment. She felt puzzled that he had a key, then annoyed that he seemed to be planning to stay.

'Someone from your office is coming round to talk to you, Miss, but they thought you'd like time to have a bath and relax first. There's some food in the refrigerator. Would you like me to make coffee?'

'I can do it myself thanks – this is my place you know.' She glanced meaningfully towards the door.

He understood. 'I'm sorry, Miss. My orders are to stay.'

'To stay? Why?'

'To guard you, Miss.'

'Am I in danger then?' Or was she under some sort of suspicion? Even under arrest? What the hell was going on?

'I think it's just routine, Miss.' But he settled on the sofa near the door and took off his uniform jacket. She saw that he was wearing a pistol in a shoulder holster – he was not going to let her leave until someone gave the word. In her bedroom she picked up the phone, but it had been disconnected.

Like Sarah, Benjamin Foo was puzzled by his reception. He was hustled away into a different car – also driven by a petty officer who was plainly not normally employed as a chauffeur – and found himself zig-zagging up the Peak. He felt irritated at being treated in this way: after all he and Sarah had been through, there was something unpleasant at not being greeted as friends and colleagues. Their reception had been cold, impersonal – and planned. It implied some kind of mistrust: it left a bad taste in his mouth. He was still searching for a reason when the car passed through an entrance in a high wall; looking back he saw steel gates closing behind him.

The building was a white villa looking over the harbour, with a modern annexe half-hidden in the trees and a high radio mast. Two young women were sitting on the grass drinking plastic beakers of coffee. He remembered it as one of the buildings on the Peak used by the CIA. A stocky man, plainly a serviceman but in civilian clothes, opened the car door and guided Foo inside, through a cool tiled hall and into an office. Rosewood desk and conference table, book-lined walls, the Stars and Stripes with a gold fringe mounted on a stand in the corner – the trappings of a senior American official anywhere in the world. Two men were in low conversation at the window; they turned to face him. Foo recognised one as the head of the CIA station, Admiral Erwin Smith: small, foxy-faced, unsmiling. The other was a stranger, tall, silver-haired but only in his forties. The pin-stripe suit was impeccable: a man taking a lot of trouble to look distinguished. He had eyes that were both cold and shifty – Foo instinctively neither liked nor trusted him.

'Please sit down.' The admiral's slow Carolina speech was friendly, reassuring, but Foo didn't trust him either. 'We're sorry you've had such a rough time.' They sat in a circle of leather armchairs, looking out on a lawn watered by sprinklers. It was like a corner of some plush oriental club. 'I represent the American government, name's Smith.' No mention of his real position. 'This is Mr Gerald Clayton from England.' The silver-haired man smiled with all the sincerity of a crocodile.

Suddenly Foo felt threatened. 'What has happened to Mr Rumbelow?'

'He is on leave.' That was absurd in the thick of a crisis.

'I should like to speak to Sir David Nairn.'

'Nairn has had a heart attack.' Clayton looked suitably grave. 'He is in hospital in London.'

Foo's suspicion deepened. 'And Mr Roper? Commander Gatti?'

'Roper is on a mission to Tokyo for two days. Gatti is on the same mission.'

Foo nodded. They seemed to have carefully removed every other British or American member of the team he had been dealing with – for God's sake, *why*? Something very odd was going on. But openly he remained relaxed. 'I am sorry to hear about David Nairn and will phone his wife later.' He looked at them expectantly. Clayton must be very senior in SIS, the little admiral was the head of the CIA station: it was up to them to make the running.

Clayton had a strange manner, half-ingratiating, half-brusque. 'We deeply regret that Miss Cable placed you in danger. It was absurd for her to travel to China under flimsy tourist cover, absurd for a woman to go at all.' He spoke as if dictating a memo.

Foo held up his hand. 'One moment, I do not understand what is going on, I do not understand what you are saying. It is my recollection that Sarah herself had grave doubts about going to China, where a white woman was bound to attract attention in the provinces – but she was *ordered* to go by Rumbelow.'

Clayton shook his head sadly. 'I fear not. But that is now an internal disciplinary matter. We are dealing with it.'

'But I am sure Miss Cable is not at fault. She is a very brave young woman – and a fine intelligence officer.'

Clayton gave him a pitying smile. 'It is generous of you to stand up for her.' What a bloody patronising bastard the man was, thought Foo. 'It is only what I would expect – but regrettably I am quite clear as to the truth.'

Before Foo could recover from his astonishment and reply, the admiral added, 'No more to be said, Mr Foo. We have something more important to discuss, far more important.'

Foo realised there was no point in pursuing it – if Sarah was being fitted up by these two, he would have to go somewhere else to defend her. He must appear co-operative. He nodded at them impassively. 'How may I help you?'

There was a long silence. 'Scorpion,' said the admiral finally. 'We have identified Scorpion.'

Foo's eyes narrowed. He felt a sudden knot in his stomach. 'You mean this time you really *know*? After all those false starts?' There was silence in the room. Through the window the panorama of the harbour seemed suddenly frozen – the ferries not moving on the water, white wakes behind them apparently still, like the vapour trails of jets in a high blue sky.

Clayton's eyes fixed him. 'Yes, Foo. This time we know.'

35

Sarah took a long bath, dressed in jeans and sweat shirt and sat on her balcony drinking lukewarm coffee. To save time at her debriefing she made some notes on the nightmare journey across China with Foo; but as three hours passed with painful slowness, she began to wonder if anyone was going to bother to turn up. On the sea crossing from Swatow she had felt exhausted – physically worn out and drained emotionally – but she was recovering rapidly. She wanted to see Nick, to report to someone from the Peak, to telephone Nairn, to get out of the claustrophobic flat. By midday she was fuming with frustration. She stomped into the living room and confronted the guard, who had told her to call him 'Brad'. It seemed a most unlikely name for someone who looked like a rugger-playing grandfather with firm right-wing convictions. 'Look here,' she snapped. 'I can't go on like this. There are people I must telephone, I ought to be reporting to my office. Anyway,' her tone became almost pleading, 'I'm going crazy locked up in here. I *must* go for a walk.'

Brad shook his head. 'Sorry, Miss, you can't leave the apartment.' He had hard little eyes and squared his shoulders showing just the slightest hint of his underlying strength. 'Please don't make it difficult for us.'

'But you've no *right* to keep me here. It's not *legal*. I'm not in the navy and I'm not under arrest or anything. Or am I?'

'Not so far as I know, Miss. My orders are to keep you here, that's all.' He settled down again.

Sarah slumped in an armchair, quietly resolving to slip out when he had to relieve himself – he had been sitting there for nearly four hours and surely couldn't last for ever? When the moment arrived and he vanished into the bathroom, she tiptoed to the door and released the catch, but the oblong of solid oak stayed firmly in place. She tugged at the door but it still wouldn't open. Then she saw a new brass keyhole low in the edge; someone had fitted a mortice lock in her absence. Horrible Brad had a key but she did not.

The door of Ivor Thomas's cell was opened that morning by a young man he had never seen before. He had an open face and his smile was friendly enough but – like Sarah's jailer – someone had chosen him for the strength that rippled under his well-cut suit. 'Captain Wells, sir,' he said briskly. 'Royal Marines.'

Thomas was still wearing crumpled fatigues as he rose stiffly from his bunk smelling of dried sweat. He yawned. 'What the hell do you want?'

'My orders are to escort you to London, sir. We are booked on an RAF transport from Kai Tak later this afternoon. If you would give me your word as a fellow officer not to – ' he looked embarrassed ' – not to try to abscond, sir – well, then we can dispense with any other escort.'

Thomas's face had lost its floridness in confinement, but he still went purple with anger. 'Why should I give you my word about anything? Tell me that! I've been locked up here for God knows how long, without any charge, without even being formally under arrest. I've been subject to humiliating questions for days on end and I still haven't a clue what's really going on.' He sat down on the bunk again. 'As I've said before, I demand to speak on the phone to Sir John Rusbridger in London. That's my *right*.'

The young marine sat down beside him. 'I'm sorry, sir, that isn't possible.' Although he was ten years younger, he made to put a comforting arm round the other man's shoulders but it was shaken off crossly. 'Your orders are to return to London under escort.'

'And what happens then?' Suddenly Thomas's eyes pleaded with him for reassurance. The rear-admiral's gold stripes, the Georgian house in Tavistock with the huge outstanding mortgage, the respect he had always craved but never earned: all were vanishing fast. He knew he was facing disgrace and again felt the naked fear he had experienced in Korea and under interrogation these last few days. 'For Christ's sake, what happens then?'

The marine looked away in embarrassment. 'I honestly don't know.' This time he didn't bother with 'sir'. 'And I shouldn't discuss it. But I've been in security some time – I expect they'll retire you on a reduced pension.' That was what Clayton had ordered him to say: *See if he buys it. I want him to be desperate to accept by the time he reaches London, to avoid the humiliation of a court martial. Of course, we couldn't really try him – he hasn't actually committed a crime – but we must get him out of the navy, lose the bastard. We nailed him for the wrong reason, but he's no longer credible as an officer, let alone a commander; he's an embarrassment.* The marine added confidingly: 'I shouldn't resist it, you know, sir. It's better than a court martial.'

Thomas nodded dumbly. He was frightened and confused. 'Can I get cleaned up and put on some decent clothes?' His face was streaked and blotchy. 'Don't want to be seen like this.' He sat down again, head in his hands. 'Don't worry.' Suddenly his shoulders heaved like a child's. 'I won't give you any trouble.'

Sarah had never spoken to Rumbelow's deputy, the grey Mason, except on the phone so she was taken aback when he arrived in her apartment at three in the afternoon. But she recovered quickly and flew at him in fury. 'Look – whoever you are – what the devil d'you mean by this? I'm a regular officer in SIS, just back after being placed in intolerable danger by an incompetent superior. I've got vital things to report, I've got personal things to do and no one has any right to lock me up like this!' Mason started to speak but she cut him short. 'No, I haven't finished – you bloody well listen to *me*! I've nothing to say to you until I'm free to come and go from here as I please. If I need a guard put him outside and take away his key. It's *my* front door and my bloody flat, or have you all forgotten?'

Mason brushed past her, out to the balcony, and sat down heavily. The air-conditioned room was cool but outside it was almost steaming with humidity. 'Okay, okay! For Christ's sake stop shouting – do you want the whole block to hear?'

'I couldn't give a damn. I'm being treated like some kind of criminal – how do you expect me to react?'

He pointed sharply to the plastic chair beside him. 'Just shut up and sit down. That's an order.'

She obeyed. 'Well?'

'I'm sorry about all the mystery. A lot has happened while you were in China. Nairn had a heart attack – '

Sarah went white. 'Oh God, no, how is he? Is he – ?'

'No, he's not dead. He's in Charing Cross Hospital and recovering well. Making a thorough nuisance of himself. But Clayton is acting head of the service and he's out here right now, determined to bring all this to an end.'

'Clayton? I knew he'd get there one day. How awful.'

Mason shrugged and gave the faintest of smiles. 'I suppose he gets everyone's prize for Shit of the Year, but for the moment he's the boss and at least he's being decisive. Rumbelow has been suspended and returned to England – I don't think we'll be seeing him again.'

'Good Lord. Poor Tom.'

Mason shrugged again. 'A switched-off head of station can be dangerous as well as inefficient – look how he dropped *you* in it.'

He was as ruthless as Clayton, thought Sarah; she hoped he was as clever. Aloud she said: 'It's still a rotten way to end – I suppose he'll be kicked out a year early?'

'I imagine so. He's not much of a loss. But let me explain about you – it's quite simple. Clayton's bringing the Scorpion thing to a head and he just wants to keep you out of danger – he'd have come himself but he's debriefing Foo first.'

'Why can't he debrief us together?'

'I really wouldn't know.'

'And why should I be in danger – what's happened to everyone else? Nick? Bob Gatti?'

'It was Nick who pressed for you to be lifted out from China – and organised it, both the abortive attempt by helicopter and last night's successful one.'

'Yes, that was amazing. I'm still confused – how did it happen?'

'The dissidents have a guy in Hong Kong at the moment, one Ling Boda. He got a message saying you'd be on that beach at five this morning – and, by God, you were.'

'Maybe I've been misjudging them – I thought they were a joke.'

Mason shook his head. 'So did I, but I'm getting more convinced.'

'Are Nick and Bob around?'

'So far as I know.'

Sarah looked wistful. 'If I've got to stay here, it would be nice to see a friendly face.'

'I'll tell them – there's no reason why you shouldn't have visitors.'

Sarah looked at him sharply. '"Visitors"? I'm not under arrest, am I?'

'No, of course not.'

'Then why is my phone cut off?'

'I don't know. I'll try to get it on again.'

Sarah studied the hillside below: the Peak tram was grinding up its track emerging into the sun from the shadow of the trees, the sound of traffic and clanking of trams filled the air, but the bustle along the waterfront was hidden by white tower blocks that showed no sign of human life, like an architect's drawing. She turned back sharply to Mason. 'You're not being straight with me – you're holding something back.'

He sighed. 'Okay. Can I have a beer or something?'

'Not until you've told me the truth.'

'Very well. It's quite simple, Sarah. We know who Scorpion is and we want to keep you out of danger until he's been arrested.'

'You *know*? It's a *he*, not a she?'

'It wasn't Mary Devereux, if that's what you mean.'

'Mary? Why do you mention Mary?'

'Oh, of course – it was while you were in China. We discovered she was having a lesbian affair and it wasn't the first – she'd lied in all her PVs because she wouldn't have been cleared and they'd have kicked her out of the Wrens. We thought she might have been open to blackmail and questioned her – just a matter of routine, really.'

Sarah suddenly felt sick. 'Oh God – poor, poor Mary. How is she now?'

'She was very broken up by it. Hanged herself in the cells.'

There was a long silence. Eventually Sarah spoke in a whisper. 'What a horrible, pointless way to go.'

Mason shrugged. 'It's all a bad business. Clayton may be a bastard, but at least he's competent – and he's trying to bring it to an end.'

Sarah wiped her forehead on the back of her hand, sweating in the heat and humidity. 'Well, for Christ's sake who *is* it? How did you work it out?'

His eyes crinkled secretively. 'The missing piece came from a Chinese kid. She was wounded trying to cross from the other side about six weeks ago and picked up by the Gurkhas. When she came to in hospital the police questioned her – the usual routine – and the WPC had the nous to see that her story might matter. After weeks of bureaucracy the report came from RHK Special Branch to us.'

There was another silence. 'Come on, then,' Sarah sounded exasperated. 'Tell me what she had to say.'

Barnie Mason gave a sly smile. 'I'll do better than that, Sarah. There's a car in the basement and you and I are going for a ride. We're going to see little Tang Ah Ming. Hear it for yourself.'

'Names,' said the admiral to Foo. 'What we need is names.' They were back in the office after the short drive to a safe house on the other side of the Peak in Mount Kellett Road. Foo had been allowed to telephone Ruth, who had reluctantly accepted that his return to Macao would be delayed for twenty-four hours. In the well-guarded house he had listened to the fourteen-year-old Chinese girl – only half surprised by the story, for he had started to see the truth on the trek across China. There was no triumph in the discovery; it was bleak, grim, tragic.

'What kind of names?' he asked.

'Names to confuse Peking.' Clayton gave a hard little grin. 'Scorpion's main task is to give Peking your order of battle. The names and addresses of the dissident leadership so that they can be rounded up and jailed or executed.'

'I know.' Foo spoke quietly. 'I wish it were not so.'

'Now that we know who Scorpion is, I want to feed him a massive dose of false information. Get Peking really confused, arresting the wrong people, destroying the credibility of Li Peng's government even further. Create mayhem, give your people a real shot in the arm before we arrest the bastard. Then he can go on for a bit – under our control.'

'So we protect my leadership? You want the names of officials that the opposition would like to see out of the way? Use the *Gonganbu* to destroy our enemies?'

'Exactly so.'

'Give me a few hours. Ling Boda is still in Hong Kong and I should like to consult him. Is that okay?'

Clayton and the admiral exchanged glances. 'By all means,' said Clayton, fingering a gold fountain pen with studied elegance. 'Someone will escort you.'

36

When it grew dark Luther began to feel more secure. The street outside was brilliantly lit and even more crowded; he stared down enviously at young Chinese and European couples scurrying to evenings at the cinema and restaurants. But when he sank back in his armchair, with both lights and television switched off, through the window he could see only a darkening sky and floating dust particles reflecting yellow sodium lamps and the rainbow colours of neon signs. He needed Josie, but at least he felt safe in the dark, a fox hiding in his earth.

He had rented the apartment in a false name, always paying the rent in advance from a local bank account in the same name, 'D. V. Miller', as he thought it best to sound British or American. Luther had taken so much care to conceal the flat – and his occasional visits to collect electricity bills or stock up with food – that he was confident the Chinese did not know of it. Despite the frustration of being cooped up, he was safe so long as he did not go outside. He needed to do so only two or three times – to collect his cash from the bank and to take a taxi to Kai Tak for the flight he had already booked to Australia. But the first time would be to telephone Josie. He could not risk doing so from the apartment for the line in Hangzhou was certain to be tapped, which would enable them to trace this number – and then the address – in Hong Kong.

At ten o'clock he went into the bathroom and carefully gummed on a little false hair to produce a drooping Viva

Zapata moustache. Crude but quite effective. When he added a denim cap and thick horn-rimmed spectacles he was more or less unrecognisable. He let himself out quietly. Weaving through the crowds to Tin Hau MTR station, he crossed to Kowloon, changing at Admiralty, and found an international telephone booth near the Peninsula Hotel. There was no direct dialling to his number in Hangzhou so he had to ask the operator for the connection, pouring Hong Kong coins into the slot so that he could talk for as long as necessary without being cut off. He had decided on a quick message: *It's me. You will guess where I am. Come at once.* He would repeat it and hang up. Josie would understand. Even if she were under surveillance, she had the skills to vanish and make her way to the frontier with Hong Kong. Like Luther she had several false passports and if she had any sense she would brave the sewage and swim the last bit across a corner of the harbour to avoid official scrutiny at a crossing point.

'Plea' wait, corer.' The woman operator's Cantonese intonation crackled down the line and he heard the click as the connection was made. The number started to ring. The glass booth stood in a busy street and the endless procession passing by ignored him; teeming crowds in Central and Kowloon always provided decent cover. The number buzzed for about two minutes, then he heard the operator's singsong voice again. 'Ve'y so'y, corer, no repry. Try later.'

Luther's fingers were drumming on the glass window of the booth. 'No – it's urgent. Please go on trying.'

The number went on ringing for another two or three minutes until the operator came on again. 'Ve'y so'y, corer, still no repry.' She broke the connection. Luther stood for a few seconds with the dead receiver in his hand, then replaced it with a worried expression.

The safe house was a suburban villa in Mount Kellett Road, solid and comfortable; the plain-clothes police guarding the place were discreet, but it had an institutional air. Sarah and Mason drove up in his Ford Fiesta and parked on the gravel circle outside the front door. The policeman in shirtsleeves who let them in made a show of examining Mason's security pass, although he must have seen him numerous times. They were shown into the kitchen – all white tiles and stainless steel, like a canteen not a private house – where a young Chinese woman in a blue and white butcher's apron was preparing lunch. 'How is Ah Ming today?' asked Mason.

The Chinese girl looked solemn. 'Just the same, sir. I'm afraid she is very down – she has had bad time.'

'She was unconscious for more than a week,' explained Mason to Sarah. 'The Chinese shot her down when she was trying to cross from Guandong – she was lucky to survive – but the bullets caught her in the shoulder and thigh, no vital organs. It was the shock that kept her out so long. When she came to she told her story to WPC Wu here, who has stayed with her ever since.'

'She was trying to escape after most of her family were arrested,' added WPC Wu. 'She is the daughter of an important official in the *Tewu* – Tang Tsin.'

'His *daughter*?' Sarah ran her fingers through her hair and screwed up her eyes as she did when puzzled. 'Here in Hong Kong? You've lost me – I don't understand.'

Mason leant on the stainless steel work-top, delicately avoiding a chopping board covered in spring onions and Chinese cabbage. 'The girl who tried to escape was Ah Ming – Tang Tsin's elder child. We believe that he sent his family to a place in the countryside outside Peking for safety about seven months ago, when he first felt he might be under suspicion. His wife, the daughter Ah Ming and his son Kwai-lan – they all went to stay with relatives out in the sticks.'

'I remember.'

'That much we knew. What we did not know was that Tang's fears were justified. He *was* under deep suspicion and the whole family was detained after a few months.

They were staying on a farmstead that stood by itself, not in a village, so there was little danger of him finding out. The farm had no phone and the *Gonganbu* made the wife and children go on writing to him every week as if nothing had happened.'

'Didn't he ever go and *see* them?'

Mason nodded. 'I thought of that too – but most of the time Tang believed he was under surveillance. It would make sense for him not to visit in case he led watchers to them. He wanted them to escape if he was arrested.'

Sarah looked around the kitchen: reassuringly ordinary, plates, knives, the carcass of a luckless duck dressed ready for the electric oven. Through the window she could see a sprinkler watering the lawn. 'Does she know what happened to the rest of the family? Or is Clayton holding that back until he's pumped her dry?'

Mason met her eyes. She had never really noticed his till then: they were pale blue, sharp but surprisingly understanding. 'She knows. I told her that her father had been a brave agent for those who want to free China – and that he has been executed. She was very stoic about it, very Chinese.'

'What about the others?'

'We don't know for sure, but Tang's wife may well have been shot too – things happen in such a secretive way in China, we may never find out. Ah Ming escaped from a camp and her brother is probably still there.' He paused, then added quietly: 'I told her she was unlikely ever to see any of them again.'

'Poor kid.' For a moment Sarah felt overwhelmed by the sadness of it all. Another trail of loss and pain for Scorpion and his masters to answer for. 'Only fourteen and alone in the world. What will happen to her?'

'Some kind of children's home for a year or two, school or technical college, then she'll have to fend for herself, same as any other child refugee. There've been enough of them down the years.'

'Shall we go upstairs?' asked WPC Wu brightly. 'Ah

Ming is waiting and after lunch I want to go on teaching her backgammon – she seems to enjoy that a little.'

The three of them climbed to the first floor, into a large room overlooking the back garden. It was comfortably furnished with modern easy chairs and the doors were open to a balcony with a red and white striped sun-blind. Through an archway Sarah saw two single beds. 'I sleep up here too,' whispered WPC Wu. 'She is afraid to be alone at night.' Aloud, she spoke to Ah Ming in Mandarin, then in English. 'You have some more visitors, little sister.'

The Chinese girl looked lost and unhappy. She was slightly built, like a bird, seeming younger than her fourteen years, and sat on an upright chair, her feet not quite touching the ground, hands folded in her lap, eyes downcast, long hair in a pigtail over one shoulder. She was wearing jeans and a blue tee-shirt. When she raised her face to WPC Wu she seemed less afraid, but she did not smile.

'Go ahead, Miss Wu,' said Barnie quietly. 'Same routine as before.'

The girl's tension and deathly stillness seemed to communicate itself to everyone in the room. There was no sound except for the splash of the sprinklers on the dark green lawn outside. The Chinese policewoman sat on a stool next to Ah Ming and spoke to her gently in Mandarin. After a few sentences she turned to Barnie. 'Now, Mr Mason, I ask her about the journey to the farmstead outside Peking.' She asked the girl a question in Mandarin, waited for the reply, delivered in a dull monotone, and translated. 'It was my uncle's farm. He grew rice and kept pigs.' The routine was repeated several times.

'We did not want to go but father made us. We travelled by train and my uncle met us in a truck belonging to the commune . . .

'It was a disgusting place, uncomfortable with smelly earth closets for lavatories. The only running water was from a standpipe, no shower or bathroom . . .

'*Father stayed a week while we settled in . . .*

'*Yes, I can remember the date. We travelled there on the fourteenth of October and father left on the twentieth.*'

This time WPC Wu repeated the question in Mandarin and the girl replied with greater emphasis. '*We travelled there on the fourteenth of October. I remember because it was my birthday. I was fourteen and father had promised to take us to the Lotus Garden restaurant near our house in Peking. He cancelled it.*'

Sarah caught Mason's eye. 'October fourteenth to twentieth,' he repeated quietly. 'Tang Tsin was in the countryside – thirty miles out of Peking, no phone, quite cut off. Remember the reports?'

The shock was like a hammer blow to the chest that almost made Sarah's heart stop. Her head began to swim, she felt unsteady on her feet, the hunched figure of Ah Ming seemed to shimmer like a mirage. She felt Mason's hand grip her arm tightly. 'Oh my God.' Her throat was dry and it came out as a whisper. 'Please don't let it be true.'

37

It had taken Luther only twenty minutes to cross to
Kowloon but the journey back was more than an hour, as
he changed from MTR to minibus to tram to cover his
tracks. In the apartment he double-locked the door,
poured himself a brandy and lay down on the bed. *Why*
hadn't Josie answered the phone? Where *was* she? The
house was in a Party ghetto and there was absolutely
nowhere else to go. He tried to be dispassionate, but
could not help feeling anxious and frightened for her – and
for himself. Instinctively he knew that he should get out of
Hong Kong at once, make for Australia, put another
three thousand miles between him and his former masters.
But he could not abandon Josie like that. She had given
him too much loyalty, too much unconditional love. His
mind became more and more confused as he lay there, an
unaccustomed and frightening experience. Eventually he
fell into a restless sleep, the light still burning.

Next morning the lynching party gathered in the admiral's
office: Erwin Smith, Gerald Clayton and, reluctantly,
Benjamin Foo. A white-coated steward served a pot of
steaming coffee, pungent aroma filling the room, and the
admiral lit a small cigar, stretching back in his leather
chair as he enjoyed planning the destruction of another
human being. 'You got me some names, Foo?'

The Chinese still looked exhausted after his ordeal on
the mainland, and uncomfortable at being mixed up with

this pair of hard men. He had spent the night in the building and hadn't yet seen Ruth. 'As you asked, Admiral. I have pinpointed six – five are men in high military and official positions, one a woman who is commander of a police district. Their arrest would help my friends in China, for they all cause us difficulty, and would cause much confusion.'

'That's good work, Foo.' Clayton sounded genuinely grateful. 'The next question is how to plant it?'

Foo hesitated, taking a sip of the bitter coffee. He hated the stuff but nobody had offered him tea. 'I had in mind that I would contrive a meeting with him – today, if that does not seem too sudden – and discuss how we might set up regular communications with these people? Avoid another fiasco?' He gave a bleak smile. 'I guess that should do it?'

The admiral held out his calloused farm-boy hand. 'Let me see that list.' Foo took a folded sheet of white paper from his inside pocket and handed it over. Erwin Smith studied it thoughtfully. 'All rightey, looks fine to me.' He passed it to Clayton. 'Gerry?'

Clayton ran his eye downwards. 'Excellent. But could you add a couple more, Foo? Make the best of the opportunity?'

'If you wish.'

The admiral blew out a ring of cigar smoke. 'Lookee here, Ben.' He was using Foo's first name deliberately, a gesture of trust, to show Foo was a buddy. 'How come you look so fuckin' unhappy an' all?'

Foo responded in a dull, emotionless tone. 'These people are my fellow Chinese. They oppose our movement, but they are not monsters. Some of them may die as a result of what we are doing – that is against all we are fighting for.' He looked at both men in turn, impassively. 'But I shall do as you ask.'

'Hell, Ben. I guess we understand how you feel, but this bastard has caused real mayhem trying to cover his tracks – Gatti's family, that Wren broad who turned out to be a dyke – ' The Carolina drawl trailed away as he searched for her name.

'Commander Devereux,' interjected Clayton politely.

'Yeah, Devereux. Sad case. Then this guy Thomas can't be too pleased at being bounced out of your navy, though he don't seem quite the man to run a missile boat. And Christ knows how many of your friends in China this Scorpion's betrayed.' Another ring of blue smoke floated to the ceiling. 'Don't you think the sonofabitch *deserves* his comeuppance?'

'He is a traitor, for whatever reason, and must be stopped. I agree with that.'

'Good. Then for Christ's sake put a bit of zip in it. Make the bastard *believe* these names, Foo, because in Peking it's *names* they're waiting for.'

'Let's work out how you can meet him without arousing suspicion.' Clayton was smoothly steering them away from upsetting questions of principle to reassuring practicalities. But they were interrupted by a knock on the door.

'Come,' growled the admiral crossly. A young woman in US Navy uniform appeared. 'Yes, Deborah? I said we were not to be disturbed.'

The girl blushed slightly. 'I'm sorry, sir. But Mr Clayton's colleague Mr Mason is on the phone and asks to speak with him urgently.'

Luther woke early, still on edge and bathed in sweat. After a shave he put on his disguise and risked the street again, hidden behind his thick horn-rimmed spectacles with smoked lenses, denim cap pulled well down. There was a queue at the bank and he had to wait twenty minutes, shuffling forward and feeling exposed as he stood out above the Chinese traders paying in bags of last night's takings. It was the wrong time and the wrong place – he should have chosen a bank in Central – for there were no other Europeans. The clerk had the ten thousand US dollars ready for him and asked for no identification except the bank pass-book. He stamped it ACCOUNT CLOSED on every page and handed it back. Luther pushed the bundles of notes into a narrow leather case. 'Thank you.'

'Yo' welcome. Next plea'.'

On the crowded pavement, Luther hesitated. Every minute outside the apartment was a risk. Every Hong Kong policeman and Chinese agent in the colony was looking for him. He had to survive until the flight tomorrow morning and the sensible thing was to get straight back. But Josie preyed on his mind constantly. He weaved through the crowds spilling into the road where the tram bells clanged angrily to clear a way. Past the Tin Hau Temple he found a row of telephone kiosks and went into the one for international calls.

Last night's routine was repeated: calling the operator to make the connection, the long wait, the buzzing but no reply. Wretchedly Luther left the booth and hurried away. A few yards along the street he felt a hand grip his arm. The police? Panicking he pulled away and struck out, feeling his fist make contact with bone.

Then he saw the old woman's face, nose bleeding, the circle of outraged Chinese faces, the furious shouting and waving of arms. She held out the coin and spat at him in Cantonese. 'Is yo' money – yo' left in phone box. Is that all thanks I get? Yo' mad or somethin'?'

Luther recovered quickly and offered her his handkerchief to wipe away the blood. He bowed deeply and apologised in Cantonese, offering her some Hong Kong notes from his pocket. She counted them quickly, nodded and the crowd started to disperse. Luther hurried away into a side street, breathing heavily, his hands shaking. That was the last risk he could take. He had gained his freedom but lost Josie. When he saw the constant stream of aircraft taking off from Kai Tak on the other side of the harbour, he could have wept with frustration.

38

Sarah passed a restless night in the apartment, with Brad on the sofa by the door. He seemed to have no difficulty keeping awake, although when she woke at about seven he had been replaced by a younger sailor who was more friendly. 'My name's O'Neill, ma'am.' He had a big smile and a Liverpool accent. 'I'll try not to get in the way.' Sarah shrugged – there was no point in protesting any more.

Benjamin Foo arrived at eight and she hugged him for a long time: the broad chest and lined Chinese face were reassuring when everything was in such a mess. They sat on the balcony, both skirting round the things that were really on their minds. 'Are you all right now, Sarah?'

'I'm okay, Ben, but I feel so bloody miserable.'

He held her hand and squeezed it tightly. 'I know. When this is over, in a day or two, will you come and stay with us in Macao? For a few days, longer if you like.'

'That's kind, Ben – but it's not over yet.' She felt tears in her eyes and, with Foo to comfort her, it seemed natural to let them come. 'I just can't face it.'

Eventually Foo stood up and patted her arm. 'I must go, Sarah, but I'll be back to take you to Macao. Soon, I promise.' When he left, Sarah went into the bedroom and watched the forecourt of the block until he appeared. A naval car was waiting for him and she went on watching until it drove away and vanished at the corner of the street.

* * *

An hour and a half later Benjamin Foo arrived on Lantau. He stood out, head and shoulders above the other Chinese in the crowd that flooded down the gangway. This made it easier for the Special Branch constable, crouched on the roof of a nearby freight shed, to focus his video-camera. In the back of the rusty van that stood at the end of the quay, Clayton squatted on an orange box before two video screens. He had exchanged his Savile Row suit for equally impeccable fawn trousers and a bush-shirt. The screens were linked by radio to the two cameras, one still following Foo, the other sweeping the waters of the bay from a hut further round its perimeter. An earpiece enabled him to hear the output from the tiny button microphone sewn to Foo's shirt; it was also being recorded on tape. Ordinary police pocket radios linked him to everyone on the surveillance team. Mason hadn't done a bad job to set all this up in twenty-four hours.

Foo was now walking down the concrete path by the long curve of beach, a crescent of silver sand lapped by the sea on his right. It was a hot, sunny morning and the vivid blue sky was reflected in the colour of the water. Sampans dotted the bay. On his left he passed small Chinese out-door restaurants with awnings of rush matting, some shanty dwellings, a concrete platform built like a pulpit for the beach guard, empty, its warning bell hanging silent. Three young Chinese police were spread out along the beach, a girl and two young men, all in casual jeans and tee-shirts.

The door of the van opened quietly and Barnie Mason slid in beside Clayton. It was stuffy in the closed space. Clayton nodded a welcome, a globule of sweat dripping from his patrician nose. 'Sorry it's so close in here, but at least we've lost that dreadful old fart Smith.' He studied the screens. A lonely figure had appeared on the second one, very small, walking along the beach towards Foo. 'They'll meet in about five minutes,' he whispered, as if his quarry – who was at least half a mile away – might overhear. 'Foo will hand over the list and it'll be on the

272

way to China in an hour or two. And we'll have lots and lots of evidence.'

'What happens next?'

Clayton did not reply – both of them were suddenly fixed on the screens as the two figures met. 'Sorry – what did you say?'

'What happens then?'

'I think we'll arrest the bastard don't you? The Chinese won't find out for a while and I want to start pumping him dry.'

At about the same time, Luther was watching a Pink Panther cartoon in Chinese; he had nothing else to do and the television was now on permanently. The air in the tiny flat was thick with blue Gitane smoke and brandy fumes. He had tried to phone Josie a third time but there was still no reply and he was loath to try again before dark. Every time he stepped out of the apartment he was taking an enormous risk. He had booked a flight to Perth tomorrow evening, two seats. He avoided thinking about the choice he would have to make if he had still not spoken to Josie, but deep down he knew that he would abandon her. It was painful to contemplate, for he was genuinely very fond of the girl; but if the choice was between Josie and survival . . . he pushed the thought away.

The ten thousand dollars from the bank was in an attaché case on the bed, his other funds were already in Australia. 'Why not go tonight?' the absurd pink figure on the screen seemed to say. But he would make one last effort; he needed Josie and she needed him, he wanted them to start the new life together. Luther was so lost in his thoughts that he did not hear the buzzer at the front door. He became aware of it gradually, an angry noise coming in long bursts. It occurred to him that, since he had no visitors, he had never heard it before – and who would be visiting him now?

With a frisson of apprehension he switched off the

television and padded on bare feet into the bedroom. The Luger automatic he kept there took a magazine with thirteen rounds. He weighed it in his hand and flicked off the safety catch. There was a strong temptation simply not to answer the door, but if it was a bunch of unwelcome visitors from Qiao Shi they would kick it down anyway. He stood just inside, but to one side, and called 'Who is it?' The buzzing stopped and he heard a muffled reply. 'Who is it?' he asked again and when she answered he recognised her voice at once. As he took the chain off and turned the lock she was standing there, thick black hair gleaming, smiling her huge Vietnamese smile. 'Thank God!' He seized her in his arms.

She giggled. 'I thought you didn't believe in him, Luther?'

Sarah too spent some of the day watching television. Bored, after a time she started to fidget and O'Neill came out from his perch by the door. Like Brad he wore the uniform of a petty officer but he was much younger and had that fresh, scrubbed appearance which she had seen in sailors before: an open face and black wavy hair. He also looked remarkably fit, broad in the chest with biceps rippling under that crisp white shirt. He could contain Sarah effortlessly and she knew it – that was why he was there.

'Can I get you some coffee, ma'am?' A friendly smile, but the confidence of all that muscle.

'No thanks, O'Neill – look, I can't go on calling you that, what's your first name?'

'Patrick, ma'am. My friends call me Pat.'

'Okay Pat – my friends call me Sarah.'

'Yes, ma'am. Is there anything else I can do for you?'

Apart from letting me leave my own flat like any ordinary member of society who isn't confined in jail or a lunatic asylum? But there was no point in asking that. She smiled sweetly. 'Have you got anything to read, Pat? All my books were destroyed in a fire on Cheung Chau.'

O'Neill fished in the pocket of his uniform jacket, hanging on a peg just inside the door. He did not pull out soft porn but a crumpled paperback of *Pride and Prejudice*. 'Would this do, ma'am? I do like Jane Austen.'

Sarah sat on the balcony for a time trying to lose herself in the book, but she felt too jumpy and irritable. How could she relax while the seconds ticked away, not knowing when the cataclysm was going to happen? There was no food left in the apartment but in the evening some plastic containers arrived from a Chinese takeaway. O'Neill spread them around the kitchen table. 'Hope you like abalone and beanshoots?' That toothy smile again as he unwrapped two pairs of plastic chopsticks. He did look devastatingly wholesome – could make a fortune as a toy-boy for the wealthy, middle-aged and desperate. Still feeling jumpy, Sarah sat down with him. 'What do you normally do, Pat?'

'I'm a writer, ma'am. I have a section in the captain's office at *Tamar* – just routine administration, that sort of thing.'

'Security?'

'Some of that, ma'am, yes.'

Sarah looked around the kitchen. She had rarely used it except for making breakfast and hardly noticed how badly finished it was: expensive units fronted in light oak, gaps showing between them, cracks in the plaster on the walls. It would never have been like that five years ago. This place had been thrown up to last about ten years – the developer wanted his money back before 1997. 'Been here long, Pat?'

'Two years, ma'am. We like it.'

'You're married then?'

'Oh yes, ma'am.' Sarah thought she would scream if he called her that again. 'Two nippers. We've got a nice flat in Kowloon.'

'Why am I being kept locked up here?'

He was not taken off guard. 'Locked up, ma'am?

'Course not.' The same boyish smile. 'My job is to guard you until this operation's over.'

'Can I go out for a walk, then?'

'I'd prefer not, ma'am.'

'Pity.' Sarah opened the fridge, pulled out a bottle of white wine and poured two large glasses; she thought he would refuse a drink if asked, but good manners and his easygoing nature would make him accept if it appeared before him. She was right. Leaving O'Neill fingering his Muscadet, she slipped out to the bedroom and found the medicine bottle of nembutal. After Cheung Chau the Wren doctor had given her some mild sleeping pills, but added the tiny yellow capsules if she felt the need to be really knocked out; Sarah had used only two of them.

Back in the kitchen she poured more wine, standing with her back to O'Neill and adding the contents of five capsules to his glass; the powder dissolved almost at once. He did not seem to notice the difference. He drank only a glass and a half, as did Sarah, so the bottle was still half-full when they moved into the living room and sat on the sofa. It was about ten. O'Neill leaned back and closed his eyes. 'Blimey, that wine's strong.' After fifteen minutes of television news he quietly dozed off and started to snore.

Sarah knew he had the door keys on a chain at his belt, but if she tried to remove them he was bound to wake up. Instead she went into her bedroom and bolted the door. She pulled on a pair of trainers, tied the laces firmly in a double-knot and added a sweater over her shirt. There were some dollar notes in the pocket of her jeans. When she switched off the light and opened the door to the balcony it was cold outside: should she add her anorak? No – that might get in the way.

The apartment was on the sixteenth floor and the narrow balcony was surrounded by an open steel balustrade; when she looked down at the street lamps and the red taillights of cars darting between the tower blocks, Sarah felt giddy and gripped the rail for balance. The solution was not to look down. She fixed her eyes on the identical balcony of the next apartment. It was only about three feet away, but the drop between was sheer to the concrete forecourt; and you'd do an awful lot of damage to yourself on all those other steel railings on the way down. Trying to breathe steadily, controlling her fear, Sarah climbed over the balustrade and stood with her feet tucked in at its bottom, both hands gripping the top so tightly that her veins stood out. The traffic noise from below would mask any noise. Only three feet across, but she was absolutely terrified. Facing the wall, she nervously reached out for the railing of the other balcony with her left hand; she had to crouch and bend her knees to grip it. Her left foot next, so that she had one hand and foot on each side, legs spread apart, weight shakily balanced about one hundred and seventy feet above the ground. All that she needed now was someone below to see her and call the police, but she hoped she was well in shadow.

She followed with her right hand and foot, moving slowly and with great care. She knew how to do it, but she was panting, sweating heavily and could feel her heart racing when she finally clambered over the railing and got both feet safely on the other balcony. She knelt down in relief, head and arms huddled on the cold tiles – partly to keep out of sight, partly to avoid the giddiness of standing up in such a narrow space – until she was breathing normally. The glass door to the other apartment looked firmly closed and she was dreading having to go back by crossing that gap again. But when she slid a credit card up the crack between the glass panel and its frame, the catch clicked back and it slid open easily. She crept in but the bedroom was empty: so was the rest of the apartment. There was no furniture – she had not known that the place was unoccupied. For months afterwards she was to have a nightmare in which, after the terror outside, she crept into the flat to find a grinning O'Neill waiting for her. But he was not there and the front door was secured only by a Yale lock. She closed it quietly behind her, pressed the button for the lift and sped down to the garage, avoiding the main entrance on the ground floor: who knows what guards might be there?

After that it was plain sailing. She walked up the ramp from the garage and hailed a passing cab. 'Stanley,' she ordered. She slid into the back seat and settled in the corner as the Datsun shot off, all the usual bric-a-brac on its dashboard vibrating in time with the engine – electric fan, Taoist charms and miniature television.

Sarah left the cab among the empty stalls of Stanley market and walked the rest of the way to Gatti's house. She knew that she had to go there, but had no idea what she was going to do when she arrived. The street was dark. On one side she could see the grey sea behind the ghostly outlines of trees, on the other the line of silent houses. Gatti's had a faint light behind the curtains downstairs. She paused, then opened the gate firmly and pressed the doorbell. It was not Gatti who opened the door but Nick Roper.

39

'Sarah flung her arms round Nick's neck and kissed him,
tears welling up in a surge of happiness and fear. 'Oh
Nick, my poor baby.'

He hugged her with that familiar patrician smile, half-
vulnerable, half-superior. 'Thank God they've let you out
– I've been trying to get to see you ever since you and Foo
arrived back from China.'

She pulled away. 'Never mind that, lover. We have to
talk. Where's Bob?'

'He was summoned to the Peak an hour back.' Still the
same classy Boston tones, although he sounded on edge.
'Haven't seen him since.'

'So we're alone?'

'Sure.' He drew her back to him and kissed her. 'Oh,
Sarah, I've missed you.'

They walked hand in hand into the living room where
the glass doors to the garden were open, curtains flapping
spookily in the breeze. Sarah shivered and went to close
them. 'Sit down, Nick, I've got something to say.' She
stood with her back to the window, looking round the
room with its modern white armchairs, the smoked plastic
cover of the music centre, photographs of Gatti's wife and
children. It was the wrong place, quite wrong, but that
was just too bad. Nick smiled expectantly: he looked more
handsome than ever, clean-cut profile, greying at the
temples, eyes tired and slightly worried. He patted the
sofa beside him.

Sarah shook her head. 'No, Nick.' She took a deep

279

breath. 'I know it all.' She spoke slowly but very deliberately. 'I *know*.'

In the long silence she could hear the ticking of the brass carriage clock on the mantelpiece, but time stood still. Before she could say anything else or touch him, Nick went white and his eyes widened in shock. Momentarily she remembered her puppy Oscar being run over when she was nine. She had found him in the gutter – whimpering, no injury visible but destroyed inside – and cuddled him until he stopped breathing, a little bundle with hurt brown eyes that stared at her like Nick's now, as if somehow she might save him. Then Nick looked away, head slumped forward. He shrivelled before her. Didn't resist. Didn't deny it. Hardly reacted. When he spoke his voice was hollow, he sounded like a stranger. 'How long have you known?'

'A day or two. That's all.'

'Who else knows?'

Sarah paused before replying. This was it – betraying her trust, disobeying the Act, the end of life in the service. After nearly ten years she would never see Nairn again. She might even end up in jail. 'Clayton and the admiral. Everyone that matters. You're finished, Nick. I'm sorry.'

He stared at her in silence. 'How? I can't believe it – *how*?'

'Tang Tsin.'

'Tang Tsin?'

'More precisely Tang Tsin's daughter – your pals put her in a camp but she escaped to Hong Kong about a month ago. She's told us a number of things but in particular that her father was with the family at a farm thirty miles outside Peking from the fourteenth to the twentieth of October last year, that he never left. Never, not once. Remember those dates? That was the week when you reported two key meetings with him. It was a lie, Nick, wasn't it?'

He made no attempt to argue or explain. 'You shouldn't be here.'

She finally sat down beside him. 'No, I bloody well shouldn't. They'll crucify me when they find out – but I wanted you to have a chance.'

He continued to stare at the floor like a wax dummy, as if in a catatonic trance. 'Why?'

'What a damn silly question! Because you *matter* to me.' She put an arm round his shoulders. She wanted him so much to be strong, the man she had loved, but he was crumbling to nothing before her eyes. She was the strong one, always had been, that was why she had stayed alone, always would stay alone. 'I don't understand, Nick. I'm trying hard not to think about all the damage you've done. But for Christ's sake *why*? How did it happen? You had everything – the world at your feet. *Why* did you do it?'

'I wish I knew.'

The tone of passive self-pity was too much for her. She struck him across the face with all her strength, leaving a red and white welt on his cheek, then seized his shoulders and shook him violently. 'Don't bloody speak to me like that! It's not the real you. For God's sake, Nick.' He finally met her eyes, looking ashamed and frightened. 'You've held me in your arms, made love to me, I *know* what you're like. At least I thought I did. You were the most exciting man I'd ever met – now I don't know *who* you are, Nick. It's such a bloody shameful waste.' She jerked her hand towards the ceiling. 'To protect you, someone knifed your oldest friend's children, Nick. Two innocent little boys. Stabbed to death before they had time to really live.' She was suddenly screaming with passion. 'Up there, Nick, in this very house. All that pain and terror – for *you*, Nick! I don't understand. Why? For Christ's sake why?'

His eyes pleaded with her. 'I didn't want that to happen.' He was coming alive again, but close to tears. 'I swear I didn't. I didn't *want* them to protect me, not like that, but I was helpless. They ignored me. When they killed Sue and the boys I was going to turn myself in, but they said they'd take you out if I did – they firebombed your place on Cheung Chau as a warning. The whole thing's been a nightmare.'

'It wasn't much fun for the rest of us, either. Poor Mary Devereux . . . '

'I was sorry about her, too.'

'Sorry? But it's not enough to be *sorry*.' Abruptly Sarah stopped screaming at him and stood up, her mind spinning in confusion. Part of her could not bear to touch him, part wanted him to take her then and there, before it was too late, part to comfort him like a child. 'Nick.' She tried to sound calm, keep her voice steady. 'I loved you. I still do. If you try, you might just get away into China. I'll never see you again – but that's what you must do.' She paused for a reply that never came and repeated it with greater emphasis. 'That's what you must do – do you *understand*, Nick?' She started to weep quietly. 'Oh God it hurts, it hurts so much, you bastard – I have to know why, why did it happen? *Why*?'

The admiral and Clayton were standing in the entrance of the CIA building when Gatti arrived. Gatti's own office had always been in one of the annexes and he had forgotten how elegant the main building could seem. It dated from the twenties, built by a tea merchant, and was entered through a hallway lined with marble columns: concealed lights picked out the stone vaulting above them. His feet clattered on a tiled floor as the two men turned to greet him. 'Bob – thanks for coming.' The admiral gestured him to come into a side room that was unfurnished except for a plain deal table and two upright chairs. It was used for interviews with agents by junior staff who shared offices. Clayton stayed outside as the two Americans sat down facing each other.

There were no preliminaries, no letting him down gently. 'I'm sorry it's me that has to tell you, Bob.' The admiral met Gatti's eyes steadily. 'The traitor is Roper. He'll be arrested at your house tonight.'

Gatti looked unhappy rather than surprised. 'I began to fear it some little while ago, sir. How long have you known?'

'Not long Bob. It must be hard for you to accept – you've been friends a long time.'

'More than friends – he was a kind of brother. It's not just hard to accept – it's *impossible*. But I know it's true. I started to sense it – no reason, no proof, just a *feeling*. Didn't know what to do.' His mouth twisted into a bleak little smile. 'Now I don't have to do anything, do I?'

'Aren't you *bitter*, Bob?' The old man knew it was time to go, but he was puzzled and concerned. 'Sue and the boys were killed to protect him, y'know. That's why I want you to stay here while the rest of us bring him in. Personal involvement always misfires.'

'I'm not bitter, just unhappy and confused. I know it's true, but this man isn't the Roper I knew at sea. He isn't the Roper I knew a year or two back. I don't understand – I need to know *why*?'

'So do we all, old friend. Maybe when we talk to him . . .'

Gatti nodded sadly. 'Maybe. But I'd prefer to come with you now, sir. I won't do anything crazy, you have my word. I know he's betrayed us all, but I don't blame him for Sue and the boys – I'm sure he didn't know. This guy has to be sick and I've been his friend.'

The admiral's thin lips tightened. 'Come then, Bob. This is new territory for me – never had an enemy agent in the crew before – I guess you may be able to help.'

The long black Lincoln was waiting at the foot of the steps. After the heat of the day the night air felt cold and a shaft of moonlight caught a line of conifers swaying menacingly in the wind. Gatti, Clayton and the admiral climbed into the back of the car, a closed glass screen separating them from the driver. 'The police will make the arrest,' explained Clayton. 'Since we're on British territory – but he'll be handed over to American jurisdiction. They're moving in now.' Gatti had a mental image of

Land-Rovers disgorging armed Chinese police to sur-
round his house. It seemed unreal – but the blood and
pain would be real enough if Nick tried to escape. He sat
on a jump-seat in front of the others, glad of an excuse not
to talk. The car purred down the drive and the steel gates
slid open silently.

40

They sat for a long time in silence, surrounded by Gatti's sitting room but not part of it. The naval neatness was alien to the turbulent emotions that flashed between them; the ghosts of Gatti's children were still crying out in pain and both Nick and Sarah were afraid to hear. She perched on the edge of the sofa and he slipped to the floor resting his head on her lap, long legs stretched out towards the cold fireplace, feet crossed as if perfectly at ease. She bent to kiss his forehead and ran her fingers through his hair. The room was partly in shadow, lit by two table lamps made from Chinese vases decorated with green and gold dragons, and Sarah had poured two large whiskies. They might have been a pair of lovers relaxing before going to bed, comfortable enough with each other not to need to speak.

'Why, Nick?' she asked again. 'I don't understand.' She spoke gently, as if they could stay huddled together there all night, but she knew they hadn't long.

'There isn't time.' He looked up at her sadly. 'Anyway I've lived the lie so long that I'm conditioned not to talk about it. I don't know if I can.'

'Don't be absurd, Nick.' Sarah suppressed her irritation. 'This is your whole life we're talking about.' She almost added *and there might not be much of it left*, but bit the words back.

There was another long silence. 'Okay.' Nick sipped his whisky and sighed. 'I believe in justice – that's all. When I was a kid we lived in a big house in Boston and I used to

285

see hoboes looking for food in trash cans on the street. I knew it was wrong, that society should be different – I guess that was the start.' He met her eyes defiantly. 'I know it sounds absurd, ridiculous, so go on – laugh.'

She stroked his hair again. 'I wouldn't dream of laughing, Nick; most of us have felt like that.' She remembered the training course at Edge on recruitment of agents. *There are three motivations for you to exploit: ideological, personality-psychological and financial. Only the second and third are generally reliable. Money can buy almost anything. Personality defects are always there for the finding – non-recognition of talent, sexual deviation, a search for adventure, malice towards a boss who is blocking promotion, inner depression externalised into hatred of colleagues, wives or society generally. But always treat ideological recruits with suspicion.* That last advice seemed to echo round her brain. 'Please go on, my love, it matters so much.'

Then the floodgates opened and he talked non-stop for more than an hour. The key seemed to be bitterness – he hated his family, resented elder brother Jan – but all mixed up with Marxist theory he'd read as a teenager and at university. The flashes of self-pity made Sarah's flesh creep, but then he was poised, confident Nick again – laughing at himself but deadly serious behind it. 'I really did think about it very deeply, you know – I felt I had to *choose*.' He laughed bitterly. 'I really believed Marx foretold the future and I wanted to be part of it. I felt arrogant as well as compassionate, joining the side that had to win – does that make it easier to understand?' He gave a wry smile, but then he was rushing on, speaking much too fast. 'I went to Princeton for a year before Yale – did I ever tell you that? – and there was this German student called Luther, of all things. Manfred Luther. He wasn't political on the surface, but when he saw I was interested he took me to meetings, introduced me to people.'

'What sort of people?'

'Just left-wing students at first. Later it was Chinese

diplomats at the United Nations, which seemed natural enough since we were in New York and they were living in the same city. They were intelligence officers, of course. Somehow the Chinese seemed more acceptable than the Russians who were the big enemy at the time.'

'But you had nothing to give them?'

'No. I didn't have anything for years. They just kept in touch. It had to be secret, but they were real *friends*.' Sarah felt the contempt creeping into her expression before she could stop it. 'Oh, for Christ's sake – you'll never understand.' His eyes blazed with anger and defiance. 'You'll *never* understand,' he repeated. 'We shared a vision – and they helped me to stay with it, even though I had nothing to give. That matters a lot when everything around you is hostile to what you believe.'

So far they had both kept the atmosphere calm, pushing down the volcano of violent emotion boiling just below the surface. But now Sarah exploded. 'You "shared a vision"? You and a bunch of foreign spies "shared a vision" – so you betray your friends and your country? You get in so deep that people have to be *killed* to protect you? It's crap, Nick. It's bloody self-deluding crap – and you know it! They were just using you.'

He flushed – with anger or shame? 'It wasn't like that. I *chose* to keep in touch with them because I thought China under Mao had taken the right road. Luther was a real friend and I've stayed in contact with him; another Westerner who'd made the same choice was kind of reassuring. Later I chose to help them in small ways. They steered me into intelligence because I had nothing much to offer as a seagoing officer – and they said I'd have more influence, which was true.'

'More influence? What do you mean?'

'This present job is the first one that's been any use to them, from an intelligence point of view.'

'I know.' Sarah's mouth set in a hard line. 'It enabled you to put Foo and me in their hands.'

'I didn't want that – '

But she cut him off with a snort and pressed on angrily. 'Proud of yourself, are you, Nick? Betraying a brave old man and the girl you were screwing?' She paused in fury. 'I loved you, you bastard, I *trusted* you. I'll never forget those moments when you came inside me, you suddenly went very, very hard and gripped me so tight it almost hurt. I've never felt so wanted – but what were *you* thinking about? Imagining how my body would feel dead?' She was close to tears, but her eyes blazed. 'Well – *were* you? They'd have shot both of us – don't you realise that?'

He stared at her defensively. 'Don't *you* realise I saved you both in China?'

'For Christ's sake, don't give me that.'

'The helicopter was my idea, you stupid bitch. The others would have abandoned you, but I made them agree and organised it.'

'So bloody what? It failed, didn't it?'

He seemed to be only half with her, gazing into the distance, speaking in a monotone. 'Then one of my Chinese contacts, a Vietnamese woman, was pressing hard for details so they could pick up you and Foo. Your friends had pinpointed a landing place near Liuzhou and said they'd use infra-red markers to guide us, so I gave the Chinese different co-ordinates for a spot three or four miles away, told them to use infra-red lamps and sent the helicopter to the same place.'

'The Chinese shot it to bits and four men from *Tamar* died, Nick.'

'But *you* lived, Sarah. If I hadn't done it you'd be in jail in China now – maybe you'd already be dead. Those marines you're so worried about had orders to shoot you and Foo if there was trouble, so that you couldn't be interrogated and put on trial.'

Sarah recoiled. 'I don't believe you. That's ridiculous – who would give them such an order?'

'Clayton did. He wanted to avoid embarrassment, diplomatic problems.'

She stared at him in disbelief. 'You're not just making

this up? It's for real, not another bloody fantasy?' Suddenly the tension seemed to subside, there was less confusion in the room – when focusing on somebody else Nick could still be rational, it was only when he gazed into his own mind that he went to pieces.

'It's for real,' he said quietly. 'They would have killed you if I hadn't wrecked the operation.'

'Then thank you.' The words hardly seemed adequate and were followed by a long silence. Of course it was true. Clayton would do anything to play things down, keep his nose clean, get Nairn's job. Nick stared at her miserably; suddenly she wanted to hug him but there was a chasm between them.

'There's more,' he said at last.

'Yes?'

He hesitated, turning to her in the lamplight, his face pale and harrowed. He looked like a waxed corpse. 'With my background and a successful career in the navy, they suggested I resign in a year or two and stand for Congress.'

'Senator Roper? Everybody's golden boy but with a private line to Red China?' Sarah curled her lip, but suddenly she saw the pattern. They could have seen that potential when he was still a student at Princeton – the fatal combination of looks and class and talent with the flawed personality, half-weak, half-arrogant. Poor Nick – they'd been manipulating him all along. She sighed. 'So you believed in Mao and they seemed to believe in you? Oh, Nick, you bloody fool – do you still believe?'

Suddenly all the weakness and self-pity were gone. She was back with the man with whom she had fallen in love – confident, strong, compassionate, masculine, even his face was looking less ravaged. He spoke very quietly, calmly, and she knew that this time it was with total honesty. 'Yes, I still believe. I'll never stop believing. It's the only way to achieve a just society.'

'How could you live with me for a year and hide it?'

'I guess I made sure we steered clear of politics? You're

a very attractive woman, Sarah – we wanted and needed each other, we shared so much else.'

'But you *deceived* me!'

'I hated that, truly I did.'

But could it be that simple? 'Did they *tell* you to sleep with me, Nick? Was I just another source?'

'No, truly, nothing like that.' He gave a wry smile. 'To be honest I've not been much of an agent for them. I'd barely started to hand over copies of documents, a year or two ago, when I realised that not too many of them were committed Marxists any more.' There was a sudden flash of bitterness. 'I believed, but did *they*? Were they just power-seekers using me for ends of their own?'

'So why the hell did you do it?'

'I started as a sympathiser, not an agent. I was ready to help in small ways, but I didn't want to be an agent.' He shook his head wretchedly. 'I felt I was letting down people around me, people I respected. I *tried* to stop – and it was then that they came on heavy. Said they'd go on supporting my career and protect me if I went on co-operating but otherwise they'd blow me.' He shrugged. 'I've been confused, on the point of calling their bluff ever since – but I knew it *wasn't* bluff.' He gave that cynical little smile, laughing at himself again. 'I think I could have faced *dying* for the cause, but just going to a federal penitentiary seemed somehow rather tawdry – even more so when it was my so-called comrades who were going to shop me.'

'You mean they blackmailed you?' Sarah wanted to believe that, badly needed a reason not to despise him.

'I guess so, but that's because they've got the wrong leaders at the moment. I chose to go with them, Sarah. I *chose* it and I'm not ashamed. I *am* a Marxist, Sarah, and I'm proud of it. I just wish I hadn't deceived you – I always hoped that somehow one day I'd share it with you, bring it all together.'

'You must be joking,' she muttered.

'No, I *did* hope, and I hate myself for deceiving you; I

hate myself far more than you could ever hate me.'

Don't bank on it, she thought, but she kissed him again and stroked the ravaged face tenderly before some instinct made her get up. She crossed the room and peered out through a chink in the curtains. The window gave onto a narrow strip of front garden, grey and empty. But she had left the gate in the high wall open and through it she could see shadows of movement. 'Wait there,' she whispered urgently. In the hall she closed the door to the living room and turned out the light, so that when she opened the outside door she would not be visible. It opened soundlessly and she padded to the gateway, silent on bare feet. Peering out she saw the dark shape of a van about twenty yards down the street and the black silhouettes of armed men, moonlight glinting on their helmets as they spread out without speaking.

41

Sarah counted sixteen figures, each carrying some sort of automatic weapon with a stubby magazine and short barrel – maybe an Armalite or an Uzi machine pistol? She closed the door quietly and ran back into the room. There was no time for sentiment or explanations; she put a finger to her lips. 'Don't make a sound, Nick. You must go – the police are outside.'

'I've been expecting them.'

She stared at him. 'You don't mean you're just going to give up? I won't have that – you're a good man, Nick. It was a good year. I don't understand how you can believe all this – maybe I'll work it out one day – and I know I'll never see you again but go, just *go*, get over the border. You must have a Chinese contact here?'

'My couriers were a Vietnamese girl and this guy Luther, the same one that recruited me at Princeton, but I have an emergency contact, a manager at the Bank of China.'

'Then go, Nick – out the back, over the wall, through the cemetery to the children's playground. If they challenge you, you'd better give up – they're armed. If not, you might just make it.'

He stood up, took a small revolver from his trouser pocket and fingered it awkwardly, as if not sure what to do with it, before pushing it into his belt. She said nothing. 'Why are you doing this, Sarah?'

'Because I love you.' But it wasn't true – they had been together a year but he was already a stranger.

'Thank you, darling. Thanks for everything. I'm sorry.' That same sad, bitter little smile. 'What a bloody silly thing to say. What a bloody silly way to end.' Then he was out of the kitchen door and hidden by the bushes in the garden. Sarah walked slowly back into the living room, topped up her whisky and sat in a corner waiting for the police. Five minutes later she heard the crunch of heavy boots and a hammering on the front door.

In Causeway Bay Josie rolled off Luther contentedly, resting her head in the crook of his arm. The tiny, perfectly formed Annamite body seemed fragile, as if she might be crushed by his muscular Saxon frame. He held her close as she smiled up at him, running her tongue sensuously across his chest. 'You *very* strong.' She giggled, sighing as his hand caressed the tight little buttocks and slid between her thighs to arouse her again. They had already made love twice in the narrow bed but this last time was slow and luxuriant; at the end she was half under him, heels drumming on his hips as she clawed him and every nerve in her body electrified to soar through a series of shuddering climaxes.

Then she lay still, peering out from under the black sampan-girl hair, eyes glinting up at him. 'You *very* strong.' She giggled. 'Turn over – let me massage you to sleep.' Luther felt exhausted as he settled on his stomach, resting his head on his arms. Josie's knuckles started to knead the muscles in his shoulders, her fingers flowed sensuously down his spine. With a practised movement, without pausing, she reached down to her crumpled clothes and her hand came back gripping the thin, razor-sharp stiletto. Kneeling astride him she raised it with both hands and, feeling that the soothing movements had stopped, he started to turn his head. As she brought the knife down with all her strength he cried out and jerked violently. Once at the shock of the cut, again as the thin steel sliced into his heart. There was no blood until she put

293

her knee into the small of his back to draw out the blade; and then it was pumping everywhere.

He was still trying to turn over, to say something; but it came out in a choking gurgle as more blood frothed from his mouth. His strength was rapidly ebbing away, eyes staring at her in confusion and pain before they went opaque and his head lolled over the side of the bed. She sprang to the floor and gathered up her clothes before they were soaked by the spreading tide of blood, turned away deliberately and walked slowly back into the main room. Staring out through the slatted blinds there were already signs of dawn behind the rooftops opposite; grey light picked out the lines of her face – alabaster smooth, rigid, sad. She would not weep, although she had loved him as deeply as she could love any other being. She had obeyed – and that was more important.

Six years ago it had been no hardship when the black uniformed cadre had chosen her from a Vietnamese army unit to be trained for work underground. Tuyet was as intelligent as she was lithe and deadly – and still bitter that her parents and all her family had died in the inferno of napalm during the war against the Americans. From Hanoi she had been sent to pose as a bar-girl in Hue where she had trapped subversives and suspected American spies with gusto; most were taken away for long interrogation, but one or two she had killed herself. When the Chinese political officer had ordered her to win Luther's trust and affection, at first it had been just another job. 'He is a loyal member of the Party and a sound intelligence officer, Tuyet, but he is not Chinese. We can never fully trust a European, so you will work with him, live with him, watch him.' The Chinese had a high sibilant intonation and delicate, rather handsome features beneath his grey hair; his name was Zhang. 'You will always know how to contact me here and later we shall all go to China, where you will have homes in Peking and Hangzhou. You will report to me every three months, or immediately if he shows signs of disloyalty.'

That evening Luther had come into the bar for the first time, tall and fair, looking and smelling much cleaner than the Europeans she was used to; he was so tall and strong that he could pick bar-girl Josie off her feet with one arm and no apparent effort. She had found him a thousand times more attractive than she had expected. But she had never forgotten her first loyalty to the Party that had liberated her country and rescued her from the life of a peasant on the land, the Party that would one day rescue all peasants from their drudgery and exploitation.

She gathered up his papers with gestures of contempt – the air-tickets, bank statements and letters were thrust into the thin leather case containing more money than she had ever seen. The list of names in Chinese characters meant nothing to her so she flushed it down the lavatory. She knew enough to see that a lot more money was waiting in Australia and that she already had a ticket to fly there, but the thought of using it never crossed her mind. She would fly back to Shanghai as soon as she could. It was nearly daylight as she dialled the airport.

Sarah squared her shoulders and opened the front door. No sign of Clayton or the admiral, just a Chinese police sergeant flanked by two constables. 'Mista Loper, preez?' The sergeant showed his warrant card, although they were all in uniform, khaki shorts and black peaked caps. All very correct, no hint that by now the house was surrounded by men with flak-jackets and automatic weapons.

'Mr Roper was here, but he left – about an hour ago,' she lied, surprised that she sounded so convincing. The Chinese looked puzzled, then snapped an order in Cantonese to the others. They shoved past her, one constable running upstairs pulling out a revolver, the other two levelled guns and kicked open the door of the kitchen. There were sounds of running outside, the clatter of metal as machine pistols were cocked, and suddenly the house seemed full of helmeted figures. A gun barrel caught her cheek as she tried to get out of the way. Sarah felt a trickle of blood on her face.

Clayton and Gatti appeared in the doorway. The Englishman's face looked murderous. 'Cable? What the fuck are you doing here?' But Gatti rushed forward and put his arms round her, dabbing at the cut with a handkerchief.

'Hey kid, what's happened? Surely he didn't hurt you?'

She shook herself free. 'Of course he didn't bloody hurt me – he's not some kind of monster.'

'I suppose you tipped him off?' Clayton shook with anger and he did not wait for a reply. 'We'll deal with you later, my girl. When I've finished, you'll wish you'd topped yourself like Devereux.' The Chinese police were spreading out in the garden, calling to each other as they searched. 'Do you know where he's gone?'

Sarah stared him out. 'I've no idea.'

'Why the devil didn't you persuade him to give himself up?'

'I tried.' Some instinctive sense of self-preservation made her lie again, and this time it sounded like it. 'But I couldn't do it.' She flopped down on the same sofa where she had nursed Nick, but this time it was Bob Gatti who nursed her. He put strong arms round her shoulders and she closed her eyes thankfully. 'Oh Bob, thank you. What's going on? I'm so scared for Nick.'

'You should be.' What did that mean? What did Gatti really feel? Had *he* loved Nick, too? Did he feel even more betrayed, even more unclean than Sarah? In this house where his children had died? Nick had hurt both of them so much. Poor Nick . . . Then Gatti stood up and led her out into the garden. The police had gone but one of their spotlights had been left in the corner, shining on bushes that writhed in the wind like tormented souls. From the hillside, the cemetery, the children's playground beyond the wall came the crash of boots and low shouts. Lights were blazing from the houses down the slope as their owners came out in curiosity.

'What did you mean, Bob?' She squeezed his hand fiercely.

'He should have given himself up. It would have caused a lot of hassle but they'd have had to put him on trial back in the States, lock him up for a few years. But the admiral doesn't feel that way.'

'You mean they'd sooner not take him alive?' Sarah spoke very deliberately, amazed at the unemotional way it came out.

'Sure. That way there's no embarrassment, no scandal, no fuss in Congress. It'll soon be hushed up and forgotten.'

She swallowed hard. 'That might even be best for him. The deception's all over now – I'm not sure he could live as himself.'

'I'd like him to have the chance.'

'After all that's happened?' They were standing close together as the noises of the hunt went further away. 'He betrayed you worse than anyone, Bob.'

'No, Sarah, he was *used*. We've all been used. It's hard to admit, but that's the truth.'

'Which way are they going?'

'Towards the sea.'

'D'you think Nick went that way?'

'I damn well hope not. If he went inland he'll have a chance, but if they trap him by the shore he's finished.'

42

Roper's terror gave way to exhilaration as he ran. For some reason the police had not surrounded the house completely, so when he pulled himself over the garden wall into the cemetery it was empty. He took off his shoes and sprinted silently between the gravestones, bruising his right knee on a corner in the dark, until he encountered a tall brick wall. This one was too high to climb. The absence of any moonlight made him feel safer, but it also made it difficult to make out his surroundings, although he had his night vision by now. He inched his way along the wall, gravel on the path cutting painfully into his stockinged feet, until an oblong of lighter grey showed him the way out.

The metal gate opened with a squeak that made him freeze, but the shouts and crashes of the search were away to his left. With luck they were going in quite the wrong direction. In the sports ground he replaced his shoes, for he would make no noise running on grass, and leant against a tree to recover from the exertion of that first burst of speed. He had to keep moving, but which way? Roper calculated that they would expect him to make for the roads back into the heart of the island, but the peninsula narrowed to almost nothing at Stanley village; if you stood above the market you could see the water on either side. They could easily block that. No, the way out was to go away from them – they were making so much din it was easy to know where they were – and find a boat. Smiling to himself in the dark, Nick Roper felt more confident

than he had for a long time. He had one simple objective –
to get away to China – and he could see how to achieve it.
Striking out across the field, a dim white shape loomed up
and he bumped into a goalpost; it made his nose bleed for
a few minutes but he jogged on, conserving his energy,
until he came to a paved road. A large, threatening mass
rose black on his left. That would be the wall of Stanley
jail. It did not trouble him – he was not going in there.

He turned right and started to run downhill, keeping to
the grass at the side of the road. Now the shouts, the
occasional whistles, were a long way off. He was aware of
an area that glared with light – mobile searchlights?
houselights turned on by puzzled residents? – but it was at
least half a mile away. There was no baying of dogs – if the
stupid bastards had used trackers he would not have stood
a chance, but maybe they hadn't thought of it, maybe they
thought he would give up easily? Without Sarah perhaps
he would, but now he had recovered from the initial
shock. He pushed the guilt and confusion to the back of
his mind. He had served his cause honestly, there was
nothing to be ashamed of – and he was going to survive.

The sea lapped quietly on St Stephen's Beach. The few
buildings overlooking it stood in total darkness. Roper
picked his way along the shore, tripping on a mooring
rope, until he found a row of boats pulled up on a strip of
sand. Now breaks were appearing in the cloud and there
was a glimmer of moonlight. He looked over his shoulder
furtively, but there was no sign of life along the beach – he
was still alone and safe. Just enough light to let him see
the boats: small fibreglass hulls used for fishing trips by
well-off *gwailos*. One yielded two oars, which he
shouldered while searching the others. He was looking for
one with an outboard engine that wasn't locked or chained
up to make it unusable.

He found it in a fourteen-footer at the end of the line.
His pocket-knife cut through the painter and the boat was
heavy as he bent to heave it into the water; but when it
finally started to slide it moved away from him fast and he

found himself running to grab its stern, up to his knees in the shallow waves. Once over the side he paddled out with one of the oars until he was bobbing up and down about two hundred yards from land. He swung the outboard down and pulled the toggle to start it. It fired third time – everything was going his way tonight – and he crouched over the tiller, pointing the boat out to sea.

The house was silent after the police had gone, leaving only two armed constables outside. Clayton returned briefly, still looking furious, but ignored Sarah; and Gatti left with him. Suddenly alone, Sarah started to feel a welcome exhaustion after all the tension and painful emotion of the last few hours. Thank God it was over. She was still alone in the empty room when she heard a car door slam outside and feet on the gravel. There was no knock – the police must have left the front door open – and she started with surprise when Benjamin Foo appeared. The tall figure stooped as he peered into the dark room and there was a great depth of concern in his eyes. 'I'm sorry, Sarah. Can I help?'

Without speaking they went into the kitchen for her to make coffee, then sat together at the round pine table, clutching two steaming mugs. Foo put his hand gently on her arm; she did not notice how he left his mug untouched and put it down carefully where he could least smell the hated aroma. There was a long silence, but she felt comforted by this wise, strong old man. Whatever the future might bring, at this moment she was overwhelmingly glad he was there. 'It must hurt a lot, Sarah – I know what it is to be betrayed. You are being very brave.'

'Am I? I'm too tired to think.' It was already two in the morning, but how could she sleep? Come to that, *where* could she sleep? Not here in the house where Bob's wife and children had died, she could never sleep here. The place gave her the creeps.

'I hope he gets away,' said Foo.

'So do I.'

Another long silence. 'What will Clayton do?' he asked. 'About you, I mean?'

'He'll fire me, that's what he'll do. He'd prefer to burn me at the stake, but he'll certainly see me chucked out of the service. I don't really blame him, in the circumstances.'

He held her hand and his eyes were full of compassion. 'I'll see what I can do. Rumbelow almost lost me to Peking so Clayton should owe me one – though I doubt he sees it like that – but you've done nothing wrong and they can't ignore everything you did in China.'

'I had an affair with a man who turned out to be a traitor – and then I tipped him off before they could arrest him. That probably makes me an accessory or something, it certainly makes me a dead loss as an intelligence officer – I knew what I was doing, Ben.'

He sighed. 'I think we should get some sleep, Sarah.'

'Not here, Ben – too many memories.'

'Yes, there must be. I'll drive you back to your apartment.'

'And I couldn't sleep, not tonight, I can't stop worrying about Nick.'

'It's strangely quiet out there – I believe he's made it.'

'Do you really think so?' She tried to stand up but stumbled; Foo caught her and kissed her lightly on the forehead.

'You must sleep, Sarah, you are dying of exhaustion. Come – my car is outside.'

Roper turned the boat eastwards, skirting south of the Stanley peninsula. All his fears had gone. He felt exhilarated and confident that he could make it to China if he followed a long curve skirting Tung Lung Chau and Tai Long Wan. It was about fifteen or twenty miles and a dark night. The further he got from land the heavier the swell; but the small boat rolled over the waves easily, slapping down into the troughs and splashing spray in his face. He started to hum *The East is Red* to himself quietly, smiling into the night at the irony. Who knows what he would find as a refugee in China, but he was sure they would take care of him. The tension passing again, he began to feel quietly optimistic.

Despite everything Sarah dozed off on the drive across the island, waking once or twice to see Foo's face lit by the blue lights from the dashboard, curling up again in the soft leather seat. He parked in MacDonnell Road and made to carry her into the apartment block but she shook her head sleepily. 'No, Ben, there's no need. Anyway I'm too large for that sort of thing.' In the flat she kicked off her shoes and flopped down on the bed fully dressed. A thought struck her. 'How did we get in?'

'They gave me your keys – I'll put them here on the dressing table.'

She turned on her side drowsily, muttering, 'So what happened to O'Neill?'

'Nursing big hangover and even bigger kick up backside.' Foo's eyes crinkled into that familiar smile as he covered her with the duvet. 'Forget about O'Neill – now you must sleep.' She felt him cradling her head, stroking her face and hair; and despite the turmoil in her mind, the fears, the choices, the pain, the questions, within a few minutes she drifted off.

Roper's boat was doing eight knots as he nosed into the channel between the New Territories and Steep Island. The outboard was popping confidently and he had found another can of fuel in a locker under the stern. At four in the morning the night was at its darkest; from long nights on watch at sea he knew it was the dead hour when even insomniacs and would-be suicides slept, when all life paused with exhaustion before deciding to struggle on for another twenty-four hours. The lights of Central and Kowloon were now out of sight, but even in vibrant Hong Kong they had been growing dimmer when they vanished behind the headland.

The fibreglass hull struck the submerged wreckage with no warning. The impact threw him headlong in the bottom of the boat, grazing his forehead. When he recovered there was enough moonlight to show the corner of a baulk of timber, black and tarred like a railway sleeper, sticking at least a foot through the splintered bow. He cursed quietly, confused and instinctively bracing himself to push it back out of the boat. The engine had stopped and there was complete silence. He was sweating with effort by the time it shifted, tearing an even bigger gash in the side; as the obstruction floated clear and cold sea rushed in he realised his mistake.

Within seconds the boat was submerged and vanishing beneath him. Roper swam clear, finding the water not as icy as he had expected, and took off his shoes, thrusting them into his trouser pockets. After a few strokes he abandoned his jacket, then struck out strongly for the black line of the shore.

43

Sarah slept fitfully, tossing and turning, tormented by nightmares. From time to time she half-woke, bathed in sweat, aware of her own voice crying out in terror. Once she saw two misty figures by the bed, bent in concern, and realised that Ruth Foo was with her husband. She caught snatches of conversation: 'The children are fine, Ben . . . I told David what was happening and he was very brave about it . . . took great care of me, his father's son . . . little Hannah was too young to understand . . . no, no, stay here as long as she needs you, the poor child, you have a debt to pay.' Sarah struggled to wake properly but drifted back into a delirium of swirling darkness, a terrible wilderness of ice and fear that turned into a graveyard where she was lying in a coffin, her body shrivelled and putrefying but Nick's face rearing above her, smiling, confident, eyes radiant then shut tight as his back arched and his head threw back, the moment of perfect sensation and perfect stillness suddenly eclipsed by mocking laughter and her shriek of terror at Nick's face now wild, insane under a green Chinese cap with a red star, spiralling into a kaleidoscope of other faces – Nairn's, Clayton's, her father's, Mary Devereux's twisted in agony, black and choking as she writhed at the end of a rope.

Sarah ran to get away but they all pursued her, panting with fear as she rushed to hide in a building that burst into flames, stumbling out to find herself trapped in a maze of barbed wire, strands tearing at her flesh, clothes still burning as she weaved wildly from side to side until she tripped and fell into a pit of never-ending blackness. As she screamed the dark exploded into a blaze of light, Nick's face leering at its centre, white as death and covered in blood.

'It's okay, Sarah, I'm here, don't be afraid.' It was Foo's voice, low and calm, and she opened her eyes in relief. Sun was filtering through the slatted blind to make a zebra pattern on the walls; she could hear the traffic outside and the roar of an aircraft taking off. He smiled down at her and she saw that he had changed – it must have happened in China but she hadn't noticed before. The same humorous eyes, the same inner toughness, but his grey hair was now white at the sides and there were deeper lines on his face.

'How long have I been asleep?'

'About fourteen hours – it's five in the afternoon. How do you feel?'

'Not bad.' She hesitated. 'Has anything happened?'

He sat on the bed and shook his head. 'No. He seems to have vanished without trace.'

'Thank God for that.'

Foo made some tea and she drank it but could not face eating anything. She tried a hot bath steaming with herbal oils, but could not relax. Eventually she dressed and Foo drove her up the Peak. They followed the footpath round the summit, looking down at the panorama of the harbour, blue water criss-crossed by the white wakes of countless motor-junks and ferries. Foo bought a copy of the *South China Morning Post* but there was no mention of last night's events in Stanley. At the western extremity of Governor's Walk they stood looking across to the misty green outline of Lantau and he put his arm round her. 'I'm sorry it's turned out like this, Sarah – I could see you'd grown very close to him.'

'I was in love with him, if that's what you mean, but sometimes I felt there was something not quite right.' She smiled bitterly. 'Now I can see why.' They walked on in silence. 'I suppose he couldn't help it, but he's left me so shell-shocked. This bloody business seems to attract so many people who can't face themselves, can only live protected by a miasma of lies and fantasy. I need more *straightforwardness* in my life, Ben – someone I can really trust, a proper home, a still centre despite the hurricane all around. I suppose that sounds silly?'

'Of course not, that's what most of us want – and you *will* find it, Sarah, perhaps when you least expect it.'

'Will I, Ben?' On an impulse she laughed and kissed him. 'You know I can't make out whether you're an old crook or the wisest, kindest man I've ever met.' Foo's eyes crinkled but he did not reply and then Nick's ravaged face came back to her and she found herself pointing across the harbour, towards China. 'Do you think he made it? Is he over there somewhere?'

'I hope so.'

'What will they do with him?'

'If they're grateful I suppose they'll give him a lousy flat in Peking and some sort of government job. It's hard to imagine him living like a Chinese – no comfort, no car, no money, whatever he may think he believes . . . and he won't be safe when the communists fall.'

'I suppose not, but how long will *that* take?'

'Probably years. This is not Europe and the army still has great power in a country where the man with a bicycle is envied as rich by the man who hasn't even a pair of shoes – but nothing can stop us now. Nothing.'

'Why does it matter so much, Ben – to you, I mean. I know you feel you belong there in some incomprehensible way, but you haven't *lived* in China since you were a boy and the bloody place has been in turmoil since before you were born.'

He stared at the mainland for a time then shook his head and turned to her with a sad smile. 'I suppose that's why it matters?'

*   *   *

The attractive Vietnamese woman was among the first passengers to board the Cathay Pacific flight for Shanghai. Ten minutes later the plane was hurtling down the runway built into the harbour, sea lapping on either side, and climbing steeply to avoid the Peak. Most of the passengers were European tourists and Josie waved away the glass of chilled champagne and shrimp canapés offered by the steward. They were flying over Causeway Bay and her face was expressionless. This time she felt no triumph, no exhilaration, just a mixture of relief and infinite sadness.

In London it was already evening and traffic was streaming across the bridge over the Thames by Parliament and past the concrete slab of Century House on Westminster Bridge Road. The headquarters of the Secret Intelligence Service was still busy and it was Nairn's first visit since his heart attack. He had come in at three, driven in the familiar dark blue Rover from Chiswick, and dictated a few requests for reports. He had spoken to Clayton on the phone to learn that his suspicions of Roper had been justified. Now he stood by the window, looking down at the traffic, as he had a thousand times before. The door to his secretary's office was closed and he was alone. He picked up an intercom and keyed the head of personnel. 'Nairn here. I've been going through some papers – I approve Goddard's next posting, to Cairo, and Cable's to London. You'll get it in writing, but I'd like you to notify them both tomorrow. Okay?'

So that was done. There was a whole service to run, but he had found a few minutes for Sarah. By the stroke of a pen he could distance her from Clayton's fury now, give her a sporting chance if she chose to stay on; but when he had gone and Clayton was in charge? *If* Clayton was in charge – but who else was there? He felt very tired and when he lit his pipe the tobacco tasted bitter and made him cough. He sighed – death was nature's way of telling you to slow up – and came to a decision. Picking up the red Federal phone he dialled the Cabinet Secretary's number. 'Nairn here. Is he in?' After a pause he was put through. 'Robin? It's David Nairn . . . yes, I'm feeling much better, thanks. Look, I need to come and see you, about the question of my successor.' He listened for a time. 'That's all very kind – yes, maybe you will persuade me to stay, but meanwhile we'd better get on with it. I'm for the knacker's yard and you need somebody fit over here. Thanks – eleven tomorrow will be fine.'

He put the receiver down sadly. Had he really made the decision? He had been in the service so long, in charge of it so long, that he could not imagine a life without it. But he crossed the room and opened the door to ask for his car; just at the moment all he wanted was to sleep.

That night Foo stayed in the apartment again, dozing on the sofa. They were both startled awake when the phone rang at five in the morning. He answered it and Sarah wandered out of the bedroom pulling on a dressing gown and yawning. 'Who is it, Ben? What on earth do they want now?'

In the light from the bedroom doorway his face was taut. 'It's about Nick. He almost reached China by boat but seems to have run into trouble and landed north of Clear Water Bay. He hid in a hut on the shore all day, but when it got dark the fishermen who owned the hut turned up and he panicked. He shot at them – they thought he was smuggling and one of them ran to a police post. He's been holed up in the hut ever since. He's surrounded by police but won't come out.'

Sarah sat down heavily, her head in her hands. 'No, Ben, please say it's not true.' She started to cry. 'You mean he was just a few miles from safety?'

'Yes.' Foo looked sombre. 'He almost made it.'

44

Sarah and Foo arrived at six in the morning, ghosts of dawn mist swirling outside the car windows. They had passed two roadblocks and noticed that the last mile was unnaturally quiet, no lights in the few houses. The police must have cleared them – there would be no witnesses to this final act. His Mercedes bumped down the track in the half-darkness until they came to a grassy bank separating it from the sea. About twenty Chinese police were standing about wearing flak-jackets and armed with Armalites or older carbines. 'Good grief,' muttered Sarah when she saw them and the long line of vehicles: half a dozen police cars, a radio truck and an ambulance.

A lot had happened in the last hour. As Foo parked, a European in the uniform of a police superintendent approached, holding up his hand for silence. 'I'm Parker,' he snapped in an accent that was more London suburbs than home counties. 'Officer in command of the siege.' Sarah winced. Siege? Did it take a *siege* to arrest poor Nick? 'Who are you two? Who gave you permission to come here?'

'Sarah Cable, Diplomatic Service.' She showed her identity card. 'And this is my colleague Mr Foo.'

Parker snorted. 'And why the devil are you here?'

'We both know him – we thought we might be able to help.'

Sarah had taken an instant dislike to Parker – he had an air of arrogance and she was in no doubt that he would do his duty without compassion or remorse. She felt Foo put his arm round her shoulders but shook it off and climbed up the bank until she was standing on the ridge, speculating on the content of Parker's orders. To take Nick alive so they could pump him dry? Or were Gatti's fears justified? Would putting him on trial cause too much embarrassment?

Although it was still half-dark Sarah could see that they were at the end of a barren peninsula in the New Territories, not far from the Chinese border. From her feet the ground fell away to a shore about a hundred yards away. The stone hut was tiny, perched on a rocky spit that jutted out into the sea; it was silent, bathed in the white glare of arc-lights, and in the mist beyond she could just make out the grey shape of a police launch standing offshore, the machine gun on its foredeck trained on the small building. 'Get down!' shouted Parker. 'You're completely exposed there.' Sarah ignored him, standing with legs apart and arms crossed, looking defiant. She did not believe Nick would shoot her. She did not believe Nick could shoot anybody. The hut was a square box with a pitched roof of corrugated iron, like a child's drawing of a house. The white beams blazing around it reflected off the rippling dark sea. On the horizon the sky was turning from mauve to salmon pink. It was going to be another hot day.

Outside the ring of light she could see only shadows, the black outlines of gun barrels and men crouching behind boulders on the slope. There was no sound apart from waves lapping on the rocks and the whirr of a generator in the radio truck; but the atmosphere was electric with tension. She sensed it in the stiffening of her own body, the knots forming in her stomach. It seemed a hell of a lot of firepower to put against one single frightened man. It seemed unreal that he was down there, alone in that silent hut. Poor, poor Nick. She remembered the gentleness of his hands, the eagerness of his eyes, too eager, too unsure. So much to give, so much compassion, so much talent, but no cutting edge. It was all so bloody unjust. She had seen him as he wanted to be – he had been man enough with

310

her – but deep down was the weakness that bastard Luther had used.

'Get down,' hissed the police superintendent again, now just below her on the side of the bank away from the sea. 'I order you to get down!' Sarah gave Parker a hard glance, then stepped back and knelt between him and Foo. On the horizon the sky was now glowing blood red – soon it would be light. 'So you both know him?' Parker spoke irritably, putting his head above the ridge and training binoculars on the hut. God knows why, thought Sarah – it was so close that you could see every floodlit detail without them.

Sarah nodded. 'We do.'

'How is he armed?'

'When he left the house in Stanley he had a revolver, an ordinary .38 Smith and Wesson, and a few rounds.'

Parker grunted. 'Is he dangerous?'

'*Dangerous*?' Sarah exploded. 'God Lord no! He's gentle and,' she hesitated, torn between loyalty to the man who had held her in his arms, and possibly saving his life. Eventually she spoke very quietly. 'And probably scared witless by now.'

'I'd expect him to surrender without resistance.' Foo's voice was hollow.

'Then why the devil hasn't he? He must know we're here – he's been holed up in that hut for twenty-four hours already.'

'He has a little pride left,' breathed Sarah. 'Just a little.'

'Pride?' Parker almost spat in contempt. 'That arsehole is a bloody traitor. I'd like to see him hang.' He slithered down the bank and marched towards a group of police and civilians clustered near the radio truck. Seizing a loud-hailer, he turned towards the sea. 'Roper, this is the Royal Hong Kong Police. You are surrounded by armed men.' The voice was metallic, and he paused for clarity between each syllable. 'I repeat, you are surrounded by armed police. Throw any firearms you may have out of the window, then come out yourself with your hands raised above your head.' The metallic voice echoed between the rocks, wisps of mist drifting from the sea and tracing eerie patterns around the stone building. 'I repeat, come out with your hands raised above your head and you will not be harmed.'

There was silence. Nothing moved in the circle of menace. Finally the crimson and grey of dawn gave way to weak sunlight that became stronger, like the lights coming up in a theatre. But the hut remained silent, apparently empty – the leading man was not going to appear.

By midday it was very hot on the rocky coast north of Clear Water Bay. Parker approached Foo and Sarah, who had found a patch of shade by a boulder. 'This can't go on.' He spoke crossly. 'Since you two know him, will one of you speak to him through the loud-hailer?'

Sarah's instinct was to refuse. It was up to Nick to decide for himself: why should she join his enemies and interfere? 'What do you want us to say?' she asked wearily.

'I should have thought that was bloody obvious. Tell him to come out unarmed and give himself up. He won't be harmed if he does. If we have to go in and get him . . . .' Parker shrugged dismissively.

A few minutes later the two of them clambered up the bank and Sarah took the loud-hailer. 'This is Sarah, Nick.' The metallic tone could only sound unfriendly. 'Please listen. I'm out here with Benjamin Foo and we both want you to know that if you come out with your hands raised, unarmed, you won't be harmed. They won't shoot, Nick, if you come out now.' She paused, comforted by Foo's hand on her arm, and tried again. 'This is Sarah, Nick. They don't want to hurt you, so please throw out your gun, if you've still got it, and come out with your hands raised. I'm here waiting for you. Please do it, now.' She wanted to add *I love you* but faltered in front of the bovine Parker. Even before her appeal had echoed away between the rocks she knew that it was futile. And again she felt those nagging doubts about Parker's orders – maybe it was *meant* to be futile?

In the silence, there was a scraping noise from the hut, a pause and the explosion of a shot. The bullet whined high in the air – it was not aimed at them – but everyone ducked instinctively. Sarah smiled and muttered: 'Good for you, Nick. Up yours, Parker.'

At five o'clock in the afternoon Clayton and the admiral settled into the leather seat in the back of the Lincoln and clung to the side straps as the car hairpinned fast down the Peak towards the harbour tunnel. 'It's gone on long enough.' Clayton's accent was cut-glass again, his fresh striped shirt and dark blue tropical suit impeccable after the hectic night. 'I hope he gives up before dark. We've banned reporters and TV cameras from the area on the grounds that they'd be in danger, but they'll find a way through. If it's going to end as front page news, we'd be better off if he'd escaped to China.'

The admiral grunted – it was always difficult to know what he was thinking. 'I guess,' the soft Carolina drawl seemed almost sleepy, 'I guess your police can finish it quick enough if we give the order?'

Even the ruthless Clayton was a little taken aback. 'This is British territory,' he said stuffily. 'He must be given a decent chance to surrender.'

'Yeah, sure.' But the admiral plainly meant *why*? 'You goin' t'give Cable a decent chance too?'

'I don't read you, Erwin.'

'You sure 'bout that, Gerry? She's a sound intelligence officer. You'd be real crazy to lose her.' For a worldly-wise man, thought Clayton, the admiral was unbelievably naive if he thought that exaggerating the hayseed in his voice could give an impression of simple honesty that concealed his deviousness.

'She has behaved quite intolerably.'

'Aw, come now, Gerry. Could have happened to any-body. I'd take it as a great personal kindness if you'd turn a blind eye. All rightey?'

'I'll think about it. What's the latest from China?'

'Food riots, unrest, an army mutiny in Shansi. I guess Foo's friends are stirring as hard as they can – but there's an odd silence in Peking, rumours of something big. Maybe Deng has finally died? They say there's a power struggle starting between hardliners and liberals who want to go the way of Eastern Europe.'

'Could that be true?'

'God knows, Gerry – I guess we'll find out soon enough. Maybe they won't need Foo's revolution after all. Whatever's going on I'd be surprised if that crew in Peking ain't shit scared. They sure as hell ought to be.'

The small hut seemed to shimmer in the heat of the afternoon and the hours passed slowly. By six the sun was lower, but still hot enough to make Sarah feel drowsy. Her back ached from crouching in one position too long. She was sitting against a boulder and shifted uncomfort-ably, trying to rub the area most affected, watching a new team of marksmen relieve the police who had been on duty for the past four hours. For herself she had been there nearly twelve and it felt like a lifetime. The tension, the blazing sun, surviving on driblets of junk food and tepid water, had all taken their toll. Her eyes stung from staring at the hut through bright sunlight and her mind was exhausted by the emotional pounding. How on earth could Nick stand it for so long? He had been in there nearly thirty-six hours. Struggling to stay awake? Terri-fied? Nothing to eat? He must have some water or he'd have passed out by now, but the tiny building would be fetid in this heat. She tried to imagine how he felt. How-ever lonely, however afraid, he had plainly found some courage at the end. She willed him to cling to it, to come out, to live – even if there were years to spend in jail, one day there would be freedom, obscurity from disgrace, some kind of new start. *Don't be a fool, Nick. Just give up – for God's sake give yourself a chance.*

She had not been asked to try loud-hailing again – and Parker had not done so either for a couple of hours. Sarah could see that he was in a huddle with Clayton and the admiral, both of whom had avoided speaking to her when they arrived. Then she noticed movement around the radio truck, a van arriving with more armed police. The preparations were obvious. They were going to rush him. *Oh Nick, you bloody, bloody fool – come out before it's too late.* She felt sick yet watched with a morbid fascination as the Chinese police strapped on thick flak-jackets and adjusted their riot helmets. Armed with machine pistols, when he had only a small revolver, it was absurd. She was concentrating on them so much that at first she did not notice the door of the hut swing open. Nor did anyone else, for the doorway was in deep shadow. A low shout from one of the Chinese police caught her attention and she went rigid at the sight below.

Nick Roper stood in the doorway, his face grey, haggard, ten years older than when she had last seen him less than two days ago. He wore a filthy white shirt, open to the waist, and the crumpled trousers of his grey suit. There were metallic clicks as thirty well-oiled weapons were trained on him, thirty bullets slid into firing chambers, thirty men mentally rehearsed police standing orders: *At the order to fire shoot without hesitation into the centre of the part of the body most exposed.* A threatening silence, no sound but the soft lapping of waves on the rocks, the generator dying as someone switched it off, a Chinese sergeant hawking to her left. Then nothing. Stillness.

Nick stood for what seemed a very long time, in reality maybe a minute: erect, proud, every inch the naval officer. Sarah was too far away to see his face, but there was an air of contempt in his bearing as he stared at the circle of steel around him, his head turning very slowly. *Oh, well*

done Nick she breathed, *show them, show them but then
for God's sake give up*.

'Raise your hands, Roper,' bellowed Parker through
the loud-hailer. 'Raise your hands and you will not be
harmed.' Nick continued to stand there, then took a pace
forward. The sun was low but its light caught his face, set
in a strange mixture of defiance and bewilderment. 'Raise
your hands,' bawled Parker again, his voice rising to a
scream. 'Right above your head, then walk forward
slowly.' But in face of the angry figure below, the order
lacked all conviction.

Afterwards there was much debate as to what Roper
actually shouted in reply. It was a low shout, hardly more
than a groan. Certainly it was derisive, full of contempt.
But there was no argument about his actions. After the
long silence, the slow movements, there was an audible
gasp of shock as Roper suddenly whipped the revolver
from his belt, fell to a crouch and levelled it two-handed
straight at Parker. Sarah would never forget that image of
him, head down, both arms extended forward, the gun
rigid.

'No, Nick, *no*!' She heard herself screaming as they
fired at him, deafened by the staccato hammering of
automatic weapons, shutting her eyes at the sight of his
body spinning in the hail of hot metal, the neat little puffs
of smoke where bullets ricocheted off the hut and the
rocks.

She opened her eyes and ran forward, ignoring Parker's
angry shouts. 'Get back, woman, stay where you are! Stay
where you are, I say!' Nick was on his back, broken
against the stone wall of the hut, his chest an ugly mass of
scarlet wounds. There was blood everywhere. She fell to
her knees beside him and cradled his head. Only one
bullet had grazed his scalp, otherwise his face was unmarked but there was nothing in his eyes and the twist of
his mouth but shock and acute pain. He was already dead.

'Oh my poor baby.' She rocked him gently, weeping
with no sound until she sensed Foo beside her. 'My poor,

poor baby.' Foo stooped to pick up the revolver, automatically breaking it open. They both stared at the six dark spaces. There were no bullets – the chamber was empty. 'Jesus Christ – he must have known. What the hell was he playing at?'

'He was going down fighting, Sarah.'

She went on stroking Nick's face. 'I think I'm glad – was it best for him?'

Foo nodded gravely. He too was close to weeping and she loved him for it. 'It was for the best.'

There was no more shouting from Parker and the Chinese police stood watching respectfully, clutching smoking weapons. She kissed Nick's forehead and Foo drew her slowly to her feet. She kissed him too as he held her tightly. 'Take me home, Ben. For God's sake just take me home.'

POSTSCRIPT

All characters and events in THE YEAR OF THE SCORPION are fictitious, with the exception of Kang Sheng.

Kang Sheng was born Zhang Shaoqing in 1898, in a small town on the coast of Shandon province. As a young man he visited Europe, studied at Shangda University, Shanghai, and joined the Chinese Communist Party in 1924. His involvement in underground agitation led to leadership of all China's intelligence and security services, a position he sometimes lost when out of favour but held more or less continuously until his death in 1975. Kang Sheng was not only a spymaster but the architect of China's nuclear weapons programme, one of the instigators of the Cultural Revolution, the lover of Mao's wife Jiang Qing and closely involved with her in the power struggles of the early 1970s. Though little known in the West, he is one of the key figures in the evolution of the People's Republic of China. His reputed ambition to succeed Mao Zedong was thwarted when Kang died of cancer on 16 December 1975, nine months before Mao's own death in September 1976.

China has a bewildering complex of security and intelligence agencies, which may be departments of the Party, government ministries or within the People's Liberation Army. The *Tewu* (Department for Special Affairs) was founded by the leaders of the Party in Shanghai in the 1920s. At first headed by Zhou Enlai, it was reorganised by Kang Sheng as the Party's worldwide intelligence service in 1938. Later came the *Shehuibu* (Social Affairs Department, *Diaochabu* (Central Committee's Investigation Bureau), *Gonganbu* (Ministry of Public Security), the responsibilities of which include the *Laogai* or Chinese Gulag, and *Qingbao* (Military Intelligence under the General Staff of the People's Liberation Army). A new KGB-style Ministry of State Security, *Guojia anquanbu* (*Guoanbu*) was added in 1983. Despite overlapping boundaries and inter-agency rivalry, they all report eventually to the Executive Committee of the Chinese Communist Party.